Choose your Lane to love!

Readers love the Candy Man stories by AMY LANE

Candy Man

"Dearly beloved, we are gathered here to celebrate the wonder of Amy Lane and the fabulousness of this freaking story—*Candy Man*."
—Joyfully Jay

"There are two Amy Lanes—the very angst-filled, need a bunch of tissues Amy and the very sweet and happy Amy. This story is firmly in the second Amy camp and my favorite kind of Amy to read."
—Hearts on Fire Reviews

"*Candy Man* is another winner by Amy Lane. I just love that she can surprise me with the way her mind works…"
—The Novel Approach

Bitter Taffy

"Combine the lovable characters with Amy Lane's rich imagination and solid prose, and you have an enjoyable way to spend some time."
—Prism Book Alliance

"*Bitter Taffy* is a light, low-angst story that I think could melt even the iciest of hearts."
—Gay Book Reviews

"I want to highly recommended *Bitter Taffy* and the whole Candy Man series. Really well done!"
—Scattered Thoughts and Rogue Words

More praise for AMY LANE

Immortal

"Leave it to Amy Lane to write a fairy tale that kicks my ass... Thank you Amy, for the gift of your words, for the gift of Immortal."

—MM Good Book Reviews

"A book that made me feel...made me live every emotional onslaught these men suffered! Bravo Amy Lane and thank you for giving me an unputdownable, gold star read I won't forget."

—Sinfully…

"I recommend this book to fans of fantasy/fairy tales and fans of the 'Queen' herself"

—The Kimi-chan Experience

Food for Thought

"This is a SWEET Amy Lane story, and those are my favorite… I loved everything about Food for Thought…"

—My Fiction Nook

Beneath the Stain

"…this was a very enchanting book and I hope to see these characters again in the future."

—Hearts on Fire

"…though this journey has been sucking the life out of me, I wouldn't change it for the world."

—Boys in Our Books

By AMY LANE

Behind the Curtain
Beneath the Stain
Bewitched by Bella's Brother
Bolt-hole
Christmas with Danny Fit
Clear Water
Do-over
Food for Thought
Gambling Men: The Novel
Going Up!
Grand Adventures (Dreamspinner Anthology)
Hammer & Air
If I Must
Immortal
It's Not Shakespeare
Left on St. Truth-be-Well
The Locker Room
Mourning Heaven
Phonebook
Puppy, Car, and Snow
Racing for the Sun
Raising the Stakes
Shiny!
Sidecar
A Solid Core of Alpha
Super Sock Man
Tales of the Curious Cookbook
Three Fates (Multiple Author Anthology)
Truth in the Dark
Turkey in the Snow
Under the Rushes
Winter Ball
Wishing on a Blue Star (Dreamspinner Anthology)

Published by DREAMSPINNER PRESS
www.dreamspinnerpress.com

By AMY LANE (CONT.)

CANDY MAN
Candy Man
Bitter Taffy
Lollipop

KEEPING PROMISE ROCK
Keeping Promise Rock • Making Promises • Living Promises • Forever Promised

JOHNNIES
Chase in Shadow • Dex in Blue • Ethan in Gold • Black John

GRANBY KNITTING
The Winter Courtship Rituals of Fur-Bearing Critters
How to Raise an Honest Rabbit • Knitter in His Natural Habitat
Blackbird Knitting in a Bunny's Lair

TALKER
Talker • Talker's Redemption • Talker's Graduation

ANTHOLOGIES
The Granby Knitting Menagerie
The Talker Collection

Published by DREAMSPINNER PRESS
www.dreamspinnerpress.com

Amy Lane

Published by
DREAMSPINNER PRESS

5032 Capital Circle SW, Suite 2, PMB# 279, Tallahassee, FL 32305-7886 USA
www.dreamspinnerpress.com

Lollipop
© 2016 Amy Lane.

Cover Art
© 2016 Paul Richmond.
http://www.paulrichmondstudio.com
Cover content is for illustrative purposes only and any person depicted on the cover is a model.

ISBN: 978-1-63476-904-4
Digital ISBN: 978-1-63476-905-1
Library of Congress Control Number: 2015918425
Published January 2016
v. 1.0

Printed in the United States of America
(∞)
This paper meets the requirements of
ANSI/NISO Z39.48-1992 (Permanence of Paper).

Mate and Mary and the kids—always.
And to Elizabeth, who likes my sunny yellow stories best of all.
And to Darrin, who welcomes me every time I walk into
Candy Heaven, and will, I think, be thrilled to get another book.

Acknowledgments

THIS IS for my friend Maria Teresa Nuno, who would answer any fool question I had about how she grew up, and who is happy to tell me what it means to raise proud sons and a strong daughter in a Mexican family.

Author's Note

PEOPLE QUESTION sometimes why my books are peopled by all sorts of, well, people. It's because I write the world around me—and I try to understand it. The character of Miguel comes from talking to my friend Maria Teresa, a proud Latina whose husband, Lalo, is one of the fondest—and kindest—men I've met. One of her jobs for the local soccer league was to talk to the vendors at Denio's Farmers Market & Swap Meet, and to translate because most of the vendors only speak Spanish and Maria Teresa is bilingual. I clearly remember taking trips out to Denio's as a kid. There was an entire world of industrious, usually friendly, hardworking people there. I was envious of the self-assurance and purpose of kids my age, when I could hardly walk across a parking lot without getting lost. I didn't realize then that this confidence came from the knowledge that without the help of the children, the families would be lost. I know this now. I also know that my community is stronger with these families in it. I know that when I was teaching, the families of immigrants were among my hardest working and often best behaved. I know that the respect I accorded them was returned to me tenfold. Miguel comes from a strong and proud tradition of hardworking immigrant families who have made this country so much better through the generations. I hope my country recognizes what a tragedy it would be not to have these families in our midst.

You Feed Them Once

MIGUEL RODRIGUEZ stared blankly at the New York transplant who had landed on his ex-crush's lawn, and then looked down the street for the ex-crush himself, who had trotted away in the sweltering heat, along with the dog of ambiguous ownership.

Rico was not coming back with Clopper any time soon.

Miguel had to look back to Mr. Manhattan, and he turned just in time to watch several drops of sweat splash down from Ezra Kellerman's forehead. The young man—roughly Miguel's age—grimaced and wiped his face on the sleeve of his polo shirt.

"So," Miguel said blankly, feeling dumb. "You, uh, want to come inside? I guess you live here now."

Those had been Rico's words before he took off with the dog to make up with his boyfriend. He'd said Ezra could have his place on the couch, and for Miguel to tell Rico's cousin Adam that it was all good.

Miguel had spent his life trying to please all the adults in a big family—he hadn't been happy about it, but he was still damned good at following directions.

Ezra looked back at him, shell-shocked blue eyes wide and a little red. Rico had been kind—because Rico *was* kind—but Miguel gathered the "I'm glad you're okay; I need to go move in with my current boyfriend!" brush-off hadn't been what the poor guy was hoping for. "Yeah, sure," Ezra responded dazedly. "Anything to get out of this fucking heat."

They had to pull Ezra's two big suitcases and his carry-on up the stairs to the second floor and into the apartment, but the cooler air hit them as soon as they opened the door. So did Finn and Adam's surprise as they walked in.

Finn was seated at the little Formica kitchen table, his mouth full of what was probably ice, given that the ice bowl was sitting right next to him. Even as they looked, he spat a stream of pink into the plastic cup in his hand. His heart-shaped face was screwed up in pain, and he kept squeezing his big blue eyes shut like he was trying not to cry. His strawberry-blond hair swacked to his head with sweat.

"Fuckin' Derek," Adam snarled, giving him a clean plastic cup and taking the other one to the sink. "Are the painkillers kicking in?"

"What happened to him?" Ezra asked, looking worried. Well, this whole day was probably worrisome. Miguel cast a surreptitious look at Ezra's knuckles. Healing scars decorated the backs of his hands—showing them to Rico had caused a stunningly vulnerable expression to cross Ezra's pale, high-cheekboned face.

"Rico's boyfriend saw you on the lawn and curbed the car," Adam said tersely. "Finn bit his tongue." He stopped for a moment and touched Finn tenderly on the cheek. "You're going to be okay, though, right?"

Finn nodded gamely and grinned, the expression surprisingly puppyish around his open mouth. "Iba gobba be fibe," he said, and Adam squeezed his eyes shut.

"Ibbit?" he mocked grimly. "Ibbit gobba be fibe?"

Finn's round eyes narrowed. "Dit."

Miguel snickered, and Adam threw him a droll look. "He could have bit the damned thing *off* and he'd still be talking."

For a moment all was right with Miguel's world. "Yes, but he wouldn't make you quite so happy, would he, *papi*?"

Adam's mouth twisted—almost a smile. Sort of a triumph. He gently tousled Finn's hair and looked up, his eyes catching Ezra. Smile gone.

"Uh, so, speaking of Rico—what are you doing here?" Adam's scowl intensified. "And where the fuck is my dog?"

Ezra's gaze darted nervously to Miguel. Wonderful. Miguel's business had failed, and he'd spent the past two months pretending he'd never even tried to be Mr. Responsible Leadership Person. Apparently now he was in charge of a stray.

"Rico said Ezra could have his spot on the couch. He, uh, told me to tell you that he was bringing Clopper back tomorrow, and that he'll get all his clothes then, and that we should get Ezra a job at Candy Heaven. And that he was going to go tell Derek that he wasn't getting back with Ezra." Miguel recited it as close to verbatim as he could get, because Rico's instructions confused *him*, and he could imagine Adam being a little surprised as well.

Not so much.

"Yeah, well, don't talk to me about Derek. I don't give a shit if he *is* my boss, anyone who would curb a convertible like that has totally lost my respect."

Finn gave an outraged whine, and Adam rolled his eyes. "Yeah, baby—and you hurting yourself doesn't help his cause either."

"Wait—Rico wants you to take me to work for *Derek*?" Ezra asked, clearly as confused as Adam should have been.

The gaze Adam leveled at Ezra would have made Miguel quail in shame. Ezra blinked and smiled slightly, like he was used to that shit all the time. Adam cocked his head then, and did something… curious.

"No," he said, drawing it out so it didn't sound abrupt. "He wants me to take you to Candy Heaven so you can work for *Darrin*. I get why you'd be confused. But right now, go ahead and stack your bags in the corner there. I'll make sure we're gone when Rico comes for his stuff…." Adam's voice deepened and his irritation clearly showed. "…and returns my fuckin' dog! You can unpack then." He glanced at Miguel. "Mik, you work tomorrow too?"

Miguel nodded. "Yeah—same shift as you."

"Awesome—then we'll bring him in and Darrin will hire him."

Miguel gaped, opening and shutting his mouth and feeling stupid, before Ezra put him out of his misery and asked the obvious question.

"Just like that? He doesn't even know me!"

Adam cocked his head again and nodded, the expression of casual acceptance at odds with Adam's height, physique, and hardened jaw. And his neck tattoos—which had always fascinated Miguel.

"He's been dreaming about you," Adam said obliquely, but Miguel understood.

"Really? Darrin's been dreaming about *him*?" And for the first time since… since he looked at Adam Macias and thought he'd never seen anyone so beautiful, Miguel let some of his frustration out. "*Him*?"

He waved his arms at the newcomer, the interloper who almost bollixed Rico and Derek's budding romance, the idiot who couldn't even wear sensible clothes when it was a bajillion degrees outside. Ezra looked back, big blue eyes wide and fringed by black lashes to set them even further apart in pale skin. He had two tiny moles by the corner of his mouth, true beauty marks, and soft pink pillow lips.

Things that Miguel only *just* noticed as Ezra grimaced and threw his hands from his chest in the classic pose of offended dignity.

"Chopped liver, am I?"

"Did you *want* the proprietor of a candy store to be dreaming about you?" Miguel asked, feeling the wound again. He *worked* there, for fuck's sake. All that fucking lonely heartbreak over a guy who had barely learned Miguel's name because he was falling head over heels for Finn, and the weirdly clairvoyant owner of the place he worked couldn't have one lousy dream about him? If Finn wasn't such a nice guy, Miguel would have spent a lot of useless time hating his guts. Didn't Miguel need some attention for *that*? Hell, Miguel's business dreams had gone up in flames—didn't he get some tea and sympathy for *that*?

But no, Miguel was the object of nobody's dreams, and this absurdly beautiful stranger just got his feelings hurt because of Miguel's attempts to mean something to *somebody*.

"I got no idea," Ezra said, shaking his head in confusion. "Maybe he knows Prince Charming. Maybe he *is* Prince Charming. Or maybe I'm just…."

He tried to sneer at Ezra, to make him feel small for wanting some attention—but he couldn't. He hadn't heard much—he'd mostly *seen* the conversation between Ezra and Rico—but he had the feeling that Ezra's heart was probably in the same state as his own.

"Lost," Miguel said with a sigh. "Yeah, no. Not chopped liver. C'mon. Let's get your luggage stashed."

"Hey, Miguel," Adam said casually as Miguel turned toward the living room, "do you want to stay for dinner? I mean, we've done a piss-poor job of thanking you for watching Clopper this weekend—"

"And Jake!" Miguel felt compelled to add. The cat wasn't any trouble, but that didn't mean it should be forgotten.

"And Jake," Adam conceded, completely serious. "Yeah—I mean, I know Derek was going to pay you, but still. You had to deal with family drama, and I was going to make that, whatyacallums, Asian salad, and that's a lotta fuckin' trouble for three people."

Miguel's lips quirked up at the corners. "But four people is just right?" Transparent. The man was transparent. But since he was being transparently *kind*, and transparently *grateful*, Miguel wouldn't shit on his parade.

"Absolutely," Adam said. He turned to Finn again and asked him to spit in the cup, and Miguel did his job as sort of a host-by-proxy.

"So, this is the apartment," Miguel said, gesturing vaguely. A hallway ran down to a bathroom on one side and a bedroom on the other. There was a generous closet next to the bathroom. The end.

"It's got air-conditioning like a fucking champion," Ezra said, nodding enthusiastically, and Miguel found his poor-poor-pitiful-me moment evaporating.

"It does," he said gratefully. It truly was about thirty-five degrees cooler inside than it was outside, and Miguel found himself a little happy that the dog wasn't there with his nova flare body and boundless enthusiasm. "Miserable out there."

Ezra nodded rather pathetically, and Miguel thought the word "miserable" might apply universally.

"Here—I'm going to set you down in front of… whatever the hell is on and let you just sort of decompress, okay?" Miguel thought perhaps he could do it—he could edge away from so much rampant pain and just let this stranger drift into his own comfort zone, and Miguel wouldn't have to deal with the fact that this poor kid had just flown thousands of miles to get dumped on the front lawn of an unfamiliar place.

"That's human of you," Ezra said listlessly, taking the remote control and disconsolately flipping through channels. He paused after a moment and turned just as Miguel was making for the kitchen so he could have a conversation of furious whispers with Adam. "Uh, so, Miguel, could I trouble you for a glass of water? I hate to ask, I mean—"

Miguel's head snapped over to stare at him and his eyes got wide. "Uh, yeah," he said. "Sure. No problem. Let me get you some ice."

That quickly, the bemused stranger was no longer a stranger. That quickly, he was a force to be reckoned with.

This apparent stranger knew his name.

ADAM WAS a fair hand at Asian salad, it turned out, and dinner was that rare combination of light and filling. They had their choice of iced tea, water, or milk, and Ezra, surprisingly enough, took milk.

"What every growing boy needs," Adam grunted. "But you're not that short, so be careful. Lactose intolerance is only a chocolate bar away." He cast Finn an evil look, and Finn smiled blandly back. Finn was not, in point of fact, eating salad. Adam had cooked him up some mushy pasta that needed no chewing and had no spice, and Miguel wondered what it must be like to love someone so much that they'd go to that much trouble for a bitten tongue.

"Yeah, well, I've seen enough of my old man and my older brothers popping Rolaids—anything I can do to avoid that, I will."

Miguel wanted to ask about that, but he'd kept that part of himself, the inquisitive, ambitious part of him, stomped flat since his business dreams had died. Sit and watch, sit and watch. But it was hard to be so passive around people who continually tried to be good people in spite of the fact that they'd gotten their hearts crushed.

An odd expression crossed Adam's face, and Miguel was suddenly *very* interested to know what Adam knew that the rest of them didn't.

"Ain't no law that says you gotta be your old man," Adam said wisely. "I mean it's one thing if you're Finn and your pops is like, solid awesome with a side of kickass, but not everybody gets that. It's okay to say 'I'm going to be somebody new.'"

Ezra smiled shyly at him. "Yeah. Well, that's the idea."

"All right, then. Welcome to our table, somebody new. This here is Miguel Rodriguez—we work together in two different places. He's a nice guy."

Miguel smiled quietly and nodded, and Adam continued.

"This here is my boyfriend, Finn Stewart—his entire family is a trip and they'll probably adopt you. Don't fight it, Ezra. Just let it happen. It'll be good for you."

Ezra smiled, biting his lower lip, and those luminous blue eyes gazed up at Adam like he was a last best hope. "And you are?"

"I'm Adam Macias. I'm Rico's cousin." Adam suddenly looked very sober, and when he spoke next, it was like nobody else at the table existed. "Rico—he told me pretty much everything, Ezra. You… you can feel safe here, okay? I mean, no bullshit getting between Rico and Derek, but… you know. Do your dishes, walk the dog, try not to run around the house naked, and you can stay here as long as you need to."

Ezra swallowed, and Miguel watched his eyes get shiny. "Thanks," he said gruffly. "I… I appreciate it."

Adam nodded and then looked around the apartment in a blatant attempt to lighten the subject. "Miguel, you sure you didn't kill the cat?"

Miguel laughed, but his eyes were still on their blue-eyed stranger, who was apparently really moved by human kindness. "I think he's sulking. He gets like that when someone takes Clopper out of the house without him."

"Huh. I had no idea. Well, Finn is so stoned he's drooling in his mush and cheese—maybe he should go say hi."

Finn startled, but Adam was right. Whatever painkillers he'd pumped into Finn, the poor guy was reduced to staring, eyes glazed, at the milk.

"Abam?"

Adam stood and looked at his half-finished salad. "I'll be back. You guys go ahead and finish. There's cookies in the jar on the counter and ice cream in the freezer—wait. Maybe just cookies in the jar. Anyway, I won't be long."

With that, he stood up and took Finn by the elbow and guided him carefully down the hall. Miguel and Ezra watched them go.

Ezra spoke into the silence. "Uhm… does he know?"

Miguel tried for innocence. "About what?"

Ezra shook his head and concentrated on his salad for a minute. "Never mind," he mumbled. Perversely, Miguel wanted to talk about it.

"No, seriously, about what?"

Ezra cautiously looked up from his salad. "That you've been… you know… pining for him or whatever? Does he know you're crushing bad?"

"I'm not crushing on Finn," Miguel said, feeling like an ass.

"No," Ezra said, keeping eye contact through a terrible blush. "Not Finn."

Miguel sighed and carefully wiped his mouth with his napkin. "See," he said quietly, listening for the door, "Adam showed up at Candy Heaven in the beginning of November during this heinous rush, right? Looking for a job. He walked in and he and Finn did that—you know, that stranger dance thing? One goes left, one goes right, and then they try to get out of each other's way?"

Ezra nodded, looking grave.

"That was it," Miguel said, half laughing. "I mean I didn't realize that was it. Darrin called Adam up, gave him an apron like he'd been waiting for the guy, and Adam worked an eight-hour shift on an empty stomach. At the end of the shift, he went up to the stock room and practically passed out, right when Finn showed up delivering sandwiches. So here I am thinking, 'Hey, this guy's cute, he's competent, he's sort of funny, I wonder if…,' and Finn is upstairs bonding with him over a hamburger—and not in the dirty way, either. Soul bonding. Adam just… just never looked at anyone else. Not me. Not Derek. It was like he walked through the door and into his guiding star, and the rest of us were just… scenery."

"Well," Ezra said, smiling a little in sympathy, "maybe you're someone else's guiding star. They just have to see you."

Miguel let out a grunt. "Papi, I'm just a twinkle in the light pollution here. *Nobody* sees me."

Ezra's expression shifted to one of profound hurt. "I've been that," he said. "Was like one person on the whole world saw me, and he…."

Aw hell. "Just walked into an inferno with his cousin's dog."

Ezra nodded, swallowing hard. "Yeah. So, uhm, whose dog *was* that thing? When Rico was in New York, he kept talking about how his cousin was watching Clopper, but everyone seems to think it's Adam's."

Miguel laughed a little. "Adam moved in and they sort of… you know… that whole guiding star thing?"

Ezra nodded. "Yeah. Had no idea it came furry. Now I do."

God, he was pretty. Pale skin—although he probably tanned, if given the chance—and dark hair, savagely scraped back from his forehead with product. A few stiff curls were rebelling against his brow and temples, and Miguel wondered what would happen if he left the product off and just cut it a little shorter. Would it be soft? Would his curls be glossy black or a more mellow brown?

"Do you like dogs?" Miguel asked, mostly to balance himself after the surge of attraction smacked him hard in the gut.

Ezra thought about it seriously. "I don't know," he said. "I've never had one."

Miguel stared at him, jaw dropped. "Everyone has dogs," he said, because his family had, like, six of them, one per kid. Of course, Miguel's dog loved his brother Berto more, but that wasn't *Berto's* fault. Berto was going to be a veterinarian. It ran in his veins.

"No," Ezra said, looking a little forlorn. "We don't have any… my dad. He's sort of a piece of work."

Miguel shifted, feeling blank and uncertain. "I don't even know what that expression means," he said.

"It means his dad is rattlesnake mean, and he doesn't need to be bothered about it right now," Adam said, apparently tiptoeing down the hallway on stealth feet while wearing a cloak of invisibility.

Ezra looked up with such naked gratitude that Miguel felt a little jealous. Seriously? Did *everybody* get a crush on Adam?

"You're not wrong," Ezra said, and then he studied the last piece of chicken in his salad like it held the secrets of the universe.

"Yeah, well, I had the female version," Adam said casually and took a bite of Finn's mushy pasta. He grimaced and went back to his salad, which was mostly uneaten. "I *had* a dog, but when I shipped out to Iraq, she had it put to sleep."

Miguel was aware that he and Ezra *both* sucked in a breath.

"That's *horrible*," Miguel said, and Adam waved it away like it must not have hurt.

"I lived. But that's why Rico wants to give me the dog, see? Wants to think it will make up for what a shitty time I had then. It *won't*, right? But it'll make Rico happy, and it wasn't Rico's fault that the time was shitty, so I let him do it."

Miguel and Ezra both nodded like this made total sense.

"But see, that's the thing. Rico says that Ezra belongs here. He's trying to make something right. He can't make up by leaving Derek, 'cause…." He grimaced at Ezra. "That's no good. Him and Derek, they work completely. Yuppie bastards, both of them, but in the best ways, you know?"

Miguel laughed. "I'm a yuppie bastard too!" he protested, and Adam shrugged.

"Then when you get your office and your suit again, *you'll* be a yuppie bastard in the best of ways. But what I'm saying is that he can't give *himself* to Ezra, just like he couldn't give *the past* back to me. But he gave something he thought was just as important. I love that fucking dog in the now, and I'll take his gift at face value. And Ezra? You must need something in this shitty apartment that Rico wishes he could give you himself. So you enjoy dinner, move his shit out and your shit in, and we'll take you in tomorrow to get you a job at Candy Heaven so you can help with the rent. It's gonna be okay. And if Candy Heaven can't help you, Finn's dad probably needs someone. I mean, Rico says you're sort of a sharp, right? Advertising, business? You gonna miss that?"

Ezra's full mouth twitched. "I tried to rip apart my office with my bare hands," he said, indicating the scars.

Adam nodded like he got it. "So that's a no. Okay. I got this to make sense—which is good, because seriously, two hours ago I was pretty sure the world was batshit insane. You guys, don't wait on me. Go move him in while I finish. Then I'll do dishes and we can watch some tube before bed." Suddenly Adam faltered, when he'd been 100 percent command just moments before. "Uh, Miguel—I'm sorry. God, listen to me, just taking over your time like that. You can go whenever—"

"You're out of ice cream?" Miguel asked, because it hurt watching Adam lose confidence that fast.

Adam sighed. "Yeah, sorry."

"Then I'll go get some," Miguel said, smiling. He stood up and cleared his plate into the sink. "Ezra, you got any preferences?"

"I'd say not rocky road, 'cause it's not kosher, but you know what?"

"What?"

"I don't think I give a shit about kosher right now. It's like the dog. I would *love* some rocky road ice cream."

Wow. Look at him. A night at Adam's table, and suddenly Mr. Independence. Miguel supposed there were worse places for him to end up.

"Rocky road it is," he said brightly, and then fled the apartment before Ezra could tell Adam Miguel was in love with Adam, and Adam could ask him why Miguel got a hard-on when he and Ezra were just talking alone.

Yeah.

Ice cream. Ice cream would make this much less confusing, he was *sure* of it!

Security Blanket

EZRA FELL asleep in front of the television around nine o'clock California time. Well, given that he'd gotten on a plane at around 6:00 a.m. New York time, it had been something of a day.

His last conscious thought was *What the hell was I thinking? Rico had no reason to wait for me.*

His *next* conscious thought was that two men he didn't know that well were helping him get up so they could fix the couch.

"Wuzz jus gonna crash," he mumbled, not wanting to talk to Rico's scary-looking cousin or the boy with the angel's face who had the crush on Rico's scary-looking cousin.

"Yeah, well, it's more comfy like this," Adam said gruffly. "Miguel, strip off his shirt and his pants and shit. It's fuckin' hot in here, and it's not gonna get any better. AC's gonna be on all night."

Yeah. What in the hell *was* that? People talked about New York sucking in the summer—and it did—but nobody talked about *California* sucking in the summer.

It sucked. It really, really sucked.

Ezra didn't want to think about everything else that sucked at the moment, so he concentrated on letting angel-faced Miguel (heh heh heh, like he was a gangster or something) help him out of his pants.

One moment he was standing blearily, balancing himself on the back of the couch, and the next moment, he was lying down on... mm... well, it was like a pillow top for a couch, so it felt, in fact, *better* than a couch. In fact, it felt better than Ezra's bed, which he'd had to put in storage when he'd made the ill-advised decision to ditch his apartment and come out here. But that was okay, because it was like magic, this new bed, and he said so.

"Magic?" said Angel-Faced Miguel. "Hey, Adam—he thinks your couch is magic."

Adam's laugh was a little bit dirty. "So far it has been. But not the same for Rico when he slept in it."

"Aw, man," Ezra mumbled. "Rico slept here? That's…."

"A gift," Adam said shortly, tousling his hair like a child. "Now hang on a minute, I'm gonna go get you a friend."

"That's nice," Ezra mumbled. "He's gonna go get me a friend." He looked up at Miguel, who regarded him soberly. "I thought *you* were my friend. Rico left and handed me to you, and hey! You had to be my friend. Like the kid assigned to the new kid at school, right? I'm a job."

Miguel let out a long-suffering sigh, like maybe that had been *exactly* what he'd been thinking, and now he was trying to think of something nice to say instead.

"No, papi," he began, and Ezra thought, *Whoa, boy, here comes the big insincere whopper!* "You were just a surprise. Too pretty to be a job, right?"

It was probably the lie Ezra suspected, but it was nice of him to make the attempt. "That's sweet," he mumbled, and at that moment a big furry, drooling sandbag plopped on his chest and lost all physical coherence.

"This is Jake," Adam said from behind the couch. "Jake is a guaranteed cure for hangovers and broken hearts."

Ezra had never owned a cat before. He'd never even had the inclination to own a cat before. He stared at Jake and Jake regarded him lazily through eyes he couldn't bother to open all the way. Then Jake started to purr, motorboating little bits of drool out of the corners of his thin spotted cat lips with every vibration.

Ezra opened his mouth to say thank you, but no, this charming California custom of trying to squash a person with a defunct cat was not to his liking, when every muscle in his back and chest suddenly went liquid. What came out was "Ahhhhhh… mmmm… zzzzz…."

And he fell asleep for the next ten hours.

WHEN HE came to, that beautiful kid with the strawberry blond hair and big blue eyes was sitting on the chair kitty-corner to him, drinking a milkshake and reading a paperback.

Ezra shifted and realized that something warm and soft was on his head and he was sweating like mad. He sat up abruptly and the warm soft thing tumbled down his pillow to wedge itself between Ezra's ass and the couch—and still it didn't move, so Ezra jumped to his feet, stumbled on the coffee table, and went over, landing on his back between the coffee table and the television, staring at the ceiling and wondering what the hell had happened to his life.

"Wow."

Ezra looked at the beautiful kid and said, "You're telling me. I didn't even know I could dance."

The kid laughed and loomed over him, offering a hand up. "You even startled the cat. Our upstairs neighbor moved in last week and it sounded like a wrecking ball. Clopper didn't stop barking. I thought freaking out the cat was impossible."

Ezra took the hand and scrambled to his feet, relaxing a little when he saw that they were the same height. Adam loomed—Finn just *was*. He glanced over at the cat, who was glaring at him from disapproving amber eyes, and smiled sheepishly. "Sorry, cat." Then he looked back at Beautiful Kid. "So your tongue is feeling better?" he asked apprehensively. He remembered the cup and the blood and the spit.

The kid managed to look sheepish. "My sister brought me some Orajel this morning—apparently I was whining in my sleep and Adam freaked out. He *really* doesn't like it when I'm hurt."

Ezra tried not to shudder. "Yeah, well, I'll make sure that you never get hurt on my watch, 'cause Adam...."

The kid let out a long-suffering laugh, like he'd heard that before. "He is *not* that scary," he said. "Now go to the bathroom and do whatever, and when you get out, I'll have some lunch ready for you—"

"Lunch?"

"It's almost eleven. Anyway—Adam has business with Derek, but after he gets back with the dog, he's going to take you to go get a job, so, you know. Shower, shit, shave, all of that."

Ezra nodded and assessed his physical person. "Number two first, then eat, then everything else."

The kid smiled and grabbed Ezra's hand. "Hey, I'm Finn Stewart, and I know you're Ezra Kellerman, and I think you and me are going to be good friends. Not besties, because, you know, me and Rico, we're like that." He held up two crossed fingers. "But you know, friends. Because anyone who makes number two number one is a guy I can talk to."

And with that, Finn turned around and gestured to the bathroom down the hallway, leaving Ezra to get down to business.

Forty-five minutes later he was dressed in khakis and a polo shirt and sitting at the dinky kitchen table. His studio in Chelsea had been about twice the size of this little apartment, but for some reason calling it a kitchen table seemed to give the little Formica thing some heft.

Which made the argument he was having with Finn over what he was wearing—or should have been wearing—feel a little more important than it sounded.

"Killing me," Finn moaned, aggrieved. "You and Rico—you're killing me. No cargo shorts? No denim shorts? It's like you're *trying* to dress yourself into heat exhaustion and looking like dorks in the process!"

"Look, why am I even getting a job anyway?" Ezra demanded at last, baffled by the idea of going job hunting in denim shorts. "Shouldn't I be... I don't know, crawling back to my father with my tail between my legs and begging to marry a nice Jewish girl?"

Finn stopped short and swallowed. "You know, Ezra, the walls of this apartment aren't thick. I've heard everything Rico had to say about your dad. You need to ask yourself if that's really what you want."

Ezra swallowed. The night before he'd eaten rocky road ice cream—not the first nonkosher food to pass his lips, but definitely an act of rebellion. It had been delicious. Not anything he *couldn't* live without, and he understood there existed scads and scads of modern Jews who ate it on a regular basis—but he'd loved it. Truly loved it. Did he really want to go back to a place where it wasn't even a possibility?

To a place where a man in his *life*—and not just his bed—wasn't even a possibility? Because that had been his dad.

It wasn't the religion, because Jews on the whole were pretty damned forgiving—no. It was Martin Kellerman, who gave credence to any idea that allowed him to control the world to his *exact* specifications. He was the micromanaging monster of every office worker and the thundering bogeyman in every child's nightmares.

He'd been the nightmare of Ezra's *waking* life, that was for sure.

"So," Finn was saying gently, intruding into unwelcome memories. "Do you *want* to turn around and go back to New York? Or do you want to do what you set out to do here and make a new start?"

"I'd hoped...." God, how embarrassing. Ezra bit his lip, because everyone he now knew was aware of exactly why he'd shown up on the lawn of a low-rent Victorian fiveplex in this weirdass little town.

"Yeah," Finn said, his voice so quiet Ezra wanted to run away. "We know. And you know what?"

"What?" He failed to keep the note of defensiveness from his voice.

"That was real fucking brave. I mean… *really* brave. You think we all don't have exes in our past? Someone we didn't want to let go? You *were* that person for Rico. He was breaking his heart over you. It took him months to even give Derek the time of day."

There had been a moment, when Ezra had been walking down the ramp onto the airplane, when he asked himself, *And what if he doesn't want you?*

He'd stopped, his carry-on threatening to veer out of control, and turned around to look for where the tunnel opened to the vast maze of JFK.

I've turned the corner. There is nowhere to go but on that plane.

Well, here he was. Rico didn't want him—but he truly had turned the corner, hadn't he?

"You really think that was brave?" Ezra asked, uncertain. Nobody had ever called him brave before.

"Yeah," Finn said, nodding. "I mean, I lost my last boyfriend because he just sort of made a unilateral decision to move somewhere else for his master's program. I… my family is here. I wasn't ready to leave them, and he wasn't ready to compromise. Leaving a place you've known all your life and going somewhere else—that's a big deal, you know?"

Ezra smiled weakly. "Yeah," he said, but he thought he could keep his voice steady for a while. "So, uhm, I need shorts?"

Finn nodded. "But that's okay. Slacks will work for the interview—I mean, Miguel and Adam are introducing you, and it's not like, you know, a Fortune 500 company. It's a candy store."

Ezra nodded, remembering all those times he hadn't been allowed to go into those places. No candy stores for Ezra, no train sets, no Legos. It had all been educational software and homework.

His father had thrown his beloved teddy bear in the fire when he was ten, because he didn't want Ezra to have any "unhealthy attachments."

"Does it have those big rainbow lollipops?" he asked wistfully. "I mean, I hear they're just cherry flavored, but, you know, when you're a kid, you think they're gonna taste like all the colors."

Finn grinned and nodded. "Yeah!" He looked over his shoulder like he was expecting an older brother or sister who would give him shit about what he said next. "My sister Mari used to buy them for me so she could go flirt with her boyfriend. You know what she said?"

Ezra shook his head.

"She said the rainbow was in the taste, but we had to know what rainbows tasted like before we recognized it."

Oh God, he looked so proud. Ezra remembered when he told his best friend—who had been Jewish too, but whose parents had done the Santa thing apparently because they just liked it—that Santa didn't exist, and if he *did* exist, he wouldn't be throwing money away on little Jew boys when there were plenty of Christians around who wanted a toy train. His father's words, verbatim, and his friend had burst into tears, and he and Ezra hadn't been best friends anymore.

So Ezra decided not to tell this grown person how his sister was probably full of shit and probably trying to shut Finn up so she could get laid or kissed or go to the prom or something.

But Finn—Finn surprised him then, because as much as he *looked* like the bubbles in soda, he was apparently the real deal.

"I know it sounds hokey—but Mari just… you know, she's got a kid, right? And she and her husband had this kid so they could *play* with him. And that all started when I was little. She just wanted to play with me. Give me a good day. So yeah, on the one hand, the lollipops probably just taste like cherry. But on the other, they probably taste like rainbow, but you have to know what rainbows taste like."

Finn smiled with his wide, mobile mouth, and Ezra suddenly understood why Adam would take time out of his night to give Ezra a cat.

Because *this* kid right here made you want to do nice things.

Ezra thought about it—him, Ezra Kellerman, the boss's kid who *could* have pulled his own weight had he not been simultaneously kissing his old man's ass.

"A candy store," he said, shrugging but not dislodging the hopeful feeling in the pit of his stomach. "Sure. Once your mad scary boyfriend gets here with his dog, let's you and me go taste the fucking rainbow."

Finn's response had a lot of teeth.

COMPARED TO Manhattan, most of "Downtown Sacramento" was a suburb. About the only thing that looked familiar from the back of the battered minivan Adam drove was the giant pile of dirt and the humongous hole in the ground behind the railroad station, near K Street.

"What in the hell are you putting there? An actual building?" Because there were a few skyscrapers on the Sacramento skyline, but compared to what he was used to? No.

"Naw," Finn said brightly. "That's the new stadium. You know, so we could keep the Kings."

"Basketball," he said with a grunt. "Ain't the Mets."

"I am fuckin' *sayin'*!" Adam exclaimed. "You play?"

"No—my people don't do sports."

Finn peered at him. "Jewish people?" he asked dubiously. "Because *I* might not be so coordinated, but we had some kids in high school—"

Ezra shook his head. "No—not Jewish people. Skinny uncoordinated people who run like an epileptic ostrich."

Finn smirked. "Oh, well that's my family's whole softball team. We've got a game on Saturday, you can play."

Ezra gaped at him. "Just like that?"

And then Adam blew his mind. "You're playing Candy Heaven!" he protested. "How do you know *we* don't want him?"

Finn sent Ezra a droll look. "Because he obviously just said he'll play better with us."

"Yeah," Adam muttered. "That's only because you enact the daddy-daddy-mercy rule whenever you get down a few points."

"Twenty points, Adam," Finn retorted. "You had us down twenty points. I figure if Ezra's as bad as he says he is, we'll only have to play, like, half an hour this Saturday, and then we can go swim in the river like normal people."

"Killing me, Finn. You are *killing* me."

"He doesn't like to show off his tattoos," Finn said, sounding smug. "I *like* his tattoos."

Ezra tried hard to look at Adam like a sex object instead of a patriarch. It was like Adam's muscles exploded in excruciatingly lurid three-dimensional color.

Oh holy God.

"I would too," Ezra said weakly. Okay. Well. He'd already had an inkling for why Miguel's crush wouldn't stop. That there was just… just sexual icing on the whole package.

Finn laughed evilly. "All mine," he said smugly.

Ezra rolled his eyes. Like there had been any doubt.

At that point Adam turned left before a freeway interchange. He turned right in front of an art gallery that Ezra marked in his head because he liked those, and then right again. And what happened next was like a wormhole in space.

A left, an odd overpass, a wiggly sort of right, and suddenly they were in a town right out of the Old West. And just when Ezra was starting to think maybe it was all kitsch and building façades, the car's wheels hit the cobblestone stretch of the pavement, and Ezra's teeth felt like they were being rattled from his head.

"Mmn…."

"Sorry," Adam grunted, and the car slowed down, making the jouncing just a little more bearable. "You didn't bite it again, did you?"

"No," Finn said tightly. "But always, too fast."

Adam barked out a laugh. "Really? From you?"

"Yeah, I know, I do it too."

Ezra looked around the tiny nest of shops and restaurants along the Sacramento River. He almost laughed at the suspension bridge that went—as Adam pointed out—to Raley Field, where the minor league baseball team played. He was used to, well, *bridges*, and this one was small, to say the least.

But then, the little tourist trap wasn't more than four blocks by four blocks, either.

"So," he said dubiously. "I'm… I mean, you guys work around here?"

"I work at River Burger," Finn said practically. "And this is my stop." Adam pulled to a halt in front of a big bronze statue of a pony express rider, and Finn gave him a peck on the cheek before hopping out. "'Kay, text me where you park, right? I'll come get you guys after your shift."

"I thought I'd show Ezra the bus," Adam said soberly. "That way, you know, he's got some freedom and shit."

Finn growled and shook his head. "You know, he could stay here for years and never have to ride the bus. You and I will make it our personal responsibility that your cousin's ex-boyfriend will never have to ride the bus. Now just text me, okay?"

With that he shut the door, leaving Adam to roll his eyes and then pull around the corner. Hey, there was another museum on the corner, this one dedicated to trains. Ezra thought that might be sort of cool to stop at too.

"What's he got against buses?" Ezra asked as Adam pulled into a big parking garage under the freeway. "Are they awful?"

"Fuck if I know," Adam muttered. "It's like he takes it personally if anyone he knows has to use public transportation. I think it's what happens when you're raised out here with all the, you know, cows and fields and shit."

Ezra nodded, remembering the vast acres of farmland under the plane as they'd landed. "Huh. Well, given what I've seen of the roads, maybe people oughtta start getting on the bus, you know?"

"I'm sayin'," Adam grumbled. He maneuvered the minivan through the garage and parked it up top. Adam took Ezra down a couple of flights of concrete stairs, and bam! They were back in the place with the statue of the pony express rider.

"So what is this, like some sort of salute to the Old West?" Ezra asked, actually curious.

"You remember the gold rush, the one in 1849?" Adam asked. "It's okay if you don't—I mean, in California we learn it like the Bible, but I get there's other states in the union. Anyway, in 1849, a guy named James Marshall found a big gold nugget and showed his boss, John Sutter. Sutter was supposedly a decent guy, but that's not the only guy Marshall told. Sutter said, 'Hey, look at this, maybe we should see if there's more!' and Marshall told his friend Sam Brannan, who was sort of an opportunistic douche bag. Brannan took out an ad in the local paper and trumpeted it on a loudspeaker and then set up businesses to charge people their firstborn for things like clothes and food."

"Charming," Ezra muttered. "Sounds like someone my dad knows."

"Yeah, well, it's the American way. Speaking of which, Marshall, the guy who found the gold in the first place, died penniless, so maybe advertising isn't the best use of your dollar. Anyway, so they start making money, and they need to build a real town, because all of the tent towns are going up in flames, and Sutter says, 'Hey, there are some nice places up the hill where the floods that happen every ten years don't reach, and one of those places—' and by the time he was done with the sentence, that douche bag Brannan had bought out all the useless land in the Sacramento Delta and then made a premium building there."

Ezra looked at Adam like he was crazy. "Doesn't it flood?"

Adam nodded. "Well, when it's not in crazy dust bowl drought, yeah. So for about a hundred years, this city flooded, and they built on top of the wreckage, and it flooded, and… well, so a lot of the city is built on the flood remains of the rest, and they just kept doing that until it stopped flooding anymore. And I guess they kept Old Town… well, old, to celebrate all that."

"So it's a tourist trap to celebrate ignorance and greed?" Ezra asked, suddenly seeing the charming little boardwalk and the façade-graced storefronts in a darker, more sinister light.

"Naw. It's celebrating the pioneer spirit," Adam said, and he sounded perfectly sincere. "They built the capital to celebrate ignorance and greed."

Ezra started to laugh. "I am going to look all that bullshit up someday," he said. "And someday, I'll take you on a revisionist history tour of New York, just to get even."

Adam shrugged. "Look, you don't want my version of the facts, maybe get a guy who didn't get his VA grant yanked because his car broke down. You make bitter citizens, you get bitter history. It's all I'm saying."

Ezra nodded, liking Rico's cousin very much in that moment. "Point taken. So, what would I find in the railroad museum?"

Adam rolled his eyes. "Oh my God, you want a monument to ignorance and greed? Let's *talk* about the railroad, shall we?"

By the time they'd walked the four blocks to Candy Heaven, Ezra wasn't sure how much of Adam's revisionist history was true and how much was just storytelling at its finest, but he *was* reasonably certain that much of California had been founded by scoundrels and thieves.

And in the entire four blocks, he hadn't found himself once asking what he was doing there and why he didn't just fly back to New York. In fact, he found himself turning his face up to soak in the sun and enjoy the smell of the warmed dusty boards under his feet.

As they crossed the street nearest the riverfront, he looked down from his sun worship and saw one of the three people he now knew in this new place. This one had dark hair, satiny brown-toned skin, an oval face, a chin with a divot, and lovely sloe eyes with a thick fringe of lashes.

Oh.

And a full mouth. Really full. Like, wide and mobile when he was talking but plump and perfect pursed together. Ezra didn't know the guy well, but he sure could look at him forever—even when his eyes were narrowed in thought and he looked pissed off and irritated.

"Angel-faced Miguel," he said, smiling slightly.

Miguel startled from his lean against a big pillar that supported the weight of the overhang.

"Mr. Manhattan," he said, the sour expression fading so he could smile back. "Adam been giving you the grand tour?"

Adam shrugged. "I do what I can. Darrin in?"

Miguel nodded and turned so he could gesture them into the double doors. He rested his hand lightly on Ezra's back for a moment, and Ezra's stomach tightened.

Oh, wow.

Wow.

Had it been that long since someone had touched him?

Well, yeah, huh. Rico had left at the beginning of April, and it was near the end of August now, so, well, five months?

Who went five months without a hug or a touch or something? Jesus, no wonder he was so enamored of the cat.

He didn't have much more time to think about Miguel then, because they got inside, and he felt a smile twitch at his lips. It was hard to believe that Rico's scary cousin worked here.

Dark paneling lined the floors and walls of the candy-by-the-pound establishment, and brightly rainbow-colored banners shielded the loft from visitors. It probably held stock, Ezra thought, and he took in the big freaky clown in the corner, as well as the giant forty-pound gummi bears along the ledge over the M&M's dispensers that held M&M's by the color.

Tacky? Well, yeah.

But also… charming. Fun. All of it designed for sweetness.

God, Ezra would have loved a place like this as a kid.

The man who stood behind the counter had a long shag haircut, bangly earrings, and a slim-cut Henley shirt over his jeans, and cowboy boots.

He also had a long face and a rather bitchy smile.

"Really?" he said, looking at Adam. "I just finished with your cousin and you bring me this?"

Adam shrugged. "Rico said you could help him. It's not my fault you like to get in everybody's business."

The man rolled his eyes, and then he seemed to take a longer look at Miguel and Ezra as they stood together.

He said a few more things to Adam that Ezra didn't understand, and then Adam called Ezra forward to introduce him.

And the guy flat-out told him that he didn't belong in Manhattan, he only thought he did.

Ezra stared at him, mouth open. *I... have you* been *there?* he wanted to stutter. Because even as they stood in the little store with the wooden floorboards and the freaky clown, Ezra was having a hard time reconciling this as part of a city, when he was used to the magnificent steps of the Metropolitan Museum of Art, or the gorgeousness that was Central Park, or the forest of skyscrapers so vast you had to hold on to a wall to look up and see sky.

He glanced out the window and saw sky.

And suddenly thought this Darrin guy might have a point.

"I...." Well, that was intelligent.

Darrin gave him a pitying smirk. "Once again Adam has brought somebody new into my life and my dreams. I can't tell you how happy I was when you started showing up in my Pixy Stix powder this last week—it was like something walked up and stomped on my toe."

"Be nice," Adam growled. "We want him to be happy here."

"Why?" Darrin asked him archly—literally arching an eyebrow and fluttering his lashes. "You're happy. Your cousin is happy. Your boyfriends are happy—why do you have it in for this one?"

Adam scowled. "He's a nice kid and he's...." He darted an uncomfortable glance at Ezra. "You know. Like I was. Sort of gun-shy of the whole human race. Look, I've got two cures for that, and he can't have Finn. Suck it up."

Darrin laughed coquettishly. "Can I feed him a cricket?"

"Are you hearing me? He's not ready for a cricket. Give him like... I don't know. Chocolate that's gentle or something."

"I am *not* giving him a laxative," Darrin snapped in honest outrage, and Adam waved his hands.

"I didn't say you should. For one thing, he's rooming with us, and, you know, Finn."

Miguel grunted, and Darrin closed his eyes. "I know more about your boyfriend's digestive system than I know about my own. Does this seem wrong to you?"

"Look—please? You needed somebody, I brought somebody. He'll be good. I said so."

Darrin pinched the bridge of his nose and sighed. "And thus the student becomes the master. Okay, fine. You know where the aprons are. Tell Carolyn to get out the paperwork. You have inventory to take— Miguel can show him around, okay?"

Adam's smile was blinding.

"Yeah, sure. That's awesome. Thanks, boss!"

Miguel took him to the left, and a little office under the stairs to the loft. Ezra glanced behind his shoulder and saw that a line of customers was forming at the register now that they'd moved away, and that Darrin was using chopsticks to offer them chocolate-covered something from a clear plastic container.

"Well, now you've done it," Miguel muttered. "He's brought out the chocolate-covered crickets. You enjoy, because I'm not eating another one of those."

"Chocolate-covered crickets?" Ezra was fascinated. "Really? What do they taste like?"

Miguel gave him a narrow-eyed glance. "Like chocolate and exoskeleton. And…." He wrinkled his nose. "And chili powder. It's weird."

Ezra did an about face and became one of the people in the line for the counter, waiting for a chocolate-covered bug.

Darrin greeted him with two raised eyebrows. "People usually have to be dared to do this."

Ezra bit his lip, feeling shy and a little stupid. But the past two days… week… month… hell, his entire life since Rico had first walked through the door to his father's business and he'd thought, *I need to get me some of that*, had been all about the new and the different.

"You know what?" Ezra said, looking into the little plastic container.

"What?"

"I'll bet that shit ain't kosher."

Darrin grinned. "Nope, sparky, it sure ain't." He popped that bug into Ezra's mouth before he had a chance to rethink it, and Ezra crunched boldly, because the only thing worse than a chocolate-covered cricket would be a cricket with all the chocolate sucked off.

Darrin watched him curiously until he was done chewing. "So?"

"So, Miguel was right," Ezra said thoughtfully, picking his teeth with his tongue. "Exoskeleton and chili."

Darrin grinned. "Someday, junior, we'll see what your real candy is."

Ezra gazed wistfully behind Darrin's right shoulder. He had three giant lollipops there, big, twisted rainbows about two feet long. "Maybe it's rainbow," he said wanting to believe, like Finn, that there really was such a flavor.

"Huh." Darrin looked over his shoulder and saw what Ezra was looking at. "Maybe it is. Tell you what. You work for me for a month, and for your month-iversary, I'll give you one of those and you can see."

Ezra had his own money—his father had paid him really well, including his rent and his car payment and parking. But while Old Man Kellerman had owned his soul, Ezra's paychecks had been his own. He probably could have bought himself a lollipop right then.

But there was something seductive in the old-fashioned reward system. It gave him something to look forward to, a different dream.

"C'mon, Ezra," Darrin said softly. "You know all about motivation, right? You can't pine after Rico forever. He moved on."

Ezra nodded, apparently perfectly comfortable with this guy knowing everything about him. Why question it? Rico had abandoned him on his cousin's front stoop—and Rico's cousin had taken him in. And now he was here, and Darrin knew about his dreams and the way he used to get through the day working for his father.

If I can make it until tonight, I'll look at porn in my apartment. If I can make it until next week, I'll masturbate. If I can make it until the end of the month, I'll go out dancing at one of those clubs where they have the sex shows. If I can do it and not embarrass myself, switch pronouns, slack off my job, maybe I'll let someone do me in a back room.

Rico hadn't been his first boyfriend—by the time he'd met Rico, he'd had a different method for being in a relationship.

If I can make it through the day, I'll see him. If I can make it through the day, I'll hear his voice. If I can make it through the day, I'll touch his hand, feel his lips, take his cock in my mouth. If I can make it through, pretend I'm normal, not tell my old man I hate him, not tell my coworkers this job is horrible, not tell my mom I'm never bringing home a girl, I can have someone in my life who loves me for me.

Ezra looked at that lollipop again and smiled dreamily.

It was *perfect.*

"Sure," he said. "I mean, I *like* cherry, you know?"

Darrin quirked one corner of his wide, smiling mouth up. "How very appropriate," he said, and Ezra looked at him hard.

"No worries, Manhattan. Just go with Miguel and get your apron and your paperwork done. Carolyn's good at the paperwork, Miguel is good with the duties—you're in good hands."

Ezra shrugged again. "Yeah, it's weird. I really seemed to have landed on my feet here."

Darrin blinked sleepily, reminding him of the furry moose who had slept on Ezra's chest all night. "Yes, well, that could be your special superpower. Now scoot."

Ezra turned and did just that—scooted around the taffy barrels to the back, where Miguel was stocking up on a bunch of small canvas bags that had a picture of Darrin on them, dressed like Willy Wonka. He was holding a lollipop.

"That's just… weird," Ezra mumbled, but then he got his head in the game and did the paperwork and apron thing before they went back to resume stocking.

When they were done with that, Miguel showed him where the stock was in the top of the loft and how to order everything in the special displays. He told him he could man the registers after he got used to the pace of the place—which was brisk—and that when it got slow, they rotated outside with free taster coupons, which usually brought people in.

It wasn't a hard job, Ezra reflected, but he noticed a few things while he was working.

One was that Miguel was good at spotting things and doing them without being asked, while Ezra was more comfortable being told what to do.

The other was that Adam was good at placing people so that everybody was working on something necessary and nobody felt superfluous or in the way. He was also good at showing up at someone's elbow when they needed help, or when a customer got tricky, or when Darrin looked like he was going to be impositioned even the tiniest bit.

"Wow," Ezra said after watching Adam zoom across the store for the fifth time to keep this tiny, waiflike, elfin creature with blue hair from having to talk to anyone the least bit male. "He's like Superman. Does he think he can protect us *all* from the bad scary men?"

"I think he wants to," Miguel said. He sighed and wrapped another batch of super sour gummi tape in cellophane. "Me, I just want to make enough money to rent some office space and try my company again."

"Yeah? What's your company?"

"I want to run a temp agency. A good one—one where the people go in for things like maternity leave or to turn an office around. Like, an elite one."

Ezra thought of his time marketing for his father's company. "That's a good idea," he said. "You need to… I don't know, hook them up with companies that don't suck, right? Like do exit interviews. I know that if my dad had to answer to *anybody* for how toxic his office was, he might have made an effort to not be such an asshole."

Miguel glanced at him sideways. "That's a good idea. That might attract good people. If they can prove that their situation is just miserable, we'll pull them out and cut off the client. It…." He grimaced for no reason Ezra could think of. "It's empowering, you know? For people to think they've been heard."

Ezra smiled. "Yeah? Good idea?"

Miguel nodded. "Yeah. Good idea. So—you used to work with Rico, right? Marketing and advertising? You got a degree?"

Ezra nodded. "Yeah. Sort of… you know, what my old man wanted."

Miguel went, "Huh," like he didn't get that at all.

"Why—what'd your old man want from you?"

Oh, that angel's face and a nostalgic smile. Sweet. "I think he would have wanted me to be happy," Miguel said at last. "He was a happy guy—I mean, played with us all the time. Took us to the soccer field, played video games, to the movies as often as we could afford it. I don't think the gay thing would have fazed him. I mean, I remember my oldest sister dating, and he was always really sweet to her and her dates. Made sure they respected her, but respected *her* too, you know? Made sure they knew what she wanted. Him and Mom, never afraid of the sex thing. I heard him once asking Mom if we should put Lydia on birth control. Mom said she'd tell him when Lydia told her."

Ezra stared at him and shook his head. "I can't decide if that's really awesome or really twisted."

Miguel shrugged. "Let's go for awesome." Those big brown eyes grew sad. "Dad died of colon cancer when I was twelve. Just melted away in a matter of months. As far as I'm concerned, pretty much everything he did besides eat red meat made him a hero."

Ezra grunted. "My old man eats beef every day. Sometimes I think God misses when he shoots."

Miguel stared at him in horror.

Crap. That sounded... well, you know, who cared about how it sounded? His shrink told him he needed to speak for himself, not his old man.

Ezra glared at Miguel and showed him his knuckles. "I lived in a cage of the old man's making for twenty-eight years. Those are the scars I got when I tore it down. I'll let go of my bitterness when it's not nearly as fun as it is now."

It was Miguel's turn to grunt. "Yeah, okay. I guess I get that. Until you live in the cage, don't criticize the animal, right?"

And that quickly, Miguel was on Ezra's good side again. "Yup. And this animal is sort of content doing this very easy job."

Miguel sighed and watched as Adam went and took care of another problem. "I'm starting to think that the job is only easy because we're not good enough people to make it challenging, you know?"

Ezra tracked his gaze. "Well, tomorrow you and me can try to save the world. Today we'll just measure candy."

He went back to work and became aware that Miguel was looking at him with some interest, and some kindness as well. "You mean that? We can try to save the world tomorrow?"

"Yeah, why not?" Ezra shrugged. "Today I landed on my feet. Tomorrow I'll go terrorize the birds. You know, like a cat, right?"

"Yeah. How was Jake, anyway?"

"Warm and purry." And Ezra could smile just thinking about it. "I think I *like* cats."

"Yeah, well, some of them scratch. I like Clopper better."

"Huh." Adam had hustled Clopper in as Finn and Ezra had been getting in the car. That had been a *lot* of active, noisy dog. "Well, I'll have to meet him to make sure."

Sniffing the Corners, Finding the Mice

THE DAY went fast, and Ezra was... well, fascinated by the people he was working with. Old Man Kellerman's office had been old-school. Suits for all parties, black, gray, pinstripe—male and female. And gender politics be damned, Kellerman was known to show a distinct preference for women in skirts. Not that he was a skirt chaser—no. Just that women should wear skirts, and that was who he would respond to. The idea of a casual Friday would have given Ezra's father apoplexy, and his office staff had a dress code that included piercings (two earrings in women, none in men) and hair color (blond, brunet, and conservatively red). Visible tattoos must be covered.

None of the people Ezra was working with now would have kept their job longer than a minute.

Adam had visible tattoos, and Katya—the tiny waif of a girl who clung to Adam's shadow for protection—had blue hair, a nose ring, and several ear studs. Joni, the stocky girl who had a terrible crush on Katya but couldn't seem to get the time of day from her, had a buzz cut and a nose ring, and Darby, the single mom, had impossibly red hair with a skunk stripe of blonde from her temples—and as many earrings as Katya, with an eyebrow ring.

Even Anish and Ravi, who seemed to be exceedingly traditional, sported sleeve art from their wrists to their elbows, much of it featuring a many-armed goddess and a god with a sword.

Not one of these people would have passed muster for Martin Kellerman, and for a moment, Ezra felt a wall of reserve erecting. His father's voice spoke in his ear—he was *better* than they were. He wore slacks and not cargo shorts and dressed like a human being, for God's sake.

And then, from behind his little erected wall of adopted disdain, he started listening to their conversation during a lull in the plentiful business.

"Gordon Lightfoot, for real?" Anish was asking, incredulity lacing his voice.

"Yeah," Darby said, arranging a bowl of lollipop flowers like a pro. "My dad used to listen to him, and when Cameron was born, Dad sang 'The Wreck of the *Edmund Fitzgerald*' to Cam all through colic. So if I could meet any celebrity, alive or dead, it would be Gordon Lightfoot." Her face softened for a moment. "I'd tell Cam it was his Paw-Paw's favorite singer, and Cam would probably sing the stupid song right back at him." She wiped under her eyes. "We miss Dad."

"You are totally making my ambition to meet Selena Gomez and charm her out of her pants seem really, really shallow," Anish said mournfully, and Darby grinned back, her moment of melancholy gone.

"That's because it *is*. Okay, Miguel, your turn—any celebrity, alive or dead."

Miguel didn't even pretend to think about it. "George Takei, because he's fabulous, gay, and funny as hell."

"But not bangable?" Darby asked, like she was making sure.

"Oh my God—he's as old as my grandfather. No—he just seems like he'd be a blast to know."

Ezra smiled in spite of himself. This was a fun game. Nobody at his father's firm would play this game.

"What about you, new guy?" Ravi asked. Ravi was a tall, thin version of his shorter, rounder cousin, Anish, but together they made one fully functional human being. "Which celebrity would you like to meet?"

Ezra grunted, not entirely surprised by the question but not prepared either. "Jerry Orbach," he said, remembering watching Turner Classic Movies during that long month in the hospital when the shrinks tried to put him back together after he'd lost himself in a thousand million pieces. "'Cause he just seems like the dad you always wanted, you know?"

"I almost wish it was someone you could bang," Miguel said, looking at him uncomfortably.

"Yeah, well, in that case I'd pick Channing Tatum," Ezra said without hesitation. The resulting round of catcalls and hoots from the rest of the employees in the mostly empty store let him know he was not alone, and he blushed, feeling pleased and, for the first time in maybe his whole life, not entirely alone in a crowd.

"Nice choice," Joni said, laughing. "I mean, even *I'd* like to at least stroke those abs, and I'm not a fan of the peen."

Ezra ducked his head. "Well, it was that or Alskar, but, you know, Channing Tatum feels like he'd be a good buddy too."

"Right?" Miguel said, looking enthusiastic. "I mean, that approachability factor—that's huge, you know?"

"And he can dance," Ezra said earnestly. Oh, the clubs in Manhattan—not the ones that were gay by reputation, because he might get caught, but the other ones, where the dancing was intense and the right stroke on your back, your hip, your thigh, meant that with a little eye contact, a little body English, Ezra might get some touch. Sometimes a hand down his spine as he bent over was enough to make him come.

But Miguel was looking at him with pity, as though dancing was no big thing. "Yeah, Manhattan. He can dance."

Ezra could almost hear the rolled eyes, and that quickly, he wasn't part of the group anymore. He retreated into a wounded silence, and that might have been it, but Adam came walking by at that moment and said, "Seriously—Finn finally took me out dancing. I'd never been before— that was *fun*!"

Ezra sent him a grateful glance. "Right?"

Adam nodded in total sincerity. "Yeah—Miguel, you should totally go. It's like… like *free*, you know?"

"Yeah," Miguel said, and Ezra threw him a quick glance, catching the wistful, wretched note in his voice that said he was helpless to deny Adam anything. "Me and Ezra'll go this weekend."

Ezra had spent a lot of time dissembling around his old man, and that was the only thing that preserved his dignity now. "Sounds great," he said, and he saved his what-the-fuck glare until Adam nodded happily and walked away.

And then he added, "What the fuck?" under his breath for good measure.

Miguel hung his head and covered his eyes with his hands. "I'm such an asshole," he mumbled. "*Such* an asshole."

"I'm saying!" Ravi said, and Anish was nodding right next to him. "I thought you had more dignity than that."

"And class," Joni added.

"I know!" Miguel wailed, shaking his head. "God—and I thought I was almost done with being stupid!"

Ezra pursed his lips. "Stupid is flying three thousand miles for a guy who's moved the fuck on," he said, and Miguel met his eyes. Ezra felt a moment of total and complete simpatico with someone. He got it—the habit of loving someone hadn't been broken yet. The hopeless yearning hadn't faded enough to remember how to act when you *weren't* in love with them.

Miguel broke the moment with a crooked smile. "So, you want to go dancing on Friday after work?"

Ezra shrugged. "Yeah, why not? I mean…." He looked around the candy store, suddenly feeling affection for the routine of the simple job and easy friendship. "I mean, anyone else is welcome, right?"

Miguel shrugged. "Uh-huh—there's a whole scene around here, live music and everything. A couple of gay clubs—Faces, Gatsby's Nick—but it's mostly just music."

"We're in!" Anish and Ravi said in tandem. "And we can bring Cy too!"

Ezra looked at them blankly. "Okay, fine," he said, thinking he liked their company. "Whoever Cy may be."

They laughed and proceeded to tell Ezra about their friend Cy from their father's store, who was apparently all sorts of funny and bisexual to boot.

"Yeah, you never know who's going to be doing the walk of shame with Cy," Ravi finished up fondly. "I'm always hoping it's a girl, because when he breaks up with her, I'll be waiting!"

"His girls are out of your league," Anish said with a pitying look. "But it's nice that he gives you something to reach for."

"Oh sure!" Ravi said with a snort. "Ever since you started dating Rebecca, you can be full of all *sorts* of pity!"

And with that, the conversation broke into a series of questions about Anish's new girlfriend, and how she was tall, blonde, and buxom, and what in the hell was she doing with Anish?

But as Anish fielded the questions—and the ration of shit—from everybody *including* his cousin, Ezra got it.

Anish was a good egg. In fact, *everybody* he was working with sat, plump and pretty, in the same good-egg carton. And he was going dancing with people from work whom he actually liked.

Not a bad thing, really.

THAT AFTERNOON, as the August sun cast long shadows that did nothing to chill the heat or calm the humidity, Adam took him home and asked him how his first day went. So normal, like he hadn't just been dropped on the guy's doorstep the night before. Ezra was in the middle of answering that it wasn't bad when a tremendous yawn almost cracked his jaw.

"Yeah," Adam said soberly. "Me and Finn just got back from San Francisco yesterday when you arrived. Gonna be an early night in the gay bachelor apartment, you know?"

"You guys are practically married," Ezra said through another yawn. "I'm just this weird hanger-on who may or may not steal your silverware."

Adam laughed. "Well, the most expensive stuff is stainless steel—you can have that, but leave the plastic, okay?"

Ezra laughed and then yawned again behind his hand. "Speaking of Finn, where is he?"

"He's closing down the store—his sister'll bring him home when he's done. I told him you were out on your feet, so it's all good."

When they got to the apartment, Adam parked the car in the little lot behind the line of Victorians, kind of an alleyway, but with a fence on one side and a line of small backyards on the other. As he and Ezra got out of the minivan, Adam paused and let out a theatrical sigh. "Yup. Clopper's lonely. I hope that dog got the dump out of his system this morning or our place is gonna look a lot more low-rent than it already did."

Ezra could hear it as they walked between houses to the front walkway. Somebody was definitely howling in welcome.

Adam had Ezra stand back as he opened the door, but when Ezra heard the big "oolf!" he looked around the corner tentatively.

The giant dog Adam had rushed into the apartment that morning was standing on his hind legs with his paws on Adam's shoulders, licking his face with interest.

"*Down*, you big moo!" Adam commanded, grabbing the dog's collar and giving it a yank. The dog complied almost instantly, and Adam squatted down to his level, rubbing his ears and his ruff while the giant silver cross between a pit bull and a pony lost his puppy mind with ecstasy. He got in a few good whacks across Ezra's thighs with his giant tail as Ezra edged past, and it was gratifying to hear Adam make the dog sit so Ezra could get by.

The dog subsided after a few, and Adam gave a sigh of relief.

"Okay, good. Let me go change and I'll take you for a walk, okay?"

"I can use the toilet like a human," Ezra said with a straight face, and Adam's chuckle warmed his heart. Yeah, he could see why Miguel would lose his mind over the guy—but Ezra could also see why it would be a fruitless pursuit. Anyone who had seen him with Finn would know.

EZRA HAD arrived on Adam and Finn's lawn on Sunday afternoon. By Friday—the big group dancing date—he felt like he'd always known them, had always known the people at Candy Heaven, had always worked a simple retail job that required nothing more or less than that he put in a good effort and smile.

Like Jake the cat—who now spent every night on his chest, purring him to sleep—Ezra had simply found his spot and made himself comfortable, happy and half-awake and only a little conscious of the passage of time.

On Friday, as he was sweeping the floor behind the chocolate counter, he heard Rico's voice outside the store, approaching rapidly, and promptly woke up. In one quick duck he was crouched on the floor next to Miguel, who was Windexing the glass countertop. Miguel glared at him in surprise, but at that moment, through the glass display case, Ezra could see Rico and another guy—pretty, sandy-haired, blue-eyed, All-American Adorable—walk around the corner. Miguel's expression changed to comprehension.

Yeah, who wanted to be sweeping the floor at their retail job when his ex walked in?

Ezra squeezed into the corner, where the counter and partition were made of wood, and held his breath. He recognized Rico's voice—warm, slightly accented from living in a home with two languages, and kind.

God, Ezra could still remember the devastation on Rico's face when Ezra had told him to go.

"Miguel!" Rico was saying happily. "Man, it's good to see you. I didn't get a chance to say thank you for the pet watching and the... you know, the person watching and everything. How's it going?"

"With Clopper?" Miguel said, obviously dicking with Rico. "He's great. Big moo, eats dog food by the metric ton—but Adam's been home for a week. You should ask him."

Ezra contained a smirk—he could imagine Rico's eyes narrowing. "You look so quiet," he said. "Who knew you were such a smartass."

"I am a deep well, papi. You just need to look below the surface, that's all."

Rico gave an incredulous grunt. "You go be a well for someone else. Just tell me you didn't murder my ex-boyfriend and bury his body in a suitcase."

"What's it to you—you abandoned him on your cousin's lawn!" Miguel shot back, and Ezra looked at his knees gratefully. Oh, that was good to hear. Ezra didn't want to say it, because he knew he'd asked for it, but oh, it was nice to hear some vindication.

"Just because I don't want to sleep with him anymore doesn't mean I don't care what happens to him!" Rico protested. Oh God, he was getting flustered. Ezra used to love it when he did that, because Rico always seemed so self-possessed. Watching him sputter and lose his cool—that was one of the best indicators of the passion that lay underneath.

Rico had been really good at making Ezra feel alive.

"And I would sort of like to apologize," another voice spoke up. Oh. This must be Rico's boyfriend. Awesome. He had a sexy baritone. Bedroom voice. Ezra was very aware that his tenor wasn't really a turn-on. He had bright morning voice—at least that was what Rico had said.

"Apologize?" Miguel said, pulling Ezra back into the conversation. "What did you do?"

"I threw a tantrum," Derek said squarely. "Which made Rico feel like he had to follow me instead of get Ezra settled. I mean, it wasn't going to be a great scene anyway, but I made it worse. I wanted him to know he's welcome here, you know?"

Oh Jesus. Ezra was hiding from two of the nicest people on the planet. What a way to be a fucking schmuck. Right then he heard a footstep on the stairwell to the loft. Unconsciously he looked up and realized Adam was at the top of the loft, looking right down into the space behind the candy counter and directly at Ezra.

Ezra cast him a green smile, and Adam rolled his eyes and then almost stopped Ezra's heart.

"Yeah, Rico?" he said, looking over the candy counter and to where Ezra assumed Rico was standing. "I sent Ezra out with the coupons and then to take his break. You might find him at the coffee place or River Burger. Go look there—and if you find him, tell him he's on break!"

"Thanks, Adam," Rico said. "Lots more help than this joker here!"

"Anything I can do to serve," Miguel said sweetly, and if the guy hadn't been helping him out, Ezra would have smacked him for being an ass. There was a rustle of pleated linen and the hollow thump of hard-soled shoes across the floorboards, and the store collectively held its breath. Ezra made to move, but Adam shook his head and belatedly Ezra could hear as Rico and Derek passed the second set of french doors.

One… two… three….

"You can get up," Adam barked. "Take the riverfront road and go around by the railroad museum and you should miss them entirely—*don't* forget the basket of free coupons as a cover, and for fuck's sake nut up and try not to be an asshole."

"Right!" Ezra scrambled up and grabbed the free-taste coupon basket and then went tear-assing out the door that opened onto Riverfront and into the three-o'clock August heat.

Oh, Jesus, he was gonna fuckin' die. It was 106 degrees outside, and as Ezra sprinted by all the languid tourists moving slowly in the hopes that the sun wouldn't kill them dead, he took a moment to be grateful for Finn and an apparently inexhaustible supply of khaki and denim cargo shorts. Finn was only a little smaller than he was, and Ezra had lost a good forty pounds since he'd gone berserk in his father's office, so the shorts fit, and Ezra might have been dripping sweat, but he wasn't dropping dead either.

Still, his chest was heaving and he could see stars as he rounded the corner to the outside café portion of River Burger, and he would have sold his soul for a bottle of cold water.

Apparently he didn't have to. An angel with strawberry-blonde hair in a ponytail and a sympathetic smile was waiting there with a water bottle, just as he practically collapsed against the pillar.

"Ezra?" she said, her voice sort of swimming around in the sweat sea in his head.

He nodded, gulping water.

"Here." With a few deft movements, she removed a white towel-looking thing from around her own neck and put it on the back of his.

Ohhhh… yes. It was *cool*, one of those Froggy things that let the water evaporate and cooled you off. Ezra almost cried, and his breathing eased even as he stood there.

"You're amazing. Can I marry you?" he gasped.

"No. You're gay and I'm taken. But follow me—there's an employee bathroom through here, and you can clean up before Rico gets here."

The tiny restaurant wasn't crowded, and Ezra followed the girl around a glass display counter much like the one in Candy Heaven. Finn gave him a wave from behind the counter, where he was standing side by side with a man who looked like a shorter, grayer version of Finn himself—he must have been Finn's father.

"Follow Mari," he said. "I'll hold Rico off—you look like hell."

Ezra nodded, grateful again for the kindness of strangers.

"'Preciate it," he said, and was ushered into the cool shade of a tiny bathroom.

"Here's a spare shirt," Mari said. "Take your apron off and put it on—it's one of my stupid brother's, so you don't have to worry about bringing it back."

Ezra nodded dumbly and stripped down, wetting the polo shirt he'd been wearing and using it to wipe off his neck and chest. "You guys are so nice," he mumbled as he was pulling on the clean shirt. "Why're you doing this for me?"

"'Cause we've all had the ex, honey," Mari said softly. "I mean, we *love* Rico and Derek, but Rico wants you to be happy. You can't be happy if you're all embarrassed and awkward. So you're going to go have a nice, civil lunch with your ex and his boyfriend, and he's going to feel like he's not a douche bag, and you're going to feel like you can get on with your life. And we can draft you onto our softball team, because Finn says you'll make us lose *way* faster, and I'm telling you, softball is *not* my game."

Ezra smiled at her, feeling overwhelmed again. "I promise I'll be the *worst* player on the team," he said fervently, and her Finn-bright smile made his chest hurt.

"Oh, you and I are going to be best friends!" she said excitedly. "Do you babysit?"

Ezra looked at her blankly. "I, uh… I don't know. I mean… I've never met kids. I wouldn't object, really, but…."

"Seriously? I was kidding! But tell you what—softball game Saturday. I'll bring Joshie. If you two get along, me and Davy might have a real date night!"

For a moment Ezra flailed; then he looked at her suspiciously. "Doesn't your brother babysit?"

Mari winked. "Yeah. He and Adam have taken a turn, and they're really good. But a new victim is always appreciated. Besides, you'll probably be watching him at the apartment, so it's going to be a team effort."

And she was trying to make him comfortable, like part of the collective.

Just like the banter at Candy Heaven (they had spent the morning debating which fast food mascot they most hated), it worked.

He smiled diffidently, and she nodded as though she'd done something important. "Good. You feeling up to a hamburger and some fries with your ex?"

Ezra nodded. "Yeah," he said, realizing he was no longer panting and Finn's T-shirt wasn't sticking to his body. "Let's go do this thing."

Mari nodded. "And don't forget to mention you're on the softball team. It always looks good if you're busy."

Oh yeah! "Me and Miguel and the folks from Candy Heaven are going dancing tonight," he realized, suddenly excited all over again. "I, uh." His warm face flushed a little hotter in the confines of the bathroom. "I've never been out dancing in a group before. It's usually, uh, you know, as a...." Smooth, Ezra! Let's confide the grim details of your shitty sex life in a complete stranger!

"Pickup?" she asked, and he grimaced.

"Forget I said anything," he mumbled.

"No, no—you and me, I think we need an ice cream and movie day. True, we'll be watching Disney/Pixar, but the ice cream still stands."

"A wha—"

"Yeah, later. Right now, talk about going dancing. Don't mention the pathetic and sad part—Rico probably knows anyway."

Ezra let out a little moan and took a step back into the bathroom. "Oh, Jesus—he *does*! How do I—"

"Because that's not all who you are! Now come on, Ezra—there will be no ice cream day at my house if there is no lunch with your ex. It's a fuckin' rule!"

With that Mari yanked on his arm and pretty much shoved him down the bathroom corridor. He burst out into what was now a *very* crowded restaurant and ran straight into a good-looking guy with sandy hair and blue eyes, wearing a Hugo Boss summer suit in a warm ecru that practically made his tan glow.

"Oh, hey! You must be Ezra! Adam sent us here, but Rico and I were starting to think we'd missed you!"

Ezra smiled gamely into the guy's All-American Boy face. "Uhm, no, uh, Derek? Right? Just got here myself, but, you know—bathroom."

"Yeah, I was just on my way. Rico's at one of the outside tables. Adam said you could take a break, so—Rico ordered sodas for us but—"

"I'll get you something," Mari said from right behind Ezra's right shoulder. It was all he could do not to startle.

"Thanks, uh, Mari," Ezra said, trying not to flail and run.

But Derek had already grinned and moved toward the bathroom, and now Ezra had no choice.

Rico was easy to spot because he was wearing another sharp suit, summer weight and tieless, like Derek's, but still very spiffy, especially in this land of mostly casual.

But as Ezra squinted, he realized Rico had gone with a different color, something warmer and less neutral than what he'd worn in New York.

Ezra had to admit—it looked good.

"Hey," he said quietly, walking up to the third white-painted wrought iron chair at the tiny little table. "Good thinking getting the shade—it's *horrible* out here."

Oh God—it really was. He must have been seven or eight kinds of crazy to haul his ass into this.

"Yeah," Rico agreed, pushing a glass of ice water at him. "I forgot how hot it got here, but this summer has *sucked.*"

Ezra smiled faintly. "But you say there's no snow, so that's a plus."

"Not down here," Rico agreed. His face softened, became gentle. "You can always go to the mountains, white boy, if you're missing it in the winter."

Ezra's breath caught. He knew it wasn't a come-on—no. But it was an acknowledgment. They'd shared intimacies. They'd been together. It hadn't been his imagination, and Rico didn't hate him for how it ended.

"I'll have to find someone to go with," he said. Then, soberly, "Someone not you."

Rico nodded and smiled slightly. "I... it took me some work to get over you," he said after a moment, and Ezra found himself blinking slowly, stupidly. He hadn't expected that.

"Yeah?" Oh, Holy Father, how was he supposed to feel?

"Yeah." Rico had sharp cheekbones and Mexican-brown skin with the most amazing big brown eyes, surrounded by thick black lashes. His beauty had always been etched in deep lines on the surface of Ezra's heart, and now, as he looked at Ezra with quiet pain, those lines started to bleed. "I just didn't want you to think you were... forgettable. Or disposable, Ezra."

"I was weak," Ezra said bitterly, tracing a design in the condensation on his plastic water glass. "If I'd been strong even a little, I would have grabbed on to you and let you pull me out of there."

Rico dragged his hand through his hair—much longer here than it had been in New York—and then reached out and touched the scars on the back of his knuckles. Ezra jerked his eyes up, pulled away from that moment when he and his father had screamed, "Just go!" at Rico and he'd actually watched another person's heart break in his eyes.

"You weren't ready," Rico said kindly. "And I was. Are you seeing a... a doctor out here?"

Ezra pulled up a corner of his mouth. "The guy in Manhattan gave me some recs, and his number for emergencies. I... I mean, I know this seems half-cocked, but...." He swallowed. He'd never promised Rico forever—had rarely even let him stay the night because he'd been so afraid his father would find out. "It wasn't. I... I told my dad I needed a few weeks after I got out of the inpatient center. And my shrink said... you know. I needed to change something—and that I probably needed to get away from my old man to do it. So I did. I told Dr. Symons what I was doing, and he sort of helped me make plans." He sighed. One of the first things Ezra was supposed to do was make an appointment with one of the people on his list. Yeah, he should probably do that. "I... I was in pain for a long time," he said at last. "I was in pain for so long that when you left, I didn't even recognize that it was more pain—that I'd hit overload." He shrugged, feeling tired, like he could curl up in a corner of a room somewhere and sleep for a week. "I'm learning how to live without pain—it's...." Oh wow. "I'm going *dancing* tonight," he said, feeling like a little kid. "With *people.* Not by myself. Not looking for a hookup. Just… with people who know who I am. It's… it's *weird.* No evading my old man's goons, no explaining where I'm at or lying about who I'm with. It's…."

Rico smiled gently like Ezra really *was* that little kid. "Yeah. You need to fall in love with someone when you're free, Ezra. It's a whole… it's a whole other kind of animal, you know? Like… like the difference between Gonzo, the totally psycho cat I had when I left, and Jake—have you met Jake?"

Oh, thank you, Rico. Thank you for the change of subject and the chance for Ezra to find his feet again.

"I'd *never* in a million years thought I could love an animal as much as I love Jake," Ezra said earnestly. "That cat is like… I mean, he's *better* than therapy. He just… just purrs and drools and loves you. You cannot *beat* that shit, you know?"

Rico laughed. "Well, it's a good thing you didn't know Gonzo— he might have put you off cats forever. He used to sit on top of the refrigerator so he could jump on my head when I walked into the kitchen in the morning."

"Oh my God! What is it with cats?" He dropped his voice. "When Finn and Adam weren't watching, I saw Jake haul out of nowhere, whap Clopper on the head with his paw, like, six times, and then while Clopper was still going, 'What in the holy fuck?' that animal took off across the hall and hid behind the toilet." Ezra had been sitting on the couch, reading one of the paperbacks Finn and Adam kept in a bookshelf in the tiny dining room, and it had taken Finn fifteen minutes to get the story out of him, he'd been laughing so hard.

Adam had gotten up and gone to get the animal, and for a moment, Ezra had been legitimately afraid. Adam was so… so *big*, and Jake the cat was just… just an adolescent, gangly and mellow most times and….

"What was wrong with him?" Rico asked, enthralled. "He *never* acts like that!"

Ezra pulled himself back to the present. "Well, Adam realized that his collar had gotten all tangled with his mouth and his paw, and apparently he was just getting the big moo's attention, you know? I guess because Clopper's his bestie—it was Clopper's job to take care of it."

Rico laughed and looked over behind Ezra's shoulder. "Come sit down," he gestured, and Ezra wasn't surprised when Derek did just that.

"Ezra was just *confirming* my point about Clopper." The way Rico said *confirming* in that meaningful voice made Ezra think this was a long-term discussion.

"See," Rico said, not disappointing him, "Derek loves dogs—and they think he's their spirit animal. They adore him. So when he asked me to move in, he was thinking, 'Yay! I'm inheriting a dog!' but—"

"But you need to leave the dog at Adam's," Ezra said, remembering Adam's words that first night, when he'd been confused as fuck and this big, terse, scary-looking guy with neck tatts and Rico's warm brown eyes had been kind. "Because... uhm...." Oh God. He didn't want to spill Adam's personal history here, even if Rico would be the one person who'd know.

But Rico gave Ezra a shrewd smile. "Yeah. Adam needs the dog," he said. "I get it."

Derek spoke up and kept an awkward silence from falling. Ezra was grateful. "So, Candy Heaven—is it all Oompa Loompas and singing, or what?"

Ezra had to laugh. "No! Man, it's... well, it's honest work, in a way," he said, thinking about it. "I mean, Rico, you know what it was like working at Kellerman's—Dad giving away good assignments like dog treats, people clawing over each other to get him to listen to their opinion. This... it's like you do the fuckin' work, and you do it with a smile, and that's just the job. So, you know, not brain work, but... but cracking a joke gets you places. Being nice to little old ladies makes you feel like a hero. Helping someone out—that's actually *your job*." He shrugged. "It's different. But it's good different."

"Yeah," Rico said. "I'll bet. It's why I like working for Derek"—he turned his head and winked—"and not just for the side bennies. It's just... all those things. It's good to feel like you get points for being a good guy."

Ezra wanted to purr. Rico got it. Rico had known his old man. Martin Kellerman had once fired a guy for telling a secretary she could go home because she was vomiting. The woman didn't have any sick leave left—as far as Ezra's father was concerned, she should have just done her fucking job. Ezra had seen the notice of termination. It said, *Overstepped bounds of authority.* He'd once denied a woman a promotion because she'd been forced to bring her five-year-old to work for a single sick day—said she was prone to "unstable distractions in the workplace." He was clever about it—nobody ever sued his ass—but compassion was not only not his strong suit, he'd laugh in the face of anyone who suggested it should be.

Ezra had been forced to carry the termination notices to the people who had displeased Martin Kellerman. He remembered that *he'd* thrown up after the first half dozen. After that, well, Ezra had just squashed the part of himself that hated it, hated *him*, into a tiny little box that he only opened when he was getting fucked against the wall of a dark alley. So then he could hate everybody, especially himself.

"I like not hating the whole fucking world," he said out loud, surprising himself. Wow—it had taken months of therapy and a trip across the country to say that. What would he be able to say after some more time in this hot, dusty, tiny corner of the planet?

"Yeah?" Rico asked, voice kind. "Anything else you like about your new life?"

Ezra nodded, and at that moment Mari brought him another ice water and a giant lemonade in a paper cup. Oh, bless her!

"The people," he said, winking at her. She grinned and ruffled his hair.

"I'll bring you guys some sandwiches—Rico, Derek, I know *your* order. Ezra, what'll you have?"

He grinned at her. "What's your special today?"

"Mushroom burger with bleu cheese. We call it 'Fun with Fungus.'"

They all groaned at the pun, but Ezra jumped right on that train. "I'll take it," he said.

"Garlic fries?"

Oh Lord. "Side salad," he decided. He'd had to use the bathroom after Finn for a week—the apartment could only take one of those events a day.

"Good man."

Mari bustled off and left him with Rico and Derek again—but he was starting to think that wasn't such a bad thing.

"So, you've got the job, the people, the cat, and the dog—anything else you like?" Rico asked.

Ezra smiled, remembering his mad dash to get to River Burger so he could save what was left of his dignity. "Yeah," he confessed. "I can wear shorts to work!"

Derek guffawed. "I think it's okay, Rico. I think he landed on his feet!"

THE REST of lunch went fairly smoothly. They stuck to neutral things—where to go dancing, what sort of dog Rico and Derek should get. Rico and Derek were funny together—they teased each other, but gently, like puppies tweaking tails. There was none of the cheerful bickering like between Adam and Finn, but that was okay. Both couples played, both couples loved, but the energy was different. The contrast was nice—and so was the company. Ezra genuinely regretted having to tell them he was late back from his break and he had to leave. He walked a lot slower this time—for one thing, if he'd tried to run in the heat after the giant lunch he'd just had, he'd get sick.

For another, he wanted to think about what he'd just done.

In a way, he wished he'd already called one of the numbers his shrink had given him, because he wanted someone to celebrate with.

He'd just talked to Rico—to *Rico*, the guy who had been his grail, his unicorn, and his biggest mistake, all rolled into one. And the world hadn't ended. The sky hadn't crumbled, and Ezra hadn't felt like shit afterward. In fact, Rico and his too-good-to-be-true boyfriend had been *kind*. And they'd encouraged kindness in *Ezra*.

And they'd talked about stuff that he wouldn't have, in a million years, talked about with his coworkers or his father or his always-fashionable mother. Silly stuff—cats, dance clubs, a guy who swore he could read your future in Pixy Stix powder.

And people his father in a million years would not have taken seriously.

But to Rico and Derek, these people were good people. And Ezra felt vindicated, like his willingness to follow Adam and Finn *wasn't* crazy, and his dependence on Miguel was good judgment instead of him simply being lost as hell.

And being kind to Anish and Ravi and Joni and Darby and everyone else at Candy Heaven was simply a matter of being a good human being. There *were* no freaks in this world. Ezra had left one of the most diverse cities in the world and flown across the country to discover that there were *no freaks*. There were kind people or there were intolerant people or, sometimes, there were people in between. But blue hair or piercings or whatever didn't make you a freak, and neither did being gay.

Ezra felt tears burn in his eyes at the power of that much simple acceptance.

So of *course* that was when Miguel caught him, about a block away from Candy Heaven up on Riverfront.

"How'd it go?" he asked, and Ezra stared at him, suddenly conscious that Miguel had been a big part of Ezra's wonky transition over the past week.

"It went. You know Rico. Doesn't make a guy feel like shit if he can help it, right?"

Miguel shrugged. "Well, you know. Who does?"

"My old man. It's his fucking life's mission." Ezra heard his voice get thick and thought, *Oh crap. I really* should *look up one of those shrinks!*

"No," Miguel said, catching his shoulder. "Seriously. Are you okay?"

Suddenly Ezra found himself face-to-face with the guy who'd been sort of dragging him around work for the past four days, and he realized Miguel might really be like Jake. Yeah, sure, Jake had been just plopped on Ezra's chest, and he'd stayed there by nature—but now Jake sought him out because he knew Ezra was warm and he gave pets.

Jake *liked* him.

And Miguel maybe sort of did too.

Ezra's eyes burned some more.

"The stupid thing is," he said, wiping his face on the inside of his shirt, "is that I really *am*. I mean… I was pretty sure I'd die seeing Rico, but I didn't, and it went okay. And I was pretty sure my heart would be all bleeding and shit, because he moved on and I didn't, but… but it is, but it's…." He took a breath and let the pain roll over him like an ocean wave. Yeah, it was cold, but it didn't knock him off his feet. "It's okay," he said through a sob he was ashamed of not swallowing. "I mean, it's stupid, right? Because I still need to call a shrink and make sure I'm not gonna fuckin' implode and I'm working for minimum wage and rooming with two guys who sort of got me dropped in their lap, but I feel…." Oh God. Oh hell. He couldn't hold it together. Of all the stupid goddamned things, now, when he finally got this inkling that he wasn't going to just wither and die from the pain, *now* he was going to fall apart.

Miguel stopped him, hand on his shoulder, and Ezra had a chance to see his almost rectangular features, square jaw, wide-spaced sloe eyes, sensitive, pillowy mouth, all of it, before they blurred and disappeared under the unexpected onslaught of tears.

"C'mere, papi," Miguel said, like he was speaking to a child. Well, he'd said he was the middle of six. He maybe knew about children, right? Maybe that explained the practiced calm he used to grab Ezra's shoulders and haul Ezra up against his chest, there on the boardwalk in the blind corner between the two sets of french doors. It certainly explained why he didn't seem surprised that Ezra just came unglued, sobbing on those broad shoulders like he and Miguel had been best friends for life instead of uneasy coworkers for about four days.

And all of those thoughts took a backseat to the warmth and the haven Miguel offered as Ezra completely lost his shit in the most unexpected time and place he would have ever possibly thought of, if he'd imagined this moment at all.

Pat the New Thing, See If It Moves

"DID YOU stock the jawbreakers?" Miguel asked, bored with this routine.

Ezra looked up from cleaning the chocolate counter and nodded. "Yeah," he said, subdued after his crying storm.

"And the bubble gum?"

Ezra didn't even flinch—he seemed to *treasure* the question and answer. He never offered any extra information and never tried to anticipate what Miguel or Darrin or Adam might want. Once, Miguel had seen him look at an empty bucket, then look over at Adam, and then look up at the loft in an agony of indecision. Ezra had *seen* the need, he'd *wanted* to fill it—but he'd been afraid that one step, any step, would be wrong. Miguel had never met the guy's old man, but he'd heard so much about Martin Kellerman that he was starting to get a pretty clear picture.

Catching a plane out to a new place to see if he could get back with his ex was the first time Ezra had ever thought for himself.

And Miguel could appreciate that—and could appreciate that the guy obviously had a lot on his mind and on his plate. And why someone who'd been punished for thinking for himself was content to let other people do the thinking for him. Apparently he was saving his *big* thoughts for meeting with Rico and Derek and dealing with a new environment and new people, and falling apart on Miguel when it all got to be too much.

Miguel still couldn't believe he'd done that. Couldn't believe Ezra had lost it, couldn't believe *Miguel* had been the one to comfort him, there in public, on the boardwalk in broad daylight.

He'd just known... known that this sweet, sort of out-of-his-element guy had kept saying he was okay—but he hadn't *sounded* okay. Miguel could have called Finn, because Finn was the guy's roommate, or he could have called Adam—because same, plus boss!—but he hadn't wanted Ezra to get handed off one more time.

Hell, they were going dancing tonight, and Ezra had sat patiently at his elbow and done everything he was asked to do without complaining. If nothing else, Miguel could call the guy a friend, right?

And it had felt good to have someone trust him enough to just come undone on him, to lean on him. He had three older sisters and an older and younger brother. The sisters, starting with Lydia, were strong, caring, nurturing, and no bullshit, and his mom had taught them everything they knew. And as for being the second boy? Forget about it. Nobody cared. He would always be the "other baby brother." If his younger brother, Berto, hadn't been such a sweetheart—and so very good at sharing his toys—Miguel might have been tempted to hate him out of sheer jealousy of having *some* place in the house. But he couldn't.

Everyone loved Berto, including Miguel, and Miguel had to be content with being invisible.

But not to Ezra. To Ezra, he was the guy who told him what to do in what was apparently a completely alien environment. Miguel caught Ezra watching his face for reactions, for cues—how did Miguel react to being teased about being from a large family? (By reminding everybody that his sisters made the best cookies in the northern half of the state, and Halloween was around the corner, that's how.) How did Miguel react when somebody brought up gay rights? (By offering them a crack at his beloved T-shirt collection, all of which espoused gay rights and marriage equality, because he loved to share the activism.) How did Miguel react when Darrin said, "You two need to stop touching each other's whiskers and play, for fuck's sake!"

Well, that last one had him sort of rocking back on his heels and squinting at Ezra's clean-shaven face as he continued to Windex the clean counter because nobody had told him to stop.

"I don't even know if he can grow a beard, papi!" he'd said automatically. "What whiskers am I touching?"

Darrin rolled his eyes. "Go catch mice," he said distinctly, and then he looked at Ezra, who was studiously avoiding everyone's gaze, and said, "You too. Maybe if one of you catches a mouse, the other one will figure out that it's not mice you need!"

With that, Darrin stalked up to the counter and sort of hip-checked Adam out of the cashier's space.

Adam went without a question, but Miguel caught him sticking his tongue out like any irritated five-year-old. And then he turned and glared at Miguel.

"What?" Miguel asked. "I have no idea what that was about."

Adam took a good look at Ezra, who had stood listlessly, staring into space, hand moving automatically while cleaning the counter during the entire exchange. He'd stopped his crying storm abruptly, with as little warning as he'd started, wiped his eyes on his shirt, and walked into the store without another word.

And hadn't spoken about it since.

Adam looked back at Miguel. "I'm starting to get *some* idea," he muttered. "How bad could it have been?"

Miguel shrugged. "He said it was fine?" He hated that his voice pitched up at the end like a question, but he couldn't help it. He'd assumed that Ezra had just... moved on. Cried, came in, moved on. But apparently holding someone while they cried wasn't the be-all and end-all of the responsibility there.

Adam scowled at him, and Miguel looked away. "He... he said it was fine," he said again, and then he looked at Ezra, who seemed to have checked out of his body entirely. "And then he cried a little bit, and now—"

"Now he needs to get the fuck out of here," Adam said decisively. "You guys are going out tonight?"

"Yeah—you and Finn coming?"

Adam arched an eyebrow at him. "Me and Finn have the apartment to ourselves for a few hours. Do you want a blowjob-by-blowjob account of how we're gonna use our time?"

Miguel felt the flush take over his body. God. Adam and sex. Who wouldn't flush? "That won't be necessary, papi," he said, ashamed.

"Good." Adam rummaged in his pocket and walked up to Ezra, stooping his shoulders automatically and making his voice soft. "Kid?" he said. "Kid, you in there?"

Ezra snapped back into his body like a rubber band against a table. "Yeah! Yeah—shit—I'm here. Sorry, Adam. Was just... you know—"

"Overwhelmed," Adam said, all candor. "Yeah, we got it. Here." He fiddled with the key ring he'd retrieved and then gave Ezra one of the keys. "This'll get you in. Remember, you gotta greet Clopper first, and maybe you and Miguel can take him out for a walk, okay?"

Ezra nodded. "Why am I going home?"

"One, you're gonna call someone. You gotta shrink or something?"

"How did you know that?" Ezra asked, sounding like a child who'd seen a magic trick.

"Blessed fucking guess," Adam deadpanned. "So, you're gonna go call a shrink and make sure your head is all in order next week, because there's no good when your head's not in order, and we promised you we'd take care of you. And Miguel is going to take you out dancing, and you need some time to get ready."

Suddenly Ezra seemed to grasp what this was all about. Miguel watched mortification claw its way up his pale throat and into his cheeks. "Nobody takes four hours to get ready," he said bleakly. "Sorry I'm such an asshole. I didn't mean to waste your time—I'll clock out, you know, don't need pay for today. I mean, I haven't been—"

Adam was squinting at him, head cocked. "What in the fuck are you going on about? Just go home and take a fuckin' breath, Ezra. Jesus. You had a bad day. You saw your ex. I'm telling you, if my ex walked in here, well… first I'd have to pull Finn off of him, and that would be a *bad* scene, and then… well, whatever it would be, it would just be bad. High entertainment for all of *you* people, but not so hot for me. So you go home and stop being our entertainment, and remember that you can deal, okay?"

Ezra's smile was a little watery but sound. "Yeah, Adam. I'll go get my head on straight."

"And call your shrink."

"I'll schedule an appointment."

Adam ruffled his hair like he was a little kid, and for a minute, Miguel wanted to defend him. Ezra was grown—he was funny and brave and smart. He didn't need to be treated like a kid!

But Ezra ducked his head and smiled, looking pleased, and then glanced up at Miguel. "You're really taking me home?"

"Uh, yeah. Bossman says we're off early, let's go home."

"Okay."

And it was just so simple, so trusting—shame swamped him for taking the easy way out after Ezra had finished his crying jag and just walked into the store. Miguel was a better person than that—he was certainly a better friend.

He slid his apron over his head and grabbed Ezra's hand, tugging him toward the door. "C'mon, papi. You know what? I think we need more than just extra time in the apartment. I think we need some time *away* from all this, you think?"

Ezra glanced behind his shoulder at the french doors of the candy store, his face set in wistful lines. "I don't know if you understand what an awesome place this is," he said, and Miguel rolled his eyes and tugged at his hand.

"You know what? You're right. I've been sort of a shitty employee these last weeks, and you're right. It's a good place. But you know what a *great* place would be today?"

"The North Pole?" Ezra gasped as the heat tried to knock their chests in.

"Close. Here—let's go get Adam's dumb dog and take him to the river. We can go swimming too, and Adam and Finn won't have to worry about the dog, and you can get your head clear and maybe a nap in before we go out tonight. What do you think?"

Ezra cocked his head in that way Miguel was coming to associate with one of Ezra's long-held beliefs about the world as he knew it back East crashing headfirst into the world he lived in now. "We're going swimming in the *river*?"

Miguel had parked his shitty Pontiac in the brick parking garage just around the corner, and Ezra waved his hand to indicate the stretch of water beyond Joe's Crab Shack, which was right next to them.

"You got a problem with that, papi?" Miguel asked. But of course Ezra did. Poor little rich boy—he probably thought people had been swimming in pools back in the dark ages.

"Isn't that... un*sanitary*?" Ezra gasped, horrified.

Miguel laughed, and what just that morning had been sort of one more duty, one more chore he'd taken on by wanting to please Adam, who didn't know he was alive, suddenly became something he really wanted to do.

AN HOUR later Miguel was wearing a pair of Adam's swim trunks (Ezra had texted him for permission, which Miguel thought was sort of sweet) and Ezra was wearing a pair of Finn's. Clopper was in the back of Miguel's shitty Pontiac, and they were heading for Discovery Park.

And Ezra was starting to come out of his fugue.

"So why?" he asked as Miguel left J Street for the I-80/I-5 interchange.

"Why what?" Miguel asked, trying to pump the AC up. Holy Christ was it hot in that red car.

"Why are you a shitty employee?"

Miguel thought about it as he took the Garden Highway off-ramp and headed for the park. "I'm not usually. I mean, I put my heart into it before Christmas, and then I worked for six months under Derek—"

"Rico's Derek?" Ezra asked, sounding surprised.

"Yeah—he's a great boss. I mean—the *best* boss. He trained me up, got me ready to run my own business, and I'd been working Candy Heaven too, and saving my money, and I started that business, like I told you. And... God. A month after I moved in, the landlord raised the rent and I was out on my ear, and by then Derek had replaced me, and suddenly... well, I was right back at Candy Heaven. I mean, I'd worked my way through school there. It was like... you know. Never going to grow up, never going to start my life." He shook his head. "I guess I sort of took my disappointment out on my job."

Ezra grunted. "Yeah. I mean, I get that. It's just...."

Miguel turned into the park and slowed down so he could pay the guy at the gate for parking. "It's just what?"

"I... I never worked with people I liked as much as I like you guys. I just... I'd think you'd take advantage of all those nice people, you know?"

Miguel grunted. "You shame me, papi." He took his ticket from the ranger and threw it on his dashboard, then pulled into the almost-empty park. He found a space nearest the river and let the car idle for a moment. "You do," he said into the sudden silence. "You're brave, coming out here. And you were brave talking to Rico. And even when you cried—"

"Oh God, can we not—?"

"Don't be ashamed," Miguel said, suddenly wondering if *that* was why Ezra had disappeared into his own head for so long. Ezra looked away, outside into the hard bright August sunshine, and Miguel squeezed his shoulder, forcing him to look back and meet Miguel's eyes head on. "Don't be ashamed for that. For crying. For falling apart. For needing some space afterward. I get the feeling...." Oh Lord, this felt like prying.

"What?" Ezra asked, guileless and sweet. Absently, he reached between the seats and scratched Clopper between the eyes.

"I get the feeling that you've been ashamed of a lot of what you do," Miguel finished in a rush. "Not that you've done anything bad, just that...."

Ezra suddenly looked away, avoiding his eyes. "You know, we should take Clopper out. He probably has to crap."

With that he snapped the lead on Clopper's collar and hopped out of the car. Clopper climbed into the front seat and then followed Ezra out.

Miguel killed the motor and climbed out his side. Well, who wanted to talk about their feelings anyway?

A few moments later, they were down by the water's edge, near one of the swimming holes. Clopper had just ploughed his way in, silver ears flopping. He jumped off the edge of the bank like those ears would help him fly.

Ezra laughed and then stuck his toe in the water and jerked it out. "It's cold," he pronounced, glaring at Miguel like it was his fault.

"It'll warm up when you get in," Miguel promised. He'd left his shirt on the bank, with his car keys, and he was wearing a pair of flip-flops he'd pulled out of the back of the car. The river bottom was sharp and unpredictable, so he'd pulled out another pair for Ezra.

Who was apparently not ready to get even his borrowed flip-flops wet.

"I don't believe you," Ezra said doubtfully. He submerged his entire foot this time and then hopped back.

Miguel was out to his upper thighs, and although he had to agree—it was cold—he wasn't going to let this visitor from New York show him up.

He took two giant lunges and then held his hands over his head and dove in. He came up gasping, but he'd been swimming in rivers or lakes for most of his life. It was a lot cheaper to take a batch of kids to the river than it was to own a membership to a gym or a private pool. His feet found the bottom, and he negotiated the rocks and pushed up.

"C'mon, Ezra," he called. "Ten minutes—it'll cool you down, and then we can throw the ball for Clopper."

Maybe. Clopper was paddling like... well, like a dog who was born to drown, mostly. Miguel thought all dogs could swim, but Clopper's ass kept sinking and he'd be stuck, upright, his front paws making these prodigious splashes in front of him while his back legs treaded water. He was sinking.

"Oh my God!" he muttered, because who—*who* took a dog out to the river to watch him drown?

At the same time Ezra said, "Is he supposed to do that?" and Clopper's head went under.

"Oh *fuck*!"

And then Ezra took three graceful steps and dove in, then surfaced cleanly right where Clopper was *re*surfacing, apparently after having aligned his head, ass, and paws.

Ezra came up sputtering river water, and Clopper woofed happily and then swam away, against the current, apparently having done this a *lot*.

"Oh-oh-oh-my *God*!" Ezra sputtered, and Miguel looked from the kid to the dog to see which one was actually going to need him.

It turned out neither. Ezra was fine—he tried to find purchase on the bottom at first, but he gave it up after a moment and treaded water instead. While Miguel watched, he extended his body and started a strong freestyle up the current toward the dog. When he got near, he started splashing Clopper in the face.

"You stupid pony! I thought you were fuckin' dead!"

Clopper barked happily and tried to bite the water, and Ezra kept splashing, just to play. Miguel laughed and swam to join him, thinking that this pale East Coaster might actually be okay.

Oh shit. "Shit!" he gasped as he drew up toward them. The current was stronger than he'd thought—he wasn't sure how Clopper and Ezra were managing to go upstream, but he was ready to kick his feet out and let the water carry him back to the inlet where they'd gotten in.

"Shit what?" Ezra turned toward him, full mouth parted, eyes wide. His black lashes were spiked with water, and for a moment, Miguel forgot everything. Lost business, retail job, inconvenient friend, stupid dog—hell, he even forgot Adam—because this kid looked so damned pretty in the river.

In fact, under the relentless sun, he was starting to look pretty and pink.

"Shit!" Miguel muttered again. "Kid, we didn't get any sunblock on you. A day like today, you're going to get cooked like a hot dog!"

"I'm twenty-eight!" Ezra protested, and Miguel rolled his eyes.

"Oh, *now* you find your dignity? I'm gonna go get some sunblock out of the car. *Dammit*, why didn't I remember this shit earlier?"

By the time he got back from the car, Ezra was already up on the bank, using one of the towels they'd borrowed from Finn and Adam. Clopper was still paddling around in the water, and Miguel remembered that easy, powerful freestyle stroke Ezra had used against the current.

"You swim like a champion," Miguel muttered, throwing the tube of sunblock at him. Ezra looked up, surprised, and the tube bounced off his shoulder. Miguel's admiration dimmed and he regarded his new friend ironically. "But you catch like a fuckin' Yankee."

Ezra's face split into a smile. "We can't all be Giants," he said, bending to get the damned sunblock.

"Ooh—baseball! We'll have to get you to a River Cats game."

Ezra blinked at him. "Well... yeah. I guess the stadium is *literally* across the street, isn't it?" He threw the towel over his shoulder and started to rub lotion sparingly on his pinkening cheeks, and then on his shoulders and nearly hairless chest.

"Here—I'll get your back," Miguel said practically but really thinking, *God, he's pretty.*

"Thanks. You want I should get you?"

Miguel grunted negative and took the tube out of Ezra's hand. For the first time, he noticed that Ezra had sort of elegant hands and wrists—like a piano player or something. "Naw—I mean, if we were gonna be out here for hours, definitely. But I'm good for an hour—dark skin and a good base tan, you know?"

"You come out here often?"

Miguel didn't answer. He'd squirted some lotion on that pale back starred sparingly with moles, and had started to rub the lotion in.

And realized, heart in throat, that he hadn't touched a man in a really long time.

Ezra was pretty, but it was more than that. He rolled his back unconsciously, like a cat accepting love. He pretty much arched under Miguel's touch, and Miguel... oh, Miguel was just so happy to be *touching* somebody.

"Mm," Ezra purred, rocking from side to side. "You got good hands."

Miguel should have just schwacked the last of it on and run away, but he just… oh man… just had to keep touching.

"You know, trying to get rubbed in," he mumbled, wishing his hands could *stop moving*.

To his embarrassment, Ezra stepped away first.

"We're only gonna be out here a little while," he said. "Here—put some of that on your face so you're not all bright red tonight!"

Miguel started smearing it into his own cheeks, hoping they'd cool down. Ezra was looking at him as innocently as a schoolboy, and Miguel could not—could *not*—afford the emotional complication of so much as a woody around this kid, this unexpected *person* in the middle of his life.

Ezra turned away and dropped his towel back in their spot, then flip-flopped his way to the edge of the water. He turned and grinned at Miguel for a second, then put his toe in. His grin went up a notch.

"Know what? You were right. It's not nearly as cold the second time in!"

And with that, he plunged into the current and swam upriver while Miguel was still staring bemusedly, feeling the tingle of Ezra's skin against his palm.

CLOPPER RAN and swam for a good forty-five minutes and was pretty damned tired after they dried him off and got him into the car. Traffic was heavier on the way back, since it was Friday night and people were off, and as they idled at a stoplight, Miguel remembered to ask.

"Where'd you learn to swim like that? When you got all girly about river water, I assumed you'd never been in anything deeper than the bathtub."

"I was on swim team through college," Ezra said, looking out the window into the city. "Geez, your city jumps into the suburbs fast."

"Yeah—it's a small city, but we like it. Do you swim *now*?"

Ezra glanced at him. "Yeah—couple of times a week, after I work out. But I've never been in… you know. Never swam *not* in a pool."

"I thought you East Coasters were all about the beach," Miguel teased with a smile.

Ezra seemed to think about it. "Yeah, no. My dad always sent me to math camp or chess camp or French camp or something. If it wasn't educational, it wasn't happening. I couldn't run for shit, I was a danger to myself with a bat or any sort of equipment—but swimming. That I could do."

Miguel grunted. "Huh. Funny how that's not on your résumé."

"What's that mean?" Ezra turned away from the window.

"I don't know—you just don't really mention the stuff you're good at." Miguel shrugged. "We were all talking about our best thing the other day, remember? You said you were good at doing what other people told you. Well, you forgot swimming. It should be on your résumé."

Ezra's smile lit up the inside of the car, and Miguel tried not to choke on his tongue. Oh wow. That smile—that should *also* go on his résumé, but maybe with a warning label or something.

"You're a good guy," Ezra said simply. "That was a stand-up thing to say."

Miguel grunted. "Just remember that, you know? When you go talking to your shrink. Remember you've got more to you than you think."

"Thank you—I'll try to keep it in mind."

Silence fell again, and Miguel worked on sorting the muddle in his chest. This kid was not… not what Miguel had imagined that first day when he'd been lost and abandoned on Adam's lawn. When he'd remembered Miguel's name first thing, like it was important, and had asked for ice cream he wasn't supposed to have.

He was just… more.

CLOPPER WAS dry by the time they got back to the apartment, which was a relief. Miguel knew that Adam and Finn had put as much time as they could into keeping the place nice, and it showed. The first time he'd been there—New Year's Eve; they'd had a few people over—it had been pretty bare, with a few pieces on the walls and an area rug in the front room. Every time Miguel had visited after that, they'd added something, whether it was Adam's art on the walls or a runner on the back of the couch. By the time Rico had come back to "claim" his apartment, it had become a home.

Ezra told Miguel to shower first so he could go through his drawers.

"I packed two suitcases and shipped two more," he confessed. "Most of the shit, it turns out, has got no practical purpose, but I've got an entire bag with dance clothes in it. I'll get you some."

Miguel hopped in the shower, wondering exactly what Ezra was going to pull out of his magic suitcases. All he'd seen so far was Ezra trying not to kill himself in shit that was too warm—he didn't have a lot of faith.

But still, he dried off, combed his hair from the part on the side, and ventured into the front room, where Ezra had draped two outfits over the couch.

"Oh wow," he muttered. "Papi, these are some *nice* clothes! Which one is mine?"

Ezra shrugged. "You pick. I'll put on the one you don't want."

But it was easy to pick. Two color schemes were at work on the back of the couch—something cool and icy, in teal and steel blue even with traces of lemon yellow in the fabric. Wow—that would look so good on Ezra. Miguel wouldn't steal it from him even if he *didn't* like the other one better.

But he did. A dark blue stretchy shrug went on first, followed by a warm beige fishnet tunic and matching slacks. The shrug would cover his arms and shoulders, leaving his stomach and back bare, and the fishnet would go over the whole thing, giving the illusion that Miguel was actually wearing a shirt. Now *these* were his colors, and Miguel, weary with pinching pennies to make his business fly, suddenly wanted to wear those clothes very much.

Ezra had even left him a pair of boxer briefs.

Miguel dressed quickly, aware that he was a guest in the tiny apartment, and when he was done, he took a moment to adjust his sleeves and wish he had better shoes.

He was wondering if there was another mirror besides the bathroom when Ezra came out, freshly shaved, his hair done, and a towel wrapped around his waist.

"Lemme see," he said, somewhat gleefully.

Miguel did a self-conscious runway pivot, and Ezra hooted. "Very nice!"

"Man, you've got some *excellent* threads here," Miguel said, fighting his blush. Ezra grabbed the other set from off the back of the couch and moved to the end so he'd have some space.

"Yeah—clothes were my thing in New York." He turned his back and spoke over his shoulder. "This whole cargo-shorts-and-T-shirt thing is blowing my mind."

"You shoulda heard Finn bitching about trying to get Rico to not dress like a corpse." Ezra was pulling on his boxer briefs, and Miguel got a glimpse of a perfect and pale behind. His stomach tightened and his voice cracked on the word "corpse."

"I feel sorta bad about that," Ezra said, turning around now that his dangly bits were covered. He moved unselfconsciously, like he was dressing in the gym, and Miguel suddenly couldn't figure out where to look.

"Why bad?" Oh thank God, the cat was on the couch, in the corner. Miguel picked him up by the scruff of the neck and held him to pet. Jake started to purr automatically, and Ezra paused after pulling on his low-slung gray jeans and grinned at him.

"God, I love that animal," he said, completely infatuated.

"That's sort of sliding down a slippery slope," Miguel said dryly, *not* staring at the happy trail of dark hair that disappeared at the V of Ezra's zipper. "But why do you feel bad?"

Ezra sighed and pulled the ice blue tank top over his head. This was a blessing, because he had shell-pink nipples, and Miguel was starting to wonder if they got darker when they were pinched—holy *hell*, when had this happened?

"See," he mumbled, tugging on the bottom of the tank and tucking it into his jeans, "my old man, he's... well, he's not really... okay, he is. He's a horrible human being. And he's sort of... I mean...." Ezra hid his face behind his hands. "He's a racist bastard, okay?" he burst out. "I mean, not to people's faces, but there I was, seeing Rico on the down-low, and every time I was alone with my old man, he's going off about why this... uh, Hispanic person, but that's not what he said, right? Why he's got to look so Mexican and—well, Rico liked to shop for clothes, and I tried to steer him to stuff my old man would like so maybe he could get the job at the end of the internship and stay longer. And the suits he looks okay in, but...."

Miguel was staring at him, not sure if he was horrified or not.

"You were trying to... *protect* Rico from your father... by getting him to buy stuff that made him look... whiter?" He drew that out to clarify.

Ezra sighed and grabbed the gauzy gray shirt that went over the ice blue tank. "Yeah. I know. I'm a fucking coward. I just...." Ezra sighed. "That's how the affair came out, actually. I... I bought Rico a suit, and, you know? Me and Dad, we went to the same tailor, and Dad saw a receipt on my desk and then asked the tailor, who started going on and on about my young man and…."

He shook his head and his eyes grew shiny. When he spoke next, his voice was congested, like this was hard to say. "The next thing I know, Dad's screaming at me in the middle of my office and we're crashing a staff meeting where Rico's supposed to be presenting."

Miguel stared, the true horror of the situation beginning to seep in. "That's… that's messed up," he said.

Ezra nodded, not meeting his eyes. "I… I mean, I cost him the internship and outed him to the whole office. I was just so ashamed, you know? I did that to him—and I was supposed to *love* him. I just figured he'd be better off without me, you know?"

"Oh papi," Miguel murmured. He dropped Jake unceremoniously on the couch, where the cat apparently lost all muscle function and just poured there like a blob. Then Miguel took two steps over to where Ezra was fumbling with the buttons of his pretty gray shirt. "Here. Here, let me, okay?"

"Yeah," Ezra whispered. "Yeah. Thanks."

Miguel could smell the body heat and aftershave rolling off Ezra's body and knew he'd be damp and nervous if they touched. But Miguel was starting to wonder—what would it be like to touch him when he was happy, those few times when he was animated, when he was talking about something that didn't make him sweat?

Or that *did* make him sweat, in the good way?

"All done," Miguel said softly, straightening the shoulders one last time and parting the V-neck so the silver Star of David could peek out. "You look great, Ezra. And… I'm sorry about your dad being an asshole, you know? But it sounds like Rico forgave you for that. And he wants you to be happy."

Ezra smiled at him with such desperate optimism that Miguel found himself praying that tonight could make it all better.

"Yeah. He asked me to come with him here, you know? But… but I… I mean, I'm still a mess. I wasn't ready then. I'm *barely* ready now. But…." He swallowed, that desperate optimism fading a little.

Miguel couldn't help it. He felt the need to comfort him, in some way.

"So," he said baldly, speaking into the space between them like they were standing shoulder to shoulder, as they often did when working. "So I live at home, with my mami. See, my older sisters, they grew up and married, and my older brother, he's living at home and going through college, and my *youngest* brother, Berto, he's just started college too. And Mami, she can't keep the house with just her income, so we all sort of pitch in. It was the house Papi bought for her, and we just... you know...."

"Want her to have something of your father," Ezra said, nodding. "Something good."

Miguel smiled and fought the urge to cup his cheek. They weren't *like* that, were they? "*Sí.* Anyway, so my mami, she knows about the gay, she knows about the sex, right? She's not stupid—she's a nurse and I think she brought *all* us boys condoms when we were in high school. But I *live* with her, and it's not respectful to just, you know, bring a boy home and bang him and let your mami know, right? I mean, if I found a boy that was forever, something would change, but until then, all us boys, we find somewhere else to go, right?"

Ezra nodded. "Of course."

"So my last boyfriend—like, last summer. I was still working at Candy Heaven and looking for an internship so I could have something on my résumé, and this guy was like—well, he's like a financial analyst downtown. So, like, a suit—"

"Like me," Ezra said, nodding. "Back when I wore suits."

Miguel shook his head, not saying it but thinking that he couldn't imagine Ezra as a shark in a suit. He'd have to *see* him in something gray with pinstripes and shiny black shoes in order to think of him any way but in his Candy Heaven casual clothes.

Or now, looking sharp and beautiful in his dancing threads.

"Yeah, well, anyway, he's a *grown-up,* right? And he takes me out to dinner and does the expensive car thing, and I'm thinking, oh *excellent,* I'm going to be a grown-up with a grown-up relationship. And one night he meets me downtown, and I've dressed up nice, and he's still wearing his suit, and I'm thinking, 'Oh my God, I'm gonna get *laid*!' and I haven't done the walk of shame since college, right? So this is a big deal."

Ezra blinked those big blue eyes at him. "How bad can this go wrong?"

Miguel shook his head. "Well, it was Friday, and first off, he takes me to this local watering hole—all they serve is bar food—and then he proceeds to ignore me and talk to his work friends and get shitfaced."

"Classy," Ezra said, nodding.

"Yeah—well, got classier. I had to drive him home, and I didn't know where he lived or anything, so I had to drive him to *my* house. I swear, I stopped at a McD's on the way, I was so hungry. Anyway, Jaime and Berto, they're all for leaving the guy on the lawn, but I feel bad—it was our third date. You just can't do that to someone you know. So we strip him to his shorts and leave him on the couch with a giant barf bucket next to his head. Well, Mami got home from late shift, and she was like, 'What in the *hell?*' and I had to explain that he would be gone in the morning. I was calling him a *cab*, right? Because we live in Roseville, and I didn't want to drive back downtown on my day off. So it's bad enough that he's there and my mami knows I've got horrible taste, but the next morning we're all drinking coffee in the kitchen, right? And my mom is coming down the stairs to ask somebody to go get milk or something so she can make breakfast, and this guy just sits up all of a sudden, looks at us—and we're all in our boxers—and shouts, 'Holy God, which one of you did I fuck?'"

"Oh my fuckin' God," Ezra breathed.

Miguel nodded. "I'm saying. So Berto and Jaime look at me, and I'm like, 'Yes, we can dump his ass on the lawn now!' We threw his clothes down the stairs and Jaime and Berto tagged him in the head with his shoes."

"You didn't want in on that action?"

Miguel shrugged. "I got him in the face with his wallet and his cell phone. But what I'm saying is, yeah. Maybe when you're grown-up you have the guts to tell your old man what you think of him. But you still felt like a kid, and you protected the guy you were with as best you could. I mean—there's worse guys to date, you know? There's worse ways to make an impression. Right now you're looking like a real prince."

Miguel had to back up. He *had* to back up. Because the way Ezra was staring at him, like he'd just started sprinkling fairy dust and moonbeams, made Miguel want to be the hero—the *real* hero, like Adam, and not just the accidental hero who got cried on because he was the right place, right time.

"Did you really tag him in the head?" Ezra asked.

Miguel shrugged modestly. "More like the ear, but yeah. God, what an asshole."

"Yeah." Ezra grabbed the towel he'd brought off the end of the couch and looked thoughtful. "You know… you're really lucky. You talk about your family like that and…." He shrugged. "You're lucky, is all. I've got two older brothers in upstate New York—I… I don't even remember the last time I saw them. I mean, the guy was a slimeball, but at least you had someone to help you dump him on the lawn."

With that he disappeared into the bathroom, and Miguel was left brushing cat hair off his mesh shirt.

And wondering when his responsibility had started to look so much like a reward.

THREE HOURS later he was looking more like a punishment for sins Miguel hadn't known he'd committed.

"So," Ravi screamed in his ear, "what do you think of Cy?"

Miguel glared at the dance floor, where Ravi and Anish's omnisexual tomcat slutty friend was pretty much leg humping everything that moved on the dance floor at Gatsby's Nick.

"I think he's lucky no one's tried to cut his balls off," he growled. Oh fuck—it was Ezra's turn to get leg humped again.

"He looks good on the dance floor, am I right?" Ravi grinned at him, waiting for approval, and Miguel gritted his teeth and nodded.

After all, it wasn't like the guy had done anything *wrong*.

They'd met downtown at the Hogshead Brew Pub and had eaten quickly and grabbed their first beer. Then it had been the big debate— Ace of Base, which had live music, or Faces, which was exclusively gay and had five dance floors, or Harlow's, which did the live music thing too, but not so much dancing. In the end, the girls had said they weren't there to pick anyone up, and all they wanted to do was dance.

Gatsby's Nick was actually closer than Faces—only about five blocks—and here they were.

In the beginning, Cy had been a nice addition. He knew Ravi and Anish, so he'd talked plenty about their apartment building and their uncle's store and their large and eclectic family and had been complimentary to Anish's buxom girlfriend, Rebecca. He'd flirted with Darby just enough to make her laugh, treated Joni and Katya as completely sexless but somehow managed to be charming so he didn't offend either of them, and chatted up Miguel and Ezra, throwing that flirty white smile—the one with just enough of a gap between the front teeth to be disarming and sexy at the same time—around with impunity. He had dark, *dark* black skin and eyes and black lashes so dark they should have been illegal.

And he moved like a jungle cat.

The whole lot of them had started on the dance floor, but Miguel wasn't excited about so many people jostling him when he didn't know them. He quickly found a table and proceeded to sit there and nurse a drink and watch his friends get dance-floor-fucked by this charming stranger.

It hadn't pissed him off quite so much when he'd thought it was just *his* thigh Cy was rubbing on. But as he'd sat and watched, Cy sidled up behind Darby and cupped the backs of her thighs as he spooned her and the two of them bobbed up and down to the music. She whirled away and he turned to Joni and Katya, hip-bumping and play-dancing with them to make them smile and then leaving them to dance on their own. And *then* he turned his attention to Ezra, and there it stayed.

For his part, Ezra turned into an entirely different animal on the floor.

Miguel had been thinking of him as helpless, a kitten in a thunderstorm—and maybe he was when he was caged in with worry about ex-boyfriends and his father. But in the center of the dance floor, he was suddenly free, and it was like watching that kitten magically transform into a black-haired, blue-eyed panther.

He danced fluidly, becoming the beat and the joy. Cy insinuated himself behind Ezra and simply moved with his body, undulating, swaying, his eyes half-closed in sensual enjoyment. Miguel swallowed against the dryness in his mouth and tried really hard not to look at Ezra's tight jeans to see if he was hard in them.

Why wouldn't he be? What's it to you if he wants to go to a club and get off or get laid? It's not like you never did the exact same thing, right?

But talking to himself didn't work. Ezra's helplessness, his *fragility*, seemed more apparent on the dance floor, when he was moving freely and unselfconsciously, than it had when he was looking at Miguel in Adam's living room, eyes wide and pleading for forgiveness.

Ezra *needed* him. Miguel had spent the past week glued reluctantly to the man's side, and he was only just now starting to understand why he'd been needed—and how he'd been falling down on the job.

Cy tapped Ezra on the shoulder and whispered something, cherry-chocolate lips brushing the pale shell of Ezra's ear in a way that made *Miguel* shudder from sensual overload. But Ezra shook his head with a little half smile, and Cy shrugged and turned away, hopping off the dance floor and toward their table with a joyous little bounce. Ezra stayed, silky liquid sex throbbing to the sound of Fitz and the Tantrums, and Darby took Cy's place behind him, although her embrace looked more like that of a mother teaching a child the steps than Cy's suggestive humping ever could.

"Hey, Angel Face," Cy flirted as he sank with a sigh into the seat by Miguel's. "You got water? You're the best." He pursed his lips and made a kissy face, which Miguel returned with a weak smile. The best? He was hardly good enough to be Ezra's babysitter.

"Having fun out there?" he asked inanely.

"Yeah—always do on the dance floor." Cy batted his eyelashes at Ravi and then leaned toward Miguel in a way that screamed "conspiracy." "So, you two," he said, pulling them in, "what's the deal with our pretty boy there? I mean he *moves* like he wants some action, but he's not exactly putting out anywhere *but* the dance floor, if you know what I mean."

Big ugly knots that had been riding Miguel's neck and chest started to unravel, unkink, and loosen. "He's just dancing," Miguel said. "He's not looking for a hookup—just had a rough breakup."

"Ain't that always the way?" Cy muttered. "Man, he is *pretty*—and brother, can that boy dance."

Miguel watched the dance floor hungrily, this time trying to take in all of Ezra's grace without that soul-crunching irritation (jealousy? Naw... irritation! Had to be!), and found himself enthralled.

"He really can," Miguel said softly. "He's beautiful."

Cy's sigh gusted across the table. "Yeah, yeah, he is. Now is he *available?*"

Miguel frowned at him in irritation. "Did I not just say no?"

"Whoa!" Cy held his hands up. "Okay, then, guard dog. You be sure to let me know when he can run without his leash!"

Miguel barely maintained a civil tongue in his head. "I'll do that," he snapped. "He's *hurt*. That's why he's out there—he's free. Can't you see it? He doesn't have a thing to worry about like that. Just don't pressure him, okay?"

Cy's flirtiness fell away, and he regarded Miguel carefully. "Yeah. Yeah, Miguel, I can see it. I'm not sure if *you* can see it, but that's okay. I'll leave your boy alone."

Miguel nodded, some of the seething anger dissipating. Cy became Ravi and Anish's friend again, happy, flirty, and handsome. And not for Miguel and *not* for Ezra.

"He's really something on the dance floor," Miguel said, watching him execute a neat turn, hands over head, and then a cool slide behind Darby.

"What's he like off of it?" Cy asked, sounding genuinely curious.

Miguel thought about it, thought about Ezra's easy acceptance of his new life and the way he listened with wide eyes and a quiet smile, as though entranced, during conversations at the store. He considered Ezra's wonder at simple pet ownership, the way he sputtered in defense of New York and his fancy clothes and how much product he used in his hair; the easy, trusting way he'd fallen into Miguel's arms as he'd cried in what must have been relief and sorrow. The scars on his knuckles and the little, petty rebellions to see if the cage he'd lived in his whole life was still there—rocky road ice cream, swimming in a river, wearing cargo shorts, working retail.

"He's… growing," Miguel said thoughtfully. "He's becoming who he wants to be."

"And who's that?" Cy asked, and underneath the bright blue eye shadow and silver hooped earrings, he was sober and curious.

"I think he's a good guy," Miguel said, watching Ezra smile at Darby in surprise as she whirled in his arms. Playfully, he dropped his hands to her hips and swiveled them backward and then forward in an imitation foxtrot. "I think he's funny and kind, and the brave is coming." He'd bought Rico suits and tried to shelter his lover from his father's bigotry. "I think he's going to be spectacular."

Cy laughed, and Miguel pulled his attention away from the dance floor to see that Cy and Ravi were both looking at him bemusedly.

"I think you're already blinded by him," Cy said gently. "But you go ahead and wait until he's spectacular."

Miguel turned away from those perceptive brown eyes and lost himself in watching Ezra dance. The song ended, and a One Direction song took its place. Darby kissed Ezra's cheek and he laughed, and then he looked up and caught Miguel's eyes. He grabbed Darby's hand, pulled her to the edge of the dance floor, and called to Miguel.

"C'mon, Miguel—let's dance! You sat long enough!"

Miguel was going to demur. Dancing, *so* not his thing—but as he was pushing himself up off the chair to jump into the melee, he realized why he *was* going.

Because he hadn't been an afterthought. Ezra had made an effort to find him, an effort to coax him onto the dance floor, an effort to see him. Cy he'd let just walk away—but Miguel he wanted.

Miguel knew that for the gift it was.

The dance floor was crowded and sweaty, which was precisely the reason Miguel had bailed before, but now, after watching Ezra's joyful, sexy grace, he thought he could manage. Darby saw him and smiled, stepping forward, and Miguel sidled between them. Ezra's hands on his hips helped him keep time, and Darby swayed happily when Miguel put his hands on her shoulders.

With two people helping him keep time and shielding his body from the rest of the franticness of the dance floor, Miguel felt sheltered and not assaulted.

And with Ezra pressed against his body, he felt...

Intimate.

Oh, yes, did he feel intimate. Darby kept time easily, and Miguel closed his eyes and forgot about the happy female body brushing him from the front and concentrated on the hot, sweaty male body cradling Miguel's bottom in a circle of hips and thighs, keeping Miguel in touch with the music, acting as a conduit between flesh and rhythm.

Throb, pound, throb. The music was sex, wasn't it? Oh, *hell* yes, it was sexy and primal, a quickie in a dark closet. But that body? Those hands at his hips, Ezra's breath against his neck, Ezra's pelvis against Miguel's ass?

That was... a long slow fuck in a moonlit room. For a moment Miguel thought about pushing away and going back to his vodka-scented ice water. He was looking out over the crowd to spot their table when he caught sight of himself in one of the mirrors in the back of the club.

Ezra had his face pressed into the hollow of Miguel's neck and shoulder, his head tilted against Miguel's neck. From what Miguel could see, his eyes were closed and he had a little half smile on his lips, and even as Miguel watched, he moved his hands from Miguel's hips to clasp around Miguel's middle.

Oh hell.

Miguel wouldn't take that happy away from him, *couldn't* take the safety, the comfort he seemed to be getting from Miguel's body.

It's probably just like Jake the cat. He's probably just getting off on my body temperature and basic humanity.

But it didn't matter. Just like with Jake, Miguel was reluctant to move, in case that perfect moment of communion was broken.

If it meant that lost look, the shattered look that Miguel had seen in Ezra's eyes that afternoon, was all gone? He could have danced all night.

THEY LEFT the dance club after another two hours, and yes, Ezra spent most of it on the floor. They dragged him to a bar that served desserts, though, and although he looked alone and worried at not having the dance floor as protection anymore, he seemed to perk up when he realized that they were not all alone walking down the wide streets of Sacramento.

"This isn't a bad scene," he said as they single-filed their way around a crowded patio so they didn't end up walking in the street. "God, there's like… like clubs all over the fuckin' place!"

Miguel stopped trying to keep up with the rest of their party—Cy was leading, and he was still as energetic as a frolicking tomcat. Miguel hung back with Ezra, knowing the way to their next destination and figuring everyone had a cell phone if the plans up front changed.

"Yeah," he said, smiling at Ezra's wonder. Theirs was not the only group moving through the sidewalks in search of a different bar, a better restaurant, someplace with dessert, someplace with music—Sacramento sported a decent variety, if you didn't go for porn or BDSM—and a diverse crowd. The people traveling the streets were often young college kids, but not always. He'd seen people in their fifties going into one of the clubs with live music and people of all ages hanging out on the patios and drinking. "It's a little more eclectic than people give it credit for. I guess twenty years ago they used to roll up the sidewalks or something, but now it's a pretty good scene."

"Looks like it—is it like this all year round?"

Miguel shrugged. "It slows down in the winter—but some of it gets busier. This isn't exactly a *college town*, but there's enough colleges and junior colleges nearby to make it sort of a college student destination."

Ezra nodded and swung his arms as they walked, probably trying to catch a breeze. There had been a nice wind during sunset, but it had died at full dark, and Miguel wasn't the only one dripping sweat between his shoulder blades.

"I'm just surprised, that's all," he said, looking around. Across the street they could see more people headed in the opposite direction, but that's not what was catching Ezra's attention. As they walked, he looked up and, to Miguel's surprise, came to a complete stop. "See?" he murmured. "That's what's surprising. Look at that—I can see sky, and the moon, and even some of the bigger stars. *That* is not something you get in New York."

Miguel paused and looked up as well. "No," he said softly. "I don't imagine so. Still homesick?"

Ezra thought about it, which was gratifying. They started walking again and then he spoke.

"No," he said, surprising Miguel a little. "Not really. I mean, right now I'd really like to show everybody my clubs *there*, but not because I miss them, just because Darby and Cy would really get a kick out of them, you know?"

Miguel smiled. "Oh yeah—you have to know, they're sort of trying to impress you. They know we're small potatoes out here, and they want you to think their town is good."

He caught a glint of Ezra's shiniest smile. "Well, if I don't get a chance to tell 'em, you make sure they know it was a great night, okay?"

"Where do you think you're going?" Miguel asked, laughing. If nothing else, they'd arrived at the club together.

Ezra half laughed. "You know, that's funny. I was… I mean, when I used to go out dancing, I went by myself. If I ever ended up with friends, I always split with them in the middle so none of my dad's employees would catch me… you know…."

"Dancing?" Miguel asked, throwing all the weight of a jailbreak into that one word.

"Yeah," Ezra agreed soberly. "Dancing. Anyway—so like now? Going to dessert and then going home? That's special, right there. I don't know if I'll tell everybody else that, but you should know."

Miguel flashed him a quick smile, liking him very much. "Thanks, papi," he said, feeling proud too. Ezra liked his town! "And I was thinking—it's pretty late, right?"

Ezra pulled out his phone. "Yeah, it's almost eleven. Hey—text from Finn. Didn't even see."

"What's it say?"

"Mm… man. He's telling me that they'll wait up for me so Clopper doesn't freak me out." He texted for a moment. "I'm fine with the damned dog. I just don't want to be on their brains during their night alone, you know?"

Miguel nodded, and before he could ask himself why, he let the impulse carry him. "You can sleep on my couch if you want. I can bring you back to the apartment in the morning."

Ezra smiled, that same genuine smile he'd shown when Miguel had suggested going dancing. "Yeah? Your mom wouldn't mind another deadbeat on the couch?"

"As long as you don't shout obscenities at her when she comes down the stairs, I think we're safe."

"Guaranteed," Ezra agreed solemnly. "Hold on a sec—lemme text Finn so they can go to sleep."

They paused under a great fruitless mulberry tree growing from a flowerbed in the sidewalk. They stood across the street from what looked to be a construction site, and the streetlights were out. Ezra leaned casually against the tree, his face caught in the glow from his phone, and Miguel kept an eye out for muggers or drunk girls who tended to stumble on the not-so-even sidewalk. The second was more likely, but the first was a possibility drilled into him by his mother. Miguel flicked his gaze to Ezra's face, lit up by his cell phone, and the details he'd seen from the very beginning—the big eyes framed with black lashes, the wide mouth and full lips, the high cheekbones and bony jaw—all seemed to rearrange before his eyes. He'd thought Ezra was a pretty kid, but with the image of that long, loose-limbed body on the dance floor behind his eyes, Miguel saw him with more depth, some character.

Something beyond beauty.

In that moment, the balmy air cooling even as they stood, Miguel thought he could spend days at a time in Ezra's company.

And he'd never get tired of seeing his face.

Ezra laughed slightly at the phone and then tucked it in his pocket. "Finn says I should probably not wake up naked."

Miguel laughed too, but something in his chest squeezed. "Probably not, papi."

Ezra blinked at him and smiled sadly. "Yeah. I think I need to be a little less broken, you know?"

Flirt, Miguel. Flirt. Make him feel like he won't feel like this forever.

"Well, when you're feeling all whole and good, you let me know. We'll go out dancing again, okay?"

Ezra smiled at him shyly, biting his lip. "You got better taste than me," he said. "But, you know. You ever feel like slumming in Manhattan, you let me know." He straightened from his slouch against the tree and started looking around for their group. "Here—let's catch up with them. I'd *really* love dessert, and that place might close by eleven!"

Together they trotted through the warm Sacramento night, going just fast enough to make talking a bother.

Which worked out well, because Miguel never had to find the words to say that there was no way to slum in Manhattan—everybody knew that. And if they didn't, well, Miguel was finding out up close and personal.

All Cats Are Aliens

MICKEY MOUSE and Ezra were on the dance floor, and Mickey sported some damned fine moves. But Ezra wasn't focused on Mickey Mouse—he was focused on three tiny mice squirming their way around the dance floor, and it was Ezra's job to catch those mice and keep them safe. C'mon, Mickey, let's get 'em!

Ezra opened his eyes quickly and closed them again.

Mickey Mouse, the dance floor, the baby mice, all of that went away.

He was on a couch—a whole different couch. That was all he knew. Instead of the easy blue corduroy of Finn and Adam's couch, this one was really uncomfortable, sort of a tapestry fabric, the kind that would go with almost every décor.

There was an air conditioner somewhere clunking its little heart out, and Ezra whimpered and nestled further into the sheet he was lying on? Under? Oh fuck. Both. He started to struggle, because the sheet had been folded like a taco, with Ezra as the kosher beef hot dog inside, and the taco had gotten tangled sometime in the night.

He wriggled and rolled, kicking with his feet and struggling with his arms, and with a heave that made his stomach muscles sing, he swung his tightly tangled legs together over the edge of the couch and stood up.

He was not prepared for the eruption of dogs that followed when he double-stuck the landing. He felt them surging like the tide around his feet, and although one of his arms was free, the other one was wrapped tight to his body. He flailed, out of balance, and was going to just sit down, but the two smallest dogs—tiny dogs, smaller than Jake the cat—had already leapt up on the couch and were *right under Ezra's ass*.

"Mother *fucker*!" he swore, flopping sideways onto the couch—but his body wasn't bending the right way because of the blankets, and he fell like a board and flipped over the back. The couch went over backward, catapulting the two dogs up and over, and Ezra once again found himself on a stranger's floor.

This time there were dogs.

The two Yorkie-Chihuahua-shih tzu things he'd almost sat on were up around his ears, barking, and there was a corgi standing on his stomach. And an eighty-pound golden lab sitting on his balls.

And two dogs that looked like pit bulls trying to make out with him, both at the same time.

Oh yeah. He was at Miguel's house.

"Mighllll…," he garbled. Oh God, that dog's breath was foul, and his tongue didn't taste great swabbing Ezra's tonsils. He turned his face to the side and tried to roll over to his stomach. "Miguel!" he called out, facedown in the carpet. "Miguel, man, little help here?"

"Hush, papi," said a woman's voice, very nearby. "He's asleep— I'll help you." And with that, he felt movement, and a pair of wide bare feet with pretty purple toenails strode away from him. He saw ankles, and what looked like a ragged pink chenille housecoat, and an unapologetically wide and middle-aged bottom, as the woman strode across the living room, through the kitchen, and to the sliding glass doors. She gave a few short commands and the dogs all stopped licking, barking at, or trying to neuter him, and flocked out the door at full speed. Oh, thank God. Nothing for Ezra to do now but flop around on this nice woman's floor like a goldfish and try not to look like more of an asshole than he already did.

"You still alive, papi?"

Ezra's face was still mashed into carpet, and the woman who still held vestiges of Miguel's prettiness was bending down and smiling at him, crinkles in the corners of her warm brown eyes testifying to a life doing mostly that—smiling.

"I'm fatally embarrassed," he said, wishing for a quick death.

"Well, if I leave you alone to pick yourself up, I'm making pancakes," she said. Surprisingly, she reached down with a soft brown hand and ruffled his hair. "Take your time—nobody's watching."

Ezra thought about it. "Don't you have two other sons who would be happy to dump me out on the lawn?"

Miguel's mother laughed, a rich, warm sound that wrapped around his chest. In a million years, he couldn't imagine his mother laughing like that. But then, he couldn't imagine his mother cooking or letting him have friends over or owning dogs either. You could bounce a quarter off his mother's ass—but that didn't mean you could melt an ice cube on it.

This woman here was nothing but warm.

"They, too, are sleeping in," she said. "And I see you heard the story of Miguel's last date to sleep here."

"Yeah," Ezra admitted, squirming out of the mummy sheet as if it was a hula skirt. "I promised him I wouldn't embarrass him in front of you." He grunted and kicked free of the sheet, then scrambled to his feet as Miguel's mother turned and walked toward the kitchen.

"I see you promised nothing about embarrassing yourself," she said, laughing kindly.

"Well, you know, me and couches. I think it's a given."

She cast him a grin over her shoulder, and he saw that she had her son's smile too. She must have been stunningly beautiful when she was younger—but Ezra was falling a little bit in love with her now. "You wake up on a lot of couches, papi?"

"Two in the last week," he said, taking stock. He was in his boxer shorts and the tank he'd been wearing under his dance shirt, so he was mostly decent. Miguel's mom didn't seem put out, so he was going to roll with it.

The living room he was walking through had seen hard use. The beige carpet was stained and the paneling had chips at the baseboards and by the doorways. The couch he'd slept on was part of a living room set—love seat, recliner, and even a couple of stuffed Queen Anne chairs in the corner, waiting for a big family gathering, probably. In the *other* corner, by the entryway, were two giant dog pillows covered in hair—yeah, the dogs were family too. There were also two big bins of plastic toys there, everything from Barbie dolls to pirate ships. He could also see oil paintings on the walls—they looked amateur, but a talented amateur, and Ezra wondered which one of Miguel's brothers or sisters painted. A giant television dominated the far end of the room, and so did several shelves full of DVDs—everything from Oscar Award winners to bad B movies, to documentaries to an entire shelf dedicated to animation.

As Ezra passed from one room to the next, he realized he was looking at a house that had seen children grow up in it and was seeing grandchildren growing. Why change the rug when the dogs were going to run inside in the winter? Why refurbish the paneling when a whole new crop of kids was going to come along and peel it? This house was made for family members to come inside and love each other.

Ezra thought about his parents' Central Park apartment, five thousand square feet of space, impeccable moldings and hardwood floors, a different room refurbished every year, and a kitchen done in steel, chrome, and black, and he wanted to cry.

In a million years, his parents wouldn't have let him come to a friend's house if his friend had lived like this.

But this warm, round woman had just smiled at him and teased him and offered to make him pancakes in her spotlessly clean kitchen with the broken tile and the battered wooden table.

"Do you like corn in your pancakes, or chocolate?" the woman asked, and Ezra blinked.

"I don't know if I've had either thing, Mrs. Rodriguez," he said politely. "Which one do you think is best?"

She laughed. "Call me Therese," she said kindly. "And I'll make them both, and next time you destroy my living room, you'll know which one."

"Oh!" Ezra said. "Yeah—be right back."

He padded back into the living room and thumped the couch over, then draped the sheet on top of it.

He got back just in time to see Mrs. Rod—Therese—pulling out pancake mix, eggs, milk, a can of corn, and a bag of chocolate chips.

"Uh," he said, wanting to help because it would be polite, but not sure what to do. "Do you need me to, uh—"

"Wash the dishes," she said succinctly. "When this is over, I want to walk away and get dressed and not have to see the kitchen again."

Ezra laughed and pulled up a stool so he could sit at the counter separating the dining room from the cooking area and the sink. "Solid," he agreed. "I can definitely do that. I'm, uh, sorry about the ruckus this morning. I'm sure a stranger on your couch isn't exactly on your list of things to do."

"You're not a stranger," she said, bending over and pulling out mixing bowls and a mixer. She set them up on the laminate counter and then started rooting under the stove for pots and pans. "Miguel has been talking about you since you arrived."

"Seriously?" Ezra's face heated. "I, uh, God. He hasn't seen me at my best."

"No," she agreed. "But he says you've been adapting. I have to tell you, I think you're good for him."

"Me?" Ezra startled enough to almost knock over his stool. "How would that work?"

She shrugged and went about cracking eggs and measuring oil and milk into the pancake mix with graceful, dancing movements.

"Miguel has always been a good boy," she said after a moment. "But I don't think he's known *why* he was a good boy. He followed directions, tried to not get into trouble. If you walked into a room where five kids were beating the hell out of each other, Miguel was the one standing on the couch screaming, 'Mami, I told them not to!'"

Ezra's face was on fire. "That sounds a lot like me," he mumbled. "I, uh... you know. Wanted to be a good boy for my father." His mother hadn't been all that involved, but his father—*he'd* been the one to lay down the law. *He'd* been the one that Ezra was trying to impress.

"Yes, well, I think Miguel wanted to be a good boy so people would know he was a good boy." She shrugged. "This is a big family, and everybody has a strong personality. Miguel was just a nice boy—he wanted a little attention was all. But with you," she said, "it's different. With you, he's been trying to be a good boy because he wants to be nice to you. I like that reason much better. He was a pompous little asshole when he was a child, you know?"

Ezra frowned. "I haven't seen that side of him," he said, thinking. "I mean, he was hurt because his business failed and all, but I don't think he was... you know... pompous. Or an asshole."

Therese smiled. "I think that's because you're *truly* a good boy. And see? You both know what it's like to be hurt and to try something brave and have it not go right."

Oh no. "He told you *everything*?" Because he hadn't realized his whole personal debacle had been on stage with more than just the people he knew about.

She grinned at him and popped a chocolate chip in her mouth before pouring half the bag into the bowl with the mix. "Of course—it's what makes it worth it to cook. I come in here to cook, and my children sit pretty much where you're sitting now, and they tell me their day. I know that Miguel goes downtown and you see him as your coworker, or sometimes he wears a suit and goes to work for Derek, but I see him as a little boy telling me stories. And this week, you have been in the stories. Is that so bad?"

Ezra shook his head. "No, ma'am. Not at all."

"So, tell me stories, Ezra. What did you do last night and yesterday? A mother wants to know."

She winked at him—just winked—and that was all it took. Ezra found the whole of the day before—from Rico's visit to Candy Heaven to their lunch at River Burger—all unfolding. He talked about swimming in the river, and how he'd only ever been in a swimming pool before, and about dressing up and dancing, and how much he'd liked the scene in Sacramento, the walking from club to club, and oh, especially the dancing. He finished up with how they'd gone out for dessert and then walked the ten blocks back to their cars, and how he'd fallen asleep on the drive to Roseville from Sacramento.

"I know it's probably not that far away," Ezra finished apologetically, "but it was… is… really different."

"Different from what?" She set the griddle on the stove and added a little oil, then turned on the heat.

Ezra shrugged, feeling that whole fish-out-of-water thing acutely. "From what I'm used to. I mean… have you ever been to New York?"

Miguel's mother shook her head, her black hair falling comfortably around her shoulders. She looked up and met his eyes, smiling so earnestly his heart swelled a little bit.

"Tell me," she urged. "I would *really* like to hear about New York."

By the time Miguel padded in, dressed in his boxers and a T-shirt, which made Ezra feel better, and followed by two guys who looked enough like him to definitely be his brothers, Ezra had been talking for twenty minutes.

He'd talked about the forest of buildings and his parents' Central Park apartment. He talked a little about Chelsea and how it was walking distance from his father's office on Broadway. He talked about striding the streets in a crowd and being alone, and how there was always something happening, no matter when you were out. He talked about the bay and crossing from one world to the next by taking a ferry or crossing a bridge, and how his favorite deli was on 45th and Broadway and his favorite Chinese takeout was two blocks down. How he'd learned to drive in the New Jersey suburbs, where you took one main thoroughfare and went from small suburb to small suburb just by driving down that one street. About how all the men wore suits and the women dressed sharp and wearing cargo shorts to the office would be considered blasphemy unless you'd just gotten fired and were collecting your shit. How the guy at the little grocery store below his apartment knew his name, and how his gym was three stories in the corner of a much bigger building. How living in downtown Sacramento was more like living in a New Jersey suburb than living in Manhattan.

And how he was starting to like it.

"See, the dog," he said as Miguel took the stool next to him and yawned. "I mean, you could have a dog this big in New York, but the park where you'd take him to play is about the size of this house right here. And *this* dog, he seems to love it in Sacramento. I can't explain it. It's like, he goes down the steps and smells the air, and he knows there's rabbits out there. I don't.... I mean, we went swimming in the river, and I just can't imagine any place even in Jersey we could do that. Maybe upstate, but I haven't been since I was a kid."

Therese Rodriguez looked up and smiled. "I understand there's lots of farmland up there. And some lovely mountains. It's just, you know, easy to get wrapped up in a city. Like it's the center of something, and you have to go outside of it to know it's not everything."

Ezra blinked at this woman who claimed never to have been to New York, and thought she was very wise.

"Yeah," he said, and suddenly his apartment in Chelsea seemed much smaller in his mind than it had when he left. Sacramento was small and still pretty rural in some ways, but he suddenly knew what Clopper felt like when he stepped out of the door and smelled rabbits. "Yeah," he repeated. "You're right. It's like, the idea of a bigger world isn't just... you know. Limited to a big city in a big world. The cool thing about a city is that there are so many different lives people could be leading there." Lives where people were out, and free, and not broken or caged. "But you forget that there are more lives outside the city than in it."

Oh, that warm, maternal smile. Ezra had not seen enough of those in his life. There had been some nannies he remembered fondly, but this kindness, this faith—hell, this *interest* in who he was—it made him want to cry.

"That's an incredible thing to say," she told him, and for a moment he thought he couldn't breathe, he was so happy. "Miguel, you need to bring him here more often. I'll cook for him and his stories any day."

Ezra turned to Miguel and grinned, feeling like sunshine radiated out from his body. "Can I?" he asked. "Your mom is the best. I mean... the *best*."

Miguel blinked a few more times, like he wasn't sure if he was awake. "Yeah," he said. "Yeah, papi—anyone who thinks my mom is the best, he's got to come back."

"Finally," the shorter, stockier brother sitting at the table said. "Jeez, Miguel—took you long enough to find someone decent."

"Yeah, well, you got such an interest in the guys I bring home, *you* find one, Jaime," Miguel retorted. "The last girl you brought here had your china picked out already and was working on the names of your first three children."

Jaime groaned. "God, and that was on the third date too. Sorry, Mami."

"Nothing to be sorry about," Therese said crisply. "I'm sure she looked sane at the bar."

The other young man at the table laughed, and Ezra turned around and got a good look at him. He was taller than Miguel and skinnier too, and he possessed sort of a gangly grace. Both the brothers had dark hair and dark eyes, but whereas Jaime had a square jaw and forehead and face to match, Berto—it had to be Berto—had the thinner face and sensitive mouth of a poet.

Of course, he was also a young man in his twenties.

"I don't think that chick would have looked sane in a psych ward, Mami. But at least she wasn't planning to join a cult, because that was *my* last date."

"A cult?" Ezra asked, not sure if he was kidding.

Berto shook his head. "I don't even… man, I mean, there's religions and then there's cray-cray, and this chick was from the church of cray-cray."

Miguel made a sound of disgust. "Yeah, I remember this one. I'm really grateful you didn't cleanse my bed with chicken blood and snake venom so you could get rid of the gay in the house and get laid, Berto. It's bad enough you stole my dog."

Berto laughed. "Yeah, well, I would have felt really guilty about Skuzzy if I'd gone through with the gay cleansing ritual. You can't have dog guilt—it's no good for anyone."

"How'd you steal his dog?" Oh, this was fun. This was like Adam and Finn talking, but Ezra didn't feel guilty for interrupting between two married people or even just for enjoying Rico's cousin as a friend when he and Rico weren't a couple anymore.

Berto snorted. "That was easy. Miguel used to come downstairs to train Skuzzy every morning—he'd use the hard pet treats, the ones that were supposed to help them clean their teeth?"

Ezra nodded, thinking that anything good for you was probably not much of a treat.

"Yeah. So I'd get up before him—this was his first year in college, and he was working and going to school, so it was on those days when he actually got to sleep in. Anyway, I'd use the *soft* treats—you know, the ones that were beef flavored with no actual beef? All the dogs loved them—Skuzzy just started liking my treats better, that was all."

Ezra looked at Miguel, who was maintaining this sort of bored expression, much like the one he used at Candy Heaven when people came in and asked him what happened to his business because they thought he was moving on up to bigger and better things.

The same expression he wore when Ravi and Anish chided him about still not being over Adam.

Oh hell.

Miguel was *hurt*. Suddenly the whole last week, and how Miguel seemed to be bored and so over his job, and so over Adam and so over dancing, fell into place.

Miguel's brother stole his dog.

Ezra looked at that stoic, bored expression and then back at his little brother, whom he obviously loved. "Uh, why'd you do that?" he probed tentatively. Maybe Miguel did something bitchy and mean to deserve it.

Berto looked sheepish. "Mostly because I was being an asshole. I'd just decided to go into veterinary school, and I was all cocky and full of myself, so I thought I'd be the dog whisperer."

"Yeah," Ezra said. "Yeah, I think you maybe owe your brother a new dog—that was sort of low."

Berto looked at Miguel and winked. "I promise, Miguel, when you move out of the house, I will get you a new dog."

"Or a cat," Ezra amended, thinking about Jake. "I sort of like cats. I'd visit Miguel if he had a cat."

Miguel's smile made an appearance, angelic and wicked at the same time. "Really? We've been joined at the hip all week and the *cat's* the reason you'd visit?"

Ezra rolled his eyes. "Hey, don't think I don't know—the only reason you've been stuck to me like glue is that Adam made you my fairy-Miguel-mother."

A funny thing happened then. It was like the bored look kept trying to take over his face again, but it couldn't. What was left when he gave up trying to be bored was raw and sort of vulnerable.

"Well," he said, "maybe at the beginning." He looked away, reached down to the counter, and snagged a pancake waiting to be served. Very carefully, he ripped it in half and handed Ezra the bigger half, the chocolate chips soft and practically dripping out the ripped side. "But now we're like, you know. Peas in a pod."

Ezra grinned back, feeling shy and vulnerable too. "Two halves of the same pancake?"

That grin made an appearance again. "Eat your pancake, papi. Then we can set the table and eat more."

BREAKFAST WAS full of conversation and laughter. Therese was a nurse who worked for a reproductive clinic, and she had stories of a woman who found out she was pregnant with quadruplets.

"She was terrified," Therese said. "And I don't blame her. Her husband was this stupid man with clothes cut too tight and hair that looks too good—no personality. He looked at the ultrasound and said, 'Well, hon, you're gonna have your hands full! I told you I wasn't changing diapers!'"

There were general groans from around the table, but not from Ezra. Therese looked sharply at him. "What's the matter, Ezra—you think the young man was right?"

Ezra shook his head. "No—I mean, *no*. It's just...." He grimaced. "I mean, I hope *she* was excited about changing diapers, 'cause when the nanny's the only one who wants to, that gets lonely."

Miguel bumped him with a knee. "Yeah, well, there's going to be four of them. I think they don't get to be lonely."

"Yeah!" Ezra cheered up. "Like you! You had three sisters too?"

"Not *had*—they didn't *die*!" Jaime said, laughing. "No, they're all still here, just as ready to get in our faces as they were when we were growing up."

"Yeah," Berto added. "Except Lydia, who lives out… God. I mean, it's like you *think* you're going to LA, so at least that's exciting? But you take a right as soon as you get on the Grapevine, and *boom*. You're out in the middle of the desert, and *that's* where Lydia lives. Why would you *do* that?"

Ezra shrugged. He could smell the river from Adam and Finn's front stoop. "Maybe there was something there that she liked," he said.

"Yeah," Berto snorted. "Her *husband*. And she's on her fourth baby, so she must like him a lot."

At this Therese let out a groan, the kind only a beleaguered woman could. "Yeah—and we still need to figure out how to get your uncle's minivan up to her. Remember? Uncle Lalo was going to trade her for her sedan, and I just don't have time!"

"Well, she's not due until September, Mami," Miguel reassured her. "Maybe one of us can do it?"

"*Could* you?" Therese asked, so obviously grateful that Ezra found himself nodding along with her sons. "Oh, Miguel, that would be such a load off my mind. She's due in *late* September, so if you could get up there sometime in the next month, that would be great."

Miguel nodded. "Yeah, sure. I'll ask Adam about the schedule today." He cast Ezra a friendly look. "What do you say—want to come with me? It's a long drive—Lydia's place is too noisy for *me*, so we could stay at a hotel for a couple of days, maybe drive into LA… I might even squander some of my hard-earned business money on Disneyland, you think?"

Disneyland? "Really?" Ezra asked eagerly. "I didn't go when I was a kid—I mean, *Disneyland*?"

"I think that's a deal," Therese said, laughing. "And you know what? If you two take the car down for me, I'll buy your tickets myself."

"Aw, Mami, no—"

"Therese, you don't have to—"

"No," she said firmly. "You're both doing me a huge favor. Miguel because he's taking the car when I can't, and you because I don't like him driving alone. You guys get your days off, and I'll fund part of your trip, deal?"

Miguel stood up so he could go around the table and kiss his mom on the cheek. "You're the best, Mami," he said, all sincerity. "You don't have to do that, but I'm not gonna say no."

"Yeah," Ezra said, feeling so grateful it made him awkward. "That's… thank you. Just, you know, thank you."

She smiled at him and reached over to pat his hand as Miguel sat back down. They continued to linger over breakfast for another half hour before Ezra and the boys cleaned up, but for Ezra, that moment, that simple human touch on his hand, stayed with him. He'd gotten used to Miguel's unconscious touches—the small of his back when they were going somewhere Miguel knew and Ezra didn't, the bumps in the shoulder when he wanted Ezra's attention. He'd learned them from his mother.

Ezra wondered wistfully if he could learn those things from Miguel.

MIGUEL SHOWERED and dressed for work shortly after that, and then took Ezra back to Sacramento. Ezra had time to appreciate the half hour the trip took, and Miguel snorted and waved his hand.

"This? This is nothing. When there's traffic, it can be forty-five minutes to an hour."

"But…." Ezra hated to finish that sentence.

"But why do I do it when there's other minimum-wage jobs closer?" Miguel asked, his mouth pulled up in the corner. "See, when I first started, I was going to school at Sac State, so going from school to the job or vice versa was actually easier when they were both down there. And then, when I was interning with Derek, I was making a decent wage and it was worth the commute." He sighed. "I lost my lease and it was just easy, you know? My safety net. I still temp for Derek now and again, and that's still near Candy Heaven for those times when I'm working both, and my friends were there."

"And Adam?" Ezra asked softly.

Miguel shook his head once, decisively. "No. Believe it or not, Adam didn't factor into it. I mean… I crushed on him. Crushed hard— and you figured that out. But… but I'm not stupid. Adam didn't even see me—not that way, anyways. But he was part of the safety net—the softball team, the people who would help me work a flexible schedule. Especially when Rico and Derek got together, you know? Not so much a crush, just…."

"A comfortable part of the background?" Ezra surmised. But it *was* pure guesswork, because he couldn't think of a single employee at his father's company who had been that for him.

Miguel threw him a grin as they drove through a shit-ton of road construction surrounding rural suburbs.

"What is this?" Ezra asked, looking around. "I can't figure out if it's farmland or strip malls?"

Miguel shook his head. "All of the above—and some really shitty neighborhoods to boot. This place, it's a mishmash. Every suburb has its own special code. Levee Oaks and Rio Linda, they're mostly white farm country. Sacramento proper is *really* diverse. Roseville *used* to be mostly brown people, and now there's sort of a split. Latinos live in the older parts of town, where they moved before everybody wanted to kill immigrants with fire, and then the rich people all moved to Lincoln and Stanford Ranch, and now the rich people pretend the brown people don't exist."

Ezra squinted at him. "Uh, brown people?"

"Mostly Mexican," Miguel supplied. "Because California is *attached to Mexico*, right? But some people emigrated from further south, so it doesn't pay to assume."

"Huh," Ezra said, realizing he'd never thought of it before. "I feel sort of stupid. You know—I just assumed people were people, and they were from down the block."

Miguel chuckled. "Yeah, well, as long as you don't scream 'Go home!' at us or try to kill us with fire, I think I can deal with that attitude. This world—it's a real mix, you know?"

"Yeah. But you know what else I know?"

"What?"

"Your mother? She deserves like, like a pedestal and a cloud and a thousand tiny invisible workers to rub her feet and clean in the corners and feed the dogs and shit. I mean, I'm sure your brothers and you try, but let's face it—you're just not good enough for her."

Miguel *really* laughed this time. "I will agree with that, my man. Sadly, we're all she's got. Well, us and our sisters and their husbands and like seven grandchildren. Wait. Six. There's *going to be* seven."

Ezra shook his head, suddenly wanting so bad to be a part of that world, where everybody got excited about a baby or a marriage or two guys driving a minivan to Lancaster. "Well, if you need to do anything for her, let me know. I want in on some of that."

"Really?" Miguel said, sounding curious. "Did you just volunteer to do yard work for my mother?"

Ezra should have felt embarrassed, but he refused to be cowed. "Man, you don't even know. That scene we just had in your kitchen? I get that she does that *every day* for you. But you know how many nice intimate conversations I ever had with my mother? How many times she said, 'Just sit there, kiddo, and I'll make you pancakes and make you feel like a real person'?"

"No." Miguel's voice was suspiciously gentle. "How many?"

"I'll let you know when it happens," Ezra said bitterly. "But I had my stupid mental breakdown in May and she hasn't called me since, so I'm not going to hold my breath."

Miguel grunted, and Ezra realized that he hadn't really talked about his "stupid mental breakdown." Not really. Oh, great—now Miguel would be afraid of him.

"She didn't call you?"

"No."

"Why not?"

"I don't know. Because I wasn't perfect, I guess. Because I was gay and I wasn't going to change my mind about it. Because my father told her not to—take your pick. I mean, she was a decent mom," he said, thinking he had to have some good to say about her. "I had birthday parties and Hanukkah presents and clothes and stuff. But... but that thing you and your family just did? Sit together and give each other shit? That would so not happen in my house."

"Yeah," Miguel said, turning down Finn and Adam's street, "well, it's not your house anymore. *This* is your house. So, you know, maybe real human contact can start occurring a lot more often."

Ezra let out a breath. Oh good. The "stupid mental breakdown" wasn't going to sit between them like a giant stone Buddha. And Miguel was right. His first dinner with Adam and Miguel in that apartment stuck in his mind. Finn and Adam had made a real effort for him to be a part of them, and they had no reason to.

It was like the touch of Miguel's mother's hand on his gave him superpowers or something. Suddenly, when he'd been sleepwalking through this week, thinking, *Oh, hey, this is dealing!* he realized he had a chance to do more than deal. He had a chance to *thrive*.

"Well, if the worst thing I ever did was let Rico go, maybe the best thing I ever did was come out here. I mean... me and Rico, we probably wouldn't work out of the closet anyway. He's...." Ezra thought wistfully of Rico, so confident and so capable and so *invested* in the work he did in Ezra's father's office. "He was born to be a businessman, you know? If not marketing or advertising, he would have been something else. He's got this... this *drive* that I just never had. But I came here wondering what made him so awesome, and if maybe I couldn't get me some of that. And I think there are people here that can help me be awesome, you know?"

"I'm starting to," Miguel said quietly. He killed the motor and they sat for a moment before the heat started permeating the car.

"Yeah, well, I'm happy," Ezra said, feeling it in his gut. "I had an awesome time last night—thanks so much for coming, and for taking me to your house so Adam and Finn could have some time. And thanks for putting up with me this week. And for introducing me to your mom."

"You know this isn't good-bye, right? We're going to work together after you get your ass in gear and shower, right?"

Ezra shot him his best grin. "Yeah. But I spent my entire relationship with Rico not saying important stuff. That shit has to stop right now." And with that, he hopped out of the car and trotted up the walkway and the stairs. He was suddenly eager to get rid of the club clothes he'd had to change back into, and to say hi to Adam and Finn and Clopper and Jake.

It wasn't until that afternoon, when they were back at Candy Heaven and working as usual, that it occurred to him:

He'd compared his friendship with Miguel to his relationship with Rico.

Ezra stopped in the middle of carrying a box down from the loft. He froze, looking out over the store to where Miguel was behind the chocolate counter, helping what looked to be a really nice lady with an order. Oh God—what if Miguel heard that and thought... oh no. Ezra *really* didn't want Miguel to feel sorry for him, or like he was responsible for Ezra any more than he already did.

He didn't notice, Ezra thought. *No harm, no foul. It's all okay.*

Miguel looked up at the loft then and waved, and Ezra nodded back.

Yeah, sure. All okay. No relationship here, folks, just a couple of guys rediscovering their keel.

"What did you just see?" Darrin said as Ezra got to the bottom of the stairs.

Ezra blinked at him. He and Darrin hadn't had a lot of conversations since he'd started working there—mostly he stuck to Miguel or sometimes to Adam.

"Uh… just remembered something I forgot," he said, feeling dorky.

Darrin rolled his eyes. "Sweet boy, please tell me you don't play poker."

No. Because poker would imply a peer group. "Nope. Do you?"

"I'm too busy playing 'fix the emotionally damaged twentysomethings,'" Darrin said with a tone of deep disgust. "It's apparently a game you can't win and that never ends."

Ezra blinked slowly. "I got no comeback to that. Maybe if geezers stopped breaking us, we'd stop bothering you."

Now Darrin was the one who did the long, slow blink. "That could be the wisest thing anyone *not* me said in here. What are you doing for the rest of your life?"

"I got no idea. I've got an MBA, but I'm not sure where that's gonna get me." He took the last two steps down to the floor and spotted the barrel he was stocking. Okay, around the toddler, through the group of tourists wearing really loud shirts, and behind the counter, where Miguel's customer was busy cracking jokes about chocolate fairies who raided her shelves but never cleaned the kitchen.

Ezra found the empty barrel and added prewrapped root beer candies, and dropped off a new stack of folded confectioner's boxes right before Miguel reached for them.

"Nice move," Miguel said, winking, and Ezra smiled back. He'd seen Miguel working hard, anticipating orders, asking Adam what he needed before Adam even looked around to see what was running out. It was like both of them walked in that afternoon with the goal in mind of being better people.

That night, after Adam drove him home, Ezra offered to take Clopper the big dorkus for a walk after dinner. Finn and Adam exchanged looks, and Finn put on a pair of flip-flops and came with him.

Ezra grabbed the lead and led the three of them down the stairs and across the walk, but Clopper got to the end of the sidewalk and sat. He cast Ezra a *very* deliberate look then, head cocked, eyebrow raised, and Ezra looked at Finn.

"I'm not good enough?" he said, a little bit hurt. "I took you to the river, jerkoff. That doesn't count for shit?"

Clopper flopped to the sidewalk, chin on paws, his sigh gusting out over the street.

Ezra sighed. "He respects the cat more than me, doesn't he?"

Finn grimaced and took the lead. "Well, Jake is a respectable cat. But it's not that. It's dog psychology. Clopper, ya big moo, get your ass up!"

Clopper pulled himself to his feet and batted big brown eyes at Finn, and then turned right and expected them to follow.

Which they did.

And now Finn was the one to sigh. "See, with Adam, he wouldn't have flopped on you in the first place. Adam is *the* alpha dog. Rico is a close second—but don't listen to Adam about Rico giving him the dog. He thinks Rico walks on water, so he doesn't see. The dog gave himself to Adam first." There was a pause while they watched Clopper water someone's hedge with an intensity that caused mud to spatter. After continuing on like they hadn't left a puddle of dog pee in their wake, Finn kept talking. "I'm third. I'm like, one noodle up on the pack hierarchy—and you want to know a secret?"

"Shoot."

"This dog pissed in my dirty laundry for a week when I first moved in with Adam."

"Oh my God!" Ezra said, thinking about that puddle.

"You're telling me—and it was like super-strength dog piss too. I mean, I was attracting dogs in heat two washes later. Anyways, I didn't tell Adam, because he still had one foot out the door at the time and I didn't want to spook him. He takes his animals seriously, right? So for a week I'd get home and find dog pee on my dirty jeans and my T-shirts. Then, one night, after my shower, I took my dirty underwear—and I cooked in them too, so they were nasty—and rubbed them all over Clopper's face."

"Gross!" Ezra said with feeling, right as they were rounding a corner. A couple of college-aged girls who were just about to kiss on their lawn retreated with a wounded look, and Ezra wanted to die, but Finn just kept talking.

"I'm saying. Anyway, the next day no dog piss. So I did that, like, two weeks straight—and if my underwear wasn't rank, I used my socks, because feet are gross, and dogs respect a healthy stench. Anyway, I rubbed my funk in that dog's nose, and he finally conceded that I was not the least important puppy and he didn't get to piss on me."

Ezra nodded, torn between going back to explain to the girls that he *wasn't* a homophobic asshole, just a homosexual ass, and processing Finn's story. He glanced behind his shoulder one more time and Finn laughed.

"Forget about it—I'll tell them tomorrow when I take Clopper for a walk. They're always out in the morning doing yard work, and we talk. Anyway, see, that's what you have to do—convince the dog that you are not the least important puppy."

Ezra recoiled. "But... my underwear is never that dirty!"

Finn's shout of laughter startled Clopper enough to make him move faster, and Ezra felt better about the walk. He was used to walking a lot more in the city—he'd been afraid he'd get fat, but walking these suburbs with their older Victorian-era houses and cracked sidewalks seemed like it could get the job done.

"I'm not saying you have to have dirty underwear!" Finn whooped. "Oh my God…. Jesus, if I laugh any harder I'm gonna pee in mine!" He chortled some more, apparently tickled beyond measure.

"Then what are you saying?"

Finn calmed down completely. "Whew… wow. That's awesome. I'm so telling Adam that—he'll wet himself. Anyway. So what I'm saying is…." And just that fast, he was completely sober. "You're not the least important puppy, Ezra."

Ezra frowned at him a little, not getting it.

Finn sighed. "Look—we get what you did last night, going to Miguel's, and Adam says you guys had a good time, and you're getting to be friends, which is great, you could totally do worse. But… but if you hadn't wanted to go sleep on his couch? If you'd felt like staying in last night, or if you'd been lonely or sad or whatever? It would have been okay if you'd come home and hung. You're an important puppy, you know? We want you to feel safe here."

Ezra swallowed against a lump in his throat.

"You guys," he said softly. "You and Adam—you're real good people. You're... you're like Miguel's mom, you know? I... there were probably friends I could have had in New York—but nobody wanted to like me at work, 'cause I was the boss's son, and I was a suck-up. And I didn't let anyone else get close."

"Mm," Finn murmured, like he was willing Ezra to talk more. "Boyfriends? Girlfriends? Best friends?"

"I had a few boyfriends," Ezra admitted. "But… I wasn't just living in the closet, you know? I was living in fear—absolute fear—that I'd get discovered. It doesn't make a person really… you know.…"

"Open," Finn said. "Yeah. I know. Well, welcome to your new life. Where you're not the least important puppy. And everyone knows you're gay and doesn't mind. And you can get the job you want and the bosses usually prefer you not suck up. We've got pollution, road construction, and some shitty politics, but you know, it all balances out."

Ezra laughed a little. "Hey, can we go by those girls' house again on the way back?"

"Yeah, why?"

"Because. It's like you said, new start, new life, right?"

"Yeah."

"I don't want to start out here with our neighbors thinking I'm an asshole. Is that okay?"

Finn shrugged. "Yeah, sure. But I warn you—it's gonna be an awkward conversation."

They walked Clopper for another twenty minutes and then returned to the little green Victorian with the two white pillars and the freshly painted porch. Ezra tried to look confident as he walked by.

The smaller of the two girls—a chubby brunette with an unfriendly glare—opened the door.

"Uh, hi. I'm, uh, Ezra Kellerman, and like, half an hour ago, I was rounding the corner and my stupid friend told me something really disgusting. And I said 'gross' really loud, and you and your girlfriend probably thought I was talking about you, but I wasn't. So, uh, you know. Not that you should give a shit, but that's one less homophobic asshole to worry about, you know?"

The girl blinked slowly. "Yeah, okay." Then she looked over Ezra's shoulder. "Finn?"

"Hi, Bethany!" Finn chirped.

"This one belong to you?"

"Yeah—he's mine and Adam's. We've adopted him. Be kind."

"Yeah, sure." She looked back at Ezra. "Human of you to come by. Just don't let that moose dog crap in our yard, we'll get along fine."

Ezra stammered thank you and backed away slowly, and then joined Finn in the darkening twilight.

"Feel better?" Finn said, a little amused.

"Yeah." He paused for a minute and closed his eyes, turning his face to the sky. "You know, it feels bigger out here. I mean, it's a smaller city, but it feels… you know. Like you can wave your arms a little."

"Yeah," Finn said, deep satisfaction in his voice. "It's why I couldn't leave when Perry, the rat, suddenly announced he was going to graduate school out of state. And I was sad for a while, and then Adam walked into Candy Heaven, and it was like, God has a fuckin' plan, you know?"

Ezra turned his head and saw Finn standing next to him, face turned to the sky. A friend who didn't think this was weird at all. Wow.

"Do you think Miguel would do this?" he asked, just so he could figure out what kind of friend Miguel was.

"I think everybody should do this," Finn said, straightening and grinning slightly. "So I'll say yes. But maybe you should ask him."

Ezra thought about that as they rounded the corner to their apartment building—to Ezra's home. That night as he was sitting on the couch listening to Adam and Finn bicker over who was hotter, the hot kid from *Scorpion* or the hot kid from *Arrow*, he pulled out his phone and hit Miguel's number.

Stupid question.

Hit me.

Do you ever stand outside in the dark and turn your face to the stars?

Yeah, sure. Everybody does.

That was nice—it was good to know Miguel did that too. *Oh.*

Anything else?

Yeah. Who's the least important puppy in your house?

Me.

Ezra thought seriously and then texted: *I think that's a lie.*

Fine, Miguel replied. *Who's the least important puppy in YOUR house?*

Me.

I think that's a lie too.

You're just saying that to be nice. But it's okay. It IS nice. Why do you think you're not important?

Because so many brothers and sisters. Nobody sees me.

Your mom sees you. Your brothers see you. I think you're plenty important.

Fine. How come you're not important?

Ezra tried not to disappear into self-pity. *Because. If I disappeared tonight, people I've known a week would be concerned, and that's nice. But nobody would be heartbroken.*

I would. We could be really good friends, and I'd miss finding out. I'd be heartbroken.

It was a lie—nobody would be heartbroken after a week, right?

Except he remembered—he'd known Rico for barely two weeks before he asked him for a kiss. If Rico hadn't kissed him, it would have hurt worse than now. At least he'd gotten that kiss.

You're a mensch, Miguel. Night.

You're an important puppy, Ezra. Night to you too.

He actually slept really well, although he dreamed about Clopper and an identical dog standing side by side, which was sort of weird. He woke up with Jake on his chest, like he'd never been gone.

Don't Touch My Patch

"YAY, EZRA! Go Ezra!" Finn screamed enthusiastically from left field, and Miguel watched in the bull pen as Adam pinched the bridge of his nose.

Ezra bit his lip and held the bat—choked way too low for Miguel's liking—and swung way back from his shoulder in an attempt to look ready.

Yeah—he was playing for Candy Heaven. The first time, they'd been up against Audrey's Toys and Antiques. Ezra had told Miguel and Adam repeatedly that he'd suck on the field, and Adam had told him repeatedly that he couldn't possibly be any worse than Finn's family. He was. He was way worse. It was a good thing their first game was against a team of spry septuagenarians, because otherwise Ezra might really have meant the difference between victory and defeat, especially since Adam had been working that day.

Of course, Adam was way better, so now that he was on the field, they were still winning against River Burger. Both teams had spent the entire game cheering Ezra on like crazy, but that didn't mean seeing him up at the mound wasn't painful, like watching a little kid run around with his pants down, screaming, "Look at me, I can fly!"

"Time out!" Adam called, and he was taking a step out of the bull pen to go coach when Miguel cut in front of him.

"I'll get it," he muttered. For the past few weeks, he and Ezra had been joined at the hip—it just didn't feel right to let Adam coach Miguel's pocket puppy with Miguel right there.

Miguel hadn't had a best friend since grade school, and he had to admit that what started off as sort of a duty for some stranger dumped on him and his friends had become a lot of fun. Watching Ezra discover the things he loved was like watching a cat approach an unknown entity. There was the patting carefully with the paw and skittering back, and then tossing around with impunity, and then finally curling up with a tenderness that astounded all onlookers.

He'd taken to swimming in the river like, well, a duck, not a cat, and of course the desire to swim was helped by the late August heat that wasn't letting up. But still, the first few times Miguel had suggested it, he'd gotten a sort of head-cocked look, an inquisitive wariness that suggested Ezra was just waiting for the river to pounce. Once he realized *he* would be the one to pounce, it was all good. The same with going out to the movies, and the same with "Hey, come over to my house for dinner tonight, because Adam and Finn are both working late!"

The first time Miguel asked him—even the coming over for dinner after Ezra had slept over—he cocked his head and considered. He would approach the outing quietly, prepared to… to what? To be rebuffed? To be yelled at? To displease Miguel, or his mother, or his baseball team?

Something—because Ezra was afraid with each new thing.

He would endure the date with big eyes and polite manners and, at the end, say thank you and then….

He'd be all over Miguel in text.

That movie was amazing—did you ever think about taking an old classic like that and revamping it?

Your mom cooks great authentic Mexican—did she teach you how?

Or, most heartbreaking, *Sorry I sucked at softball. If you and Adam don't want me to play, you know I don't have to.*

And after they texted about it and talked about it the next day or two at work, Miguel would ask him to do something else, and Ezra would rub his whiskers against the idea and purr, and it would all be okay.

So after a couple of weeks, he no longer expected to be kicked off the softball team. But he didn't expect to get a hit either.

"Kk, papi," Miguel said gently after asking permission to approach the batter's box. "Remember, we talked about this—you have to choke up on the bat."

Ezra regarded him unhappily from under the hard plastic batter's helmet. "You know, that's great when you say that, but I have no idea what that means."

"You've watched baseball your entire life—"

"I could *bet* on the Mets," Ezra said defensively, "but I couldn't tell you why they won!"

Miguel let out a little grunt of frustration, but after nearly four weeks of knowing Ezra, he didn't growl or snap or any of the things he might have done before. "Here," he sighed. He looked up at team River

Burger—led by Finn's dad on the pitcher's mound—and said, "Is it okay if we have a little batting training here?"

"Not a problem," Mr. Stewart said, relaxing from his pitching stance. He had curling gray ginger hair around a sweet oval face and looked like he *could* be the leader of a family of happy elves. Which he was. "In fact," Finn's dad said as he dropped the ball and came trotting up to the batter's box, "I think I can help you."

Miguel stood behind Ezra and pulled at his hips, adjusting his body, and then bent down and nudged his lead foot until he could move quickly if he actually made contact with the ball. While he was doing that, Finn's dad adjusted Ezra's arms and hands. When they were done, they both stepped back and checked him out.

"Howzitlook?" Ezra asked from gritted teeth.

"Good," Miguel pronounced. "You ready to hit the ball?"

"No." Ezra straightened up and dropped the bat. "You guys, my arms are killing me. Can we just let me strike out and get on with the game?"

Across the field, Finn guffawed, and Mr. Stewart let out a snicker.

"I'll do my best to oblige you," he said solemnly and turned back toward the pitcher's mound.

Miguel did not feel like taking his shit. "Don't give up," he snapped, eyebrows drawn.

"Does it bother you so much that I suck?" Ezra asked, and although the corners of his mouth were quirked up, Miguel was still remembering that text, the one that said *I'll quit if you need me to.*

"I don't care if you *suck*," Miguel responded. "I care if you *try.*"

Ezra shrugged. "Yeah. Okay. I'll try. Now move. It's hot out here."

They were playing at Discovery Park this time, and although there was a breeze off the river, as they were standing in the sun of the baseball diamond, all that really got them was humidity.

Miguel scowled. "Yeah, it's hot. We can go swimming afterwards *if* you just *try* to hit the ball."

Ezra rolled his eyes, and Miguel suspected that if he really *were* a cat, Miguel would be talking to the one pink eye.

"Don't give me that shit, papi," Miguel muttered. "Have you seen me at work this last month, steppin' and fetchin'? That's your fault. I just want to see some back."

Ezra twitched his upper lip. "Get out of my way, here, I'm trying to play ball."

Miguel went back to the dugout, where Adam was standing stoically, arms crossed, chewing a wad of bubble gum and watching the field. Miguel stood next to him, crossing his arms and leaning against the edge of the gate.

"He choked up like you said," Adam observed.

Miguel grunted.

"And he's fixed his hips."

George pitched and Ezra swung, his forehead knit in concentration. *Whiff*!

Miguel grunted.

"What do you want from the guy? Perfection?"

Oh hell. No. "Way to go, Ezra!" Miguel cheered. "Good eye, good eye!" The rest of the bull pen took their cue and reluctant applause broke out, even from Darby, who was on third and dying to come home.

Ezra relaxed into his stance again, but Miguel could see a slight smile on his face in addition to that furrowed brow.

"So, did you decide what you wanted from him?" Adam asked.

"Yeah. I wanted him to try."

George Stewart pitched again, the ball making a perfect arc from the mound to the box, and Ezra swung…

And hit!

For a moment the entire softball team was silent as the ball wobbled off the tip of the bat and sailed straight for Finn, who was out in left field.

On his phone.

"What in the fuck," Adam muttered. "*Finn*! Heads up, asshole!"

Finn raised his face from his camera just in time to see the ball heading for him, and he responded by throwing his glove—and his camera—in front of his eyes.

The ball bounced off his glove and onto the field amid the cheers of the Candy Heaven team and the outraged shouts of his own family.

Adam was clearly torn. For once he wasn't stoic, ordered, or in control—and he wasn't cheering his own guy either. Instead, almost beside himself, he was waving his hat around and sputtering while Finn scrambled for the ball and lobbed it to his sister.

As soon as Finn had cleared the ball, as Ezra rounded first in front of an irritated Rico and tried for second, Adam found his voice.

"Jesus fucking Christ, baby, what in the *hell* were you thinking?"

At that moment they all heard a very familiar electronic noise from Adam's duffel bag, and he paused midrant as Finn waved sheepishly from the field.

Ezra slowed down at second as Darby came in home—mostly unnoticed, poor thing. The chaos on the River Burger field and in the dugout, and even in the stands, where Derek was going fucking insane with Clopper, Finn's mom, Darby's kid Cameron, and Mari's kid Joshie took a long time to die down.

And Adam didn't move, instead staring bug-eyed at the man of his dreams.

"Uh," Miguel ventured, "are you going to check your—"

"Oh, look!" Darrin cooed. "Adam, do you want to see the text Finn sent?" He was wearing a tie-dyed T-shirt with *Candy Heaven* stenciled on the front over a pair of cutoffs, and his hair was up in a ponytail under his hat. He never actually went out on the field, but he always showed up to cheer everybody on.

That got Adam's attention. "How do you even know my passcode.... Never mind. Sorry I asked. Yeah. Sure. Whatever. I'm dead. He's killed me. My heart stopped because he was sending me a text on the baseball field. I've jumped off the cliff of what the fuck—why not look at the fucking text!"

Darrin smiled broadly. "Maybe because the rant in the meantime is so fucking precious I can't stand it. But Katya's up, so cheer for her first, then look."

Adam turned to dutifully cheer Katya on, and Miguel took the opportunity to look around at Adam's phone.

And choke on his tongue.

"Oh holy Jesus...."

Darrin grinned happily. "You're like... like little twins!" he said, and Miguel barely remembered to cheer as Katya bunted to first and Ezra ran to third.

He checked back in time to see Darrin pushing on Adam's phone. "Oh, hey—there we go. To Ezra, George, and Mari. Oh! And the dumb yuppies—they need a picture too." Darrin hit Send with a flourish, and Miguel turned back to Adam with a groan.

"What?" Adam asked, not taking his eyes from the field. Ravi was up next, and he'd been their worst player before Ezra had joined. It was like everyone in the batter's box needed Adam to cheer them on or they'd completely lose their minds and forget that they could function as a team without him.

Maybe they couldn't.

"I don't want to talk about it," Miguel muttered.

"No, seriously—what was the picture? Was someone tugging at their strap or picking their nose?" Suddenly Adam chuckled. "Please tell me Rico was picking his nose. We'll blow that up and put it on the refrigerator. He'll *never* live that down!"

Miguel chuckled, because hey, he had brothers, and nothing really trumped a good booger pic when you were dealing with family, but then he sobered.

"Nope. Not boogers."

Adam had his arms folded in front of him again, and after Ravi swung and missed, he turned to Miguel curiously. "No, seriously. What was it?"

Miguel's arms were folded too—again—and he tried hard to drop them down to his hips or to his sides or anywhere else, but they wouldn't go.

"It was us," he muttered. "You and me, standing together. We've got the hats, the shirts, and I'm actually six feet tall, so I don't look too much shorter than you."

Adam groaned. "And we're Mexican."

"And we're Mexican."

So brown hair, brown eyes, and they both had square chins. Miguel's nose was a little bigger—but then, so were his eyes—and his mouth was fuller, but it didn't matter.

"We looked like twins," Adam muttered.

"With the brims in our faces, yeah."

Adam shook his head and Ravi struck out, groaning and walking the bat back with a muttered "Sorry, boss."

"You did your best, man," Adam said. "Now everybody clear out of my way, I'm gonna go yell at Finn."

He didn't hear the general chuckle in the dugout that indicated nobody believed that Adam yelled at anybody, especially Finn.

"So," Finn was saying as the Candy Heaven bench grabbed their gloves and streamed out, "did you see it? Wasn't it cute? You and Miguel, you looked like twins—that was great, right?"

They heard Adam's sigh across the field. "Yeah, baby. 'Twas awesome. Give me your phone."

"Wha—"

"Mr. Stewart, give this to your wife when he's on the field, 'kay?"

"God, yes. Finn, I swear to Christ you almost made me shit my pants. Adam was gonna plotz. Just… just… argh!"

Finn grinned, completely unrepentant, the little shit. "I love you, Daddy. Can we call the game now?"

"*No!*" With that he stalked off to his wife, a lovely woman with ash blonde hair sitting in the stands looking stylish and svelte—when Clopper wasn't trying to lick her face off.

Finn sighed and shook his head. "He must be pissed. That usually works."

Miguel scowled and handed Ezra his glove before he had to trot into the dugout.

"Did you see?" Ezra asked like a little kid. His eagerness faded almost before he was done talking. "It wasn't very good."

Miguel was going to give him pointers and tell him how to fix it next time, explain that it took practice. One look at the half turn of Ezra's shoulders, and he realized that with some people that would work. But Ezra was a cat, and like all cats, he needed his strokes or he would take his needy, fuck-off self somewhere else.

"It was great, papi," he said sincerely. "I mean, last time you struck out every at bat, and this time you hit one. You must be really proud."

Ezra smiled, his eyes half-closed. "Yes, yes, I am," he said, and then tapped the brim of his baseball cap down. "Can you believe Finn and the camera phone? Why would he do that?"

Miguel suppressed a groan. "You'll see when you check your phone. Now out to left field, and remember to hold your glove up to catch the ball, not to protect your face, okay?"

Ezra gave him a wide-eyed nod, and the game went on.

CANDY HEAVEN maintained the winning streak they had firmly established when Adam started working there, and the end of the game had a lot of people jumping in the river to cool off.

Miguel swam out with Finn, and together the two of them watched as Adam and Ezra kept Cameron and Joshie from going in past their ankles.

Mari, after checking with Ezra, gave Joshie a kiss and swam out toward the middle, where a little bit of treading water could keep them upcurrent.

"Look at them," she murmured. "They're the greatest babysitters ever." She scowled at her brother. "Adam would have to be or he'd have beaten you senseless, moron."

Finn gave her a look that clearly said "talk to the fuzzy butt" and then grinned at Miguel. "It was a great picture, wasn't it?"

Miguel was going to give him shit about it—he was. But he'd actually studied the picture as the game wrapped up, and he'd realized something important.

He and Adam really *were* alike. It had taken him the time with Ezra, trying to be there, to anticipate the things Ezra needed, trying to be a good guy instead of looking for what was in it for him, to make Miguel understand that maybe his fixation hadn't been a crush or unrequited love after all.

Maybe, just maybe, it had been hero worship, with a smidgen of attraction thrown in. And who wouldn't be attracted to Adam? Dead lesbians were probably attracted to Adam Macias—but noticing how a guy was built didn't mean it was true love always.

Maybe it just meant the guy was built, and that Miguel and Adam had more in common as people than they ever would have as lovers.

So although it had been a piss-stupid move on Finn's part, sometimes a guy needed a piss-stupid move for shit to make sense.

"It was a great picture," Miguel said, meaning it. "Ezra thought so too."

Finn grinned, and then one by one they all lifted their feet and let the current carry them into the inlet. It was time to let Adam and Ezra swim out, and then everybody was moving to one of the picnic tables and barbecues to help with dinner. The sun was going down, they'd get kicked out at dark, and time was getting on.

It was Friday night, and on Monday Finn and Adam were starting school. Miguel hoped Ezra was ready for their comfortable rhythm to change—he'd been getting used to having his roommates nearby, and that wasn't going to be so easy from now on.

THE HEAT was so bad, even *Ezra* begged off dancing. Adam and Finn were having an animated film festival at their apartment, and that was a better option. They were watching as many animated films as they could stand, starting off with a French one called *The Illusionist*.

Normally Miguel would have thought that sounded like, well, a waste of time, really. He'd had to sit through animated films a bajillion times with his sister's kids, and he was about over them, but two things stopped him from blowing it off completely.

Well, three.

The first was that Adam had studied to be an animator, and Miguel was curious as to why that was such an exciting field. He wanted to hear Adam talk about what made animation so interesting. Not because he was still crushing on Adam, because that was pretty much over with the picture (which had gone viral—even his mother had seen it), but just because. He was starting to realize that the attitude he'd adopted when his business had failed, the one that said he was bored with everything that didn't benefit him and it was all beneath his time, was pretty much bullshit. Watching Ezra's cautious wonder reminded him that he was still young and still had plenty of enthusiasm to give.

The second was that he wanted to see the movies through *Ezra's* point of view, because as far as he could tell, Ezra's father had bypassed any and all opportunity to make his son a happy child. Miguel was on the lookout for one more thing to make Ezra happy, one more thing to talk to him about, one more thing to keep their growing friendship alive and thriving.

The third was that he couldn't possibly stand another night watching Cy and Ezra dance. Oh yeah, sure, Ezra danced in that sinuous, throbbing way with anyone who got on the dance floor with him, male or female, but with Cy, it was different.

Every time Miguel saw Cy and Ezra vibrating together on the dance floor, he wanted to grab Cy by his irritating hair extensions, yank his head back, and clock him in the jaw.

Of course, as soon as Cy got off the dance floor—or Miguel got on and between Cy and Ezra—the need went away. Miguel had been spending an awful lot of time getting felt up by strangers so he could protect Ezra's sinuous, writhing, half-naked body from a guy that he actually liked.

No, Miguel couldn't figure it out either, but although he'd gotten better at dancing, it still wasn't his scene. When Ezra said he wanted to hang with his roommates and watch cartoons, Miguel was 100 percent in his corner.

Of course, after the first movie, Miguel decided that Adam was a jerk and Ezra was nuts. The movie came to its poignant, painful ending, and out of nowhere, Ezra started to sob.

Uncontrollably, like he had after lunch with Rico, and he hadn't cried since, in spite of seeing Rico and Derek a couple of times a week now.

Miguel folded him against his chest, aware that Ezra hadn't called his shrink yet, and that everybody cried at movies, and that Finn and Adam didn't seem too upset.

And aware—very aware—that Ezra's liquid, loose-limbed body felt very comfortable in his arms.

Ezra recovered after a few minutes and retired to wash his face. When he came back, they told him they weren't going to watch *Ernest & Celestine*, and instead they would watch *Megamind*. Miguel insisted, actually, saying sad foreign films weren't really a good idea right now, and maybe if they could get him to laugh until he threw up, he'd feel like his weekend had been achieved.

So this, horsing around on the couch, squashing him against the arm, smashing his carefully slicked-back hair, *this* all felt like a bit of normalcy. Great, you had your catharsis, let's have some laughter endorphins as well, right?

Miguel would so much rather have Ezra laugh than cry.

So he shoved at him and wrestled, and threw his arm over Ezra's legs and mocked him when he whined like a weenie for some personal space.

"Finn, make him stop!" Ezra complained, shoving at Miguel's leg sprawled across his lap.

"Stop being a baby. Where were you going anyway?" Miguel shoved a hand against the top of Ezra's head, like his brothers did to him, and wiggled his butt to make Ezra even more uncomfortable.

Ezra glared at him and threatened to dump popcorn on his lap.

"Yo!" Adam barked. "Children! Knock it off! Miguel, I'll call your mother. Ezra assures me she's a perfectly normal human being, so you behave!"

Miguel cackled and straightened on the couch a little, but he didn't give Ezra back his space. Ezra was really good at setting up this invisible wall between him and the world, but in the past month, Miguel had made a point of knocking it down.

"You radiate heat, you know that, don't you?" Ezra observed, squashed against the side of the couch. It was the first week of September, Finn and Adam had been in school for a week, and temperatures had been in the hundreds. Their poor little transplant had been fighting a losing battle against wilting in the late-summer oven that was the valley.

"I am *not* giving you your space!" Miguel retorted as Ezra beat futilely at his leg. "They've got the AC cranked until it's criminal. Now stop pretending you don't like it and cuddle."

"Oh, good Lord," Finn groaned. "You guys, Adam loves this fuckin' movie—now both of you settle down, sip your sodas, and get into the movie groove before the Xbox dinosaur gives up the ghost!"

Ezra squinted at the thing for a moment and then cried, "Turn it off! Turn it off! Finn, the red ring of death! Man, turn the damned thing—"

The Xbox overheated and the television went blank.

"Fuck."

Finn hit the remote, and the four people in the living room groaned. "Aw, man," Adam muttered. "Crap. Okay—let's put some towels between that thing and the DVR and maybe it'll cool down. Finn, you and I'll take Clopper for a walk, okay?"

"Ugh. Can we try cooking an egg on the sidewalk?" Finn muttered. "That sounds fun too."

Ezra continued to shove at Miguel's leg, insistent, but pretty feeble on the whole. "Look," he said in exasperation. "You need to get off, because we're going out for ice for the freezer and the sodas, okay? And ice cream."

"Oooh." Finn turned big eyes their way. "Can you get root beer floats?"

Ezra grinned like it was the perfect idea. "Sure. Let's all wander out and come back in an hour, and see if that thing doesn't cool down and we can watch the next movie."

"Deal," Adam agreed. "Break!"

Ezra scrambled off the couch, his slightly large cargo shorts threatening to slide down his scrawny ass as he did, and Miguel followed him, slouching and languid, behind him.

"Really, papi, you're that excited about getting out into the heat?"

Ezra didn't answer him, just checked his pocket for his wallet and house key and then grabbed Miguel's hand and pulled on him.

They trotted down the stairs and across the lawn, the steamy autumn swelter smacking them like wet wool as they went, but that didn't seem to dampen Ezra. He stood, dancing from foot to foot he was so excited, and as soon as Miguel got in the car and turned it on—and cranked the AC—he hopped in next to him.

"So, which market's best for the ice cream?" he asked.

"Where's the nearest electronics store that won't rip us off?" Ezra asked, all excitement.

Miguel blinked. "Uhm...."

"See, I've got money—I mean, besides what I make at Candy Heaven—and I... I mean, Adam and Finn, they've been good to me, you know?"

Yeah, Miguel knew. They ate dinner as a group, they watched movies, they walked the dog. Miguel got the same feeling hanging with Ezra and his roommates that he got going home to his brothers. Sure, living with people in close proximity could be irritating as hell, but mostly he was just glad they had his back on any given day.

"You do laundry and walk the dog," Miguel said. "You know, pay for the groceries, bring home takeout—you're a good roommate."

"I don't know if they'd say that—Adam's underwear keeps disappearing when I use the downstairs washer and drier."

Miguel rolled his eyes. "That's just apartments, buttercup. People steal shit all the time—Adam would *give* his underwear away to know someone he likes is helping with his dog."

Ezra's face lit up. "Yeah? Seriously? That's nice of you to say. I... you know. I got my own room in college, 'cause my dad was a fuckin' snob mostly, and since my grades didn't get me into Harvard, he wanted me to be like, the king of Syracuse. Anyway, lonely. But I just… I want to do something nice. If I tell them I'll get them an Xbox, it'll be no good. But if we go out for ice cream and come back with a new Xbox and ice cream and just, you know, bam, set it up and shit, I think they'll take it."

Miguel blinked, something else about Ezra fitting into place. He was meticulous, actually, about making sure he bought groceries or brought something whenever he came over to Miguel's mother's house to eat. Sometimes it was flowers, sometimes it was dessert from the grocery store deli—but it was always something.

Courtesy.

Miguel wasn't great at it. Ezra seemed to do it automatically, and maybe that happened because he hadn't had many real friendships. He had courtesy, probably the one thing that had been bred in him to the bone, and he would be courteous to people until he was sure he pulled his own weight.

Something Miguel didn't worry about—not at Adam and Finn's, not at Candy Heaven, not when he worked for Derek.

He'd been sure he could pull his own weight. No one had ever made him doubt it.

So Miguel got it—it might not have been Miguel's move, but he got it. Ezra was bringing a thing to his new friends and dropping it in their entertainment center before they had a chance to say no.

It was only courteous.

Target was uneventful, although Ezra was impressed about how big the Target was in the middle of the city.

"Man, our stores are mashed together in small buildings," he said, putting the ice cream in the cart with the root beer and the brand-new Xbox. "Even the apartments don't hold much. I mean, you keep talking about how small Finn and Adam's apartment is, but they live like royalty compared to what they'd get living in New York. My last boyfriend before Rico, he was a teacher. He lived in a bed-sitter with a hot plate on top of his tiny refrigerator. It was the top of an eight-story walk-up, and the ceiling sloped so you could only stand up straight in like two feet of the apartment. I think the whole reason he broke up with me was that he knew my apartment was pretty big, but I wouldn't take him there because my dad had his people watching over me all the time."

Miguel laughed, trying to lighten the moment. "I'd break up with you too, papi—all that space and you didn't share."

Ezra grunted, and they pushed the cart toward the entrance to stand in line. Miguel paused for a moment to sweep in some cookies and a gallon of milk, his treat.

"Yeah, but see?" Ezra said, like they were just continuing the conversation. "I mean, he fired Rico—and he would have done the same thing with this guy too, even though he was out to his staff. Just complained about him until the school board pulled him out. I mean, I could barely relax with him, even in his tiny apartment—just kept expecting the hammer to fall down."

Damn. "Well, you're better off here. That's no way to live." Miguel meant it too.

"Yeah, well, you and Adam and Finn, you've been really nice. I just want you to know I appreciate it, that's all." Ezra looked at the cart and then behind him at the grocery stacks. "Do you think they'd want chips?"

"Yeah, fine. Get dip too. They can eat crap food next week, they'll have it for days." Ezra was back in two seconds, and Miguel carried on the conversation. "It's easy to be nice to you. You're fun. You send me stupid cat videos and tell me dumb jokes. We're totally good."

Ezra threw a shitload of chips and dip into the cart. "You're easy. I can't believe you don't get laid more often. And we can bring whatever's left on the trip with us—we're still going to your sister's next week, right?"

"Yeah, good idea, papi." They'd both gotten work off, and the timing was perfect—with Finn and Adam tired from their new schedule, it would be good if Ezra got out from underfoot. "And I'm finicky," Miguel said. "I have to know the only asshole near a guy's dick is the one he's supposed to have, and he doesn't mind me pounding it. Anyone else need not apply."

Ezra blinked at him in that sleepy, half-aware way he had that usually meant he was processing something. The line advanced, and Miguel started unloading everything onto the check stand.

"So you're totally a top?" he asked, like this didn't make sense.

"So far, yeah," Miguel confirmed.

"That's weird. I didn't know people did that anymore. I thought verse was the new gay."

Miguel laughed, but the pit of his stomach was tight, and his entire sexual area was beginning to ache. He and Ezra didn't *do* the dirty joke thing, they didn't *do* sex confessions, but now that the can was open, Miguel couldn't see the conversation for the big worm with only one eye. He smiled greenly at the kid behind the counter, who smiled brightly back.

"I just like making sure nobody gets hurt, that's all," Miguel grunted.

Ezra grunted back. "Yeah—nothing kills sex faster than screaming, 'Ow ow ouch stop it!'"

The kid behind the counter started to laugh. "Uh, supplies to help make that not happen are right over there." He stopped and looked meaningfully at Ezra, who stared blankly back. "I'll go get some and add them to your pile. Be right back."

The kid disappeared, and Ezra squinted after him. "What the—did we forget onion dip?"

Miguel gaped at him. The kid wasn't bad-looking—lots of brown hair, green eyes, and a sweet, full-lipped smile—but Ezra was oblivious in the extreme.

Thank God.

"No," Miguel said shortly. "We did not forget onion dip. And there will be no dipping anything in anything, do you hear me?"

Ezra cocked his head just as the kid came back with a twelve-pack of condoms and a generous bottle of high-end lubricant. "Then why did we buy onion dip?"

"Will this do, sir?"

Ezra's blank look gave way to complete surprise. "Miguel, why are you getting rubbers? I didn't think you had a date!"

Mother of God.

"They're not for me," Miguel muttered, giving the clerk a fulminating look. "They're for my brother."

"Berto?"

"No, Jaime. He's a total slut. Needs rubbers all the time. This is a weekend bender for him," Miguel lied, deadpan. He made a mental note to tell Jaime that he'd just been thrown under the bus, thump-thump, but he wasn't sorry at all. Yeah, sure, the Target clerk *looked* harmless, but he obviously had designs on Miguel's recovering kitty cat, and Miguel had already resolved not to let Ezra get hurt on his watch.

"Sure," the clerk muttered, casting a look in Miguel's direction. "I buy prophylactics for *my* family all the time."

"I bet you're up for brother of the year," Miguel replied blandly. "Here, Ezra—you get the Xbox and batteries, I'll get everything else. I've been hanging out with Finn and Adam a lot these last days, and I haven't even offered for groceries."

"Yeah, okay," Ezra said, handing the clerk his card. "Just make sure to take your brother's stuff out of the bag—that could get awkward."

"You are telling *me*," Miguel muttered. He maintained a stony silence as the clerk rang up the rest of the stuff, and glared as he handed over the card.

Ezra had wandered off and was looking disinterestedly at the magazines on the check stand in front of them, which gave the clerk room to hiss, "If you want him so badly, you'd better let him know. If he comes in here alone, I am all over that."

"Classy," Miguel hissed back. "He is recovering from a broken heart—he doesn't need anybody right now!"

"The best way to get over a broken heart is to have somebody else fix it!" the guy snapped. "God, I hope your brother enjoys the rubbers, but personally I can think of a better use for them!"

With that the clerk shoved bags in his hands and gestured imperiously for him to go.

Miguel muttered to himself all the way out to the car, when Ezra said, "Hey, what's the matter—did you forget something?"

Miguel regarded him, big blue eyes wide and without agenda, lush mouth parted and nearly smiling, and his irritation faded to a dull roar. "Yeah, papi. I forgot what I was doing for a minute. I remember now."

"Good—I hope you're never that mad at me."

Oh God—that earnest nod and guileless smile, and suddenly Miguel could only hope that he'd never be as irritated at Ezra as he'd been at that slutty, man-stealing asshole of a clerk. "Yeah, papi, me too."

They got back to the apartment before Finn and Adam, which made Miguel think that maybe they'd stopped for a quickie while the company was gone. The new Xbox was all set up with the DVD in it by the time they came through the door, bickering amiably. Ezra hid the old one in the box behind the entertainment center. It wasn't until they were almost done with the second movie that Finn said, "Wait a minute, why didn't it overheat again?"

"Because Ezra bought us a new one," Adam said drolly. "And he was trying to be all secret and quiet about it, but you had to go blow it. Classy."

Finn gaped at him and then at Ezra. "You didn't have to—"

"Of course he didn't," Adam said. "He wanted to. It was nice." He looked at Ezra and winked. "'Preciate it. You didn't need to, but it was a nice gesture."

Finn got up from the couch and started to fondle the Xbox. "Look— it's really the new model, does all the bells and whistles if we hook it up to the cable box," he said. "Netflix, Amazon Prime, Hulu, the works...." He grimaced. "*After* we pay tuition."

"Sayin'," Adam confirmed, but Finn looked so crestfallen, he added, "but they have sales all the time. We'll watch the mail, okay?"

Finn perked up, and Miguel stood, ready to drive home. Ezra got up to walk him out, and together they ventured into a night that had cooled off considerably from the dripping hot afternoon.

"I forget," Ezra said, half to himself.

"Forget what?" Miguel drew near his car and paused, turning his face to the breeze that was whipping up from the river.

"Forget that a college education and living expenses are a rough gig sometimes. I mean, my father wasn't a prince, and I'm glad I didn't go back—but it hasn't been all bad, right?"

But he sounded like he was hoping for approval, and Miguel wasn't sure he could give that.

"You know," he said, "my sisters were still at home after my dad died, and they all worked retail and brought home their paycheck so mom didn't lose the house. Jaime was fifteen, and he got a job. Berto and I both talked to some of the vendors out at Denio's, and we spent every weekend until I was old enough to get a work permit running errands so we could bring home produce for the rest of the week."

"Wow," Ezra said, sounding impressed. "That's... that's a family effort. That's... that's amazing."

Miguel nodded, remembering those days. Many of the produce vendors at Denio's were immigrant workers, and few of them spoke English. Miguel and Berto had translated and helped them fill orders— and they had gone home with bags and bags, not only of groceries but of things like specialty soaps and premade carnitas when the burrito people had extra. They worked their asses off, but Miguel had never doubted, not once, that his community would take care of him or that his family would be there.

"That first year, when Mami was so sad," he said, the memory taking him by surprise, "Berto, Jaime, and I spent a week after school working for one of the jewelers. We stocked and stacked and even worked the forge, even though we were too young. So for Christmas, we could get her something really pretty—a silver necklace with six tiny diamonds. I mean, now, Jaime could probably buy it for his girlfriend of the week, but back then it was a big deal. Mami still wears it, you know? For special occasions."

"That's sweet," Ezra said softly, and Miguel searched his face in the light from the porch.

"Yeah. It was. It wasn't an easy time, you know? But... but I think of you growing up all alone, no roommates for college even, not able to take anyone home to your family. It makes me think I had the best childhood ever. Makes me think *all* boys should work at the auction on the weekends, or *all* boys should have too many kids in their family. I was never alone, Ezra. I think Adam was alone a lot—but even then, he had Rico, and you know that Rico had him. Finn—you've *seen* his family. No—I mean, it's nice that you want to help with stuff, especially since you're part of their household. I think that makes you a really decent human being. But you had it worse. Don't try to tell yourself to buck up and that your childhood was okay because you had enough to eat and shit. You were all fucking alone. I wouldn't trade my family for a free ride to Syracuse. But I would have worked at Denio's my whole life if I'd known you didn't have to be alone for your whole life, you know?"

They were standing on the sidewalk in front of his car, his beat-up, hope-it-makes-it old-style Pontiac, and Ezra suddenly turned his back and took a step up the walk.

"That's real nice," he said, his voice thick. "That's maybe the nicest thing anybody wished for me ever."

Oh no. Miguel could hear it—he was crying.

A month ago Miguel would have let him wipe his eyes and go back inside. Wasn't any skin off Miguel's nose, right? Wasn't his responsibility if Ezra was hurt inside? But that was a month ago, and since then not only had Ezra gotten under his skin, but the idea of being the guy who would help somebody like Ezra had worked its way there too. That picture of him and Adam standing side by side—they hadn't just *looked* alike, there'd been that suggestion that they *were* alike. The reason that people followed Adam and Derek was that they took care of the people around them without being asked.

Miguel wanted to be *that* guy. He especially wanted to be that guy for Ezra.

Miguel took a few steps and grabbed Ezra's shoulder. "C'mere, papi," he said gently.

Ezra came easily, without a fight, and Miguel held him and Ezra tucked his face against Miguel's shoulder. He didn't sob—he maybe shed a couple of tears. But mostly what he did was trust and relax against Miguel's chest and believe that Miguel would be there for him.

It was a pretty sweet feeling, actually.

"It's okay if you're sad," Miguel whispered. "I get that. But you've been with us for a month—and I think you're learning to let go of Rico. I hope you're learning to let us in."

"Why?" Ezra asked, and it was a logical question, but it still made Miguel cringe. "I… I just showed up and—"

"And we had room in our hearts for you. Isn't that enough?"

Ezra sighed and straightened. "I think you're really good people," he said after a moment. "You in particular, because you've sort of let me tag along and be your friend and meet your family—and I love that, and I don't want it to stop." He turned and took a step away, and Miguel grabbed his bicep again and pulled him gently.

"Then why are you leaving when you're still sad?" he asked kindly.

Ezra was stiff in his arms, though, and not limp and trusting like he had been. "There's nothing special about me," Ezra said. "I… haven't earned this place here. I mean, you bring home a stray cat and feed it, you're not going to love it like one you went out and picked just for you." Ezra struggled again to move, and Miguel tightened his arm around those narrow shoulders.

"That's bullshit," Miguel rasped. *Please. Anything, but please don't walk away thinking like that. Don't think I'd do this for anyone else and want it the way I do with you.*

"It's not your fault—"

Miguel dropped a kiss on his forehead and hoped that would shut him up. He shivered against the electricity of Ezra's skin on his lips and held tight in his heart to what he was doing here. "You know, Mami feeds outside cats. And some of them come inside, and some of them we love—but some of them stay strays and hate us forever. You're an inside cat, Ezra. You came in because we fed you, gave you a safe place to sleep. But you're staying because you're happy, and it makes us happy to make you happy."

"Finn and Adam," Ezra mumbled. "Because Rico made them."

"And because you're a good guy. Rico loved you because you were a good guy. He wanted you to be happy, and that didn't change just because he fell for Derek. C'mon, man." Miguel shook him a little using his one arm around Ezra's shoulders. "We like *you*—not the responsibility, the man."

His shoulders relaxed again, and Miguel breathed a sigh of relief.

Miguel didn't have to say anything—not now. Didn't have to commit himself—not yet. Didn't have to tell Ezra that he was special, particularly to Miguel, and that nobody else was as special as he was.

Miguel needed time in his heart, that was all. Time to rearrange his world without the habit of thinking he loved Adam. Time to know if Ezra was over Rico or just looking for the rebound guy to help him *get* over Rico.

Time to make sure that when Ezra sighed and melted into his chest and accepted comfort, he wanted Miguel and Miguel alone. Time to guarantee he was not just taking love from the first sucker who stroked him and took him home.

Because this thing, this creeping heat over Miguel's body, this progressive need to see Ezra, to catch his texts or to hear his New York accent making wary and wry observations, this could be stemmed, right? This wasn't irrevocable.

Except he couldn't seem to let Ezra go. He'd turned in Miguel's arms, and they were standing, holding each other on the sidewalk, practically dancing with Ezra's arms around Miguel's waist and Miguel's arms around Ezra's shoulders. They both had work in the morning, and Miguel had to drive all the way up to Roseville, and Ezra was going to have to take Clopper out one more time, and Miguel floundered for other reasons he should let go, just sigh and walk away, because not one of those things was compelling enough to break the moment.

A half an hour later, as he was walking into his mother's house with a small bag of prophylactics and lubricant in his hand, he still couldn't remember the moment in which they'd let go.

Catnip

EZRA RECOGNIZED the handsome young waiter from Fat City. He came in every day for a bag of gumballs and a chocolate truffle.

"You're gonna rot your teeth," he chided gently, and the boy—who had a square jaw and big brown eyes like Miguel, but not as much character in the mouth and too much space between the eyes—smiled.

"Aw, that's sweet—you care," he bantered, and Ezra replied without thought.

"I do. It would be a shame if you got a cavity and couldn't eat any candy anymore!"

The boy leaned against the chocolate counter, blocky, muscular body molded against the glass. "Yeah, that would suck. So how come you always eat at River Burger? I mean, I'm just down the street—I'm closer!"

Ezra laughed. "'Cause Mari and me we have a deal—I get sandwiches and she has an emergency babysitter card over my head."

This wasn't entirely true—Ezra paid for his sandwiches, and Mari was still looking for *time* to get a date so Ezra could babysit and pay her back for that day of kindness with Rico and Derek. But Ezra had met Joshie and played with him before and after a couple of the softball games. Even if Candy Heaven wasn't playing River Burger, Finn's family still showed up to cheer Adam on. Ezra and Joshie really had bonded—the little kid was inquisitive and liked to play, but he also had no problem just relaxing languidly against Ezra and talking.

It was just that Ezra *liked* going to River Burger for lunch—he saw Finn and Mari and their sweet dad, whom everybody called "Mr. Stewart" even though they were all grown-ups. Why would he want to screw that up by going to a really nice restaurant in his work clothes—most likely alone?

"Yeah, but, you know, you could eat with *me*," the guy wheedled.

"Does he even know your name?" Miguel said from his spot stocking barrels.

Ezra looked over and smiled. It was hard not to smile at Miguel—besides the angel face, he was also a good egg on the whole. Hanging out with him, being friends, learning the ropes around his new town—all of that would have been so much lonelier without Miguel's help. It was too bad he was still gone over Adam, or Ezra would think about….

No. No—better that he not.

Miguel was too nice a guy to get involved with a hot mess like Ezra. If nothing else, hanging with Miguel's family and Finn's family, and even Rico and Derek, had taught Ezra that his concept of how real people spent their time had been way, way damaged by his childhood. He'd always assumed that people worked first and lived second, and that the home was a showcase to intimidate business clients and show other people how you spent your wealth.

But the past month, he'd lived largely on his salary from Candy Heaven (with a few exceptions, like the Xbox and his contribution to the first month's rent in August, before he'd gotten paid) and had spent his spare time in an apartment with pretty art on the walls and dog and cat hair on the couches and people who were nice to him inside.

He was starting to think that maybe his childhood and young adulthood had it all wrong. When he thought back to his time in New York, working twelve-hour days to be the guy his father wanted him to be, working with strangers who hated his guts because he was the old man's kid and puppet, squeezing relationships into pockets of time he could get away from what felt like 24/7 surveillance and his father's iron-fisted clutch of his personal life—God. All of it, even going out with Rico and then running back home so his father's paid man could report that he'd been home by ten—alone—seemed… gray. Prison gray. It hadn't been a life, it had been a sentence, and holy fuck had he done his time.

Miguel had been part of teaching him what living a real life was all about. Ezra would really rather eat a sandwich in the little park two blocks down, Miguel by his side, than go out to eat with….

"Gordon," he said suddenly, surprising both Miguel and Gordon. Ezra had rung the guy up at least three days a week for a month—sometimes he used his card. "His name is Gordon, but Miguel and I got plans for lunch today—we're going on a road trip to Disneyland in two days and we have to plan. Sorry!"

Gordon grinned and winked. "No worries, papi. You let me know if you and"—he looked narrowly at Miguel, as though he'd done something wrong—"this one ever *don't* have plans. I'll help you do lunch right."

He winked again, took his candy, and sashayed out. Miguel followed him with his eyes and a decidedly unfriendly look on his face.

"You will *never* go out to lunch with him," Miguel said, something going on with his chest that made it sound like a motorboat was rumbling. "And I don't like the way he calls you papi."

Ezra blinked. "You say that all the time," he said. "The Puerto Rican boys in the clubs said that in New York. What's the big deal?"

Miguel glared at him, shook his head, and stalked off, muttering to himself. He grabbed the free-taste coupon bucket and left the store, presumably to go do his rounds and give away coupons for free candy.

Ezra watched him go. "Jesus, I didn't think it was a big deal," he said out loud, feeling hurt. "I mean, I know I'm not great at this whole West Coast transition, but I didn't think—"

"Oh. My. God." Darrin huffed, walking by and overhearing. "You really are as virginal as you look, aren't you?"

Oh please! "I've had plenty of sex," Ezra told him. "I've had your sex and his sex and everybody's sex. I'm a slut, I swear."

Darrin rolled his eyes. "Oh, sugar—there's a difference between a slut and someone who is just looking for the right hand to scratch his whole body. When you itch that bad, you'll take anybody—but when the right person does it, you only need the one. You're a virgin because you haven't found the right one, that's all."

That was absurd. "Have you *not* seen me recovering over a broken heart?" he asked, almost outraged. He'd lived in New York and had a nervous breakdown, for sweet Christ's sake. What did a guy have to do?

"No," Darrin said thoughtfully. "I really haven't seen any evidence of a broken heart. Bruised, definitely—but you didn't even know where your heart was before. How could it be broken?"

Ezra shook his head, too bewildered even to stutter. "Not know where my heart was? Isn't it… you know, in my chest?"

"That's a muscle that pushes blood, genius. Where's your *passion*?"

Unbidden, Ezra remembered the last time he and Rico were together. They were gentle—always so gentle. Exploratory. Ezra had sat astride Rico's hips, taking Rico inside him.

But Rico's face blurred in Ezra's mind, and he couldn't remember anything they'd said or anything they'd done that had made the moment special. It had been a cock and an ass, and even Rico's deep brown eyes were fading.

"I don't have any," Ezra said with a shrug, thinking sadly that must be true. He'd had *something* inside him, *something* that had snapped and battered at the portable sides of his cubicle at his father's office, but he couldn't ever remember thinking it was passion. "I am… passionless."

"Hm," Darrin said, jaw squaring mutinously. "I think you're wrong, and I think we should discuss this on Monday."

"Monday!" Ezra sputtered. "Miguel and I are off starting Monday—we're driving down to Lancaster and seeing his sister. This is a big fucking deal! You can't make me work Monday—I'll quit!"

Darrin laughed and walked away while Ezra was still sputtering. Before Ezra could get someone behind the counter so he could follow Darrin across the store, his boss returned, this time with a big rainbow lollipop.

Ezra paused and stared at it longingly.

"Recognize this?" Darrin taunted.

"Yeah," Ezra said, absurdly hurt. "It's the lollipop you said I could have after I worked here for a month." It was a kid's thing, right? The rainbow at the end of the rainbow? What adult in his right mind worked a job for candy?

"Well, Monday is the end of your fifth week. You can either go on your little jaunt to Disneyland with Miguel, or you can have your lollipop. What's it gonna be, sweetness—make your decision."

Ezra swallowed a lump in his throat. He'd *wanted* that lollipop—he clearly remembered that. He remembered talking about lollipops with Finn, and how the stupid candy confection had become some sort of symbol of everything Ezra had missed in his life until right now.

"There's lollipops in Disneyland," Ezra said, pretty sure it was true. "And you suck."

Darrin laughed and leaned forward, right into Ezra's space. "I *do* suck, not that you'll ever see. And *you* can take your lollipop *with* you to Disneyland, on one condition."

Ezra regarded him suspiciously. "What's that?"

"That if you're so *passionless*, you tell me exactly what it was that you just showed me when I said you had to come in to work on your vacation."

Ezra gaped at him, flailing his hands. "Uh... I mean... me and Miguel, we've planned this!" They had, too. They were going to leave at three after work on Sunday, stop for lunch at the Black Bear Diner, and get to their hotel in Lancaster in the wee hours of the night. Apparently Lydia's house was small, so they had the hotel booked for two nights so Miguel and his sister could visit, and then they had three nights booked at the Tropicana, which wasn't a great hotel, Miguel said, but was *right there* and they could walk back and forth from the park. Ezra had been appalled at all the hotel fees and the park fees and had tried to pay more than once, but Miguel had put him off.

"Derek gets us an employee discount," he'd said when Ezra had protested again, "and I'm still officially on his roster, so that makes the tickets cheap for Mami. And I still have my business discount for AAA, so that works too. Don't worry, *mijo*, you can buy us some food while we're there, and you'll be even."

"Yes, I know," Darrin said now, touching Ezra's nose now like he was a little boy. "You kids planned a trip to Disneyland, and I was being the big bad boss and it wasn't fair. But you didn't cave, did you? No, you threatened to quit, because it was *important*. That's passion, little britches. You gots it." Darrin handed him the lollipop with a meaningful wink. "You have the reward to prove it. Now you just have to ask yourself where your heart is to have so much passion."

Ezra just regarded him with big eyes, stuck on the part where he'd just told his "big bad boss" no.

"I did, didn't I?" he asked, hand in front of his mouth. "I told you no!"

Darrin grunted. "Adam!" he called, and Adam, who had just walked in through the front door from his last class of the week, called out "Yes, boss!" without a hitch in his breathing.

"I need you to do me a favor."

Adam walked to the counter, backpack still over his shoulder, eyes dark with exhaustion, and still he said, "Yeah. What do you need?"

"I need you to take over dreaming about stupid lovelorn assholes for me—I am about fucking done."

To his credit, Adam didn't even blink. "Does this mean I can start napping in the office like you do? I'm telling you, I'll dream about purple ponies for you if I can just catch twenty minutes of sleep."

"Catch an hour," Ezra said quickly, and both Darrin and Adam looked at him in surprise. Well, yeah. Self-motivation was not usually Ezra's strong suit, but Adam looked so tired! "I'll put off my lunch. Me and Miguel can talk after work."

Adam didn't even look at Darrin to ask him. "God, Ezra, I appreciate that so much. Are you sure?"

"Yeah," Ezra said. "Darrin?"

Darrin looked thoughtfully at Adam and nodded. "Yes, that's fine. You go ahead. And forget about the dreaming, boy wonder. I can deal with that until you get out of school."

Adam grunted and wandered off.

Together they watched as Adam trudged into the little office, presumably to tuck his backpack under his chin and catch forty winks.

"Ezra?" Darrin asked, all hint of his playful Machiavellian self gone for the moment.

"Yes, boss?"

"Have you thought about your big stupid dog and drooling fur monkey while you're gone?"

Yeah. Yeah, that was true. Ezra had been doing a lot of the pet ownership now that Adam and Finn were *both* in school and working full time. It was going to take them a little while to get past that whole exhaustion thing—he remembered *that* from school, at the very least.

"I've got it covered," he said, not wanting to think about how he had it covered.

Darrin looked at him and smiled faintly. "Yes," he agreed. "You do. And I promise that it won't hurt even a bit. Do you believe me?"

Ezra blinked at him slowly. Darrin knew exactly who he was going to have to call. "Yes, boss, I do."

Darrin patted his cheek gently and wandered off to talk to some customers. He was actually really amazing at talking to them—he played with the little kids and asked them what their favorites were, and told the adults to have a sweet day. Whatever Darrin's other "abilities," Ezra couldn't deny that this boss really loved what he did—and that what he did was make people happy.

Given Ezra's last boss, he had a sudden, profound sense of gratitude for his quirky, interested, enigmatic new boss. Darrin didn't actually have to give him a lollipop to get him to want to do things for the people in this store.

Ezra smiled and rubbed his finger around the edge of the rainbow lollipop in his hand. It didn't hurt, though, did it?

He sighed and at that moment, Miguel stalked back in.

Ezra pulled him over with a jerk of his chin. "Could you take over for a minute?" he asked without preamble. "I'm going to go call Rico, okay?"

Miguel's expression, if anything, got darker. "Why? Why do you need to talk to Rico?"

"Because you and me are going to be gone, and I want to make sure someone looks in on Clopper and Jake when Finn and Adam are gone all day. Rico's logical—I don't know if Adam's called him yet. They've been busy."

Miguel's expression lightened. "Yeah," he said slowly. "Good idea. That makes sense."

Ezra grunted. "I hope so, because talking to my ex is still not my favorite."

"Hurts?" Miguel said, his mouth trembling a moment, and vulnerable.

"Mm...." Ezra thought for a moment. "No. Just awkward. I'm still living at his cousin's house like dead weight, you know?"

"Not so much dead weight if you're looking after his animals," Miguel said, and he smiled.

Ezra had no idea how long he'd been waiting to see Miguel's smile today, but oy! It felt like it had been forever.

"No," Ezra said through a Death Valley mouth and Sahara throat. "Not dead weight."

Or something like that. *C'mon, Miguel, let me see that smile again!*

Ezra remembered the generic smile Miguel had given him on that first day, to let Ezra know it was all going to be okay. *This* smile was warmer and so much more personal, and Ezra realized he'd do anything for it. Work Adam's shift? Work Miguel's? Walk Clopper every night for a month? Oh God, just let Ezra know what sort of dues he had to pay to see that smile again, every day, just for *him*.

Miguel kept smiling. "Good. So you know. Go—go make your phone call. But no falling apart."

"Promise."

The east side of Candy Heaven was in the shade this time of day, and Ezra tucked himself against the wall and watched as people walked by. The crowds of the summer were gone, but Candy Heaven still did a brisk business in the morning. Right now it was late afternoon on a Thursday, and nobody was moving quickly. Ezra's gaze lingered on the bridge, sort of a Sacramento icon. Miguel had taken him across it one lunch, shown him Raley Field, and they'd eaten under a tree in the park overlooking the river. It had been a hot and sticky day, but the breeze had been nice, and Miguel had laughed a lot.

For some reason, the times when Miguel laughed or teased a lot were sticking with Ezra more than usual. Ezra could remember Miguel's last joke crystal clear—and he really was forgetting the exact shade of Rico's eyes.

Which made pulling up his number and hitting Call a whole lot easier.

"'Lo?" He sounded preoccupied.

"Yeah, Rico?"

"Hey, Ezra—you still settling in all right?"

That was nice. But then, Rico was always kind. "Yeah. But I'm not sure if Adam told you—Miguel and I, we're running a sort of errand for his family on Sunday—"

"Disneyland?" Rico confirmed, sounding amused. Well, yeah. Rico wasn't a roller coaster guy, was he? "Yeah, I heard. Finn is jealous as hell, so you know. He hasn't said anything because he wants you to have a good time, but he's wanted to take Adam forever."

"Yeah, well, maybe we can all go together sometime," Ezra said, realizing he'd like that. Friends—he had 'em. "But right now I'm just worried. Finn and Adam are running the ragged edge, and I've been doing a lot of the walking and cat box scooping and stuff. I mean, if there's any way you could walk Clopper at night, I think that would make their life a little easier while I'm gone."

"Of course," Rico said. "So, Adam having a tough time with school?"

"I think he's taking classes up the ass," Ezra said. He hadn't had to work through school—he didn't know how Adam did it. "But you know, starting something new—it's always rough. I just didn't want to leave them high and dry, you know?"

"Yeah. That's really considerate, Ezra. But you were always good at that."

Ezra took a moment. "I was?"

"Oh yeah. I mean, I don't think I would have waited forever for you to get out… but you're sort of a catch, you know?"

"No," Ezra said, remembering Rico's gentleness, remembering how every moment was precious—but not remembering feeling important, even when Rico said "I love you."

"Well, you are," Rico said softly. "It makes me really happy that you seem to be settling in here. Let Derek know if you ever want to work in marketing or advertising again. He's not really an employer but more of a matchmaker—you could pick your own contracts."

Ezra tried to lock his brain around working in his field again, doing something not at Candy Heaven, and his breath came short and his palms started to sweat, and he remembered those last few moments before he'd come unglued and his cubicle had sprouted ugly iron bars and the staff rules pinned behind his computer had looked like blood stains.

"Not yet," he apologized on a gasp, and as soon as he said it, his breathing evened out. Okay. Good. "I'm just getting better," he added, and saying that made him feel good too.

"I'm really glad," Rico said, and he sounded so sincere.

"I'm really glad you're happy too," Ezra said, and oh, thank you, God! He meant it. "I… I was a mess a month ago, but I'm a little saner now. I… if you've been staying away from Adam and Clopper because of me, you know, maybe don't."

"Thanks, Ezra. Text me when you get to LA—and Adam too. We want to know you guys are safe."

"Sure. Thanks, Rico—and take good care of Jake. I think he kind of likes me, you know?"

"Yeah. I think you're right."

Rico signed off, and Ezra gave a prayer of thanks. It would have been honest to point out that Jake was sort of easy and that he slept in every corner of the house, and even on Clopper when no one else was there. But it felt good to think that the dumb cat liked Ezra best. There hadn't been a whole lot of that going around in Ezra's life.

MIGUEL HAD a thing on his phone—an app that told them which way was quickest down the freeway—and they ended up on Hwy 99 for the trip down. Ezra thought it looked pretty bleak, just a string of towns in the desert like dust-bowl pearls, but Miguel told him that I-5 was worse.

"Yeah—at least you've got Oleander bushes in the center here. *And* you have towns. On I-5 it's all alien landscape, like the moon. There's stretches there where the only green for fifty miles is the rest stop, and the rest stop has a rattlesnake warning on it."

"A what?" He was sitting next to Miguel in Uncle Lalo's used minivan, enjoying the extra room for his feet—but he couldn't hardly believe he'd heard that last right.

"Okay, so last time Mami and I drove down to visit Lydia, we stopped, and there was triangular signs that told us to watch out for rattlesnakes. Rattlesnake warnings. I mean... *rattlesnake warnings.*"

Miguel shuddered, and Ezra laughed. It had been a good trip for that—laughing.

"Man, my older brother hid a snake in my bed when I was, like, four," Ezra said, dredging up this memory from God knew where. "It was only rubber, and I remember my old man telling my mother that I'd be fine, because what were the odds of me seeing a real snake in Manhattan. I... I mean, I haven't really thought of snakes since, but I'd probably lose my nut, you know?"

Miguel frowned. "Okay, A, that sounds like a totally shitty thing to do to a little kid. My mami and papi, they had a strict policy. The baby, he got the whole world, and it was our job to make sure that happened. So for a whole five years, I got to be the baby. Then it was Berto's turn, and that's just the way it is. And you'd think that Berto would have grown up to be an asshole, but not a chance. He's like you—he plays with the babies and the little kids like he's got to give back, and I'm okay with that."

"Yeah," Ezra said, not sure how many times or ways he could say this, "but that's because your family is awesome."

"Yours was worse than not awesome," Miguel said darkly, pulling around a sedan in the right lane. Miguel wasn't an aggressive driver, per se, but he did *not* like to sit behind the slowest guy on the road. "Your father—kicking in the nuts is too good for him. But besides that," he added before Ezra could gasp in surprise or shock, "is that you never really mention your older brother—"

"Two," Ezra said. "Gregory and Chaim."

"You know," Miguel said, looking at him delicately, "for a guy who claims his faith was not a big deal, your family sounds an awful lot like it was a big deal."

Ezra shrugged. "Yeah, I think they just didn't have a lot of imagination. You know how your mami goes to mass once a month and tries to get you guys to go to confession?"

"Yeah, especially now that the new pope is trying to get people all okay with gay—she's all excited about that."

"Yeah. Well, my family doing that for temple would imply we'd have to spend too much time together. My older brothers help run dad's other companies—I haven't seen them in years, but they write a mean expense report, you know?"

"God. So all you've got from your older brothers is that they put a rubber snake in your bed?"

Ezra shrugged. "I think I have nephews and nieces. I know I was on point for a card and a gift. I had a kickass secretary at the time—she sent them."

"That's *horrible*!" Miguel protested, and Ezra felt that familiar ball of hurt in his stomach.

"Look, I'm sorry. I wish I had better things to report. I wish I was the kid brother who took time out of his life to help his older sister with her family—I'm sorry I'm not. I just… you know. Every word out of the old man's mouth was how much I sucked and how Gregory and Chaim were better people than I was. And I never told him I was gay, but you know what? That didn't stop him from using the word fag over and over and over and fucking over again."

Ezra snapped his mouth shut, almost biting his tongue. Oh, he'd tried hard not to spew bitterness about his father. He'd been acknowledging the way he'd grown up—he had. He'd seen Finn's family and Miguel's family and had recognized the world was different—that was fine.

But now… oh, he remembered this feeling. This trapped feeling, this *blazing anger* again. Oh no. He didn't want Miguel to see this. This was the part of him that was fragile, the part that had come apart in his cubicle, the part that had stood, naked and numb, on Adam and Finn's lawn.

"I'm sorry," he mumbled, realizing that his voice had risen and that Miguel was casting him shocked looks as he negotiated traffic.

"What for?" Miguel asked, still sounding a little dazed.

"I didn't mean to sound mad—I'm not mad at you, you know that, right?"

"Yeah. I do. You're mad at your old man, who sounds like a real motherfucker. I have no problem with that. I don't have a problem with you not talking to your brothers either, papi. I'm just pissed *for* you. I'm so fucking angry. You show up at Adam's all broken, and all the people who should have been fixing you, they were the ones doing the breaking. I am not okay with that, Ezra. I am *pissed as fucking hell*—and every now and then, you show me that *you're* pissed too, and I swear, I'm so relieved. It makes me so much happier that you know it wasn't right. I only had my dad for twelve years, and that makes me mad, but he *loved me* for all twelve years, and that makes me happy. He loved the big kids too—and he loved them so much, when he died, he told them to pass down all the good times so me and Berto got some extra. I mean—*that's* a father to me. *That's* a man." Miguel swallowed. "I think of you trapped in that cubicle, coming fucking unglued like a cornered animal, and I want to tell your father what a real man is. Don't even get me started on a mami who wouldn't comfort you when you were scared."

Ezra smiled, knowing it was sort of wobbly but not caring. "That's really nice," he said softly. "I mean, I'm not even angry anymore, because that's such a nice thing to wish. I'm just, you know. Embarrassed. I don't want the whole world to feel sorry for me."

"I don't feel sorry for you," Miguel muttered. "I'm *pissed* for you, but I don't feel sorry for you. Not anymore. You're... you're a friend. You know—someone you want to play with. Like little kids. You don't feel sorry for your playmate. I'd rather come get you from Adam and Finn's and play with you than about anything in the world."

Oh, that was a nice compliment. Ezra's cheeks burned. "It's the best thing about my time here," he confessed shyly. "Hey—can we get ice cream?"

They were coming up to a town with one of those full-service gas stations as well as some fast-food places. Miguel laughed—of course they could get ice cream, and he pulled off the road to do just that.

They both ignored the fact that it was a clumsy segue, a way to get Miguel off the topic because Ezra felt exposed and vulnerable and he didn't want to talk about that anymore.

They found other things to talk about, though, and between that and Miguel's iPod, which featured a *stunning* amount of hip-hop and dance music, they stayed awake and alert down 99 to the Grapevine, and then off the Grapevine and down the razor-straight roads to Lancaster. Ezra was left with the impression of vast dark gray skies and flat mesa desert underneath. It was an alien landscape from what he was used to, on so many levels. As they pulled out their packs from the back hatch, he felt compelled to ask, "So what does your brother-in-law do here?"

He'd seen several "churches" that looked more like compounds, as well as a few *super nice* houses out here in the middle of nowhere, two of them with their own helicopters and landing pads. Ezra had put together three scenarios from *CSI* and *Criminal Minds* in their first five miles off the Grapevine.

"He's a doctor—don't worry. He fixes up the cray-cray, but he doesn't take part."

"I didn't think he was part of the cray-cray," Ezra defended. Then his voice leveled out. "I was just sort of wondering if there was any to worry about."

"I think it's mostly the usual," Miguel said thoughtfully. "First aid for farm equipment stuff, maintenance for long-term illnesses, the occasional pregnant woman." Suddenly he laughed. "Most of those would be his own wife."

"Yeah," Ezra said dryly. "I'm sure he thinks that's *hilarious*."

"Heh heh heh…."

"God, it's late. I promise you, tomorrow morning, you won't think that's so funny."

"I'm gonna text it to Lydia right now," Miguel said, nodding wickedly, and Ezra rolled his eyes.

And suddenly remembered that he had people to text too.

Miguel hit the bathroom first, and while he was there, Ezra pulled out his phone, pinging Rico, Adam, and Finn in the same shot.

Made it. Miguel thinks he's hysterical at 2 a.m. I should record him.

Rico: *I can't imagine Miguel thinking he's hysterical. Want proof.*

Finn: *Miguel always thinks he's hysterical. Only record him if he's truly funny.*

Adam: *Have a good time. What's your father's first name?*

Finn: *Ignore Adam. We'll ask Rico.*

Rico: *Martin. Why?*

Adam: *No reason. Any brothers?*

Rico: *Adam, you and me. Now.*

Miguel came out of the bathroom wearing sleep shorts and a tank, and Ezra glanced up at him and frowned.

"What's up?"

"I don't know. Mom and Dad are having a conference without me."

Miguel came over to where he was sitting on the bed and frowned at the phone too. "Huh," he muttered. Ezra turned to look at him and realized he'd washed his face and brushed his teeth. He smelled good—a little sweaty and earthy from the trip, but also minty and soapy. And with his dark hair no longer slicked back from that beautiful angel's face, he looked vulnerable and sweet—and dead sexy.

"Huh what?" Ezra had lost track of what they were talking about anyway. He felt Miguel's breath against his cheek, and he realized that unlike his nights on Miguel's family's couch, they were *alone* in a *bedroom* together.

And he was getting close-up exposure to lots and lots of Miguel's golden brown skin and the stringy muscles underneath. They looked… delicious.

"Uh… huh. I forgot something in the bathroom," Miguel said, turning back around.

"What'd you forget?" Ezra asked, bewildered. His phone buzzed, and for a moment he ignored it.

"My phone," Miguel called back, his voice muffled by the closed door.

Ezra turned his attention back to his own phone.

Adam: *We all want you to have a wonderful time. Be sure to text us before you start back, so we don't worry. Take pictures of Mickey Mouse for Finn, and Darrin wants ears. I mean that's imperative—he's threatening to fire you without them.*

Ezra laughed.

Deal. I'll remember, I promise.

He signed off, and just in case, he added "Mouse Ears" to his calendar for three days later.

"Hey, Miguel!" he called. "Are you going… you know… poop?"

"No, I do that in the morning," Miguel called back.

"So, can I brush my teeth?"

"Oh." He sounded surprised by the request. "Oh yeah."

The door opened and Miguel walked out, his phone by his side. "Yeah. Sorry about that. Texting Mami. She says hi."

By the time Ezra got out from his own night routine—which included, embarrassingly enough, putting in his retainer—Miguel was in his bed under the nylon comforter with his light out.

"Huh," Ezra said, crawling into his bed. The sheets weren't bad— not the Westin, but not bad—and the mattress wasn't too lumpy.

"Huh what?" Miguel's voice sounded isolated and tinny in the dark, like he was speaking from a radio.

"It's like I can feel the car still moving when I close my eyes," he said, his skin vibrating with the road all over again when he said it.

"Yeah—that's why hotels have pools. A good swim gets rid of that, you know?"

"After the river, I don't know if a pool will be big enough." Ezra laughed quietly. "Especially a hotel pool."

"You should swim in the ocean," Miguel said sleepily. "My papi's last summer, he took us down to see our *abuela* in Mexico, and we stopped at the beach by San Diego on the way back. We swam all day—Mami couldn't put enough sunblock on all of us. Papi had to rent hotel rooms that night, because he'd been planning just to stop, right? But we loved it so much, he let us stay and called in to work the next day." Miguel's voice dropped a little. "I wonder, you know? If maybe he felt sick then but didn't want to say anything. It was a great day. Lydia had just graduated from college, and she met Bobby on that beach. He wanted to take her out right then, that night, but she stayed with us kids in the room to play games so Mami and Papi could be together."

Miguel laughed then, sleepily, but still like the memory was a good one.

"What's funny?"

"Bobby. He brought us pizza that night and made us promise not to tell our parents. He played card games with us until midnight and kissed Lydia's forehead at the door. I don't think Papi was fooled for a minute, and I don't think they did... you know. No having sex in a hotel room with the kids next door. But it was probably the only thing that got them through traffic the next day, that time alone without kids."

"That makes him a good guy," Ezra said, thinking that his assessment of that term had changed a lot since he'd arrived at Sacramento.

"Yeah. I think it sealed Bobby's fate too, you know? Lydia might have just blown him off, but he was ready to be part of her family from the very beginning." Miguel paused so long that Ezra almost drifted off, the bed still vibrating like the car under his fingers. "Sort of like you and Mami."

Oh, that was nice. "I love being part of your family," he sighed, barely holding on to consciousness. "Would be great if you loved me too."

Behind his eyes, the brown minivan continued to rumble off into the night, the pavement humming softly under the mattress, the headlights illuminating just enough of the road to show they were still on the way.

Hiding Rodents

WOULD BE great if you could love me too.

Miguel had driven from Sacramento to LA a lot of times—he was past being haunted by the car on the pavement and the engine noise.

But Ezra's mumbled wish for love? Yeah. That was going to keep him awake for a while.

Well, that and the fucking texting nightmare he'd let himself in on.

Okay, guys, what gives? he'd typed as soon as he'd hit the bathroom. Ezra might have grown up in a dysfunctional family, but Miguel could recognize a family emergency a mile away.

Adam: *Ezra's father showed up on the doorstep this morning.*

Rico: *Holy God.*

Finn: *Jesus, why us? Fucking again. It's a curse.*

Rico: *Adam, don't fuck with him. He's mean.*

Miguel: *Are we going to tell Ezra?*

Finn, Rico, Adam: *NO!!!!!!!!*

Miguel: *He's an adult—you guys know that, don't you?*

A pause then, well timed, because that was when Ezra had needed to use the head. By the time he'd gotten out, the conversation had continued.

Rico: *Yes. He's an adult. But this is the happiest I've known him. His dad can't touch him right now, and he can't touch any of us for holding out. We can put him off for weeks.*

Miguel: *And the point would be?*

Finn: *You tell us, Miguel. You're an awesome guy, and we appreciate your company, but we've seen you more in the last month than I've seen you in four years of working in the same place.*

Adam: *Finn, go talk to the dog.*

Finn: *Sayin'!*

There was another pause, and Ezra came out of the bathroom. Miguel tucked his buzzing phone under his pillow and talked to him until Ezra fell asleep, his heavy breathing just shy of an actual snore.

By the time that happened, Miguel was ready to deal with what Finn had not-so-subtly been hinting—at least on the phone. However, there'd apparently been a big telenovela happening on his phone while he'd been talking to Ezra, so Finn's last sally seemed moot—all Miguel really needed to read was the last text.

Adam: *IT'S MIGUEL'S CALL BECAUSE I SAID SO. FINIS!*

Miguel: *Thanks, Adam. Sorry Finn—I don't need to hang around so much.*

Adam: *You're welcome, and I have Finn's phone and Rico has signed off. You are always welcome, Miguel—whether you and Ezra become a thing, or Ezra goes home with his father or what. ALWAYS WELCOME. You'll treat Ezra right because you're a good guy.*

Miguel: *Thanks again, Adam.*

He thought for a moment and decided that if Ezra was strong enough to do this next thing, Miguel should be too. *You know, I used to have the biggest crush on you. I don't think that ever would have worked—but I'm awfully glad we're friends now.*

Adam: *Yeah. I'm glad we're friends too. And it wouldn't have worked, because you're totally in love with Ezra.*

Miguel laughed, but not happily. *Night.*

Adam: *It's okay if it's true. Night.*

He set his phone on the charger and closed his eyes against the strain of reading in the dark. Yeah, Adam was the big dog all right. But Miguel was starting to feel like he could bark loud too.

EZRA WOKE him up early in the morning, sitting on his bed in a pair of swimming trunks and a T-shirt, a towel in his hand. "Hey, Miguel?"

"Whatdfulkoarcrap?" Oh God—mornings had never been his thing.

"Yeah, you can go back to sleep in a sec. I'm gonna go swim—I slept like ass and I need something to make my skin stop buzzing. Anyway—I'll stop at the complimentary breakfast on my way in, so just chill. Text me if you want anything."

"Yumf." There was *lots* of stuff Miguel wanted—he wanted to tell Ezra about his father, he wanted to see him swim in a pool where Miguel could watch him move under water, and he wanted a kiss on the cheek or the lips or something before he went, because that was just nice.

What he got was a sweet smile and a hand tousling his hair. Well, that was affectionate. Platonic but affectionate. Well, yeah. Miguel wanted to be the big dog, he'd have to make the next move, right?

He closed his eyes and imagined putting his hand on Ezra's bare thigh, imagined stroking the pale skin of his leg under the coarse, sparse black hair. He imagined sliding his hand up, feathering across Ezra's concave stomach. Not a six-pack, no, because no muscle, but soft, flat, slender. Imagined brushing his thumbs across Ezra's pink nipples, listening for his gasp of pleasure, kissing his ribs to see if that tickled or turned him on. Dreamed about kissing his neck, feeling the few silky hairs that passed for stubble on his jaw, capturing his mouth and diving inside.

Miguel moaned, mostly asleep and all the way turned-on, just as he heard the door close.

Oh God. He couldn't remember wanting someone this bad in his entire life.

He fell asleep just when he closed his hand on his prick, and dreamed of Ezra's soft pink mouth.

HE WOKE up an hour and a half later, half panicked. His phone buzzed and he snagged it, trying to remember where Ezra was and why he was in a strange place. He saw Ezra's avi pop up—a giant lollipop, because yeah, sweet—and sighed in relief.

Do you want a waffle?

Yes.

He sat up in bed and yawned, then stood and threw last night's T-shirt over his tank and shuffled into his flip-flops. He'd just started to brush his teeth when his phone buzzed again.

The waffle maker and I are having a thing. Sorry it's taking so long.

No worries. I'll be there in a minute.

Okay—I've got help with the waffle iron. I may triumph after all!

Oh, that was nice, he had help.

Miguel scowled at himself in the mirror. Yeah, a lot of people wanted to help Ezra. Target clerks, Candy Heaven customers—*Miguel.*

Oh, Jesus, maybe Ezra had enough fucking help as it was!

It took Miguel about ten seconds to spit out his toothpaste, wash his face, grab his key, and run out of the hotel room like all hell was after him.

When he got to the courtesy breakfast room, he was not surprised in the least to see Ezra, wide-eyed, being chatted up by a guy wearing a polyester work shirt and a pair of jeans. They were working together to scrape burnt waffle off of the waffle iron with little plastic knives, and Miguel thought irritably that it could possibly take them another hour to get the damned thing clean.

The guy was talking to Ezra slowly in Spanish—so far they'd covered the word *gofre* for waffle, *pegada* for stuck, and *aceite de aerosol*, which was apparently the nonstick cooking spray Ezra had forgotten to use.

Ezra was nodding earnestly, saying the words with decent inflection, and looking at the guy with the plastic knife like he held the secrets of the universe.

Miguel didn't even hear the sound coming out of his throat until the young worker—handsome, of course—turned toward him in surprise.

A slow, sly smile bloomed across his pretty, thirtyish features, but the next words he spoke were in *very* quickly pattered Spanish.

"You want your boy, come get him—he seems to think he's fair game."

"He doesn't know any better. He's recovering from a broken heart," Miguel snapped back in Spanish, but of course, Ezra appeared to be *over* the broken heart, didn't he?

I wish that you could love me too.

Unless, of course, *Miguel* was the one breaking his heart, and wouldn't that just suck?

The young custodian rolled his eyes and snorted. "I'll help him get over his broken heart, *pendejo*—you just need to get out of the way!"

Miguel growled louder. There were two waffle irons, actually, and he stalked up to the already crowded counter, elbowed between Ezra and the interloper, and opened up the one Ezra *hadn't* gummed up with waffle mix. He sprayed a fuckton of nonstick on the damned iron and muttered, "Get me a cup of mix, would you, Ezra?"

"Yeah, sure." Ezra moved to the dispensing machine, eager to please. "Sorry about the mess-up. He seems to have a trick to getting the crap off, but I just didn't feel right leaving him, you know? I can't even apologize for fucking up his kitchen equipment."

Miguel took the paper cup of waffle mix from him and nodded grimly, then dumped it on the iron and swung the thing shut, flipping it over and starting the timer for good measure before he translated Ezra's apology.

"He says he didn't want to leave you alone to clean up, and he didn't know how to apologize, so how about you say it's okay and I don't tell him you were trying to get in his pants."

"You sure?" the guy had the stones to ask. "Fifteen minutes, I make his broken heart go away, and you have a shot, free and clear. I bet he'd be a *sweet* ride, even in fifteen minutes."

Miguel swung to the guy and bared his teeth. "I will rip out your balls without a knife, *pendejo*. Fix the fucking waffle iron and go the fuck away."

The guy laughed softly and started to apologize to Ezra in broken English. "No worry, I go fix. Here." He unplugged the thing and pulled a cloth out of his back pocket, detaching the two sides of the already cooling waffle iron and walking away with them, presumably to a kitchen area nearby.

Ezra thanked him profusely and waved, and behind Miguel, the waffle iron dinged.

Miguel turned toward it, feeling a dangerous combination of irritation and desire. Just look at him! He was wearing swimming trunks and a T-shirt, for fuck's sake, and his curly hair was waving around his head without product. His blue eyes were wide and clueless, and his mouth was parted with a half smile—

How could he not know he was giving straight men for miles boners just by mouth-breathing and hoping for the best?

"What a nice guy!" Ezra said, his enthusiasm as grating as the other guy's lasciviousness. "I think we should get him something at Disneyland, you think?"

"Don't you fucking dare," Miguel growled. And then before Ezra could look all hurt, "And besides, he's probably not going to be working when we come back, right?"

Ezra nodded. "Yeah, I just felt bad—I mean, how stupid do you have to be—"

"You're not stupid, papi!" Miguel snapped, adding butter and dumping a little plastic tub of syrup on the waffle. "Here, go eat." He shoved the plate in Ezra's direction with little grace.

Ezra shrugged, doing a poor job of hiding his hurt. "But, you know, the waffle was for you."

Miguel tipped his head back and let out an "Aurgh!" and when he looked back, Ezra's eyes were big and shiny and his lower lip was trying not to quiver, and Jesus fuck, all Miguel had wanted to do was give the guy some time and—

Miguel grabbed him by the T-shirt and hauled him against his body, plundering his mouth in a kiss of sheer frustration.

Ezra sighed and opened his mouth in complete surrender, melting against Miguel's chest like he belonged in that exact place.

Oh holy hell, did he taste good. Fruit and bagels and cream cheese—that was what he'd eaten before his misadventure with the stupid waffle iron, and it was just exactly what Ezra *should* taste like.

Miguel pulled back and framed Ezra's face with his hands. "Only me," he muttered. "All these men trying to get you to flirt, to smile, to take off your clothes—only me, you understand?"

Ezra nodded and nipped at his lower lip. "I was so hoping you wanted me," he said breathlessly. "You want me, right?"

Miguel's body was going to explode, and not in the good another-word-for-coming way either, but in the bad, cartoon body-is-a-firecracker way. He ground up against Ezra's thigh and moaned into his neck.

"*So* fucking bad, papi. You've been driving me insane, you know that, right? Fucking apeshit, wondering who was going to be grabbing your ass next when it needed to be *me*!"

Ezra's moan in his ear set everything in his body tingling. "I wanted it to be you," he said gruffly. "But you needed to want me. I came all the way out here for someone who didn't want me—if I was gonna try it again, it had to be for someone who wanted me."

"I want you," Miguel muttered. "Oh Lord, do I want you."

He turned and grabbed Ezra's hand, then dragged him from the breakfast room and around the hotel, clattering up the stairs with a few stumbles along the way.

"We just left your breakfast!" Ezra complained breathlessly when they stumbled to a halt by the door to their room.

"I'll eat later," Miguel muttered, hauling out his wallet and his key. "C'mon, work, c'mon, work." Because the key cards weren't always functional, which would really piss him off now. But the light turned green and Miguel burst into the hotel room, Ezra hot on his heels. Miguel kicked the door shut and turned to grab the hem of Ezra's shirt and yank it over his head.

"*Yes*," he hissed, because all of that pale skin was *his*. Yeah, sure, other men had tasted it, but nobody had owned it, not like Miguel was going to. He traced Ezra's collarbone with his mouth, interspersing the caress with little nips, and fed his hands on the smoothness of Ezra's sides, the silken indentation of his stomach, the tiny pebbled nerve centers of his nipples.

Ezra held on to his shoulder with one hand and cupped his neck with the other, fusing their mouths together while Miguel's palms charted all the territory he'd been marking with his eyes over the past month.

When he slid his hands down Ezra's back and under his still-damp swim shorts to cup his ass, Ezra made a hot, aroused keening sound and humped against Miguel, grinding their cocks together through their clothes.

Miguel broke away for a moment and rasped his cheek against Ezra's so he could whisper in his ear. "You want it?"

"Yeah…," Ezra breathed.

"I top."

"Yeah, please."

"I want to blow you first," Miguel told him frankly before bending so he could take a nipple in his mouth and suck. Ezra moaned and wobbled, his knees probably deserting him, and Miguel straightened and grabbed Ezra's hair, pulling him up. "You take it," he whispered harshly. "I've been going home and beating off thinking about you. Some nights you were down on the couch, but I wasn't going to hurt you. So you take it—you stand up and take my mouth on your cock until you blow, you hear me?"

"Augh…."

Miguel lowered himself to his knees and pulled down Ezra's swim trunks, burying his head in Ezra's thigh and suckling on the sensitive skin there when Ezra's cock flopped out.

"Fucking damn," he breathed in appreciation.

"'S average," Ezra told him, and he *believed* that.

"In *porn flicks*!" Miguel shot back. God, seven inches long if it was a cock! "It's *perfect*!"

"Kinda skinny," Ezra corrected, and Miguel glared at him and sucked the entire damned thing in his mouth in retaliation. "Oh dear God!" Ezra swore. "Oh hell, Miguel! Fuck—"

Miguel pulled back and wrapped his fist around it, stroking mercilessly. "No complaining," he grated. "I'm going to suck you until you come, because I *need* it, you hear me, Ezra? I *need* to taste you, feel you in my mouth, I've fucking *craved* it for a *month*. I craved it since I saw you on Adam's lawn, dammit!"

Ezra's fingers clenched in his hair, and he tried to drag Miguel's head back, but Miguel fought him. Yeah, he knew Ezra was pissed too, but Ezra would give. That was why Miguel was so damned backed up—because Ezra needed somebody to take the damned lead!

Miguel forced his head down again until Ezra was buried in the back of his throat, and Ezra's yank on Miguel's head turned into a massage, a plea for more.

"Why didn't you say something?" Ezra begged above him.

"We'll talk later," he panted, Ezra's cock slapping his lips and glazing his mouth with spit. "You come right the fuck *now*!"

And with that he started a furious rhythm, fist and mouth, bobbing his head as fast as he could, hand squeezing hard enough to make Ezra scream—and beg for more.

He bucked in Miguel's grip, hips stuttering as he tried not to fuck Miguel's mouth, and Miguel wasn't having any of that gentleness crap. He let spit trickle on one of his fingers and then slid it back into the cleft of Ezra's bottom.

Oh yes—there it was: home.

A brief massage, a little thrust timed just when Ezra was deepest in his throat, and Ezra cried out, "Oh, *fuck*!" and spurted down Miguel's throat. He beat feebly on Miguel's head and Miguel pushed himself up, swallowing, some of Ezra's come still dripping down his chin. He looked Ezra in the eyes, his groin aching with desire, his hands shaking with need.

"I. Want. You." Each word was a tortured breath, and Ezra nodded, mesmerized. Miguel framed his face again and pulled him into a kiss that Ezra returned boldly, taking it all, the fierceness, the command, even the come trickling down his chin.

Miguel kissed him more, softer, sweeter, feeling safer now. Ezra wasn't going anywhere—Miguel had him. He would stay Miguel's forever, as long as Miguel didn't let him go.

Ezra's shaking eased, and Miguel pulled away, rubbing his cheek against Ezra's. "Bend over the bed, baby," he whispered hoarsely. "I brought condoms and lube."

Because he never *did* give that package to his brother. No, Miguel had tucked that away in his backpack, hoping, maybe, that this, this right here, was going to happen.

Ezra leaned over the bed and sucked on two fingers, then moved them behind him, stretching. Miguel paused while rifling through his backpack to admire that sight—and oh, it was pretty—of Ezra, one shoulder bent back, his face raised with his eyes screwed shut in pleasure.

Oh yes. Ezra loved this—*loved* this. How could he not know? How could he say things like "verse is the new gay" when part of him just *begged* for assplay, *begged* to bottom.

Miguel had no idea, but that noise was going to stop right now.

"You don't need rubbers," Ezra rasped. "You said it's been a while for you—you were tested?"

Miguel nodded, remembering those late-night talks. Yeah—that had come up.

"I was tested after Rico," Ezra gasped, talking obviously difficult as his busy fingers kept working. "We're both negative, windows and all."

Miguel actually whimpered. Oh damn—the boy was right. He was right, and Miguel would have him skin on skin, raw and real, and no screwing around with commitment if they were ready to take that step.

They *were* ready. This sex was their first time—of *many*, not a maybe next time or maybe again. If Miguel knew anything, it was that he and Ezra, they were in each other's pockets now—they had the thing inside them that was meant to last.

Miguel couldn't imagine a day when he didn't wake up and talk to Ezra.

He grabbed the lubricant and walked behind him, treasuring that sexy moment. Ezra bent over, his fingers stretching his ass wide for Miguel, making sweet little sex grunts as he thrust his hips back to take himself deeper.

Miguel dumped some lubricant on Ezra's fingers and Ezra moaned, spreading it around while Miguel undid his shorts and shucked his shirt.

His own cock flopped forward, not as long as Ezra's but thicker, probably more painful if he didn't stretch Ezra right. He bent forward and kissed the small of Ezra's back and then traced his lips along his buttcheek. He finished up with a little suckling of the nearly hairless flesh of his bottom and let it go with a pop.

"Let me stretch you," he said against Ezra's skin. "I want to make sure I fit."

"Can I see?" Ezra begged, and of course he could.

"Turn around and sit down, baby—you want to taste?"

"Oh God—*please!*"

Damn, Ezra was good at following orders. He turned around, opening his mouth greedily. He saw what was coming and opened it wider, stretching his lips to take Miguel in. Oh… oh…. Miguel watched as he slid slowly past those puffy pink lips and the head of his cock was engulfed in wet heat. Oh… oh yes. He loved getting a blowjob—*loved* it—but not many lovers offered because he was such an aggressive top.

But Ezra had—he'd begged—and Miguel was so glad he had.

"Oh, Ezra—papi, you're good at this. Yeah—deeper? Can you go deep—*yes!*"

Halfway down, Ezra had to stop, and he pulled back in a hurry, his eyes watering. He made a few more thrusts, taking Miguel in as far as he could, and now Miguel was the one who felt a wobble in his knees.

He grabbed Ezra's hair gently and pulled him back. "I don't want to come in your mouth," he said, rubbing a thumb along Ezra's swollen lip. "I want inside you so bad. Are you ready?"

"Yeah," Ezra whispered, eyes wide.

He stood again and bent at the waist, burying his face and hands in the rumpled sheets of Miguel's bed.

Miguel prepped him some more, stretching with two fingers, then his thumbs, pushing him to the edge of pain and then backing off. Finally Ezra was squirming, pleading, choking on half sobs as he begged Miguel to fuck him.

Miguel was begging the same thing in his head.

Slowly. So slowly. He took Ezra's cues, and whenever he stiffened up, Miguel paused, rubbing his back, kissing his shoulder blades, telling him softly how good he was doing, how wonderful he felt. Finally, after forever, the head of his cock breached the muscle ring, and Ezra groaned—thank God, not in pain—and thrust back.

Both of them breathed, "*Yes!*" before Miguel heard Ezra begging some more.

"Faster."

"Thank you so much!"

He thrust all the way forward, listening for Ezra's noises, and then pulled back until the bell of his cock caught. And forward, and backward, time-honored rhythm of something that people had been doing before time was measured.

It hadn't gotten old since then.

"More," Ezra whispered harshly. "More. Faster. Harder. More."

"*Augh!*"

Miguel's hips snapped forward and back, building speed, building pressure, going faster and harder. Some of his frustration spurred him on, but mostly it was the enormity of the thing, the fucking *huge* weight of wanting this man, craving him, desiring him with every atom of his being, while he'd seemed indifferent for so long.

Ezra groaned and his shoulder dipped as he moved his hand to his cock, and Miguel choked back his own sob and pounded with all he was worth.

Ezra tightened around him, whimpering into the pillows for one more release, and that set Miguel off, pouring hot and slick into Ezra's body while Ezra made his "come" sound again and spent himself against the sheets. Miguel couldn't stop immediately, though, just because he'd hit his climax, and his hips still thrust into Ezra's willing, sated body, even as Miguel stroked his hair back from his face and whispered subtle words of encouragement.

"You're beautiful," he said into the shell of Ezra's ear. "God, that was the best. You're amazing, wrapped around me. I could touch you forever."

He wanted to heap praises on him, sing his virtues to the sky, let him believe that he was important and cared for and desired.

And then Ezra simplified all of that, boiling it down to the one thing that was most important, and so simple.

"Love you, Miguel," he panted against the bed. "Love me too?"

Of course he did.

Cats and Kittens

EZRA STARED at the cheap comforter and tried to remember when he'd ever felt as possessed as he did at this moment.

And just like that, all other lovers ceased to exist.

The club hookups had never been. The sweet teacher he'd been trying to protect was a dream. Even Rico, whom he'd flown cross-country to try to win back, was relegated to a friend's cousin, with no further meaning than that.

But Miguel, who told him filthy things with that angel's mouth and who was still shuddering with orgasm, breathing harshly on his neck—Miguel was real and solid. His come was sliding down Ezra's thighs and his cock was still lodged solidly inside Ezra's body.

There was no one else. When Ezra closed his eyes, Miguel's face was the only one he saw.

"Yeah, papi," Miguel said softly in his ear. "I love you."

"Not at first," Ezra clarified, because it was important. Miguel wouldn't lie to him—this was a test.

"No. Not at first. But I knew you were special, even that first day."

Ezra melted further onto the bed, Miguel squashing him and reassuring him at once. "How?"

"You knew my name, papi. You recognized my face. My whole life, I thought I'd always be the fifth child of six, the second banana, the face in the crowd. But you—you were dead on your feet and you remembered my name, and you remembered my face, and you thought I was your person."

Ezra nodded, closing his eyes against the burning. Yes. *Yes*. He'd known Miguel was his person—not a lover, not then, but Miguel had been the person he most wanted to follow, to rub against, to be with. "You are my person," he said, his throat thick. He closed his eyes tightly, and still they came, tears of relief, of gratitude, of joy.

"Hey, what's wrong?" Miguel asked softly. He slid to the side, tracking wetly against Ezra's backside and not ashamed of it either. With a little prodding on Miguel's part and scooting on Ezra's, they were both lying on the rumpled sheets, the nylon comforter kicked to the floor.

Miguel rubbed a gentle thumb along the crease of Ezra's eyes, wiping away the moisture.

Ezra shook his head, not sure if he had the words. "I'm just happy," he said, his voice rasping in his throat. "I'm happy, and I'm so…." Oh no. He didn't want to say this word, but it was the one he was looking for.

"Anxious," Miguel supplied bluntly. "You're worried. Because here we are, together, and when we get home, your life is going to be up in the air."

Ezra nodded, his lower lip wobbling. "Yes," he whispered. "I'm still a mess, Miguel. I mean—look at me. I'm crying at movies and I thought about putting on a suit the other day and…." Oh God. He let out a little sob. "I just… I could be working at Candy Heaven for the rest of my life, and how am I gonna be a grown-up and have a relationship and…."

"Sh," Miguel whispered into his ear. "Don't think about that. Not right now. Right now it's just you and me and that thing we just did. And the thing we just did was beautiful, okay?"

Okay. "Yes," Ezra agreed. "Yes—that was… that was like reinventing sex for me. I didn't know it came like that."

"Yeah—that was like a whole new flavor," Miguel agreed, his full mouth pursed and serious, his round sloe eyes wide over his bold nose.

Ezra found his tears easing up and knew he was smiling. "Like lollipops," he said. "Like—if you just taste them, they're supposed to just taste like cherry. But if you *believe* they're more than that, they really taste like rainbows." Silly little kid story, yes, but this… this had been *special.* This had been rainbow-flavored sex, and Ezra had never had that before.

"Yeah," Miguel said, jumping on board that train with both feet. "Yeah—this was special because it was us. Exactly. So we're going to hold on to that. We're going to clutch it in both hands. I can't move out right now because Mami needs the rent for the house. You need to stay with Darrin and Adam and Finn—they're good for you, but you haven't been there enough."

"I still need to grow," Ezra said, feeling wise for maybe the first time in his life.

"Yeah," Miguel said, brushing his cheek with a thumb again. "So there's gonna be us, and it's going to be complicated, and you may have to come over to my place for sex and then spend the night on the couch, but we'll be together, okay?"

Ezra nodded, so happy suddenly, he couldn't even pin all the source of his happiness on Miguel. It was just that Miguel *got* it. Ezra was still finding his feet, adjusting to all of the things he didn't have to be afraid of, and Miguel got it, that he wasn't ready to give up his safety blanket, his new friends, his *breathing room*, even though they were in love.

But then Miguel's expression shifted, became unaccountably sober, and Ezra's heart sank.

"You're not going to say you want to date other people," he asked, suddenly terrified. "Because—"

"*No!*" Miguel snapped. "Jesus, papi—you are definitely mine, do you hear me? If you trip in the middle of the street in Old Sac and an old married banker gets out of the car to help you, the first words out of your mouth need to be 'I've got a boyfriend,' do you hear me?"

Ezra squinted at him, laughing. "Uhm, oookaaay...."

"If you are standing behind the counter at Candy Heaven and some rock star gets out of his car and says he wants a barrel full of candy and you sitting like a bow on the fucking top of it, the first words out of your mouth need to be 'I've got a boyfriend'—repeat that, okay?"

"I've got a boyfriend," Ezra repeated dutifully. "I hear you."

"I don't think so," Miguel said, getting more agitated. "These last weeks, I've been trying to get a handle on this feeling in my chest, how when I see your name come up on my phone it's like my whole *life* makes sense, including why my business fell through so I was back at Candy Heaven, right?"

"Right." Ezra nodded. "'Cause that's how I felt when I knew we'd be working together."

"Well that's special for you, papi, but every time I got all happy, some *asshole* would try to pick up on you, and you'd be like, 'Oh, me? But I don't have a cock and an ass and there's no way I'd be interested if half the gay population of Sacramento wants to bang me! No, I'll just give them candy and buy chips from them and help them chip crap off an archaic waffle iron while Miguel loses his fucking mind!'"

Ezra was laughing so hard by the time Miguel finished his little rant that he couldn't breathe. "Oh my God—you're so full of shit. I swear, nobody wants in my pants but you!"

Miguel kissed him then, their bare bodies lining up, their desire throbbing, filling, hardening between them. The kiss ended, and Miguel sighed into Ezra's neck. "You keep thinking that, baby. You keep thinking that nobody wants in your pants but me, because I'm the only person *getting* in your pants, you understand?"

Ezra was nodding, happy, thrusting up against Miguel again, when Miguel sobered like he had to tell one piece of bad news before they were done.

And that was when Miguel's phone, which was still on the charger next to the bed, started buzzing like crazy.

"Aw, *fuck*!" Miguel groaned. He reached over Ezra's shoulder and unhooked the thing from the charger. "Crap—that's my sister. She wants us to come over *now* and not in the afternoon, and she wants me to bring her coffee and donuts and hash browns. Jesus, heifer, you are pregnant, not feeding an entire army." He scowled and started to punch something back into the phone, but the phone buzzed some more.

He pressed Call and then settled back on the pillows with the phone in one hand. Imperiously, he patted his shoulder, and Ezra followed him, laying his head where Miguel indicated.

"Lydia?" he said suddenly. "Yeah, woman, I got your texts. Did you want anything for, you know, your husband and children that *isn't* refined sugar?" Whatever her reply was, he rolled his eyes at Ezra over it. "Yeah, well, a dozen donuts isn't going to do it. Ezra and I want donuts too—the waffle iron wasn't working, we need sugar and carbs. Yeah, Ezra—Mami told you about him, right? Yeah, well, forget that part about friend. Boyfriend. So, like, remember how we were only a little awful to Bobby? Yeah, you have to be *not awful at all* to Ezra. He didn't grow up with family—he doesn't know how awful we can be."

Miguel listened some more and then, with absurd tenderness considering how brusque he sounded on the phone, bent his head and kissed Ezra's temple.

"I'm serious, Lydia," he said after a moment. "You'll see. He's really good with kids—watch him play with them, you'll get it. You can't mess with him like you do with Rosa or Ella or the other boys.

Yeah, no—if you break my boyfriend, I'll be seriously angry, like Papi was that one time you hurt Mami's feelings, okay?"

The voice on the other end was suddenly quiet and somber.

"Yeah. You understand. I knew you would—you're the best big sister in the world. But we're coming over, okay? Yeah. We'll bring your donuts and stuff. Lots of it, no worries. It'll be good."

He signed off and set the phone down on his end table, and then hugged Ezra close to him like they had all the time in the world.

"We good?" he asked soberly. "I wanted more time—I wanted to spend all morning in bed with you, make love to you so many times you forgot everybody else's name, you know?"

"I don't even know who they are," Ezra said sincerely. "And all morning in bed would be nice. We'll have to do that one of these days we're on vacation, okay?"

"Yeah, Ezra—about that—" His phone buzzed angrily and he checked it. "Jesus *Christ*, woman!" he muttered. "Yes, we'll remember the fucking whipped-cream filled!" He sighed and looked at Ezra, and Ezra realized how possessive his gaze was, how much he still wanted them to touch each other and explode.

Ezra smiled and winked. "I get it," he said happily. "You have family. That's awesome. Let's go be a part of it!"

"Yeah," Miguel said, sounding sadder than that plan warranted. "Yeah. Let's do that."

Excellent—Ezra was looking forward to it.

JOSHIE, MARI'S kid, was awesome—he was cute, thoughtful, clever, and used to being the one child among scads of adults and older cousins. He was adorable.

Lydia's three kids, Jessica, Brock, and Ariel, were cute, diabolical, and used to being three kids raising hell with each other and only with each other, and never shall the interlopers part them.

They were *terrifying*.

And Ezra was having the time of his life.

When they'd first gotten to Lydia's house, he'd been more interested in the topography than the children. Lancaster was essentially on a high desert mesa, and the dusty road carved its way through tumbleweeds and not much else. But after Miguel took a right off the main drag, they ended up in a small housing development of maybe two-by-two blocks, the only sign of a prefab suburban area anywhere. There were yards— some with lawns and some with rock gardens and succulents—and each house sat on what looked to be a bare half acre.

The house Miguel pulled up to had a rock garden with succulents, but as they parked, Ezra spotted a pool and a patio in the back. This was awesome, since it was around ninety-five degrees out, and when they'd stopped in the small town outside the hotel room, Ezra had started dripping sweat under his arms and down his back.

Hot.

Like the bowels of hell, when Satan was having a barbecue on his asshole. Holy God, what *was* it about this state?

"You bring your suit?" he asked Miguel, feeling wistful. His morning in the pool had been terrific, but he'd left his pack in the room.

"Yeah, and yours too, and you know what else I brought?"

"I have no idea," Ezra said. "My mind is a blank. You have fucked the common sense right out of me."

Miguel laughed and grinned wickedly. "Excellent—I'll strive to do that more often. But I brought sunblock, because you have no base tan. How is it we've been taking you to the river twice a week and you have no base tan?"

Ezra rolled his eyes. "Who says I don't? I'm just a white person, that's all."

Miguel started to laugh then, low and rippling, like he'd never heard anything that funny. He was still laughing as he parked the car and still laughing as he opened the door and grabbed a bundle of clothes and shoved it under his arm.

Ezra followed the laughing idiot, his hands full of takeout bags and a giant box of donuts, and wondered exactly what he'd said.

Miguel knocked on the door like he owned the place and had forgotten the key, and when the most enormously pregnant woman Ezra had ever seen opened the door, he greeted her with a careful hug around her belly and a friendly insult.

"Hello, heifer—could you be any bigger? Are you sure you're having a human baby? Maybe you got abducted by aliens, you think?"

"Hello, little brother. I changed your diapers—are you still sticking your thumb up your ass and screaming, 'Look at me! I'm a shish kebab'?"

It was Ezra's turn to cackle. "Please tell me that's true," he said, following Miguel in.

Lydia—had to be Lydia—smiled sweetly. "Sadly, no—but not because we didn't try." She was shorter than her brother by about six inches, and her belly was not the only round thing about her. Her brown face and brown eyes were as round as a doll's, and so were her hands and her feet. The first thing made her beautiful, but the second....

"Yeah," Miguel muttered. "The whole world keeps trying to shove something up my ass. C'mon, woman, let's go sit down. You need to be on your feet like this one needs to be out in the sun."

She grunted and turned to waddle through the house, leaving Ezra to close the door. "Yeah, you're telling me. Bobby makes me take my blood pressure every two hours—it's insane."

"Is it high?" Miguel asked, his snark toned down by his concern.

"Only a little," Lydia reassured him. She came to the kitchen, which was laid out a lot like the one at Miguel's house, with a counter separating the cooking area from the dining room and a sliding glass door overlooking a shaded patio. In this case, the yard on the other side of the door was mostly a swimming pool, and instead of six dogs, there was one dog—a gigantic German shepherd—and three kids and a dad, all swimming in it. "Bobby wants me to get into the swimming pool more, which is probably a good idea." She shrugged. "In the pool is wonderful—getting *out* of the pool is not something I want you to have to see."

Miguel rolled his eyes and took some of the takeout from Ezra to set at the table. "Like it bothers me to watch you beach, whale woman. Do what your husband says and take care of yourself."

She rolled her eyes with the exact same expression. "I don't see *you* listening to anybody so much, right? What did Mami say? And Abuela? They said to wait another two years to start your own business, remember? You do remember that, right? Because I was sitting here, getting all ready to tell the whole world I was pregnant, and *bam*! You lay out the new business thing, and besides the fact that my baby is suddenly named Nobody Cares, the whole world is telling you that this is a bad idea, your funding isn't solid, it's going to fall through. Did you listen?"

Ezra glanced at Miguel and saw... conflict. Yeah, sure, he was irritated at being lectured, but he was also... happy? Contrite? Wow. Maybe just conflicted.

Suddenly Miguel held up his hand and said, "Enough! Hold on a sec, Lydia, I need to get something straight." He stood up and put two firm hands on his sister's stomach. *"Mamacita?"* he said, obviously to the baby. "You need to listen to me—this is important. Your name is *never* Nobody Cares. You may think it's Nobody Cares because you get lost in a big family, but in this family, *everybody* cares, you understand? Even if you're doing something fool-stupid because of pride, *everybody* cares. You might not notice it, that's all." He patted his sister's stomach and glanced up soberly, and she quirked her lips back.

"I can't tell that story anymore," she conceded.

"Only if you tell this one," he said, and she nodded.

"Classy move, little brother. Now introduce me to your classy boyfriend and let me eat donuts."

Miguel got up. "Lydia, this is Ezra. Ezra, this is Lydia. Lydia, be nice. Ezra, I swear she doesn't bite. I'm going to get milk."

They sat staring at each other for a moment before Lydia's round face split in a white smile. "Oh, you're pretty. I mean, Miguel's no slouch—he got Mami's looks, you know? But you're prettier than he is. I bet it drives him crazy."

Ezra shook his head. "No—Miguel's been really patient with me. I was sort of a fish out of water when I first landed here, but he showed me the ropes at Candy Heaven and let me hang out with him when we weren't at work."

Lydia nodded. "Yeah—usually, he's a good guy. After the whole business fail thing, he tried to pretend that wasn't true, but you can't just erase that for good."

"No, but you're giving it a good try!" Miguel complained from behind the counter.

"Shut up, we're bonding here," Lydia shot back pleasantly. "So you just got here? How long do you plan to stay?"

Ezra felt like he'd just fallen through a slow-motion hole in time. "Uh," he said, except it drew out like "uuuuuhhhhhhhhhhhhhh," and in the two million years it took to say that one syllable, he remembered his and Miguel's entire conversation that morning. Miguel assumed he was staying. *He* assumed he was staying.

And just like that, he no longer thought of himself as a New Yorker.

"Until this place hurts me," he said earnestly. "I left New York because I got hurt there. So far, no pain. I'll stay until it hurts too much."

"Mm," she said in surprise. For a moment they regarded each other, assessing, and he already liked her, but he knew *she* was drawing conclusions. "Miguel, did you hear that?"

"Yeah," Miguel said, surprising Ezra because he was right behind Ezra's seat. The milk appeared in front of him, along with three clear glasses, and Miguel's hands, cold from the refrigerator, descended on Ezra's shoulders.

Mm—that feeling, that grounding, comforting feeling of Miguel's touch, hadn't changed since that morning.

"You feeling like leaving right now, papi?" Miguel said softly.

Ezra looked over his shoulder and smiled. "No. As long as you want me, I don't think it will hurt that bad."

Miguel leaned forward and kissed his temple. "Good," he said.

And then the sliding glass door opened and all hell broke loose.

Ezra hadn't been paying attention to what was going on outside, but apparently all of the kids had dried off, and suddenly three pairs of pittering, pattering little feet came charging through the kitchen, and little wet brown humans, chattering in two languages at the same time, swarmed over the kitchen table and around the seated adults.

For a moment Ezra stared at them in shock, and then the tiniest, a little girl who weighed about twenty pounds and wore only a swim diaper, scrambled onto his lap and regarded him with giant cartoon-character brown eyes under a straight, flyaway shock of black hair.

"¿Dona?" she asked. "¿Dona, por favor?"

Well, that didn't take a native Spanish speaker to translate, did it? "Uh, sure. Powdered sugar or sprinkles?"

"Teek-teek-teek-teek-teek," she said, making her fingers flutter.

Ezra was reasonably sure that wasn't a real word in either language, so he took a guess. "Pink sprinkles it is," he said soberly, pulling one out of the box.

"Gracias. ¿Dona para ti?" She broke the donut cleanly in half and gave him his share of the goods.

"Gracias," he told her. He was using one hand to steady her on his lap, so with donut in hand, he dragged a glass of milk toward the two of them. "Let's dunk on it, 'kay?"

"Okay," she said, clear as day. "Dunking in milk tastes good. Jessica, *¿has visto al hombre bonito de Miguel?*"

"Sí," the older girl at the table said, looking up from her chair. She had hair long enough to braid, and it held some frowzy blonde in it, probably from her father's genes. "He's very pretty. Mama says Miguel is in love this time, so you can get attached." The tiny one on Ezra's lap turned and patted his cheek.

"Like him," she said simply and then turned back to her donut and milk.

The little boy, who had a round face much like Lydia's, looked at Ezra dismissively. "He's okay. I don't know how pretty he is. Do you like to swim, *tío*? Daddy says he's tired."

Ezra finally got a look at Bobby and found a big, bluff guy—probably had been really pretty in high school but was not just solid, serviceable ex-jock. Not fat, no, but probably because he exercised as often as he could and only let his wife talk him into donuts sometimes.

"Daddy was the only doctor in the hospital last night," Bobby said mildly, and Ezra could see the dark rings of exhaustion under his eyes. "Maybe let Daddy have a nap, and he won't be such a killjoy."

"Daddy's earned a nap," Ezra said to the boy—Brock, probably, since he was the only boy. "But yeah. Miguel brought my trunks, and I need some sunblock—"

"You sure do," the boy said. "I've never seen a white person so white before."

And Miguel burst into laughter again.

"What?" Ezra said, and suddenly Bobby and Lydia were demanding to know what as well.

Miguel held his hand to his mouth and shook his head. "No, no—you guys don't get it. See, before we came in, I told Ezra he needed sunblock, and he said, 'Yeah, I'm a white person.'" Miguel broke into howls of laughter again, and Ezra was very relieved to see that the rest of the table just stared at him.

"Yeah," Lydia said after a moment. "I don't get it either." She shook her head. "That's okay, Ezra, I think he means well. But sure. After breakfast, if Ezra's game, you guys can go out swimming—"

"And I'll clean up," Miguel said firmly, "and Bobby will go to bed."

Lydia nodded, smiling tiredly, and Bobby let out a groan of gratitude. "Best. In-law. Ever."

"And don't you forget it!" Miguel challenged.

The swarm of children—not so intimidating now that Ezra could start talking to them and learn that Jessie was the older one and Ariel was the tiny one who seemed to think he was pretty—all chattered at the table in that heady rush of two languages, and Ezra ignored the adults and tried to keep up.

After breakfast he changed into his trunks in a bathroom down the hall from the kitchen and emerged just as Miguel was coming down purposefully, with sunblock in his hand.

"Yeah, yeah," Ezra said dutifully, turning so Miguel could rub it into his back. "I'm the whitest person you know."

"Not just the whitest person I know," Miguel corrected. "The whitest white person I know."

"I have no idea what that means," Ezra grumbled, and Miguel leaned over his shoulders and kissed his cheek.

"Good—because it means you don't really see the divide, you know? Between brown people and white people or black people and brown people. You see the *people*, but even though you know what it's like to be different, you don't *treat* anybody different."

Ezra grunted. "Should I?"

Miguel kissed his other cheek and cupped Ezra's shoulders. "No, papi. Everything in Sacramento was new to you when you arrived—you just accepted all of it, whether it was me and Finn talking in Spanish or the fact that cargo shorts are business attire. When Rico got here, he was *freaked* about Darrin reading his future, but you? You just assumed that was part of the guy with the dangly earrings. When you said you were a white person, I was laughing, because you're not, like, *exclusively* white. You're more like *inclusively* pale. I like that about you, okay?"

Ezra smiled at him, feeling like he was too happy to think about anything as serious as brown and white or black and white with too much of his brain.

"I have been happy so little," he said after a moment. "It just didn't occur to me to think beyond the fact that these people make me happy, so I'll love everything about them. Is that wrong?"

Miguel's hands worked on his back for a few moments, and then he said huskily, "Turn around, okay?"

Ezra did, and Miguel continued to rub sunblock into his chest, even while Miguel leaned forward and took his mouth softly.

He pulled back and smiled, then leaned forward to rub noses. "You're a really good person, Ezra. Any color, your heart would be pure gold, okay?"

Ezra grunted. "My father's heart is probably pure gold. I'd rather mine just be muscle."

Miguel grunted back. "Papi, that reminds me. I was going to talk to you this morning, but, you know…."

Ezra closed his eyes sleepily. "Yeah. That."

"But anyway—"

"¡Tío Ezra!" The tiny one, squealed, running through the hallway. "¡Tío Ezra!" And then she erupted into such a thoroughly language-blended version of events that even Miguel was shaking his head.

"Sounds dire, Ariel," Miguel said dubiously. "Tío Ezra will come down and deal, okay?"

Ezra nodded but looked at him, troubled. "Okay, yeah. Miguel, this thing—"

"Later," Miguel said, pursing his lips. "I promise."

Ariel grabbed urgently at his hand and hauled him out to the kitchen, where Jessie and Brock waited patiently by the sliding glass door to the pool. Together, the three of them pushed, begged, cajoled, and bickered until he was in the pool, armed with a water squirter and trying gamely to peg them all with the streams of water while they shrieked with approval.

Tío Ezra, huh?

He liked that title. He liked it very much.

They played for a good hour, but then Brock splashed Ariel one time too many, and she started to cry. Ezra didn't know much about kids, but he was pretty sure they got tired—eventually—like the rest of the world. Ariel could swim like a champion—just this teeny little girl bobbing in the pool like a cork—so he picked her up and grabbed Brock by the hand and made them get out, Jessie in the lead. Well, she was a little bossy, wasn't she?

He calmed them down and dried them off and asked Jessie if Ariel had a nonswim kind of diaper and maybe a T-shirt she could wear.

"Sí, Tío Ezra," she said soberly. "I'll go up to my room and change and bring that down for you, okay?"

"You are an awesome big sister," he assured her, fairly impressed. He didn't remember ever being that self-assured.

He got them all inside and saw that Miguel and Lydia were in deep conversation. Something about the way Miguel's brow was furrowed and Lydia glanced harriedly at him made Ezra think they were talking about him.

Miguel nodded at him. "In a few minutes, 'kay?"

"Sure." By the time he got Ariel changed to watch a cartoon, she was nodding off, and he set her carefully in the corner of the couch, dead to the world. Jessie was stretched out on her stomach, coloring in front of the television in a sort of languid way that suggested she'd be asleep soon too, and Brock had found his own spot on his back, arms spread wide before the world.

Ezra looked at the kids and thought about what a blast he'd had with them, and thought about how tired Lydia and Bobby were.

Yeah, it had to be rough, raising three kids and getting ready for the fourth. Suddenly he wanted to help. He liked this family—he'd felt good being involved in their lives, even if it was just for takeout and to play in the water.

He wondered what it would be like to take them to Disneyland—would it be the happiest place on earth for them? Really?

So when Miguel came into the living room and held his fingers to his lips, inviting Ezra down the hall toward what looked like a guest bedroom, Ezra went almost eagerly.

"Hey," he said, as soon as they were in the bedroom, "do you think we could take the kids with us?" Suddenly he remembered who he was. "No—that would be stupid. I mean, why would your sister and brother in-law just throw us their kids and send us to Disneyland—"

"Because they're tired and desperate for some rest before the new baby gets here?" Miguel said, half laughing but mostly still looking grave. "Yeah, I told Lydia I'd ask you. Don't worry—I actually have experience with them when I'm *not* being their favorite uncle, and my other sisters have their kids too. You'll meet them when we go back home—there's a big celebration for like, half their birthdays at the end of September."

Ezra felt like Hanukkah and Christmas had a birthday party at Disneyland. "Seriously? We can take them? That's *awesome*. I mean, I'm terrified, right? Because... dude. Ariel—I'm afraid she'll float away. We can like, tie a string to her wrist or something because—"

"Strollers, papi. That's why they were invented. But before you get too excited, I have to tell you the big bad thing, okay?" Miguel grasped his shoulders and turned them both around, then backed Ezra up until he was sitting on the bed. "You all prepared? Can we do this?"

Ezra regarded him, not sure which thing made him feel more like the little kid: the being happy because he could take a bunch of kids he hadn't known two hours ago to Disneyland or the being worried because Miguel looked *so* serious.

"Yeah," he said, trying to feel adult and succeeding mostly in feeling about Ariel's age, all big eyes.

"Okay, so Ezra, do you remember how you ended up on Adam and Finn's lawn?"

Ezra blinked. "Well, yeah. I knew Rico let his cousin stay there when he came out to New York for the internship. I mean, I had an address and hailed a cab. Why?"

"Where'd you get that address?" Miguel asked, like he was *willing* him to make the obvious connection.

"Rico's employment records—my dad keeps those files for two years and *oh my God*!" Ezra bounced off the bed like a jack-in-the-box. "My *dad* is at *Rico's old apartment*?"

Miguel sucked air through his teeth. "Yeah. Yeah, he is—with your older brother. Uh, Adam has been putting them both off since last night. He, uh, called the cops—"

Ezra blinked. "*Adam?*"

"Yeah, I know. You'd think he'd be the last person to make that phone call, but apparently they've done this before with Rico's family."

"Oh God!" Ezra wailed. "They've been nothing but nice to me, and I set the hound of hell on their *doorstep*. I am *scum*, I am *horrible*—they're going to *hate* me, Miguel. I finally have friends and a place I love and a boyfriend I don't have to hide from the world and I just fucked everybody over and—"

Ezra was exploding, panicking, freaking out. Six hours away, his father was coming down like a jackhammer on all the parts of his life Ezra had been proudest of in the past six weeks, and oh God, if Miguel took him back, his father would see them together and *know*, just like he knew a bespoke suit for Rico meant something. Just the way Miguel *looked* at him meant something, and no, he couldn't let his father ruin this for him, he couldn't—

Miguel clapped one hand over his mouth and the other on the back of his head.

"Breathe," he commanded, and Ezra took a deep breath of warm air. "Now let it out." Ezra complied. "Good. Now breathe slowly, with me, okay?" Ezra nodded, and together they took slow, deep, even breaths until Ezra felt like he could function again.

"Okay," Miguel said. "So are you calm now?"

Ezra shrugged and nodded. His heart was still pounding, but at least he wasn't lightheaded anymore.

"So," Miguel continued, "you need to look at the things that this is, and not the things you're afraid of. First of all, Rico, Adam, Finn—they love you. You're the little brother they never had. They're putting your old man off, like I said, and calling the cops, because he's got no ground to stand on. So don't worry. They were all for me not telling you until we got back—they wanted you to have a good time, ¿sí?"

Really? "Remmfff?" he asked, and Miguel took his hand off his mouth.

"Yes, really. You didn't fuck up, baby. This isn't your fault. Your dad is a piece of sh… work. Let's go with work right now, because there's little kids sleeping down the hall. But seriously. Your people have your back, okay? They're not mad. They're not upset with *you*—and they're not going to tell him where you went either. So far all he knows is that Rico used to live there, and Adam is scary when he gets mad."

"That's…." He swallowed. "That's so nice," he said, feeling this sort of awe welling up in his chest. "For me?"

Miguel half smiled. "Yeah, baby. For you. So they wanted you to go have a good time, and I am all for that. But I thought we should tell you first because, you know. You're a grown-up and you have to make those decisions for yourself, right?"

Wow. "That's amazing," he said, admiration sweeping him. "You really—I mean, this is your trip too, and you're just going to put that in my hands?"

Miguel kissed him, quick and clean, and cupped his neck with warm palms. "Of course," he said. "Family is important—even if it's clearing up bad family, you know?"

"Yeah," Ezra said thoughtfully. His first impulse had been to jump in the van and drive screaming back to Sacramento to….

To do what? Go back to New York with his old man? Forget he was gay, and in love, and happy for the first time in his life? Forget that his old life felt like a prison, like he'd never seen the sky, or seen in color, or even knew what sex felt like, because the life, the job, the hiding, had all been so very bad for him?

"I'm not going back," he said, and it was like he truly realized it for the first time.

"Good," Miguel said, smiling, but Ezra wasn't sure he got it.

"No—you don't see. It's like I told your sister, I'd have to be hurt to leave here—why would I want to leave? Sacramento feels *good*—everything, you especially. If we go home to tell him that I'm not going back to New York, I just let him ruin… like, the best time in my life *ever*. And for what? Because he's being an asshole to people I care about? Why does he get to do that? No." Ezra fumbled with his still-damp swim trunks and then growled a little in frustration. "Here—give me my phone."

Miguel pulled it out of his pocket, because of course Ezra had handed it to him before he jumped in the pool, and Ezra brought up his blocked numbers, which were pretty much all of his family and old work contacts.

There had been over two hundred attempted calls to his cell.

"Oh," he said, grimacing. "I maybe should have looked at this app before he flew all the way cross-country to see me. Okay." He took a deep breath and sank down onto the queen-size bed in the pretty blue-calico-decorated room. Then he looked up at Miguel and held out his hand, feeling weak and stupid, but maybe Miguel didn't see it that way.

He took Ezra's hand and then sat down next to him, throwing a warm, powerful arm over his shoulder and leaning his temple against Ezra's.

"Let's do this thing, okay, papi?"

"Yeah." Ezra's hands shook as he typed in the number, and he was pretty sure Miguel saw. But he didn't stop, and he didn't hesitate, and he didn't back down.

Progressive Littermates

MIGUEL DIDN'T want to say anything, but in truth, he was so very proud of Ezra.

"Hello, Dad?" His voice was firm, like his hand wasn't shaking and sweating as it clutched Miguel's convulsively. "Yeah. It's me."

He held the phone away from his ear as it exploded in an angry, tinny rant, and Ezra met Miguel's eyes grimly and hung up.

Then he blocked the call.

He swallowed. "We need to give it ten minutes," he said, his voice scratchy. "Dad used to give people five, and they'd calm down and talk to him—he'll be ready for five, but not for ten."

He took a deep breath and wiped the sweat off his forehead, and Miguel knew Ezra wasn't going to make it for ten minutes. In ten minutes he'd be a sobbing heap in the corner, so miserable with anxiety he'd say anything, *do* anything to make that feeling stop.

It was exactly how Miguel had felt when he was bluffing the guy at the bank about having another venue lined up for his business.

Miguel had lost because he hadn't held any cards, but Ezra *had* cards. He just had to have the strength to use them.

"Give me the phone," Miguel said softly in his ear. "C'mon, gimme."

Ezra handed it over without a qualm, and Miguel appreciated that trust. He stood up and said, "Okay, I'm gonna lock the door—I want you to take off your pants, okay?"

Ezra's mouth fell open. "I'm sorry?"

"Your swim trunks, Ezra. Take them off. I'm not even joking." He turned his back and walked to the door, hoping Ezra wouldn't fail him here. This would only work if Ezra agreed to be dominated, agreed to be distracted—otherwise Miguel was going to have to make him go out and swim laps.

He clicked the lock on the door and listened—Lydia had been going down for her own nap when he came back to talk to Ezra, and he figured the only two people awake in the house were in this room.

Good.

He turned back around and Ezra was sitting on the bed, naked from the waist down. His cock—beautiful, straight, pale—was semierect and stiffening as Miguel looked.

"Just remember one thing," he said, feeling insanely confident.

"What?"

Miguel took the three steps to the bed and sank to his knees, then looked up at Ezra with hope that this would work. "Don't make any noise," he said, grinning wickedly. Then, without preamble, he took that lovely, hardening cock into his mouth.

Miguel had given blowjobs since he was fifteen and still working at Denio's. A pretty white boy selling knockoff jeans had taken his break one day while Miguel had been coming out of the bathroom. They'd made eye contact and there'd been heat, and the next thing Miguel knew, they were all over each other. He'd already known he was gay, although he hadn't told his family yet, and the feeling of Alexy's cock in his mouth had been a euphoric thing, a brilliant, filthy awakening.

Through boyfriends and hookups, he'd waited for that euphoria, that power, and that submission to another person's needs, all wrapped up in one, to return.

He'd been sadly disappointed, until now.

Ezra was the perfect blowjob receiver just like he was the perfect bottom. Sensitive, responsive, willing to take that mouth on his body and simply experience what Miguel had to give. He controlled his breathing to harsh pants, and Miguel pumped his shaft and lowered his head, quick and dirty, but Miguel wanted more. He wanted full capitulation. As soon as he began to fondle Ezra's balls, to skirt his finger behind them, Ezra gasped, biting his palm, and tangled his fingers in Miguel's hair.

Miguel grasped him, hard and full in his palm, and looked him in the eyes. "No noise," he cautioned just as he slid his finger over Ezra's still-tender entrance.

Ezra grunted, closed his eyes, and muffled a moan in his cupped hand. Miguel heard something that sounded like "Bastard!" and smiled as he lowered his head again.

Oh, papi, you wanted to be over your nerves when you talked to your old man? You were going to be *over* your nerves. They were going to be dumped down Miguel's throat, and swallowed, and disappeared. Miguel promised, didn't he? Promised to love him? And Ezra promised to stay as long as it didn't hurt. Well, Miguel was going to make sure it didn't hurt, not even if the hurt chased him down and tried to grab him by the throat.

Ezra's cock bottomed out in the back of his throat and he swallowed, reaching down and caressing Ezra's entrance again, and this time breaching just a little, finding him still loose from their morning. Ezra began to shake, pounding on Miguel's back with his free hand, and before Miguel could even think about coming up for air, Ezra climaxed, hard and fearlessly, just like Miguel had hoped.

Miguel swallowed and cleaned him off, then wiped his lips on the inside front of Ezra's trunks. Ezra flopped back onto the blue calico comforter, and Miguel pulled his trunks back up and did the little lace on the front. Then, while Ezra was still recovering, he pushed himself up on the bed and plopped his head on Ezra's shoulder.

Ezra looked stunned and replete, and he turned dazed blue eyes to Miguel and searched his face. "Proud of yourself?" he asked after a moment of watching Miguel smirk.

Oh yes. "Are you nervous anymore?" Miguel asked, smiling with all his teeth.

"No. Hard to be nervous when you just sucked my brains out of my dick like a straw."

"Heh heh heh…."

Ezra snickered back. "You've got such an angel's face," he said, gentle reproof in his voice. "But you've got a *really* dirty mouth."

"Are you complaining?"

A slow smile bloomed across Ezra's face, relaxed and joyful, and Miguel felt an amazing sort of pride. "No," he said softly. "No."

Miguel pushed up on one arm and kissed him, come-breath and all, and Ezra kissed him back without reservation. The kiss ended when Miguel pulled back and glanced at the clock on the delicate white end table. He sobered and looked at Ezra with purpose. "It's been thirteen minutes. You ready?"

Ezra nodded without thinking, and Miguel pulled the phone out of his pocket and sat up. Ezra sat up next to him and—probably still in sort of a postcoital trance—hit the number without any preparation at all.

Miguel could still hear the angry yelling on the other end, but it wasn't quite as loud.

"I'll hang up again, and I won't tell you when I'm coming back," Ezra said, sounding as relaxed and as cool as a trained negotiator. "If you want to meet with me—at all, ever—you need to shut up and listen."

The noise on the other end of the phone stopped.

"I'm not in town right now. I'm on a trip with a friend and we're staying with his family, and no, I'm not going to leave early."

The noise started up again and Ezra hung up, but he didn't look nervous this time.

"This is going to be a *long* conversation," Miguel said dubiously, but Ezra shook his head.

"Naw—this time is just to remind him that he's the one who wants to talk to *me*. It only needs to last a minute or two." Ezra smiled shyly and set the alarm on his phone. "How many kisses do you think we can get in under two minutes?"

Miguel traced that shy smile with his thumb and wondered how many times he'd seen that expression on Ezra's face before it started punching him in the stomach. Had he just been tapped at the beginning, and the full "hooha!" of the punch hadn't hit him until later? Or had the punch been just as strong at the beginning, but he'd had his stomach flexed and his defenses up? A person could only do that for so long before he had to relax his guard.

Miguel had no idea, but as he claimed Ezra's mouth again, kissing long and slow and druggingly, he thought that so far each kiss, each touch, each acknowledgment that they were together, seemed to make them a foregone conclusion, destiny instead of the slow, cautious getting to know you that they'd actually been.

Ezra got bold, sweeping his tongue inside Miguel's mouth and then pulling back to suck on his lower lip, teasing it with his teeth. Miguel let him and then went in for his own intrusion. His cock got firmer and achier with each kiss, and when Ezra's phone went off, Miguel panted against his shoulder.

"Augh, papi," he muttered, "you're going to kill me. Remember, *I* didn't get no calm-your-blood-pressure blowjob!"

"Yeah," Ezra said smugly. "I am fully aware." He straightened on the bed and without preamble hit his father's number again. This time when he held it up to his ear, there was only a harsh syllable in greeting.

"Yeah. So Dad, like I said, I'm not in town. You can't bother people about me—they're good people, and they've been kind to me, and you can't. I'll let Adam call the cops on you and Greg again, and I won't bail you out. You'll have to fly your lawyer from New York to do that—enjoy."

The next sentence was a short pithy bark, and Ezra caught Miguel's eyes and nodded. Yeah. This was where they'd arrived at.

"I'm not sure when I'll be back—it was originally four days, but we may add an extra one or two, so we'll see. I'll call you the day we get back and we can meet the next day."

Bark, snarl, pause.

"Yes, the day after. I don't want to meet with you when I've been in a car all day—and I'm not meeting with you at the apartment. That's Finn and Adam's home, and mine now too, and I don't want you there."

Yipe! Yipe! Yipe!

"No, Dad. Our house wasn't a home when I was a little kid, and that didn't change when I was older. *I* made a home, and *I* get to say who I want in it. Adam and Finn get to have a say too, and we all agree that you're not wanted. I'll meet you someplace not personal. I don't want you anywhere near my personal space, and that's final."

Growl.

"Well then maybe you should have been nicer to me when I worked for you, or hey—when I was a little kid and needed a dad, that would have been great! Right now it's too late. I quit your company and I've got some business matters I need to clear up with you and Greg, and then we'll be done. If you want to send me a Hanukkah card, that would be really sweet, but I won't hold my breath."

More snarling, but it had lost its heat.

"I'm killing my mother? Really? *Her* number isn't blocked on my phone, and I don't have one phone call from her. Does she even know I'm gone? Yeah, well, I'll take your word for it. For now, stay away from my friends, stay away from my apartment, and in case you figure out where I work, stay away from those people too."

And then he hung up.

Miguel hugged him so hard he probably creaked a few ribs. "You were *amazing*!"

"Yeah?" That shy smile—yup. It was getting more powerful with every use.

"Absolutely. But what business things? I mean…." Miguel felt bad for even thinking this way—*he* had been the one who'd wanted Martin Kellerman out of Ezra's life the most. "No personal things?"

Ezra shook his head. "No, not really. I sort of need to...." He grimaced. "Actually, I need to call my accountant. I hired one that my father fired—'cause he was gay, actually, but the guy didn't know that. Dad just said he wasn't a good fit during his probation period, and that was the end of it. But anyway, I need to talk to him and settle up some financial stuff." Ezra chewed his lip, suddenly as insecure as Miguel had seen him since that first day, lost on Adam's lawn. "So you know how I've got money to do stuff?"

Miguel nodded.

"If I have to live on my Candy Heaven paycheck... I mean, that's gonna be a lot of us watching movies on Netflix, you know?"

"Yeah—we don't make a lot there."

Ezra shook his head. "No. But that's okay with you?"

Miguel shrugged. "Will it bother you to be poor?" he asked, thinking probably yes.

"I just...." Ezra shook his head. "I guess the one thing I ever had going for me was my dad's money, you know?"

Miguel took back every jealous moment he'd ever had over rich people who seemed to have more than he did. "That's not why Rico came here breaking his heart," he said gently. "That's not why Finn and Adam protected you. Don't worry, Ezra—there's more to you than that."

Ezra grinned. "Well, I still need to talk to Ted. I'll shoot him an e-mail tonight, okay?" Suddenly he seemed to remember the whole reason they'd been making out in Miguel's sister's guest bedroom. "So—if we're still going to Disneyland, does that mean we get to take the kids? Because I'm telling you, that sounds *amazing*. I mean, at least for one day, right? Wait—no, two. So we can stay down there and get up early and do the late thing and—"

Miguel's chest felt sore, like maybe his heart had gotten a workout it wasn't used to. "Yeah, baby. We can take them for two days. Lydia asked us to, actually, but I told her we had to clear up the thing with your dad first. So... yeah."

Ezra smiled, that free-and-clear agenda-less smile that Miguel had come to treasure. "This is gonna be *the best thing*," he said, nodding sincerely. "Miguel, you do the best stuff *ever*."

How could you not love a guy who was leaving a fortune in New York so he could be happy in Sacramento? How could you not love a guy who thought two days in Disneyland with his boyfriend's nieces and nephew was the best time ever?

If it was possible, Miguel didn't want to know about it. All those months spent fruitlessly chasing a dream about Adam, and the reality of Ezra was so much sweeter than anything he'd imagined.

THEY WENT back to their hotel that night right after dinner. Bobby barbecued for them while Lydia made coleslaw and pudding, and they ate out on the patio. Even with Ezra's efforts during the day to play with the kids, while Miguel talked to his sister and brother-in-law, Miguel could tell they were wiped out.

Two days—with Ezra's help, he could give them two days to rest, to finish shopping for the clothes and diapers the new baby would need, and to get their thoughts and their collective shit together for the coming challenge. He knew his mom was coming as soon as the little peanut popped out, so he didn't feel bad about leaving after that, but he *did* feel good about what he and Ezra were doing.

That didn't mean he didn't take sweet advantage of their last night alone in the hotel.

It couldn't be *too* dramatic—they'd been pretty active that day, and besides being satisfied, they were also tired. But that didn't stop Ezra from exploring Miguel's body slowly, taking his time. He exclaimed over each new thing—Miguel's thick black groin hair and his smooth chest.

"I wax it, papi. Yeah, I admit it—I'm that vain. Do you hold it against me?"

"No, not at all. You can take your shirt off for me at any time."

He spent a *lovely* amount of time stroking and licking and nibbling on Miguel's solid erection. "Damn. Just… I mean, it's got a curve! Like the guys in porn and everything!"

"How much time do you spend watching porn in a week, sweetheart? I'm not judging or anything, but I just sort of want to know."

"This last month? None. All the months before? Tons. I've got no idea how much porn I'll watch when I've got a boyfriend I can kiss in public."

And then, when Miguel expected a cresting wave of a climax, Ezra shoved his knees apart and spread his asscheeks and….

Oh man. In porn they might have called it a rim job, but to Miguel, the angels wept and the heavens sang and his *entire body* tingled with each throb of his cock. There was no dialog when Ezra was tongue-fucking Miguel's asshole, because Ezra's mouth was busy and Miguel was beyond words.

Instead, he clapped a hand over his mouth and *screamed*, especially when Ezra seized his other hand and wrapped it around his own cock.

No words—none. Just breathless little shrieks of orgasm that probably took points off his man card, but it was *so* worth it.

He came, spattering his chest, his stomach, hell, some even hit his chin. He let go of his cock and grabbed Ezra by the hair, tugging him up, up, over Miguel's body.

Ezra ignored the semen and lay on top of him, perching on his sticky chest and grinning, his face glazed with spit.

Miguel grabbed another handful of hair and pulled him down for a kiss, and promptly lost himself in the heat of his mouth. Ezra moaned softly and ground against his hip, and Miguel realized that giving the rim job made him hard.

Oh, man, that was a turn-on—someone who got an erection from giving pleasure. Miguel kept kissing him and Ezra rutted against him some more, the slender lines of his pale body undulating gracefully. He threw his head back, his mouth slack with arousal, and Miguel grasped both his nipples in a long, slow, pinch.

Apparently that was all he needed. He bit his lip, his face contorting with climax, and Miguel felt the heat of his come add to the mess on both of them. He collapsed then, limp and sated, and Miguel rubbed his upper arms with shaking hands.

"Wow."

Ezra looked up at him, eyes half-closed, a sated little smile on his face. "Yeah?"

"Damn."

"Good?"

Miguel remembered that first moment, that first look, how he'd wanted to leave Ezra alone, just… just get him into Adam and Finn's place and dust his hands of the whole situation. Absurdly, he felt heat behind his eyes, and he pushed Ezra's hair back from his face and used his thumb to trace his bruised, swollen, and slick lips.

"I could have not seen this," he said thickly. "A guy who would take my sister's kids to Disneyland and think that was a reward. I could have missed this."

Ezra smiled crookedly. "So glad you didn't," he said earnestly. He bit his lip and rested his cheek on Miguel's chest.

Miguel left it at that and contented himself with running fingers that trembled through Ezra's hair and over his back for silent minutes until they were both ready to go wash off, but he felt that moment of "almost didn't" keenly in his stomach. For a little while, he'd tried not to care about anything—and he could have missed this by becoming the worst version of himself.

If there was a motivation for being the best version of himself, this feeling of Ezra, limp and languid, content in Miguel's arms—*that* was all Miguel needed.

BOBBY DROPPED the kids off the next day, and when the flurry of putting car seats in the minivan and getting their backpacks out of the hotel room had passed, Miguel found himself at the helm of the brown Toyota familymobile—but this time with the family. Bobby's last words as he got exhaustedly into his little sedan were "We packed enough diapers for a month—just don't feed her too much fruit, or she'll go through them all!"

And then he was gone. Ezra turned to the kids—Ariel in the middle seat and Jessie and Brock in the far back—and said, "This thing's got movies—your dad brought some, right?"

And oh, thank you, Disney/Pixar/Dreamworks/Sony, because they heard nothing but movie dialog and delighted laughter for the next two hours, with a break at McDonald's before they got back on the freeway.

Miguel had been to Disneyland a couple of times, both as a kid and as an adult. His father's family lived not too far over the border in Mexico, and they used to save for three or so years, come down and visit Miguel's abuela, who used to watch telenovelas with a ferocious dedication, and then go to Disneyland for three or four days on the way back home. Disneyland became a catch-all for Abuela and family vacation and generally joy as a whole. Jessie and Brock and even little Ariel had all been to Disneyland several times, and their excited chatter would have made him smile under ordinary circumstances.

But circumstances weren't ordinary, and this time he had Ezra to watch.

Ezra was worth watching.

His eyes opened wide and round, and the oddest expression—half of wonder and expectation and half almost of fear, like this moment would be taken from him—was written on his pretty face as they drove by. Brock and Jessie could identify some of the rides from the outside, and he kept saying, "Yeah? Is that it?" as though he'd *heard* of the Matterhorn and the Tower of Terror but he hadn't actually believed they existed.

The Tropicana was right across from the park, and they had planned to check into the hotel and then walk, and Miguel almost regretted pulling into the parking lot. He sort of wished he could just drive his boy to the front gates and turn him loose. Would Miguel's boneless kitty cat run hell-for-leather like an excited puppy into the magic kingdom?

Probably not, Miguel decided, watching as Ezra very conscientiously helped unload the kids and their stuff from the car. His kitty was a grown-up kitty right now—but then, given the fascination he was showing with every exchange with Brock, Jessie, and Ariel, he was a grown-up kitty who very much enjoyed playing with kittens.

They dumped their stuff in the okay room—Miguel was almost glad there would be no romance for the two of them in the next two nights, because he wanted better for Ezra—and then pushed off for the park.

Later, when the two of them started the meat of their relationship, after the honeymoon beginning, he would look through the pictures on his phone taken over the next two days and sort of glow with the promise of them.

Ezra bought everybody mouse ears at the very first shop they came to, and every picture, whether it was of Ezra tickling Ariel while they waited in line, or Ezra and the kids sharing a cookie in Starbucks, or even all of them, Miguel included, having their picture taken with every character from Donald Duck to Stitch, featured Ezra in a pair of basic Mickey Mouse Club mouse ears, that shy smile on his face and a look of such profound adoration for the little people he was playing with that it brought a lump to Miguel's throat.

His mother texted him in the early afternoon while he was in line getting them drinks by the Haunted Mansion ride, and he sent her the picture of everybody with Minnie Mouse.

Very nice. You and Ezra look very happy together. Uhm, should I ask?

Miguel looked at the picture again and realized that while Ezra had Ariel on his hip and one hand in Jessie's, Miguel was standing with one hand on Brock's shoulder and the other one on the small of Ezra's back. There could really be no question, could there?

Miguel blushed.

Very perceptive, Mami. Yes. We're officially a thing.

Good. He's my favorite.

Miguel looked at the text and frowned. *Of who? All your boys? All my boyfriends?*

Choose one. I like him best. I'd pick him over you in a heartbeat. I never liked you anyway!

Miguel stared at the text in outrage and then realized his mother was kidding him.

Jesus, Mami!

Then don't be stupid, mijo. But of every boy you've brought home, this is the one you look at like your father looked at me.

Miguel got to the front of the line then, so he was not obliged to answer her, but the more he thought of the comment, the more he blushed.

"What?" Ezra asked when he came to them in line. They were not yet at the porch of the building, so Ariel was still happy in the shade of her stroller, and Jessie and Brock were enjoying their lemonade.

"Mami said something very wise," he said thoughtfully. Then he snapped out of it. It was bad enough they were at the "I love you" stage so early—but to be in the "I think you're the love of my life" stage now....

No.

Even the mildest, lowest-key kitty would bolt with too much of that.

They'd established a plan of sorts for the two of them, a way to conduct their relationship around their lives until all the threads were ready to tangle.

Miguel thought maybe Ezra needed that. If you opened a pet carrier and shoved a cat in, he'd destroy you in the effort to get away. If you opened a pet carrier and put in some food, he'd sleep there forever and ever.

Still, that night as they lay in the hotel room, the three kids on one bed, Miguel and Ezra on the other, he wrapped his arm around Ezra's middle and buried his face in his neck and closed his eyes and dreamed.

He'd never really thought of his future before—not with a man and a family. When he'd been planning his business, that dream had been all about him at the forefront. There hadn't been another person in that dream.

Now when he thought about that dream, he wondered—would he and Ezra work as well in real life as they worked together selling candy?

Sell Out

IT WAS hard to say good-bye to those kids.

They were sleeping when Miguel pulled up in front of his sister's house. Ezra lifted them out, one at a time, and walked each kid into his or her bedroom. Ezra was grateful for the time to tuck each kid in and pull the covers over little shoulders.

"Night, Brock."

"Night, Tío Ezra."

"Night, Jessie."

"Night, Tío Ezra."

"Night, Ariel."

"Buenas noches, Tío Ezra, voy a ver que mañana y tu puedes llevarme a Disneyland para siempre jamás."

"Uh, yeah. Night, sweetheart. I'll see you soon. Next time you visit your grandma, I promise."

She sighed and rolled over, clutching the stuffed Stitch Ezra had bought her. "Yeah, okay. I like you like Abuela. You're both good."

She fell asleep, and Ezra turned out the little white lamp, which had a base painted with pink ponies. He thought, his heart a little full, that this parenting gig was a pretty sweet deal. It was a thing he'd never even thought to look at before coming to live with Finn and Adam and eating at Miguel's mother's table.

He came out of the room and went down the stairs to find Miguel standing by the door, hugging his sister, who had gotten tearful between one kid and the next.

"Miguel, I can't even tell you. The last two days—they saved my life."

"Yeah, I hear you. I'm the best brother ever. By the way, after all this, with me and Ezra bringing the van down, Mami managed to get off work two extra weeks. So you hang in there for a couple of days and you'll have Mami. Of course *we'll* have to live without her until October, but you and the new *mija*, you'll be all good."

Lydia cried a little harder, and Bobby came in at that moment and took her gently out of Miguel's arms.

"You and Ezra are the best," he said, calming Lydia down with the gentlest of touches on the back of the head. "She's *close*—I think she'll go into labor before the end of the week—but just having these two days.... I can't tell you how much that helped."

"What are awesome brothers for?" Miguel shrugged nonchalantly. Then he looked up at Ezra and beamed, and in that smile, Ezra saw the whole of their new relationship, as well as the past two days spent forging ties with family that Ezra had never known could exist. "And their boyfriends," he said softly.

And oh! Ezra hadn't known he could still blush. "Yeah," he mumbled through the heat in his face. "And their boyfriends."

"Well, nice-guy hug," Lydia said, leaning into Ezra from her husband and giving him a sniffly kiss on the cheek. "I know the kids weren't what you'd planned, but I'm telling you, taking them for us— that was like hero stuff right there."

Ezra was so pleased, he couldn't even look at her. "Hero stuff," he repeated. "Nobody has ever accused me of that!"

"Well, they should." Lydia patted his cheek, and then Bobby took him in for a hug, and before Ezra could recover from the embarrassment, Miguel was leading him by the hand through the windy dark to the sedan they were driving back to Miguel's house the next day.

"That was a little abrupt," Ezra reproved as Miguel backed out of the driveway. "I wanted to tell them what the kids did, 'cause, you know—Brock got to do the Jedi thing, and that was pretty cool, and Ariel got her picture taken with Jasmine, and—"

"I texted Lydia pictures all day. Don't worry—they didn't miss a thing," Miguel replied. "Do you realize how much sex we haven't had in the last two days?"

Ezra smirked. "Yeah, that's at least forty-eight hours of orgasms we've missed out on—that's a fuckin' *shame*."

Miguel just glared at him and shook his head. "Yeah, you laugh, but we're going to get home and be squeezing sex in between all the people we're living with. I just *found* you, papi. I don't want to go back to not *having* you again."

He sounded so distraught, and Ezra realized a few things.

"You really *do* love me," he said, full of wonder. And equally as important: "You trust me not to go back with my old man," he finished, his voice sinking to a whisper.

Miguel couldn't really look at him, because he was driving, but Ezra could sense the flicker of attention his way, even in the dark. "Yeah," he said, like there was no question. "Why would you?"

Ezra swallowed. Oh, yeah. Confession time. He and Rico had never had confession time, because he'd never believed it would last. But Miguel—he needed to know how it ended, didn't he?

"Because that's what I did with Rico," he said, feeling the shame in his gut. "Rico—he didn't just let me go, you know? He asked me—twice—to come with him. I just… I just thought, you know. I couldn't. I didn't get happy endings. I… I mean, I got us busted—the stupid receipt on my desk. I got him fired. So he asked me to come with him, and… I just still saw myself trapped." His voice sank, and he remembered that day, being hustled away from Rico's apartment by his dad's goon. "I… I don't think I saw a way out of there until I started ripping the place up with my bare hands."

Miguel reached across the seat and squeezed his knee.

And then shot an arrow through Ezra's heart.

"I worry, you know," he said softly.

"'Bout what?"

"You haven't called your shrink, baby. I fell in love with you a little at a time—I didn't hardly see it until I was inside you. And I can't tell if you're okay or not. I mean, I know you got out of that trap and you've been finding your feet again. But…." His hand tightened. "I would hate it if you took apart Darrin's store because your heart was screaming and you had no words."

Ezra swallowed, his heart suddenly so full that he couldn't even breathe.

Miguel turned into the hotel parking lot and parked the car. Ezra had brought his glasses—he'd offered to drive—but Miguel seemed to take pride in it. Maybe because he'd been a little kid being driven by all the adults. Ezra had been given his car and turned loose on the world—he'd never known where to go. He liked it when Miguel drove; it seemed the natural order of things.

And now Miguel was asking him in a very real way if he was fit to drive his own person.

"My heart hasn't been screaming since I left New York," he said on a deep breath.

Miguel killed the engine and the lights, and together they sat in the parking space and stared at the bright Best Western sign that lit up the desert night.

"Is that true?"

Ezra could barely hear him, so he turned sideways and admired his profile against the glare. That full mouth, the bold chin, the strong planes of his face—Ezra had seen him from the very beginning, had known he would be the one to drive.

"Yeah," he said, remembering the past six weeks, the camaraderie of rooming with people who were kind to him, the unguessed-at fulfillment of having a job where not killing himself didn't get him screamed at and working hard got him friendship and some props—even the simple joys of a dog to walk and a cat that thought he was okay.

But even before that—it was that moment he got on the plane and thought, *You can only go forward.*

"I… I went forward. I'm here. I'm living life different, and it's mine."

"So not a trap?" Miguel asked, like he was making sure.

"Yeah. Not a trap."

Miguel turned toward him and cupped the line of his jaw. "You let Rico go. That's okay. Maybe you loved him, but it wasn't enough. I won't let go, papi. If I'd been Rico, I would have grabbed your hand and yanked you out of that office, out of that place. I would have bought your ticket and damned all my stuff and pulled you on board that plane. See, thing is, neither you nor Rico had a blueprint for how to do this shit right. You needed someone to show you. I'll show you. Someone comes along that grabs you in your gut, you don't let it go. I've had lots of guys—I won't lie. But you looked at me, and you knew my name, and you just stuck. Now I'm not letting you go. So I need to know—are you okay in here?"

He held his other hand to Ezra's chest, and that feeling of fullness burned past Ezra's throat and into his eyes.

"Yeah," he whispered, nodding. Tears spilled over, and he hated them, but they felt cleansing all the same.

"You sure?" Miguel rubbed the salt water across his cheek with a rough thumb.

Ezra nodded. "Yeah. I just... I've never... I just never thought someone would keep me, that's all."

Their foreheads touched and Miguel rubbed their temples together. "I'll keep you. You face your old man like a soldier, okay? Because he's not getting you again." Miguel's voice thickened and he captured Ezra's hands, rubbing his thumbs roughly on the scars that covered Ezra's knuckles. "The thought of you tearing apart your office like a cat stuck in a box—that breaks my fuckin' heart. That's not ever gonna be you again, ¿sí?"

"Sí," Ezra parroted, entranced by the idea. "You'll protect me?"

"Yeah, but I won't need to. Don't worry. You won't need to be alone."

Ezra nodded, and a part of him—the guarded part, the part that had worried for the last two days if telling Miguel that he was in love hadn't been a mistake—went limp, melted back into the shadows that house all lovers' fears.

"Okay," he said, willing to simply be a part of Miguel's plan. He'd never been great at planning—it was one of the reasons his old man had hated him in the office. All those years trying to anticipate what Martin Kellerman would want, chasing his tail, running over his own feet, all because when it came to people he cared about, he was without a road map for how to behave. His brain shorted out, he couldn't reason—all he was left with was a burning desire to please and the knowledge that he couldn't.

Rico had been the first person, really, that he'd been able to please.

Darrin was the first person to tell him that he was capable of pleasing himself.

Miguel was the first person to tell him that he didn't need to make that plan alone.

The thought made him giddy.

Miguel brought his hand up and played with the six-pointed star Ezra had worn since his bar mitzvah.

"This mean something to you?" he asked quietly. Miguel and his brothers all wore a small gold cross—Ezra assumed they got them at confirmation.

"It means I'm Jewish," Ezra said, feeling dumb.

Miguel flashed his white grin in the moonlight. "I mean, do you listen to all the rules? Some of the rules? None of the rules?"

Oh.

"My parents gave it to me," Ezra said, feeling stupid. "It was… man, it was the last time I thought, even for a minute, that I mattered."

Miguel reached behind Ezra's neck and fumbled for the clasp in the dark. The chain slithered down, but the charm stuck on his neck, held there by the faint sheen of sweat they both wore in the darkened car. Miguel swept it up carefully and held it in his hand, then lifted his own chain off his neck and slipped it over Ezra's head.

"Oh my God!" Ezra gasped, thinking this was probably blasphemous.

Miguel lifted one side of his mouth and fiddled with the clasp around his neck, dropping his hands when it was secure. "No, not God." He touched the gold cross at Ezra's throat. "Berto and I went through confirmation before my papi died. He put this around my neck about two weeks before he passed away. My parents, they weren't great on rules, you know? There was no being a virgin for the girls and no having to be macho for the boys. I was gay, it wasn't a thing. But when we went through catechism, I was mad. My papi was dying, and sucking up to God wasn't going to save him. I asked Papi why it mattered."

"That's a good question," Ezra said, impressed. Even as a kid, that was Miguel, taking the lead.

"Yeah—he thought so too. He said that symbols mean different things to different people. I don't want to take over your god, *papacito*. But my dad, he told me that this meant we all believed we were under the same umbrella. It meant we had faith, there was kindness in the world, and there was a plan. So not the rules—you're still Jewish, I'm still Catholic—but kindness and faith and a plan. So I'm giving you these things, okay?"

Ezra nodded and reached out to touch his silver Star of David, resting gently on Miguel's clavicle.

"What am I giving you?" he asked, thinking mournfully of the worry for Ezra's mental health, and Ezra's dad, who was a nightmare, and how they were both going to have to work really hard before they got to live together and be a couple.

"You're trusting me that you matter," Miguel said fiercely. "You matter to me. I tried not to let you—I tried so hard to just be an asshole and not let you touch my heart. I sucked at it. You matter. Not just to me, but I'm the most important, okay?"

Yeah. "Yeah," Ezra said, and for a moment he thought he was going to cry some more, but Miguel's mouth touched his gently and then captured him in full, and his body had other, better things to do than cry.

Oh... oh yes. *This* was the kind of kissing he'd been wanting to do as he and Miguel had pecked each other chastely on the lips and then snuggled on the bed next to the kids' bed. This was all-consuming, Miguel's lips crushing into his teeth, his tongue assuming dominance, his hands all over Ezra's throat, his shoulders, his chest. Ezra keened and thrust his hands under Miguel's T-shirt, suddenly wanting *all* of their skin touching. He brushed a thumb over Miguel's nipple, then pinched, and Miguel pulled back and nipped him sharply on the lower lip.

"Out of the car," he ordered. "Into the air-conditioned hotel room. We've got a lot to do tonight, okay? You go in, you jump in the shower, you get out, I'll jump in—"

"No shower sex?" Ezra asked, a little confused. He'd never actually had shower sex, but it seemed like a logical extension of the plan here—

"No," Miguel said flatly, shaking his head. "I know it sounds all romantic, but you know what? When you're young and stupid or having hate sex or even makeup sex, I can see the appeal. But this isn't like that. I want you clean and naked and spread out on the bed. I am going to take you apart, papacito. I'm going to make you scream. And when you're all screamed out, I'm going to make you come so hard, you forget everybody's name but mine. You say Rico is just some guy? Good. You're gonna forget his name tonight."

He scowled at Ezra, aggressive and certain, and Ezra nodded, completely ensorcelled. Of course. Miguel could do that. Ezra's body would be cleansed of meaningless hookups and relationships he'd doomed to fail with his own cowardice. He'd be Miguel's, inside and out, and the doubts that had made him able to let Rico go, those would be burned away.

Faith and a plan.

His fingers traced the unfamiliar emblem at his neck.

Okay, he could believe in that.

HE SHOWERED quickly but carefully—wandering around an amusement park any time of the year left you with swampy creases and murky pits, and he scrubbed those places as hard as he'd ever cleaned in his life. When he turned off the water, Miguel thrust a towel at him from outside the shower.

"Dry off and lie down," he said seriously, and Ezra had to smile.

"You're not even going to look at me?" he teased, peeking around the plain hotel shower curtain.

Miguel glared at him, naked and waiting to get in the tub. In the bright light, Ezra got to appreciate every plane and angle, the heavy muscles at his flanks and shoulders, and he was going to reach out and run a finger from his nipple to his happy trail when Miguel grabbed his hand.

"No playing," he muttered. "See my cock?"

Ezra looked and realized that it was engorged, dripping, the impressive curve fully outlined against his thigh. "Yeah," he said through a dry throat.

"I *want* you, Ezra. So bad. But we're doing this right. It's going to have to last."

Ezra nodded and dried off quickly, stepping out of the tub so Miguel could get in. He went to the bed—a king-size this time—and pulled back the covers, then lay on his side in the middle and let the cooling air wash over his skin.

His nipples pebbled and his cock filled and his body throbbed with anticipation. Miguel didn't make idle threats, and tonight Ezra was going to be taken care of.

He'd never, not in his whole life, been taken care of.

He closed his eyes against the yellow light of the hotel and imagined touch, imagined knowing that he could wake up every morning next to the warmth of a man who wanted him.

He had good memories now, of Miguel's hands on his body, his rough, filthy commands in Ezra's ear, his intensity and concentration on Ezra and only Ezra, until Ezra came apart in his arms. He shivered, the emotional arousal of knowing what was coming, building everything— the pleasure, the sweet bite of pain, the desire—until Ezra's anxieties ceased to exist, and it was only their flesh, their hearts, merged together.

Unconsciously he clasped his hands over his head so he wouldn't use them on his body. He was too close, just from anticipation, to even touch himself.

The bed shifted under Miguel's weight, and Miguel's hand came up to cover his eyes. "Keep 'em closed," he whispered, nuzzling Ezra's cheek with his own. He'd shaved, but his body was still damp and sweet-smelling from the shower, and Ezra took a deep breath, filling his lungs with steamy wet man like smoke.

"Should I worry?" he asked, mostly kidding. "Is this where you break out the kinky shit?"

Miguel laughed, low and dirty. "Someday, yeah. Someday we're going to buy out a sex store and you're gonna be vibrated, plugged, handcuffed, and blindfolded, but not today. You keep your eyes closed, okay?"

Ezra nodded. "My wrists—"

"Yeah." Ezra felt Miguel's hands spreading his knees, propping them up, and anchoring his feet. For a moment the room went cold, and then the light went out and the red tinge in front of Ezra's eyes went dark.

And Miguel's body was back, and Miguel's hands, his maddening, inquisitive, bold, and merciless hands.

He made a pass over Ezra's stomach and Ezra sucked it in—he knew he wasn't fat, but he wasn't muscular either, and when Miguel stopped and pulled in a mouthful of skin right by his belly button, Ezra laughed.

"Tickles!" he gasped.

"Stop hiding from me!" Miguel said after releasing the skin with a pop.

Ezra closed his knees, feeling suddenly vulnerable. "Not hiding," he muttered stubbornly, and Miguel, ever patient, shoved his knees apart again. Gently, but there was no mistaking his intent.

Miguel closed his mouth over Ezra's nipple, and Ezra pressed the flat of his feet against the bed and arched his back. Sparks exploded behind his eyes as Miguel sucked and released, and nibbled on the end and released, and sucked some more.

Ezra couldn't help it—he moaned, and his hips bounced off the bed and his cock splatted against his stomach in a little wet spot formed by precome.

"I...," he panted, "am going to come."

"Go ahead," Miguel taunted, moving his mouth to Ezra's other nipple. He sucked that one in and left the other one to dry. Ezra clasped his hands tightly together, tortured by the aching in his cock, in his ass, wanting Miguel's attention on *those* parts, and still...

Sort of loving being teased.

Miguel pulled especially hard on his nipple, though, and for a moment Ezra teetered. One breath, one rock of his hips—he could smack his cock on his abdomen a couple of times and just come!

But where was the fun in that?

He whined and locked his hips down, concentrating instead on all of the other sensations there for the taking.

Miguel's torso half covered his own, and Ezra felt heat and the pleasurable friction of skin on skin. Miguel slid his free hand silkily over Ezra's upper thighs, then behind his knees, then over his calves, every caress bringing exquisite attention to the place he *wasn't* touching.

"Here, baby, suck on this," Miguel murmured when Ezra let out one too many whines. He popped two of his fingers into Ezra's mouth, and Ezra had a pretty good idea where they were going, so he got them good and wet.

Miguel surprised him, though. He didn't immediately shove them where, well, where things went during sex. Instead he took those wet fingers and traced them along Ezra's ribs, along the tops of his thighs, and every so slyly, along the length of his dick.

And then stuck them back in Ezra's mouth while that teasing trail dried, making *all the skin* sensitive and ticklish and *aroused as fucking balls*!

Miguel turned his head so his ear was pressed against Ezra's stomach and his tongue was… well, it *felt* like it was sticking out near the head of Ezra's cock, but Ezra couldn't be sure. He rippled his stomach and rocked his hips up as far as they could go and… oh… oh…. Oh God, there it was….

Miguel lapped twice and Ezra had to release the tension in his stomach so he could breathe. His hips sank down against the bed and Miguel's tongue disappeared.

Ezra grunted outrage against the two fingers in his mouth and then rolled his stomach and his hips again, wanting to feel Miguel's tongue.

Yes! There it was! A few laps, teasingly firm slaps of his tongue against Ezra's crown, and oh *hells*, Ezra was going to *die* if something didn't happen soon.

Miguel pulled his fingers from Ezra's mouth and Ezra found himself gibbering, begging, *needing* those expected touches with unexpected force.

"You gonna… oh please, Miguel, just… my ass… man, please…."
He clenched and released his muscles, begging to be filled, although he knew Miguel couldn't see. "My cock… man, please… I'm dyin' here… please don't…."

Miguel disappeared and Ezra let out a half sob.

But he kept his hands clasped above his head and his eyes shut.

The bed shifted as Miguel moved, and Ezra felt him, head between Ezra's knees, shoulders shoving at his thighs as he made himself comfortable.

Ezra wanted to lower his hands, to shove his head, *force* him to take Ezra's dripping cock into his mouth. Oh *Lord*, was there anything dirtier than wrenching your fingers in your lover's hair when he had your dick buried in his throat?

But Miguel had told him to stay put, and it had become a point of trust now. Ezra took a few deep breaths and calmed his squirming body and waited, just waited to see what Miguel would do next.

For a moment he felt hot breath on his balls, and then Miguel lifted his hips and shoved a pillow under his lower back, leaving Ezra's ass, taint, and balls open and exposed.

When Ezra felt Miguel's palms parting his cheeks and his wet tongue darting in without preliminary, he couldn't control the moan that escaped.

Yes. Yes, please. I'm laid out here for you—nibble me, sample me, suck me, eat me, fuck me*!*

Miguel's chuckle resonated against his skin, and then, oh holy hell, he delivered. His tongue lapped and rimmed, teased and penetrated Ezra's asshole as Ezra lost his fucking mind. His cock sat full and aching on his stomach, bouncing with every breath, but for a moment he could only concentrate on the dreamy pressure of Miguel's soft organ against his sensitive skin.

He wanted more. *Needed* more. Miguel was right—he craved the bite of pain, the dark pleasure of being invaded, dilated, forced to accommodate someone else's body inside his own.

He started to gibber again, to beg, and this time Miguel didn't stop his mouth with anything. It was just Ezra's voice making sobbing, broken pleas into the darkness, and then…

"*Yes!*"

Miguel thrust his thumb inside, rough enough to temporarily fill Ezra's need. While he did that, he lifted his head and then lowered it in one motion, engulfing Ezra's cock and taking him deep.

Ezra howled, his fingers biting into each other with the terrible urge to grab Miguel, to control, to make.

Miguel pulled his head up and let Ezra's cock thwack him softly around the mouth and cheeks when he spoke. "You can let go of your hands now—but only if you grab your nipples, 'kay?"

"'Kay," Ezra sobbed, and his fingers ached from clasping each other, but God, his body *needed*. His own hands felt alien on his body, as though he shouldn't be touching himself even with Miguel's permission, as though he was completely owned. He found the swollen flesh of his nipples and squeezed roughly, needy, just as Miguel lowered his head and sucked Ezra's cock *hard* and added his other thumb, spreading Ezra wide.

Ezra screamed, pinching himself until he left marks, his ass coming off the bed as he drove himself deeper into Miguel's throat, then rocking down as he impaled himself more definitively on Miguel's thumbs.

Everything, oh, God, just fucking everything!

But still, still he couldn't come. His whole body was clenched, bowed, needy, and he couldn't figure out what he was waiting for, because the weight of his orgasm was backing up against all his nerve endings, until the point of pain. Miguel released his cock and pulled out of Ezra's body, and Ezra gasped, writhing with the emptiness and the gut-clenching want.

"Keep your eyes closed," Miguel instructed. "Keep 'em closed until you can't do it no more."

Ezra heard the snick of a bottle and had just figured out that Miguel was lubing himself when that broad, curved cock was breaching his entrance. He pinched his nipples harder and let out a feral grunt, bearing down and taking that thing as far as it would go.

Miguel chuckled above him. "You are fucking pushy, you know that?"

But Ezra had no humor right now, he had only need. "Oh God... oh God... fuck me... c'mon, fuck me... please, Miguel, I can't... I can't... I can't...."

"You *can*," Miguel commanded, thrusting into him with incredible force. "And you *will*."

Ezra let out a groan from deep in the pit of his stomach, something loud enough to wake the neighbors and make them complain. *"Yes!"*

Miguel shoved at his thighs, spreading him out even more, and continued to rock him with hard, even thrusts.

"You ready, baby?" he demanded through gritted teeth. "You ready for me?"

Ezra had no words. He moaned, pinching harder and tilting his head back.

"Stroke your cock," Miguel ordered, and Ezra felt that curious displacement again. Not his body. He was touching it, but it was Miguel's, owned exclusively by him, claimed and marked and made his. His hand on his aching cock felt as delicious as a stranger's, and his entire body shuddered as he stroked in time with Miguel's next thrust.

"Good?" Miguel panted, still pounding.

"Munghn...."

"Yeah?"

"Oh... oh... fuck. Fuck. Fuck me faster...."

"Whose are you? Tell me," Miguel said, unrelenting. He placed his hands on top of Ezra's thighs for a moment and changed his angle, and his next thrust went *up* and hit Ezra's prostate just *right* just as Ezra screamed, "Yours! Oh God, I'm yours! Yours!"

"Yes!" Miguel howled, nailing that spot again and again and again until Ezra's muscles all rippled and every synapse in his brain fired at once and come spilled from his balls through his cock to land *everywhere*—chest, stomach, cheek, forehead, lips. His ass contracted and he darted his tongue out, tasting himself, and the salt and the bitter rocked him into the second wave of climax, even harder this time, squeezing Miguel so tight that for a few strokes he just rutted, not moving, locked into place.

"Hnungh...." Miguel thrust hard into his body, sliding through to the hilt and then climaxed, tucking against him, until Ezra forgot about following orders and just wrapped his arms around Miguel's shoulders and patted his neck and his upper arms in vague comforting motions as he tried to put the world back together in his head.

Miguel shuddered some more and collapsed limply, and Ezra was the only one in the world then who could protect him.

Their breathing grated, harsh and uneven, and then it mellowed, synchronized, calmed.

Ezra felt Miguel's lips on his own, and he opened for a gentle, exploratory kiss. Miguel pulled back and let out a rusty chuckle. "You can open your eyes now, papi," he said softly.

Ezra did, seeing Miguel's face easily in the faint glow from around the blackout curtain, after having his eyes clenched shut for so long.

"Hey," he said, tempted to look away. He'd closed his eyes and let Miguel have him, let Miguel take him over, body and soul. He knew all Ezra's flaws in excruciating detail. What if there was something there, something horrible, a flaw in his private places, a horrible thing he did when he came, a sound he made that caused all erections to wither— maybe there was something awful that would make Miguel regret owning him. He could be sent back to the shelter of friends bereft, empty after this unexpected foray from friendship to love.

"You're mine now," Miguel said, startling him into searching those rich brown eyes.

"Yeah," he whispered, remembering how not even his own hands felt right on his body when Miguel was inside him.

"We're gonna stay locked together in our hearts, okay?"

Ezra nodded, mesmerized. Not sent back to the shelter. "Okay."

Miguel rocked his hips, his cock still lodged inside Ezra, awash in the sticky warmth of come. "Like we're locked together here, but inside," he said soberly, shifting on his elbow and placing a hand over Ezra's chest.

"Yes," Ezra agreed, fervent. "Yes. Locked together."

"Remember that when we get home and you have to deal with your people," Miguel continued inexorably, like he wasn't going to let Ezra out of this lecture. He rocked his hips again, and Ezra clenched hard, just to feel him inside. "We're locked together. You have a place. You're not just some stray who ran away—you're a man who moved, and you found a home, and I wanted you and you said yes. You're mine now, you understand me?"

Ezra nodded, remembering all those times Jake had claimed his chest as his territory. When he was in the apartment, he was Jake's human, and there existed nowhere else for that cat to be. "And you're mine," he said, thinking that nobody else could ever, ever be allowed to see Miguel helpless, spent, having poured himself into another person's body.

Never.

Miguel nodded and wrapped his arms around Ezra's shoulders, placing gentle kisses on the corner of his mouth, on his chin, on his neck. He kept rocking inside Ezra the whole time, until Ezra realized he'd grown hard again and they were fucking once more.

But this time was gentle. This time they owned each other. Miguel stroked long, and his cock hit just the right place all over again. This time when they came, it wasn't to screams and howls like animals mating, it was to soft grunts, gentle words, sweet squeezes and touches, each one helping the other over the crest.

This time, when they were done, Miguel lay on top of him and licked playfully at the come still sticking to his skin from the first orgasm, until Ezra giggled and they rolled off each other to wash up.

This time Ezra kept his eyes open the entire time, locked on Miguel's, until they both had to close them, trapping the moment for all time, this heartbeat of being inside each other, their bodies as locked as their hearts.

THE DRIVE the next day was interminable.

Ezra had been able to put off the anxiety of talking to his father when they were playing in Disneyland, or—of course!—in bed, but he flat-out couldn't do it when they were staring down endless and alien stretches of Highway 99.

Then Miguel stared that scary man in the face and growled.

"So, papi, where are you going to talk to him?"

Ezra grunted. "Uh... I don't—he'll probably want to have dinner or something."

"Then you pick the place."

Ezra let out half a laugh. "The only place I know is River Burger—and Gatsby's Nick or Faces, but those places don't serve food."

"Well, that's fine," Miguel said, hitting cruise control so he could stretch his legs. "River Burger it is. We'll tell Finn, he'll reserve a table, Mari will wait on you—it'll be good."

Ezra blushed and shifted uncomfortably. "You know... maybe you all don't want a front-row seat to me being...." Shamed like a child. Browbeaten like a cocker spaniel. Eviscerated so all his faults lay spread across the little white-painted wrought iron tables of River

Burger like cow guts, ready to be thrown into the trash pile with the viscera of his self-esteem.

Miguel grunted in a no-bullshit, my-word-is-law sort of way that Ezra would not have suspected from him before he'd fucked Ezra blind.

"Your comfort zone, papi. That's fine if your people are around you. Your whole life, you've been surrounded by him and his world and his people. You have your own place now. No one disrespects you in your own house, you understand?"

"Okay," Ezra said, feeling a black hole open under his feet. "But what if… you know… nobody wants to *be* my people after this?" His hands were cold and sweating, and he was breathing shallowly, just like he'd been when Rico had suggested he go back into corporate life. "I… I mean, I wasn't a great person in my dad's office. What if that person comes back?"

Oh God. This was a horrible idea. If it hadn't meant his old man badgering his friends, he would have told Miguel to just let him hide out in the crappy hotel in Lancaster until the whole thing blew over.

He couldn't catch his breath.

Miguel turned his head for a moment and without warning cut across the slow lane of traffic in time to make the off-ramp they were passing. "Are you going to throw up?"

Ezra tried hard to control his breathing. "No," he breathed. "Yes. Maybe. God."

Miguel took the first right and parked in front of an ampm/McDonald's, probably because it was the first place he could find. He put the car in park and rolled down the windows and turned in his seat and grabbed Ezra's hands.

"Look at me, papi. C'mon, *look at me*."

Just like the night before, Ezra did what he commanded. Oh God, there was something about his eyes, dark and warm and direct…. Ezra clung to his gaze like a lifeline.

"Looking," he said, trying to maintain his breathing.

"Okay, you know how you told Rico to go and you stayed with your father?"

Ezra nodded, because hey, not forgetting that.

"I will *never* tell you to just go."

"I'm not a good person," Ezra whispered. He'd done that. He'd told Rico to just go and broken his heart.

"You were trying to protect him," Miguel said, rubbing the backs of Ezra's scarred knuckles with a gentle thumb. "But see? You needed me instead. I would have protected *you*. I can protect you, papi. It'll be okay."

"He makes me feel like I'm nothing," Ezra confessed, feeling stupid. "Everything I've got here—my couch in Adam's front room, the job I didn't get from my old man, hell, the stupid cat who likes me—those *mean* something to me, Miguel. How do I…. What if he makes me feel like that stuff's nothing too?"

Ezra's vision went under in a cold wash of black, and he really *did* think he was going to throw up. All of the happiness he'd built up in the past six weeks threatened to go under in the onslaught of fear.

Miguel's lips nuzzling his temple and the faintly sweaty heat rolling off his body brought Ezra back. "C'mon, baby," Miguel pleaded. "He's just a man. Maybe back in New York he was some sort of petty god, but he's gonna show up here in his suit and his shiny shoes, and you're gonna show up in your cargo shorts and a T-shirt, and who's gonna belong here, right? And I'm going to be there. He can say what he wants—do you think I'm an angel? Do you think I'll just get all hurt and sit there and take it? I'm stronger than that—and if you're not yet, that's okay. You just hold on to my hand and we'll be strong together."

Oh, that was promising.

Ezra had tried so hard to be strong for Rico, but he hadn't known how to ask for help. Rico hadn't known he'd needed it. But Miguel knew—Miguel had known Ezra was weak from the start, and he'd been beside him helping him be strong.

"He'll be awful," Ezra whispered, warning. "He'll… he'll be racist and snide and…."

"But you're not," Miguel reassured him, holding him tighter while he worked out his shivers. "C'mon, you think I don't know you by now? The first time I met you, you sat across the table from Adam, who looks like scary Mexican guy, and you didn't even flinch. First time you ever said my name, you were polite and respectful. My mother loves you—and Jaime and Berto would have beat the shit out of you if you were any sort of asshole to her. So it's okay if he's that dumb. You're not. I don't know why—I mean, you were apparently raised by snakes—but somehow, baby, you came out good."

Ezra thought about it, tried to pinpoint what made him not believe what his father said about people like Rico or Cy or Miguel. "He was just... mean to me," he said after a moment, some of his fear receding. "He was mean to me, and I just... it felt like the people he was mean to, we should be on the same side."

Miguel's laughter was warm—kind—and the tremors that had rocked Ezra as they'd pulled off the road eased up. "Sounds smart," he said softly.

"Not so smart," Ezra said, his voice harsh in his own ears. "Work sucked. I'd try to be nice to the other employees, but they hated me because I kept trying to please the old man...." He started to shake again, and Miguel whispered in his ear.

"Baby... baby, don't worry. We can do this. You aren't that person anymore—I mean, wait!"

He sat up suddenly and grinned. Ezra sort of welcomed the space between them, because it was getting hot in the car, but he missed the comfort of Miguel's heat too.

"What?"

"You *are* that person," Miguel said, smiling a little. "You're kind. You've always been kind. You've always been a good person, baby. You just didn't see it until you left, that's all." That smile went up in the corners. "You just needed room to grow."

Ezra thought about the space in Sacramento. Yeah, sure, the boardwalks of Old Sac got crowded, but nothing like the streets of the garment district during rush hour. Yeah, Sacramento had its own streets, and God, did the cars zoom down them, but it had more trees and more sky to balance out all that speed.

"I should take you to New York sometime," he said wistfully. "It's... there's great things there, you know? I mean it's true—you don't see the tourist stuff when you live there—but that didn't mean I didn't like taking business contacts out and showing them a good time. The theater district, restaurant row—it wasn't all bad."

"No," Miguel said. He opened the car door and gestured for Ezra to get out too. "I'll bet it's glorious," he continued as they walked into the convenience store. A cold drink, Ezra thought gratefully. A cold drink and some sugar, and maybe some trail mix. Good idea, Miguel! "I want to see it—I want to see it through your eyes."

Ezra thought about that—a trip, just the two of them, Miguel seeing all the tourist things that made grown men into little kids. That would be fun.

"But we'd come back home here," he said, staring blankly at a wall of chocolate. The words came out of nowhere, but Miguel seemed to understand exactly what was going on. He moved behind Ezra and put a hand in the small of his back.

"Yeah, papi. This is home. You and me, we'll face down the big scary demon, and you'll stay here at home."

Ezra closed his eyes, envisioned Adam and Finn's apartment and the big trees lining their block. He pictured Jake the cat, and Clopper, and Darrin his boss, and the candy store across the river. He imagined Miguel's mom's house and the way she invited Ezra to come talk to her, like any other of her sons.

"Okay," he said after a moment, all of those visions fixed firmly in his brain. "I can do this. River Burger. I'll ask Finn tonight when we get home."

They were in the middle of what even Ezra could recognize was nowhere, so not a place for Miguel to kiss him or nuzzle his temple or do any of those kind, reassuring things. But that hand on the small of his back was warm and real, and it wasn't going away.

"Good plan, papi," Miguel said softly. "We'll run with that, okay?"

Ezra's fingers searched out the new charm at his throat. Faith and a plan. No rules he didn't believe in. He could do this.

He could.

Marking Territory

MIGUEL CAME inside Adam and Finn's after they got home and listened to Ezra very casually ask Finn if he could meet his dad at River Burger.

Finn and Adam both looked at Miguel, who nodded, and Finn responded that yeah, that'd be fine, he'd make sure Mari would be there and so would his brothers, and they'd save a table, and his dad would be ready to cook extra special, and....

Miguel lost track of the ands.

Finn was covering for the fact that they were all thinking the same thing. River Burger was going to be the most hopping joint in Sacramento if they had anything to say about it.

"So sure," Finn finished up breathlessly. "Go ahead. It'll be fine. As long as it's after three."

Ezra didn't ask why. He was sitting on the couch, sprawled out in the air-conditioning—because September was still sucking, that's why!—with Jake purring on his stomach. The cat had staked Ezra out as soon as he'd walked through the door, and Miguel wondered if the cat had ever gotten the Cats Don't Get Attached memo, because *this* one sure did love Ezra something fierce. Ezra patted the cat a few more times and then reached into his pocket to dial his father's number.

Miguel looked at Finn and mouthed, "You'll be there, right?"

Finn nodded urgently, and then the entire apartment went silent as they all shamelessly listened to the conversation.

"Yeah, uh, Pops? Four o'clock—I'll be on my break, I'll take it late." Pause. "No, I'm not telling you where I work—but we're meeting at a place called River Burger. It's a good place." He gave directions then, finishing up, "It's right across the street from the bronze pony express rider—it's sort of cool."

The bitter, barking whine Miguel had begun to associate with Ezra's father came through loud and clear, and Ezra held the phone away from his ear. When the tirade wound down, he held the phone back, and his voice assumed a hardness that Miguel had never heard.

"You know what, you're right. I don't give a shit if you think it's cool or not. But *I* like it—*I* think it's cool. You and Gregory can meet me there, or you can fly back home and fuck yourselves, but I'm done giving a shit what you think about me. See you tomorrow, asshole."

He pounded the End Call button, and for a moment, Miguel was *pumped*. Look at him! He was animated and strong—Martin Kellerman didn't have a *hope* of living up to his son's iron will.

The moment passed and Ezra slumped down onto the couch again, the phone falling next to him unremarked.

Miguel bent and kissed his temple. "I'll just plug this in for you, okay, papi?"

Ezra turned a blank face to him. "Yeah. That's fine—thanks, Miguel."

"You staying for dinner?" Adam asked. He was sitting at the table, either doing homework or working for Derek, Miguel couldn't tell. Whatever he was doing, he was still hell-bent on taking care of his family.

"Yeah, sure. Tell you what—you let me know what we're having, I'll cook."

Some of the tension on Adam's face eased. "You are a stand-up human being, you know that?"

Miguel winked. "I hope so—gotta be to take care of our boy." He reached down and tilted Ezra's face up so they could meet eyes. "Calm down, baby. We'll take care of you. It's going to be all right."

Ezra nodded, but his eyes were still focused on outer space, and Miguel sighed and kissed his forehead.

Helpless, that was how he felt. Absolutely helpless.

He vented his frustration by invading Finn and Adam's kitchen, but fortunately they had plenty to invade. The best thing was a big box of grilled hamburger patties, probably brought from Finn's job. Add some salad mix, some cheese, sour cream, some chili powder and garlic… damn. No tortillas. Wait, here, hello—tortilla *chips*. Well, they were men—this would practically be health food.

And there in the fruit bowl next to the fridge, could it be?

"Avocados!" Miguel practically crowed into the quiet room. Finn and Adam were so intent on their homework they barely looked up. Ezra glanced at him and smiled. "You guys are my *favorite*!"

"Glad you approve," Adam said dryly, gaze still in front of him.

"Where's Clopper?" Miguel asked, unloading the fridge. "He at least laughs at my jokes."

"Rico's got him for the afternoon," Finn said, stretching. "Because you guys called and asked him to, which was really awesome of you." He set his homework down on the coffee table and paused in front of Ezra, handing him the remote. "Watch something, okay? The silence is driving me bugshit." Then he moved to the kitchen and started pulling out little serving bowls. "Tacos, right?"

"Yeah—with guacamole."

"Oooh—here, there's salsa under the cupboard."

"I like you people—you do shit right," Miguel said, just happy to have some company. Ezra's quiet unnerved him.

"So, good trip?"

Miguel nodded and assembled his ingredients on the counter. "The best. I've been there like twenty times in my life, but I can't remember having so much fun."

"Here, let me turn on the heat for the meat," Finn said, showing his teeth at the rhyme.

"Yeah, thanks. Throw in the burgers, we can chop them up into ground beef and I'll add seasoning."

"Taco salad," Finn said, reading the situation aright. "I like it. So why was it so good?"

Miguel looked up from the frying pan, where he was cutting the meat with the spatula. "'Cause Ezra, of course," he said, not feeling self-conscious in the least.

"You guys officially a thing?"

Miguel blinked. Yeah. They'd been "just friends" when they'd left, right? "The best thing," he said gruffly. "The thing I've been waiting forever to happen—*that* kind of thing."

Finn nodded and opened the bag of salad mix on the cutting board so he could chop it a little finer. "Yeah. You guys, friends first. That's good. Promising."

Miguel grunted. "Complicated."

Finn used the edge of his chef's knife to scoop the pile of salad into a big bowl, and then started to smash the tortilla chips. "You mean 'cause he's here?"

"Yeah—me and my brothers, we don't bring dates home, you know?"

Finn *hmm*ed and dumped the tiny tortilla pieces in with the lettuce. "Yeah. And you can't leave your mom in the lurch—you're all still making house payments, right?"

"Yeah. You wanna skip the guacamole, add the sour cream and salsa like dressing, and we can slice the avocados up and throw them in with the cheese and ground beef?"

Finn gave an ecstatic little shudder. "Yes, yes, and yes. I love it when my dinner all comes from one bowl."

"Your turn to do the dishes?"

"You know it! Well, Ezra's a good roomie—he can stay here as long as he needs to. But...."

Miguel looked up from the meat at Finn's pause, because it sounded important.

"But what?"

"Just know—as long as you guys still play softball and be our friends and shit, it's okay if you steal him."

Miguel grinned. "You're stuck with me for life." He sobered and looked to where Ezra was flopped sideways on the couch, watching an old episode of *Sons of Anarchy* with listless eyes. "I just hope...." His chest went cold, followed by his stomach, followed by his bowels. He'd never actually realized what that saying meant until just this moment. He swallowed and tried not to shiver. "I hope he... I hope he's the same way."

Finn grunted. "Here, you finish up. I'm gonna go make some phone calls. I think we can make tomorrow a little easier on him." With that, Finn left Miguel to cook while he trotted down the hall, blowing a kiss at an oblivious Adam.

Or at least it *looked* like Adam was oblivious, until he glanced up from his studies with a wink and caught the kiss before going back to work.

Miguel had hope for the two of them—that much playfulness, what wasn't to love?

"Ezra," he called, hoping to break through the sort of inert terror that seemed to be possessing him. "You want to come set the table?"

Ezra popped up like he'd been poked in the ass with a sharp stick. "Yeah, sure. Sorry. Zoning out. I'll be right there."

His usually languid grace deserted him, and for a moment he reminded Miguel of one of these YouTube videos where the cat falls off the television. This was *not* Ezra relaxed and happy in his home. He clattered to the kitchen, and Miguel turned down the heat on the warmed ground beef and turned to grab him around the waist before he could reach for the plates.

"Papi," he said quietly, "you have got to relax."

Ezra nodded at him, his eyes limpid, and then buried his face in Miguel's shoulder. "I just keep thinking, you know? He put me through school so I could help him with his business—and I'm throwing that back in his face! I mean, look at Adam and Finn—they're working so hard, and he handed me that shit for free—"

"Yeah, but baby, you gotta ask yourself if you wanted it. I mean, one of my sisters gets a clothing discount from her job at Macy's. I could get you a tuxedo for, like, twenty dollars. But what in the fuck are you going to do with a tuxedo right now?"

Ezra grimaced.

"Don't tell me…."

"Yeah. I told you I had a lot of useless clothes."

Miguel had to laugh. "Well, maybe someday you and me will go to a fancy dinner and we'll find a reason for your tuxedo. But you get the point, don't you?"

"It wasn't something I wanted, and it wasn't something I needed for something I wanted," Ezra replied dutifully.

Miguel sighed and suddenly thought of a really important question. "Ezra… papi, what did *you* want to be when you grew up?"

Ezra thought about it seriously and then looked up with an expression that sort of punched Miguel in the gut. "I wanted to be a kid," he said, sighing. Then he brightened. "And I have been, right? Rooming with friends, Disneyland, babysitting—wow! That's a really good question—I should think more about that stuff, you know?"

Miguel resisted the urge to smack his forehead with his palm. "I sort of meant do you want to be *here*," he said, after fumbling for word choices for a moment. "You know, so when you talk to your dad, you're not just saying, 'Fuck you, Dad, I'm not playing with you no more!' You need to be saying, 'I'm sorry, I have a different plan for my life than you did, and I can't do that back in New York.'"

Ezra pulled away—not out of irritation or disgust, but because suddenly he was self-animated and autonomous. "Huh. You know—

that's a really good question. Thanks, Miguel—let me think about it. I want to have an answer when I meet him tomorrow, you think?"

Miguel nodded, relieved, and stood back to let him move around the kitchen, his motions almost dancelike as his attention was taken by other things.

DINNER WAS much appreciated by everyone, and Miguel felt good about his deed for the day. Ezra walked him out to his car, per usual, but this time Miguel needed to kiss him, leaning up against his car, his hands in Ezra's back pockets as they took each other's mouths slowly. The early fall air blew cool against their skin, although the day had been warm, and Miguel placed a series of butterfly kisses along Ezra's jaw, just to remind Ezra that he had someone in his arms, someone right there, to support him.

"This is better and worse now," Ezra murmured.

"What?"

"Saying good night to you."

Miguel laughed, trying not to think about it. "Yeah—it's gonna suck driving back without you now. I'm going to look forward to when you can spend the night on Mami's couch."

Ezra nodded and kissed his mouth, taking the rare moment of initiative. "Tell me we can do this," he said softly.

"We can definitely do this," Miguel replied, his eyes burning with the need to make Ezra believe.

"Then it's done," Ezra said. He nodded soberly. "Faith and a plan— isn't that what you told me?"

"You remember that?"

"Yeah." Both of them raised their fingers to the new, unfamiliar charms at their throats. "Yeah," Ezra said softly, kissing Miguel's fingers as they stroked his Star of David. "It's an important thing. It's the first time anyone told me I could control my own destiny, you know?"

Miguel smiled and rested his forehead against Ezra's. "Who controls it?"

"We do," Ezra said, his voice as certain as Miguel had ever heard it.

"When do you work tomorrow?" he asked. It was a small detail but an important one.

"Ten to six."

"I'm supposed to be there at twelve. I'll get there early so you and me can take our breaks at the same time. Don't worry—I don't have to sit at the same table, but you're going to have friendly faces there, okay?"

Ezra nodded. "Hey, do you think if I asked, Adam could take me to a bank on our way to work?"

"Yeah, but why for?"

"My accountant e-mailed me back," he said vaguely, and then he was kissing Miguel again in what had to be their good-bye kiss, and he made it good.

It must have been good, because Miguel was lost in it all the way home. It wasn't until he was getting ready for bed and missing Ezra like crazy that he thought to wonder about it.

He really did trust Ezra to bring himself home.

Four Feet and a Tail

"Do you really want to do this?" Adam asked quietly before Ezra got out of the minivan and went into the bank. Ezra had needed Adam's help in finding a brick-and-mortar branch that would do what he needed.

"Are *you* sure?" Ezra asked, trying not to let anxiety claw his gut. "I mean, I'm not paying much rent now, but this is going to take away my margin."

"You're not a freeloader, Ezra," Adam said, turning to look at him. God, him and Rico with those eyes. A different shape than Miguel's, but warm and brown and strong. Ezra was lucky he liked Miguel's better. "You're a member of the household—pet care, food, cleanup. Me and Finn really lucked out having you with us these last weeks. We don't need your money to appreciate you."

Ezra nodded and swallowed. "That's really nice of you to say," he replied past the lump in his throat. Oh God, he was really going to do this. "It's the only reason I'm feeling this brave right now."

Adam grunted. "You *are* brave. You think I haven't been there? Broke and starting over again? It's not easy. But it's less hard with friends and backup, and you got that. You're going to be okay."

Ezra nodded. "I'm going to be okay," he repeated, trying to believe it. His hands and feet were icy, but maybe that was because the temperature had dropped and it was sixty degrees outside.

Adam made a sound that wasn't impatient—but it *did* remind Ezra that time was marching on.

"Okay," he said after a moment. "It's time for me to go stand on my own two feet."

"Four feet," Adam said, lips twitching. "Yours and Miguel's."

Ezra's hands began to tingle with some warmth and feeling. "Yeah. Four. Okay. Back in ten."

It took fifteen, mostly because he couldn't convince the teller that he wanted a check for an amount that big.

"But sir, that doesn't leave very much in your account!"

He'd seen Adam doing finances at the beginning of September to figure out if he and Finn had enough money to buy books. It turned out they didn't, and Finn had unashamedly asked his family for book money. It was no big deal—at least for Finn—and Ezra had seen Adam's wistful surprise at that too.

But Ezra knew how much money his friends were making, and he knew that even if they threw him out on his ear tomorrow, he was still in a better spot than they were financially.

And they were still in a better place in their lives.

"Some families don't make that much money in a year," he said soberly. "I'll be fine."

The cashier looked at the amounts again and shrugged. "Yeah, but who are you paying off? A mob boss?"

"Worse," Ezra told her. "Family."

Ezra had gotten his first wallet for his birthday in seventh grade. He'd kept it for two years, until it had fallen out of his pocket at school. His father had spanked him with a belt—not the first time, but definitely the last—for his carelessness, and Ezra had never lost or forgotten his wallet again.

That didn't stop his hands from shaking as he placed the cashier's check carefully in his wallet and then slid his wallet into his back pocket.

"You look like shit," Adam said as he got in the car. "I've never seen a white person turn green before. Let's stop and get you a coffee or breakfast or something before we hit work."

"Yeah, okay," Ezra said. Then he half laughed. "But you'd better make it McDonald's and not Starbucks, okay?"

"I hear you loud and clear," Adam said, pulling out of the parking lot. "But then, you've been going to McDonald's for weeks now."

Ezra thought about that—it was true. Sort of like Jake—he didn't care if it was Friskies or Eukanuba as long as it was in the bowl at chow time.

The shaking in his stomach calmed down.

"I like McDonald's," he said simply. "I mean, not for every meal, but yeah. The coffee's not bad."

They were stopped at a light, and Adam turned and winked at him. "That's a good way to think about it."

Indeed it was.

STILL, EZRA'S anxiety never did go away. A Monday in late September was not exactly prime tourist time, and while Ezra tried to engage in some meaningful activity, the truth was Adam had brought *his* schoolwork to do at the counter, just in case there was time.

There was time. There was time for Ezra, Miguel, and Adam to get unbearably jumpy in a very limited amount of space.

Ravi arrived when Miguel had been scheduled, and as he clomped into the relatively quiet store, he made such a racket that Ezra dropped the unsealed bag of small jawbreakers he'd been filling, Miguel bumped his head on the bottom of the staircase as he straightened, and Adam startled and pushed his book off the cashier stand.

The resulting clatter had Ravi clutching his chest like a silent movie heroine and Darrin stomping out of the back office where he'd apparently been doing the books.

"What in the seven names of sweet hell…." He swung then, glaring from Adam to Miguel to Ezra, all of whom were busy picking up objects or rubbing sore foreheads. "What in the hell is hanging over your heads?" he snapped, apparently reading the electrons in the air. "And why don't I know about it?"

"It's no big deal," Ezra muttered defensively, reaching between two barrels for a tiny jawbreaker. "My father is meeting me today—"

Darrin made a really *interesting* sound. It was like a cross between a jungle cat and Clopper if he'd seen a jungle cat. "*Your* father?" he asked neutrally.

"Yeah." Ezra rounded up the last of the tiny jawbreakers and scooped them into his cupped hands, then knee-walked the three feet to the trash can and let them rattle into it like rain on a tin roof. "Uh, my dad. He, uh, well he wants me to come back with him, but I'm—"

"Please," Darrin said, his voice dropping as he offered Ezra a hand up. "Please, baby, *please* tell me you're planning to tell him no."

For once he was not being charming or snarky. Darrin was 100 percent compassionate, 1,000 percent sincere.

Ezra nodded. "Uh, yeah. I've got a, uh, plan. You know. A plan. 'Cause Miguel said it would be easier to tell him no if I told him what I was going to do instead."

Darrin cut his eyes sideways to Miguel, who managed to focus on the two of them through the rising goose egg on his forehead.

"Miguel said?" Darrin asked, some of his usual snark in place. "And that's important to you?"

Ezra blushed. "Yeah. You know. Uh, lollipop kisses—he's got 'em."

Darrin nodded soberly. "They don't just taste like cherry," he said, completely serious. "They taste like the whole rainbow."

Ezra took his first full breath of the entire day. "Yeah," he said, smiling and fighting the urge to just fall apart. "You get it!"

"Yeah." Darrin patted his cheek. "I totally do. So when is your meeting with the bridge troll, little Billy?"

Ezra didn't even have to ask what he meant. "Four o'clock. I think Adam and Miguel were hoping they could come with me."

Miguel had come up behind Ezra and laid a comforting hand on the small of his back, and Adam was standing on Ezra's other side—not intimately, but like he had a right to be there.

"Of course," Darrin said thoughtfully. "Adam, can I talk to you in the back for a minute? But yeah—we've got two more people coming in, and this place is a tomb. Take an hour if you need it. I'll, uhm." He grimaced. "I'll look forward to hearing how things went."

Ezra nodded, and Darrin summoned Adam with a perfunctory jerk of his chin. Miguel watched them go with assessing eyes.

"What do you suppose they're going to talk about?" he asked, almost to himself.

"Me," Ezra said simply. "They're worried. It's nice. Nobody's ever worried about me like that."

Miguel let out a drawn out breath of his own and pulled Ezra a little tighter. "I'm worried too," he confessed.

Ezra put his hand on the back of Miguel's neck and kissed his temple. "Don't be." He was not used to reassuring people—he tried to make it good. "Faith and a plan. You bring the faith, I'll bring the plan, okay?"

Miguel nodded, and they stayed that way for a minute.

"I'm trusting you here," Miguel said after a moment. "I know we haven't been a thing long, but I would…." He shook his head. "I remember Rico when he was trying to get over you. I'd make him look okay, and he wasn't. Not by a long shot."

A customer came in then, and they parted. Miguel didn't look at Ezra as he turned to help the college students in for a sweet break. Ezra watched him for a moment, trying to catch his breath.

Rico had been wrecked. For some reason, that meant something. Rico had said it too, a couple of times. Miguel would be wrecked. Darrin cared. Adam and Finn wanted him to stay. Miguel would be hurt worse than Rico.

Ezra mattered to people.

He held on to that for the rest of the day. When three forty-five rolled around, Adam finished running his last bit of stock and turned to where Ezra was finishing with a floor sweep and Miguel was wiping off the chocolate counter.

"'Kay, guys. Let's roll."

Now that some of the heat of summer had eased up, Ezra was starting to really love this part of the city. The breeze off the river kept the temp down, and the sky above the bridge was this amazing color blue. Small, yes—but he'd felt like a face in a crowd in Manhattan. Maybe someone like his father, or someone *bigger*, in person, in heart, would be comfortable, would maybe thrive. Hell, Adam could have done it no problem, but Adam fell in love here. Rico too.

Ezra had been thinking—ever since Miguel had asked him what he wanted to be when he grew up—and he was coming to realize something about himself.

He didn't want big. Miguel did, and Ezra could sit at his elbow and be the boyfriend of the big bad business entrepreneur as long as Miguel would let him. But Ezra wanted small. Ezra wanted to play with children—or hell, he wanted to play with adults. He had a couple ideas for what that could mean, what kind of education he'd need, but that wasn't the point. The point was, seven weeks earlier, Darrin had told him that his heart wasn't *really* in Manhattan.

Spooky how often that man was right.

The three of them walked quietly and steadily until they got to River Burger, and Adam let out a sigh of relief when he saw that Mari had set up three tables in the shade.

"That's my girl," he muttered.

"Three?" Ezra looked around, wondering who else was going to be there. He'd assumed Miguel and Adam would sit separate but—oh. Oh wow.

A beautiful red Mustang convertible drove up, top down, and Rico hopped out of the passenger side. Derek stayed long enough to put the top up, and then both of them trotted up the boardwalk.

"Is he here yet?" Rico asked, sounding partly anxious and partly eager. "Because I was sort of hoping we could all be seated before he showed up."

Derek smiled at him. "Showing a tactical advantage. I'm so proud."

Ezra grinned weakly at them both. "Yeah—yeah, that's a good idea. But we should hurry, 'cause the old man invented it."

Yes, yes, he did, but in this case, Ezra had home field advantage too, because his father—going against everything Ezra knew about the man—showed up two minutes late.

He texted on the dot—apparently they'd just found parking over on the Candy Heaven side of the area and were on their way to River Burger, and when Ezra looked up to tell Miguel that, he smirked.

"Home field advantage," he said, and Ezra smiled, feeling a little stronger now. At that moment Mari walked out with appetizers for their three tables, and Ezra looked at the basket in front of him, surprised.

"I didn't order—"

"Deep-fried pickles," she said pertly. "They're a new thing. You taste 'em now, and if they suck, let your dad eat them. If they're *good*, then you can be all smug like you've always known they were great and where the hell has *he* been."

Ezra grinned at her and she dropped a basket off for Rico and Ezra and one for Miguel and Adam. Finn was behind the counter with his father and his older sister JoBeth, who looked like an older, less perky version of Mari.

"The pickles are awesome!" Finn called over the counter. "Swear— Dad and I worked on 'em all summer. You like, give me the signal and we'll dump hell-pickle-fire on your table. I'm sayin'. Anything for a friend."

So when Ezra's father rounded the corner, Ezra's older brother hard on his heels, Ezra himself was in the middle of a deep, happy belly laugh—and one of his new favorite things to eat, because fried pickles really were freakin' awesome.

His father looked, well, ordinary, in the clear, bright light of Sacramento near autumn. He was wearing a black pinstripe suit, and Ezra's brother was wearing its twin—American cut, so boxy as fuck, and both of them had wide, shiny dress shoes. Gregory's tie was blue. Martin's tie was red. Gregory still had curly brown hair coming to a widow's peak; Martin had lost all but a fringe of hair years ago, and he kept the fringe trimmed tight to his head.

Both of them looked hot and uncomfortable and sort of bound up, considering they were having lunch at a sidewalk café in a place where a lot of people wore cargo shorts and miniskirts to work. Even Rico and Derek, both of them in pale lightweight suits that matched the climate, looked as though they belonged.

Martin and Gregory approached the table, and Ezra stood and gestured them over. He wasn't expecting a hug and his father didn't give him one. Instead, they shook hands gravely, as though this were a business luncheon, and then they all sat down.

"What's this?" Martin Kellerman asked sourly, eyeing the basket.

A thousand years ago, Ezra would have quailed. He would have mumbled, "Just an appetizer" and looked away. But not now. Now he grinned and swiped one of the slices through the ranch dressing on the side and popped it into his mouth.

"Fried pickles, Pop. You should try them—they're *amazing*."

"Yeah?" Gregory asked, interested, but Martin glared at him, and the oldest Kellerman boy stopped, hand extended, and went back to staring hungrily at the appetizers.

"I'm not eating anything that's fried," Martin Kellerman growled. "Do they have something decent for lunch?"

"Turkey club on rye," Ezra said glumly. "But that's not what I'm having."

"What are you having?" Gregory asked curiously, and Ezra smiled at him. He thought of Miguel's family and how much the brothers loved to be in each other's lives, and suddenly he missed his brothers. They could have meant so much more to each other if only someone had shown them how.

"I'm having the bleu cheese mushroom burger, because it's awesome and I missed it while I was gone," he said. "Mari will be over in a minute—why don't you guys study the menus?"

They both looked at the little printed pages with the day's specials on them, and Gregory set his down after a moment and tried to make conversation.

"So now that you're back, are you going to tell us where you went?" he asked, and again, Ezra heard sort of an eagerness there. Ezra wondered how mad they'd both get if he told them, and in that moment, he experienced a curious surge of power.

He could piss them off. Or at least his father. With just the simple truth, he could piss him off.

It was heady stuff, and he would admit later that he used his sudden knowledge for evil.

"My boyfriend and I were driving a car down to his sister's house. She's having a new baby, and they had a line on a minivan, so we did a car swap down in Lancaster and then took her three other kids to Disneyland so Lydia and Bobby could get some sleep before the big event, you know? The kids were great—I mean, *great*. We had the best time—rode the rides, ate the food, saw the shows. Miguel says we can go again, just him and me—there's this app you can get on your phone, right? Where you put in all the rides you want and it gives you a schedule for how to get on them all in one day? Miguel says it sounds like video games in real time, so we sort of promised each other we'd go back next year—"

"The fuck you will," Martin snarled, slamming his menu down. "You're not going to fucking Disneyland with your new fag boyfriend, because you're coming home with us."

Suddenly all of Ezra's people were staring at Ezra's table like it was the epicenter of the plague. And then Finn's dad came around the counter and walked right up to Ezra's dad like Martin Kellerman didn't think he was a big furry deal.

"Mr. Kellerman?"

"Yeah?"

"I'm George Stewart—this is my restaurant. Ezra is always welcome to stay, but you need to tone down your language—"

"What in the fuck—"

"Yes, you can fucking say *fuck*, Mr. Kellerman, but you *can't* say the other f-word. My son is gay, his boyfriend is sitting right behind you with Ezra's boyfriend, and his cousin—who you might know—is sitting in the table next to theirs, with *his* boyfriend. We've got a very rainbow vibe here, Mr. Kellerman, and I have the right to refuse service to anyone who tries to make my friends and family feel like shit. So you have your meeting, but you do it in a civil voice, and you watch your language."

And with that, Finn's dad turned on his heel and headed back for the grill. Adam was the one who started the applause, but it picked up speed, and by the time Mr. Stewart got behind the counter, *everybody* in the café was whistling and clapping. Mr. Stewart gave a modest little bow and went back to work, and the applause died down, but Ezra's father had gotten the point. He glared around him, particularly at Rico, who gave him a specific finger of salute back, and then turned to Ezra like it was all his fault.

"I am surrounded by—"

"Don't say it, Dad," Ezra warned soberly. "He will kick you out. Adam is about to grind your face into the street if you don't calm down, and his boyfriend will help him, and Rico's here and he's got reason to hate your ass—"

His dad glanced behind his shoulder, skating over Rico almost guiltily, and finally saw Adam, who was snarling, the skin drawn back from his cheekbones with the force of his feral smile.

Martin Kellerman startled. "Who in the fuck is *that*?"

"That's Rico's scary cousin, and I'm rooming with him and Finn. They've got the best couch in the world—one of those pillow tops, better than a bed, I swear." Okay—babbling. But not scared. He wasn't afraid—he was sharing.

"You're *rooming* with two guys and"—Martin Kellerman flailed—"*dating* a third?"

"I'm sleeping on their couch, Dad. They work and go to school and play softball and go out with Finn's family—it's not like they'd have any time for orgies even if that was their thing." Ezra rolled his eyes like he'd never had the nerve to do when he was thirteen. Felt good, actually—like he was stretching his sarcasm muscles.

"But Ezra," Greg said from his elbow, "what do *you* do?"

"Help," Ezra said, smiling softly. "I have a job, I pay rent. I help with the animals and dinner. They've got this dog that weighs more than me—he's a real sweetheart, but he needs to be walked and taken out to the river to play. They've got a cat"—his voice dropped—"he's like… like a sleep bomb, you know? You'll be lying there thinking you can't sleep because the world's coming to an end, and this cat will get on your chest and start to purr and that's it—lights out. It's like a superpower. I love this fuckin' cat. Someday Miguel and I are going to move out and I'm going to have to leave that cat behind, and *that's* gonna suck."

"Ezra, this is bullshit," his father said in the same voice he used to tell competitors that it was time to get down to brass tacks. "I paid for your fucking education—you owe me better."

Ezra smiled, but it was a sad smile, and he missed the empowering sarcasm. "Yeah," he said, almost to himself. "I knew you'd say that."

At that moment Mari stopped by their table, and Ezra placed his order.

"Garlic fries?" she asked, because they were a specialty, but Ezra shook his head.

"Side salad." He patted his stomach and she squeezed his shoulder.

"Dad's making you a special dessert," she said, and although she spoke in a normal voice, her words were just for him. "When your"—she glared at Ezra's father—"*meeting* is over, we'll get you something that'll help that, okay?"

Ezra smiled wistfully at her. "You guys are awesome," he said, and then he remembered the art of banter, which he'd also picked up over the past two months. "Or is this just because I keep trying to let you win at softball?"

Mari laughed. "Nope. All love, sweetie. Besides, if Dad *really* wanted to win at softball, he'd play the son-in-law card and make Adam play for him."

"Thank God," Ezra said with fervor, "because it's the only time I've ever gotten to play."

Mari took the other orders at the table and moved on to Adam and Miguel. Miguel was watching Ezra, gnawing his lower lip, and Ezra gave him a wink he didn't feel before turning back to the business at hand.

"Dad," he said soberly when Mari was done, "here's the thing you need to know. I'm not *ever* going back into your office. Miguel's trying to start a business, and I might be able to *help* him, but I'm not *ever* going to wear a tie again, nine-to-five, weekends and overtime. Ever. If you brought me back home and tried to make me straight, I'd go out and get a job in a bakery on the West Side, maybe a bedsitter in Greenwich with some roommates—but I'm not going back to the office."

His father opened and closed his mouth like a fish, and Ezra tried to ignore the icy wash of fear and nausea that threatened to overcome him just *talking* about his old life.

"If you drugged me, threw me in a van, and woke me up in a suit in my old office, I'd hang myself from one of the light fixtures by my necktie," he elaborated. "I'd choke on my own vomit to fucking end it all." He closed his eyes and tried to take deep breaths, and couldn't. He thought consciously and raised his fingers to the unfamiliar charm at his throat.

Faith and a plan.

He looked up and caught Miguel's eyes, and Miguel touched his own new charm, and Ezra drew some strength.

Ezra turned to face his father and brother again.

Gregory looked shaken. "Really?" he asked, breaking through a heavy silence. "You hated it that much?"

Ezra nodded at him and rubbed a fingertip over the scars on his knuckles. "You weren't there that day," he said, for the first time in months bringing himself back to that moment when his cubicle walls felt coated in his own blood. "If I'd been able to think at all, I would have bashed my head against the window until I fell out." His voice choked, because *oh God* he'd been desperate, but he was stronger now.

Adam thought he was brave.

Darrin cared about him.

Finn liked his company.

Miguel loved him.

Miguel loved him.

"I know how not to feel like that anymore," he said softly. "I do. I mean, I probably need more work, and I *still* haven't called a shrink because, well, I've been busy, but in a way, getting here was proof that I've gotten better. Man, it's like a rat in a cage. He'll gnaw his own skin trying to get out, but once you let him out, that wound goes away, you know?"

Gregory regarded him for a moment and then turned his attention to their seething father, whose venom was, for the moment, boiling over onto Ezra.

"Yeah," Gregory said softly, voice cracking. "I kn—"

"Shut the fuck up," Martin said to Gregory, and Ezra looked at him in sympathy. "And you—you're making me fucking sick. I didn't raise you to be this fucking weak. I didn't pay for your education so you could get in touch with your fucking feelings. You've got a *job* to do, or did you forget about that? Did you forget that you grew up in luxury and you fucking owe us for that—"

"Hold that thought, Dad," Ezra said, reaching into his back pocket. "Here."

He placed the check on the table and waited until his father took it before he let go.

"What in the hell is this?"

He'd never heard Martin Kellerman sound confused before, and he'd thought the moment would be more gratifying.

"It's my college education," Ezra said, looking at the check. "You can have it back."

"What?" He blinked, and for a moment Ezra might have thought he looked hurt, but he managed to mask that.

"My college education. I mean—the car and the condo are in your name, and I figured that's twenty grand to add to that. But that's five years' tuition at Syracuse, plus dorm fees, right? Plus books, incidentals, lab fees, that sort of thing. But, you know—you paid for me to go to college so I could help with the company. I don't want to do that, so, well, there's your investment back. Maybe you can adopt a poor high school grad and keep him in indentured servitude for ten years or something. For someone else, that money would be worth it. But not for me."

"Ezra," Gregory said, apparently the only one still able to speak, "that's—that's a *lot* of money!"

Ezra shrugged uncomfortably. "Yeah, but, I mean, what'd I spend it on? Dad paid for the condo, paid for the car—yeah, they were all business expenses, but they weren't *my* expenses. All I had was my salary and a fuckton of clothes. I mean, seven weeks here, I could have lived on just a little over minimum wage. Yeah, I was sleeping on a friend's couch and he and his boyfriend eat a lot of River Burger leftovers, believe you me, but we get by. And we're happy. And not once have I felt the urge to beat the walls in with my fist or jump out of a fucking building. This check is worth it to me to make sure I *never* feel like that again."

"But what are you going to do?" Again, it was Greg doing the asking.

Ezra looked at his dad and shook his head, and then turned to his brother. "Well, I figure that I'll apply to state college next year—maybe work on my teaching degree—"

"Like they'd let a faggot teach," Ezra's father said under his breath.

"It's not against the law, Dad," Ezra said patiently. "Not even Hasidic law, okay? I know, I looked it up. Anyway—maybe grade-school teacher, or maybe not. Maybe I'll just keep working for Darrin and help Miguel when he gets his next business loan. I mean, if I'm just cooking up marketing plans and shit for someone I believe in, I think I could have fun with that, so it doesn't freak me out too much. Maybe I'll take some online courses and choose a whole new career path—the job isn't the point."

"Go ahead and tell me, genius," Martin snapped. "What's the fuckin' point?"

Ezra looked his father in the eyes. "The point is, I can find a way to be happy that doesn't include you. And you don't have a fucking thing to say about it. Not anymore."

The silence was absolute, but Ezra didn't flinch. Martin backed down first, and while Ezra's father was building up something to say in his dragon cave brain, Mari danced in with their food baskets.

"Here you go, Ezra," she chirped, and Ezra looked up at her gratefully.

"You're a lifesaver, Mari."

"You can save your own life, baby," she said and bent at the waist to kiss his forehead before setting down a fourth red plastic basket on the table. "Here, this is Miguel's—I think he should come join you."

Ezra beamed at her. "Thanks, sweetheart. That's a good idea." He looked over and met Miguel's eyes. "Miguel, come on over. I want you to meet my brother, Greg. He's not the one who put snakes in my bed— he's sort of a nice guy."

"Oh God," Greg laughed. "I'd forgotten about that. That asshole did the same thing to me—I had to go to a shrink to stop twitching at garden hoses."

"Pussies," Martin Kellerman sneered, but it barely registered.

Miguel walked over, and Ezra stood and kissed him on the cheek. He turned to face his family, and saw that his father couldn't even look at them.

Well, that was fine. He didn't have to look. The point was, he'd seen.

"Greg, this is Miguel—he's working to start a temp agency where the temps get to rate their employers, so they have some say too. Miguel, this is my brother Gregory, who runs the New Jersey office and plant. He's got a wife and *three* kids—I had to go look that up," he said apologetically to Greg. "I'm sorry—we just never visit."

Greg smiled, embarrassed. "I'm the older brother," he apologized. "I didn't realize you'd gotten this interesting."

Miguel sat down and they ate and chatted—and ignored the seething cauldron of hate and disdain that was Ezra's father.

It wasn't pleasant, but then, he wasn't spewing venom or orders, so it didn't have to be.

They finished their sandwiches and Ezra pulled out his phone to check the time. Across from him, Adam did the same, and Ezra let out a breath of thanks.

"Greg, Dad—my break is about over," he said, his palms breaking out in sweat all over again. "And I'm really… well, Greg, I'm glad to see you."

Martin Kellerman actually looked surprised at that. "Nice," he said. "What am I?"

"Chopped liver," Ezra returned firmly. "But I'll send you a holiday card if you like."

Greg snorted. "God, Ezra, you have grown some *balls*!"

Miguel's hand on the small of his back gave him strength. "I'm happy," he said, begging this to be the end of it. "It's easier to be strong if you know why you're being strong."

At that moment Rico and Derek stood up, done with lunch and waving Mari off for dessert. Rico came directly to their table and nodded politely at Greg.

"Ezra?" he said with a smile. "You staying around?"

Ezra nodded. "Yeah," he said. "That okay?"

Rico bent and kissed his cheek. "That's awesome," he said sincerely. "Adam and Finn love you to pieces. I'm so glad you landed on your feet."

He turned to shake hands with Miguel and was about to leave—probably without saying anything—when Derek put a hand on his shoulder. "Hold on a sec, I've got some shit to do," he said pleasantly. Then, oh God, Rico's boyfriend must have had titanium balls, because he tapped Ezra's father on the shoulder.

"Mr. Kellerman?"

"What?" He didn't bother to get up.

"I'd like to thank you for firing Rico and being a complete bastard about it and even fucking up your son until he had to come running here to heal. I'm telling you, I got *the* best employee because you were an ignorant asshole, and better yet, I got a boyfriend out of the deal too. And Ezra is the nicest guy in the world—your loss is totally our gain, so, you know, continue to be an asshole. By all means keep throwing great people out here—we'll love the crap out of 'em, and you can go back to your empire and be alone."

And with that, Derek Huston turned on his heel and stalked away. Rico followed, a completely besotted look on his face, and Ezra and Miguel exchanged amused looks.

"Yeah," Ezra said, because he'd gotten it the first time he'd met Derek. "I'm not anything like that."

Miguel shook his head and seized his hand to kiss his knuckles. "Which is a relief to me, papi. I worked with him for six months, and I didn't even crush."

Ezra's smile was slow, and it felt like it took over his entire body. "Only took us seven weeks," he said, and Miguel chuckled, low and suggestively.

"'Cause I felt like I knew you forever," he said, and Ezra had to glance away.

His father was staring at the two of them in bafflement. No poison in his eyes—not this time—just a complete inability to comprehend. "You don't even know these people," he muttered. "You've known me your entire life."

"Yeah," Ezra said, wishing they had time for that dessert Mari promised. "But did you know me?"

Mari came over to the table and Ezra pulled out some cash. She waved him away. "I'll send your dessert home with Finn," she said. Finn had come out from behind the counter to kiss Adam, and the few other customers in the café were all *awwing* over Adam's discomfort. "We're glad you'll be here awhile." She kissed his cheek and gathered up the baskets while Ezra finished up with his dad.

"Take care," he said simply. "Greg, I'll unlock your number, okay? If someone needs to get hold of me, you do the calling and I'll get back to you."

Greg nodded and shook his hand. "Give me your address," he said. "I'll send you Gloria's holiday letter—she writes a good one, right?"

Ezra's mouth quirked. "You've never sent one to me," he said. "But I'd appreciate one now."

Greg gaped at him and shook his head. "God, kid—you got cheated in the family department. I'm not fucking kidding. Finding your own was the best thing you could have done."

"Fucking *nice*," Martin Kellerman snapped, but Greg grabbed his arm and pulled him away from the cheerful little white tables and general camaraderie of River Burger.

"Take your check, old man," Greg said grimly, his words carrying above the hollow thump of their hard-soled shoes on the boardwalk. "I hope it's a comfort to you in the old age home, because I don't know who's going to visit you when you get there."

Ezra watched them go, a sort of shock washing over him.

"They left," he said dumbly, because he'd dreamed about this moment but had been sure it could never happen.

"They did," Miguel said. "You okay?"

Ezra nodded and then looked at him dolefully. "I was thinking about investing that money in your business," he apologized. "I'm sorry. I just figured he'd...."

Miguel squinted at him. "What in the hell are you talking about? You *earned* that money, papi. Paying your old man to leave you alone? That was my favorite way to spend it."

"Yeah, but now I'll be broke." It was hitting him, really. He'd learned to be a good employee in the past two months—and wasn't that a fortunate thing. "I need to get back to work!"

Miguel laughed and pulled him in for a kiss on the cheek. "Yeah, we all do. But don't get too upset about the money. You didn't see, but Derek and I talked a minute while you were occupied. Guess who's going back to work in a suit and tie?"

Ezra's heart fell. "So you won't be working at Candy Heaven anymore?" Aw, *man*!

"Part time," Miguel said as the two of them waved bye to a madly waving Finn and started walking up the boardwalk toward Candy Heaven. "Don't worry—you and me, we're not going away just because we won't be at work so much." He squeezed Ezra's hand. "In fact, it'll give us more reasons to see each other afterward, okay?"

Ezra nodded, feeling surprisingly confident. He'd just told his old man to go away—and he *had*. Ezra was free. Ezra could do *anything*.

"Those workplace romances, they don't work out anyway," he said facetiously, and he was rewarded by Miguel's laughter.

"Yeah, sure—you keep telling yourself that," he said, still chortling. "Maybe I'll believe you."

He grabbed Ezra's hand, in spite of the residual clamminess, and together they continued down the boardwalk. They didn't dawdle—it turned out they really did like where they were going. But they didn't mind the trip either.

Cat-Dog, Cat-Dog....

DARRIN HAD called Adam aside to ask if he'd had dreams.

"Dreams?" Adam asked, that maddeningly practical face wrinkling in confusion. "Have I had... dreams?"

"Of Ezra!" Darrin snapped. "Of Miguel. Of people coming to Candy Heaven—you know, dreams!"

Adam regarded him suspiciously. "Uh, isn't that your department, boss?"

Darrin smacked him on the arm, the sound echoing in the tiny little office space. "Yes, yes, it is."

"Have you stopped having them?" Adam asked, sounding a little upset.

"No!" Darrin said in horror. "No. My dreams continue unabated, you blasphemous chimp. But... but I had a dream about Ezra last night...."

"What sort of dream?" Adam sounded panicked—and well he might. The last time Ezra had faced down his father, well, Darrin had been cleaning up that mess in one way or another for the past few months.

"Don't worry," Darrin said softly. "I mean, I worry about him too. But he and Miguel finally got their asses in gear, and I think he's got the strength. No, this was something else."

"Something I'm going to understand?" Adam asked suspiciously. That deadly attractive face radiated a combination of skepticism and reluctant belief, and Darrin sighed.

"Yes," he said after a moment, feeling sad. These young people, they came, they went, they came back, they faded from his life. He knew everything about them, and they were always (yes, always!) grateful for his haven, his meddling, his kindness.

But always, they were fated to move on to bigger things. It was the pain all good teachers faced, he supposed, but he'd never claimed to be a saint.

"I'd hoped it would be you," he said after a moment, sadly. "I was hoping you'd have the dreams, and you'd be the one to stay. But...." But

Adam had too many other gifts, really. Art, animation, leadership. "But no—a couple of years, maybe. I'll enjoy them. Pay attention to Ezra in the next few months."

"He's my roommate—do I have a choice?"

Darrin laughed, because Adam really was precious. "He's your friend, and he'll continue to be after the roommate thing ends. Trust me, if he starts talking about dreams, you're going to want to know."

Adam had learned by now. "If he starts dumping sugar packets on the table and drawing, I'll be sure to let you know."

"Pixy Stix, you heathen. Sugar packets are for amateurs. Now get back out there and study your classes on my dime."

"Since you mentioned it...." Adam started for the front but paused at the door, looking over his shoulder at Darrin with suddenly astute eyes. "Boss?"

"Yes?"

"Staying here, being your second banana—it's not a bad fate, really. I wouldn't mind."

Darrin winked. "I would. You'd be depriving the world of intelligent children's programming. Now go away."

Adam nodded and left, but he took the lingering sadness with him. Sweetness was a thing Darrin valued, and Adam had just dumped a truckload of it into his office. He was going to savor.

"EZRA, PAPI, wake up." The voice was familiar, but the red and blue lights flashing through the blinds were not.

"Therese? Is someone in trouble?"

"Yeah, you need to get up so you and Miguel can get an apartment."

"But I thought you loved u—"

"Ezra, papi, wake up."

"Holy crap, where am I?"

Ezra blinked hard against the dream, focusing on the now familiar furniture of Therese's living room, no red and blue lights included. "Oh," he mumbled, still torn between the dream and reality. "Sorry—did you just get home?"

She was still dressed in her nursing uniform, as she'd gone back to work at the beginning of October, when she'd gotten back from visiting Lydia and Bobby and their new baby, Ramona. It was the first week of

November now, and Ezra had lots of practice running from Miguel's bed at one in the morning so he could be asleep on the couch when Therese got home. Weekdays, when Miguel worked for Derek, Ezra stayed at Finn and Adam's with as many date nights and snuggles on the couch as they could manage, but on the weekends, when Therese would be at work, he and Miguel had the house to themselves. Ezra didn't even want to *think* about the brotherly blackmail Miguel had inflicted on Jaime and Berto to get them to clear out for at least one night of the three, but Miguel did seem to be the only one picking up dog shit every day, so Ezra assumed it would balance out.

"Yes, mijo, I just got home," she said wearily, "and you and Miguel are breaking my heart. Go upstairs with him—it's sweet of my sons to be so respectful of my delicate sensibilities, but I get the point. You're not a hookup, you're family—go sleep with your family, okay?"

Ezra pushed up off the couch, trying not to disturb the dogs, who had all taken to sleeping at the floor by his feet. "Yeah," he mumbled, wincing as he stretched his body just the wrong way. "Yeah… ouch… sure…."

He heard her sigh behind him as he walked up the stairs. "Sorry, don't mean to be a pain in the a—" Oh, was that the wrong choice of words. Miguel had been in fine form that night—excited about work, frustrated by their weekly separation, generally wanting Ezra on the whole. The resultant pounding had been… well, memorable. Ezra couldn't remember ever being fucked quite that hard or that earnestly in his entire life.

"You're not," Therese sighed. "In fact, I'm glad you're here. Get up early tomorrow morning, I need to talk to you."

Ezra made a wounded sound and paused on the landing. "Not anything—"

She shook her head and patted his cheek, looking happy and tired at the same time. "No, not anything bad. In fact, something really good. But it's going to be a change. In the meantime, stop in the hall bathroom on your way to Miguel's room. There's some witch hazel pads on the back of the toilet—they'll help."

Ezra nodded, not registering, really, what witch hazel pads actually did. "Yeah, sure, thanks a… oh my God."

Therese laughed softly and passed him on the way up the stairs, muttering to herself in Spanish. Ezra spoke a few words now, and he knew stupid young men figured large in what she was saying but wasn't really sure about the details.

Well, she apparently knew enough about details for both of them.

And she also knew about home remedies, because witch hazel pads really did ease the burning, and thus soothed, he crawled in next to Miguel's warm body, already half-asleep.

"Mm," Miguel murmured, wrapping an arm around his waist. "Nice to have you back, but Mami—"

"Woke me up and told me to go to bed," Ezra returned on a yawn. "Night, papi. Love you."

"Love you too."

Ezra closed his eyes convinced that sleeping next to Miguel was the only way to sleep, and glad that he'd get to do more of it. That old Beach Boys song played in his head, the one about being married and not having to wait so long, and on that note, he fell asleep.

THE NEXT morning, he heard the gentle rap on his door and crawled out of bed slowly, trying not to wake Miguel. It was Sunday, and they both had a short shift in the afternoon, and Ezra would go home with Adam. In a way, he thought this must be what it felt like when a child had shared custody with both parents.

In another way, he thought this was sort of bullshit, because he really wanted to sleep with Miguel on all the fucking days.

But Miguel was patient, and Ezra could be too. He'd waited through a life he'd hated so he could warm his soul in bright spots of sunlight. He could walk in the sunlight with friends so he could savor deep pockets of joy.

Turned out, they didn't have to wait much longer.

Blearily, he followed Therese down the stairs so he could park himself at the counter and watch her begin the sweetly familiar routine of making breakfast. Today it was french toast, where she added just the tiniest kick of chili with the powdered sugar, cinnamon, and cocoa that she sprinkled on crispy fried bread.

She had the coffeemaker on a timer, so while she was waiting for the first batch of french toast to cook, she poured a jumbo-size cup for him and added cream and sugar.

He smiled at her and accepted it—he'd tried, more than once, to help, and he'd finally just had to deal with the fact that caring for people, even him, was in her nature.

"Gracias," he said humbly, and sipped tentatively. Oh yeah… that shit was real.

"Is nothing," she replied modestly, and then she checked the cooking french toast and adjusted the heat. "I need to ask you something, papi, and I need you to not panic or think the worst, okay?"

Ezra looked at her with a sinking heart. Oh God. He'd overstayed his welcome. He bit his lip hard to keep it from quivering and nodded. She had been more than kind.

And she was not fooled for a minute. She shook her head and reached over the counter to pat his hands before backing away from the stove.

"I can tell you're panicking," she said kindly. "Hear me out. Are you better, papi? I know when you first showed up here and you and Miguel were 'just friends' that you were sad and hurt and broken. I need to know if you're happy now."

Some of Ezra's panic eased. He smiled at her and nodded. "Oh yes," he said. It had been almost two months since the meeting with his father. The time in between had been hectic—a lot of shuffling around from Sacramento to Roseville and back—but it had been wonderful. "I… I never knew family could be like this," he confessed shyly. It wasn't *all* good, of course. Adam got grumpy and Finn took up the bathroom and there were nights when he and Miguel *really* wanted each other and, short of getting laid in Miguel's car (which they'd tried once—hadn't been comfortable), there was nowhere to go. Customers were bitchy sometimes, and every now and then his coworkers could *really* get on his nerves, but….

But he always came back in his heart. He always remembered what it was like when the walls had been closing in, and he always remembered that he had the freedom to leave at any time.

He chose to stay—who wouldn't? Miguel treated him with all the reverence he'd ever dreamed of in a lover, and with all of the power he'd never thought he needed.

Adam and Finn were brothers he hadn't known he could have, and Miguel's mother….

Well, Sunday mornings were his favorite.

"I'm *so* happy," he said after a moment, when all the happy tried to rush out of his mouth at once and got blocked by the lump in his throat. "I'm…." He cried so easily, but sometimes he cried from happiness. His eyes burned, and not because he was sad or anxious or stressed. "I didn't know," he finished simply.

She smiled at him and turned the toast. "So," she said, "you and Miguel—you said you would stay until it hurts. It doesn't hurt, so you'll stay, right?"

"Absolutely," he affirmed, and she laughed slightly.

"Good. Because I want you at my table every Sunday morning. Every other Sunday at the least. You are the only son I have who isn't too lazy to get up with me, yes?"

Ezra smiled, trying not to duck his head. He was pretty sure the other boys slept in on purpose now so he could have his turn to talk. "It's worth it," he said.

"That's good to hear." She busied herself for a moment plating the toast that was done and egging new bread to put in the pan. She moved to shaking her trademark blend of yum onto the finished product before she spoke. "See, something has come up—something good, actually. Bobby has been looking for a position up here in Sacramento for a long time, and he finally found something he's excited about. It's in Roseville, and it would only make sense for the whole family to move in here, since it *is* a house made for a big family."

Oh. Ezra blinked. "So the kids will be here?" he asked, feeling like a little kid himself.

Theresa laughed. "Of course. But it's going to be crowded, and there's no need for all my boys to stay here to help me pay the mortgage, you know?"

Ohhhhh....

"You need them to move out."

She smiled sunnily. "Jaime and Berto couldn't find a place fast enough," she confirmed. "They lined up a place in Sacramento yesterday— they're so excited, it's disgusting. They're planning on taking three of the dogs even, which is fine, because now I can get another cat. But," she said, stopping herself from rambling, "I was worried about *you*."

"Me?"

"Yes." She put two of the pieces of french toast on a plate and covered them with butter and syrup and then handed the plate over the counter. "Eat, papi. The boys will be down soon enough, and this way you won't have to fight them off." Ezra dug in, because *french toast* made *just for him*, and she continued. "You haven't had enough loving," she said simply, looking at him seriously from under a tangle of mostly black hair. "I needed to make sure you and Miguel were happy, that you wouldn't run if we shifted your home. Because Miguel, he'd do anything to see you smile. Even stay here in this house that is about to become *much* smaller, just so you and I could talk on Sunday morning."

Ezra took another bite and tried to ignore the fact that he was crying all over the place: happy tears, sad tears, just emotional tears. His whole life he'd been told to keep them in—but here, in front of Therese or in front of Miguel, he could be safe.

"We can still talk on Sunday mornings," he said when he could speak.

She handed him a paper towel without a word, and he mopped his face.

"Always, Ezra. My counter is *always* open."

He gave her a watery smile. "Then, you know, me and Miguel should start looking for a place."

She beamed at him, and at that moment Miguel thumped down the stairs wearing sweats drooping at his hips and no shirt or slippers. The chill of the November morning made his tiny nipples almost purple and his muscled chest was covered in gooseflesh. Ezra wanted to drape himself over Miguel's shoulders and warm him, skin to skin, and to kiss his neck, and run his hands through the hair that was sticking out in sixty-eleven different directions.

But he couldn't—not here in Therese's kitchen, talking to Therese.

He could do that when they found a new place, he thought happily. Someplace in Sacramento, walking distance from Finn and Adam so he could still walk Clopper and pet Jake and they could have dinner on Thursday nights like they did now.

"Morning," Miguel said, blinking. "Aw, you started without me?"

Ezra grinned and patted the seat next to him. "C'mere. You and me can share. Your mom's got news."

TWO NIGHTS later, he and Finn were playing video games on the couch when Clopper started barking like mad. They looked toward the window that faced the street and saw the cherry lights outside.

"Holy crap," Finn muttered, pausing the game. "I wonder what's up?" He stood and stuck his face out the window that faced the street, and Ezra stood to join him.

"Get in here," Adam snarled over Clopper's racket, surprising them all with his vehemence. "Jesus, people, has nobody ever told you not to get involved?"

Finn didn't get upset or flustered. He looked at Adam with infinite patience instead. "No, baby. Nobody ever told *us* not to get involved, and *we've* never been shot at for being nosy. Nobody has guns out," he said, peering back outside, "but... huh."

"Huh what? Clopper, *down*!" The dog subsided and Adam stood from the table where he was doing homework and peered outside next to Finn. "Wait... isn't that the guy from upstairs?"

"The one that didn't give out candy for Halloween?" Finn asked. "And had that really awful letter telling the trick-or-treaters that they were going to burn in hell?"

"That's the one."

Ezra peered over Finn's shoulder as they all watched the guy getting hauled downstairs in his boxer shorts and a tank top—and handcuffs. "I wonder what he did?"

"How do you know he did anything?" Finn asked, looking at him. "People get arrested all the time when they haven't done anything."

"Yeah, but that guy was an asshole—I sort of hope he's guilty."

"I think he used to steal shit out of the drier," Finn conceded.

"Ya think?" Adam asked caustically. "Aren't those my underwear?"

"Oh God—yes! You can see the red stain where I washed them with that shirt!"

Finn and Adam both looked at each other and quailed, and Ezra held his hand over his mouth.

"Oh gross."

"Ew."

"Man, I'm buying new shorts!"

"Oh," Ezra interrupted. "Ouch—man, he banged his head on the cruiser."

"Yeah, but we still don't know—oh *fuck*!" Adam's horror was well founded. A clatter past their apartment indicated several officers parading down the stairs before appearing on the lawn.

ATF was emblazoned on the back of their black jackets, and each one of them was carrying a yellow gun case of what were probably illegal guns.

"Oh geez," Ezra said, eyes big. "I had no idea. I mean, he was a little creepy, but he looked so quiet!"

At that moment a knock sounded at the door. The rest of the night they spent talking to the ATF about how their quiet neighbor who was a little creepy and stole their underwear out of the shared drier downstairs had never waved a gun or distributed nihilistic propaganda to anyone in the apartment.

"ARE YOU kidding?" Miguel asked, wide-eyed, when he came to pick Ezra up from work the next day. Adam and Ezra had related the story about creepy Anton Geldoff and how he'd been hoarding weapons for… well, paranoid reasons, mostly, and was probably pleading out to multiple firearms violations that would get him imprisoned for five to ten.

"We shit you not," Ezra said, nodding. "But oh! I forgot to tell you the best part!"

"There's a good part?" Miguel looked at Adam accusingly, like somehow Adam would have known that the neighbor in the upstairs loft had been a Grade A scumbag.

"Yeah," Adam said, nodding seriously. "There totally is a good part."

"What's the good part?" Miguel's brown eyes were as wide as a child's, and his soft, mobile mouth was parted in expectation.

God, Ezra loved him. So often he was so strong, but sometimes, when Ezra needed to see it most, he was just as wonderstruck as Ezra was most days. It was a beautiful thing.

"The good part," Ezra said smugly, "is that his apartment is going to be available to rent after Thanksgiving. It's smaller than Finn and Adam's, but—"

"Oh my God!" Miguel whooped, just like Ezra had known he would. Right there, in the store, in front of most of the crew, he leaned over the chocolate counter and kissed Ezra hard and with purpose, until the world melted and it was just Ezra and Miguel killing it in the little city.

Miguel pulled back, and Ezra beamed at him dreamily. "Yeah," he said, just bursting. "And you know what's weird?"

"Besides, you know, the whole 'busted for firearms violations right over your head' thing?" Miguel shot back, shuddering.

Ezra shrugged. He'd lived in a big city. There was always worse. "No—not that. It's that I dreamed the whole thing," he said, remembering that vision of Miguel's mother telling him he had to wake up and move, with the cherry-top lights in the background. "I mean, not... *dreamed* dreamed, but I saw... you know, signs?"

"Signs?" Darrin asked from across the room.

"Yeah," Ezra said, thinking about it with wonder. He shook his head. "I mean, I'd say it was clairvoyant, but lately I've been dreaming about this... well, he's sort of a disgraced soldier, and I must have seen him on television, because I sure as hell don't know him *here*."

Darrin motioned for Darby to take his place so he could move from behind the front register. "Describe this soldier," he said, hip-checking Miguel and Adam out of the way.

"Huh." Ezra closed his eyes and tried to summon the dream from the night before. "Brown hair, sort of a long-bridged nose, green eyes... a really nice smile, but sad, you know? Like he'd done something really wrong."

"Yeah," Darrin said, as though this made total sense. "He *has* done something very wrong. I hope Adam's got his big-boy panties on, because he's showing up right after Thanksgiving."

Adam looked from one of them to the other, and Ezra shrugged. "I got no idea about that," he apologized.

"Fuck to the no," Adam muttered and turned around and walked away.

Miguel and Ezra looked at each other. "Huh," they said in tandem.

Darrin sighed. "It appears, children, that I am needed." With that he followed Adam across the store, and for a moment Ezra felt some concern. Whoever this guy was, he'd seemed genuinely hurt—but then, so had Adam. Should he get involved now? Should he just wait until the guy showed up and see what Adam needed from a friend?

Then Miguel shrugged. "Don't worry about him, okay? I mean, yes, worry, 'cause he's a friend, but we have two weeks to deal with whatever the hell that is," he said practically. "Right now, papi, I want to take you to dinner; then you and me can plan how to move into your crazy ex-neighbor's apartment. I am telling you, waking up next to you every morning is going to be my best Christmas present *ever*."

Ezra's knees got a little wobbly. "You say the best things," he told Miguel in complete sincerity. "I will totally move all your stuff if you just keep promising forever to me."

Miguel chuckled low in his throat, and thoughts of dreams and an upset Adam all faded. "I'll promise forever even if I have to make Berto and Jaime move all my stuff," Miguel said, an evil little smile on his face.

Ezra could have just leaned into him, dimples and all, but he remembered that he was off. "Back in a minute." He trotted around the counter, under the stairs, and to the back cashier room so he could retrieve his jacket. November had hit, and while it wasn't nearly as cold as an East Coast winter, it wasn't sweaty September either. He scrupulously declined to listen to Darrin advising Adam seriously in the back corner of the cashier room, grabbed his jacket, and ran back to Miguel.

Yes, there would be crises—but he could handle them now. He had a whole bright, shiny future with the man he loved waiting for him—he could handle anything.

"Hey," he said while Miguel helped him slide his arms into his quilted wool coat, "Miguel! I just had a thought."

"What, papi?" Miguel threaded his fingers through Ezra's, and Ezra thought with pride that walking down the boardwalk of Old Sacramento while hand in hand with his boyfriend was something that would *not* get old.

"We can get a cat! We can, right? We can get a cat?"

Miguel laughed, and together they left Candy Heaven, planning for a bright future that Ezra could almost see.

Swishing Tail In Wait

WELL, DARRIN thought, of course Adam was upset. Who *wouldn't* be upset when you learned that the guy who betrayed you—in the worst possible way—was coming to confront you?

Darrin was one of the few people besides Finn who had ever really seen Adam rattled—and oh hell, was Adam rattled now.

"My boy," Darrin said, taking the usual sting out of his voice, "you're going to have to calm down."

"I'm totally calm," Adam bit out. "Just tell me when he's coming and I won't be here."

"It doesn't work like that," Darrin replied in annoyance. "You know that. Look—he's coming to find you. You need to make sure Finn's ready—"

Adam hid his face in his hands. "Do you remember the last time someone came to town and was mean to me? *Do* you?"

Darrin winced. "Wasn't there, I don't know, mothers in jail? I seem to remember that. Yes. It was weird."

Adam stared at him in apparent despair. "Weird, he says. Yeah, it was fucking weird. It was a fucking nightmare, okay?"

"Well that's why you should warn him, right?"

Adam groaned and scrubbed his face with his hands and then stood up. "This," he said boldly, "is not happening. And Ezra took off and the floor is understaffed." And with that, he turned on his heel and went back to the front.

Darrin watched him go without surprise. Adam was strong—so much stronger, really, than Ezra—but he still had weaknesses, tender spots, places that needed to be protected.

Well, the good news was that Darrin no longer had to do that alone.

He'd been hoping—yes, he had. But it wasn't going to be Adam, he'd reconciled himself to that. Ezra, gentle Ezra, had the gift. And he had a need for a destiny in which he brought joy.

Darrin knew just the place—and lucky Ezra, he already worked there. Maybe with Ezra's help, the ghost from Adam's past wouldn't be such a disaster after all.

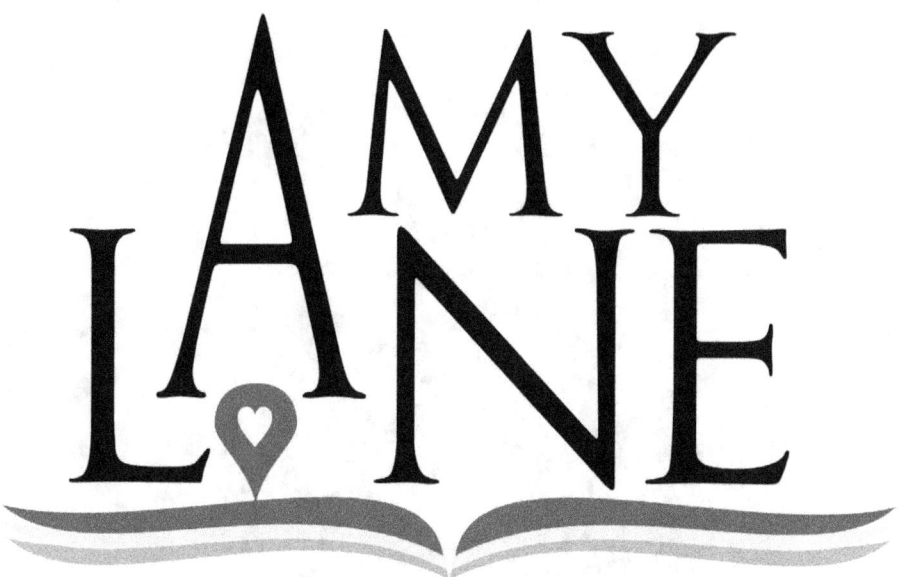

Choose your Lane to love!

Yellow

Amy Lane Lite
Contemporary Romance

Available at
www.dreamspinnerpress.com

A Candy Man Novella

Adam Macias has been thrown a few curve balls in his life, but losing his VA grant because his car broke down and he missed a class was the one that struck him out. One relative away from homelessness, he's taking the bus to Sacramento, where his cousin has offered a house-sitting job and a new start. He has one goal, and that's to get his life back on track. Friends, pets, lovers? Need not apply.

Finn Stewart takes one look at Adam as he's applying to Candy Heaven and decides he's much too fascinating to leave alone. Finn is bright and shiny—and has never been hurt. Adam is wary of his attention from the very beginning—Finn is dangerous to every sort of peace Adam is forging, and Adam may just be too damaged to let him in at all.

But Finn is tenacious, and Adam's new boss, Darrin, doesn't take bullshit for an answer. Adam is going to have to ask himself which is harder—letting Finn in or living without him? With the holidays approaching it seems like an easy question, but Adam knows from experience that life is seldom simple, and the world seldom cooperates with hope, faith, or the plans of cats and men.

www.dreamspinnerpress.com

A Candy Man Book

Rico Gonzalves-Macias didn't expect to fall in love during his internship in New York—and he didn't expect the boss's son to out them both and get him fired either. When he returns to Sacramento stunned and heartbroken, he finds his cousin, Adam, and Adam's boyfriend, Finn, haven't just been house-sitting—they've made his once sterile apartment into a home.

When Adam gets him a job interview with the adorable, magnetic, practically perfect Derek Huston, Rico feels especially out of his depth. Derek makes it no secret that he wants Rico, but Rico is just starting to figure out that he's a beginner at the really important stuff and doesn't want to jump into anything with both feet.

Derek is a both-feet kind of guy. But he's also made mistakes of his own and doesn't want to pressure Rico into anything. Together they work to find a compromise between instant attraction and long-lasting love, and while they're working, Rico gets a primer in why family isn't always a bad idea. He needs to believe Derek can be his family before Derek's formidable patien ce runs out—because even a practically perfect boyfriend is capable of being hurt.

www.dreamspinnerpress.com

AMY LANE is a mother of two college students, two grade-schoolers, and two small dogs. She is also a compulsive knitter who writes because she can't silence the voices in her head. She adores fur-babies, knitting socks, and hawt menz, and she dislikes moths, cat boxes, and knuckle-headed macspazzmatrons. She is rarely found cooking, cleaning, or doing domestic chores, but she has been known to knit up an emergency hat/blanket/pair of socks for any occasion whatsoever, or sometimes for no reason at all. Her award-winning writing has three flavors: twisty-purple alternative universe, angsty-orange contemporary, and sunshine-yellow happy. By necessity, she has learned to type like the wind. She's been married for twenty-plus years to her beloved Mate and still believes in Twu Wuv, with a capital Twu and a capital Wuv, and she doesn't see any reason at all for that to change.

Website: www.greenshill.com
Blog: www.writerslane.blogspot.com
E-mail: amylane@greenshill.com
Facebook: www.facebook.com/amy.lane.167
Twitter: @amymaclane

BLaCKBiRD KNiTTiNG iN A BUNNY'S LaiR

AMY LANE

Sequel to *Knitter in His Natural Habitat*
A Granby Knitting Novel

After three years of waiting for "rabbit" Jeremy to commit to a life in Granby—and a life together—Aiden Rhodes was appalled when Jeremy sustained a nearly fatal beating to keep a friend out of harm's way. How could Aiden's bunny put himself in danger like that?

Aiden needs to get over himself, because Jeremy has a long road to recovery, and he's going to need Aiden's promise of love every step of the way. Jeremy has new scars on his face and body to deal with, and his heart can't afford any more wounds.

When their friend's baby needs some special care, the two men find common ground to firm up their shaky union. With Aiden's support and his boss's inspiration, Jeremy comes up with a plan to make sure Ariadne's little blackbird comes into this world with everything she needs. While Jeremy grows into his new role as protector, Aiden needs to ease back on his protectiveness over his once-timid lover. Aiden may be a wolf in student's clothing and Jeremy may be a rabbit of a man, but that doesn't mean they can't walk the wilds of Granby together.

www.dreamspinnerpress.com

A Tale of the Curious Cookbook

Emmett Gant was planning to tell his father something really important one Sunday morning—but his father passed away first. Now, nearly three years later, Emmett can't seem to clear up who he should be with—the girl with the apple cheeks and the awesome family, or his snarky neighbor, Keegan, who never sees his family but who makes Emmett really happy just by coming over to chat.

Emmett needs clarity.

Fortunately for Emmett, his best friend's mom has a cookbook that promises to give Emmett insight and good food, and Emmett is intrigued. After the cookbook follows him home, Emmett and Keegan decide to make the recipe "For Clarity," and what ensues is both very clear—and a little surprising, especially to Emmett's girlfriend. Emmett is going to have to think hard about his past and the really important thing he forgot to tell his father if he wants to get the recipe for love just right.

www.dreamspinnerpress.com

Every dreary day, Zach Driscoll takes the elevator from the penthouse apartment of his father's building to his coldly charmed life where being a union lawyer instead of a corporate lawyer is an act of rebellion. Every day, that is, until the day the elevator breaks and Sean Mallory practically runs into his arms.

Substitute teacher Sean Mallory is everything Zach is not—poor, happy, and goofily charming. With a disarming smile and a penchant for drama, Sean laughs his way into Zach's heart one elevator ride at a time. Zach would love to get to know Sean better, but first he needs the courage to leave his ivory tower and face a relationship that doesn't end at the "Ding!"

www.dreamspinnerpress.com

www.ingramcontent.com/pod-product-compliance
Lightning Source LLC
Chambersburg PA
CBHW051638260626
47170CB00004B/1226